Jean Busby is semi-retired and lives in the city of Saskatoon, Saskatchewan, Canada. She was raised on Saskatchewan farms near Melfort and Hudson Bay and lived in the City of Prince Albert for over a decade. Aside from careers as a realtor, florist, and legal secretary, the mother of two and grandmother of five attained a Master of Science in Nursing while working as a registered nurse, nurse manager, and educator. Jean's lifetime interest was writing and history and in earnest, she took to the task after her semi-retirement. She loves music and spending time with family and friends and playing the piano and painting with acrylics.

Jean Busby

ROOTS & THE REMITTANCE MAN

AUSTIN MACAULEY PUBLISHERS™

LONDON * CAMBRIDGE * NEW YORK * SHARJAH

Ordering Information
Quantity sales: Special discounts are available on quantity purchases by corporations, associations, and others. For details, contact the publisher at the address below.

Publisher's Cataloguing-in-Publication data
Busby, Jean
Roots & the Remittance Man

ISBN 9798891555945 (Paperback)
ISBN 9798891555952 (Hardback)
ISBN 9798891555976 (ePub e-book)
ISBN 9798891555969 (Audiobook)

Library of Congress Control Number: 2024909168

www.austinmacauley.com/us

First Published 2024
Austin Macauley Publishers LLC
40 Wall Street, 33rd Floor, Suite 3302
New York, NY 10005
USA

mail-usa@austinmacauley.com
+1 (646) 5125767

I wish to credit those authors whose works inspired and educated me in the writing of this book. Thank you to my family for their best recollections and support through roadblocks, frustrations, and revelations. I tried to prioritise actual memories, even if they conflicted with the written word. Thank you to library staff at Saskatoon's Frances Morrison Library and to their Writer in Residence, Di Brandt. The efforts of Melfort's St. Paul's Lutheran Church, the Melfort & District Museum, the Prince Albert Historical Museum, and the R.M. Offices in Bjorkdale and Tisdale were appreciated. Sandra Moulton and David Gunderson's research of incredible and award-winning genealogy provided the foundation. Local history books shared a wealth of information along with tips from the Saskatchewan Writer's Guild. Bringing the character's stories to life was a rewarding and thrilling experience.

Table of Contents

Preface

This work is fictional but based on truth and family legend. The names are changed and without proof of how actual events occurred, the details were ripe to expand upon. Breathing life into century-old, spirited pioneers, painted a picture of how a family tree came together and highlighted their courage and ingenuity. Finite clues like headstones, singular photographs, newspaper clippings, and knowing their places of origin left room for characters to unfold. Fictitious secondary characters enhanced the story. We can never truly know previous generations other than through genetics, stories, or legacies of land or heirlooms. After five generations, plucking out the pieces to bring them back to life was a journey to anoint my soul.

Disclaimer: This work is based on truth with a fictitious bend and attempts to follow historical timelines. I tried to recreate certain events, and concocted others. In order to protect the privacy of real individuals, I changed names and fabricated or omitted identifying details. The evolution of these lives is the product of my imagination, and from researching the events of the day. Since it is not my intent to harm any person or persons, please know that any potential infraction was unintentional.

1

Spinning Wheel and Hope Chest

Muskoka *1867–1892*

"Thank ye for the shit shat, ma'am," the bride's father slurred.

"He's either gubbed tired or not used to me homemade wine!" Uncle Hugh whispered.

"Feelin' guilty, are ye?" Auntie Vi raised an eyebrow.

"Naw, 'tis well past time me strait-laced brother cut loose!"

Before they could blink, the bride's father announced, "Me and Lizzie are stayin' on 'til fall."

The Muskokans exchanged looks and the bride, Tessa, exclaimed, "Maybe ye can help clear the land." The groom, McLaren, not quite so convinced, whistled under his breath.

When Tessa tossed her bouquet, it hit a plain girl square on the knee. Having elbowed her way to the front, the old maid clutched her prize, waiting to see which bachelor caught the garter. To her delight, Uncle Hugh's hired hand, the one with a chip on his shoulder, caught it and she grabbed his arm.

"'Twilt be quite the couple if she marries that gommy!" McLaren, winked.

By the wee hours, the wedding dance wound down, and Tessa's parents looked a bit green.

Uncle Hugh stepped in, "George and Lizzy! Yer room is the spare one on the right where we put yer luggage."

"Oh nae!" George, a reverend himself refused, "we're stickin' close to our girl!"

Auntie Vi was floored, "Are ye sleepin' in the honeymoon bunkhouse too?"

"We're nought leavin' our daughter's side!" Lizzie retorted spiriting her daughter, away by the arm.

Both Auntie Vi and McLaren flinched, then she hissed, "That's not fair!"

Uncle Hugh snickered, "Ye have to laugh, or ye'd cry. No groom needs an audience getting into his bride's knickers!"

Tessa blushed and her heart sank. McLaren was red as a beet. Fairly naïve as to what was to come under the sheets later, she knew one thing. It was supposed to be private. She thought of how she and McLaren met, her tripping over a root and him coming to the rescue. It was 1866 and both worked on her uncle's farm. They spoke a mix of Scottish Gaelic and English and his easy manner made her smile.

"Yer the new niece from Baltimore, miss?"

"Aye, sir."

"A'm from Vaughn, near Toronto."

"Nice to meet ye, sir!" she called over her shoulder, scurrying away.

Now, given their wedding celebrations were over, Tessa and McLaren broke free and slipped away to the bunkhouse. Amid creaking knees and giggles, he carried her across the threshold. Overtired, their giddiness bordered hysteria when her parents came bumping along behind.

Once inside, her father whined, "Me stomach's growlin'! Cannae, we get a sandwich in this place?"

Tessa looked around spying the strawberries Auntie Vi had laid out on the newlywed's pillows. That was the extent of the food.

"There's sandwiches leftover in the house," McLaren offered, "a'll run get some."

Awaiting his return, the parents chattered away, making small talk but after a time, Tessa's imagination wandered to she and McLaren's second encounter.

"Do ye believe in fate, miss?" he'd asked when they'd met on a wooded path.

"A'm not sure a ken, sir."

"Think of the year! 'tis the signin' of Confederation and changin' the province's name."

"Ye mean Canada West to Ontario?"

"'Tis not official 'til July but by then, a predict we'll be merrit."

Caught by surprise, she gave a nervous laugh but something inside her shifted, "Yer givin' me goose bumps, sir!"

"Aw! 'tis only yer blood pumping from the hike."

"Ye mean sloggin' through mud!" and she lifted her skirt and petticoats enough to show caked boots and a wee bit of hose-covered leg.

"This is me favourite fishin' hole!" he cleared his throat and changed the subject. As they sat on a log bridging the stream, his smile captivated her. "We've lots in common, don't ye think? Both children of Scots immigrants. Meself, eventually, a want a homestead with bairns all nearby."

She felt her heart swell, "Aye."

"A want a dozen!" he pressed.

Tessa loved that he shared his innermost thoughts, "A too want bairns close by, nought far apart, like me own family, but maybe nought a dozen."

His steel blue eyes enveloped her and she remembered how their heart-to-heart turned to tentative hand holding, then tender embraces, and finally smouldering kisses. She sensed him struggling to maintain his composure and wondered how long before they couldn't tow the line.

Back in the bunkhouse, her parents blathered on. What was keeping McLaren?

The occasional yawn was the only sign of any petering out. Tessa sighed, trying to avoid hearing of people she didn't know and trained her thoughts elsewhere.

Uncle Hugh had said, "A farmer must be bull-headed, a jack of all trades, and ready to fight stones and stumps."

Indeed, McLaren was all those things plus used foul language away from polite company. Indeed, Tessa stumbled into the house with scorched ears more than once after overhearing him.

Vi, doubled over laughing, "The worst a've heard him say was, 'a nod's as good as a wink to a blind horse'."

The chippy hired man, pitchforking cow dung, spread farmyard gossip like manure, "Pish!" he said, "she kens when he visits the loo."

Evenings, by lantern light, Hugh and McLaren blinked through pipe smoke, watching Tessa pump the spinning wheel and Vi embroider crewel motifs.

"Hugh gave me the braw spinnin' wheel when we got merrit," Vi beamed.

Tessa sensed the bewitching undercurrents between her aunt and uncle, guessing it was all about the thrill of the chase, no matter what age.

In fact, McLaren said, "A could watch ye pump that spinnin' wheel all day."

The farm hands made fun of them, saying things like, "He hasnae taken a wee gander at her fer over an hour! 'Tis time those two dafties got merrit." That Tessa heard loud and clear.

Indeed, McLaren got down on one knee 29 March 1867, and Tessa, with no hesitation, said yes.

Auntie Vi, on the other hand, came close to falling off her chair. "'Tis a sign! Right when Queen Victoria signed the British North America Act," she clucked, "now, the provinces of Canada, Nova Scotia, and New Brunswick, form the Dominion of Canada Federation!"

When McLaren returned to the bunkhouse with the plate of sandwiches, Tessa pulled herself back into reality and unusually ravenous, they all dug in.

Not long after, Tessa's watery-eyed father said, "Time fer bed Lizzie!" and herded his wife off to the adjacent bed like she was a child. The bridal couple breathed a sigh of relief.

Tessa said to McLaren, "Actually, a never expected to see them come from Baltimore. 'twas Auntie Vi and me openin' me hope chest and adjustin' me grandma's handsewn gown." She showed him the now filthy hem.

He admired it, trickling his fingers down her arm, "Even after all the dancin', 'tis still beautiful," she couldn't help but feel shivers shooting in every direction.

"Even if it's a smidge yellowed, she rued, nattering on worse than her mother. "'Twas gorgeous layin' across the bed, backed by a dreamy crochet coverlet," nervously, she tried to buy herself time."

"And what of yer bridal shower?" he seemed to grasp at straws too, "me stag was a real smoker!"

She laughed inwardly. Was he scared to death too?

"We made toilet tissue bridal gowns and drank tea and cordial."

He laughed with hesitation, "We braided lassos and smoked cigars."

"Some ladies felt like party poopers draggin' their men home early."

"A couple of revellers kept me from me bed all right, until a sprinkle of rain scattered them!"

"This mornin' at the manse," he smiled, "in me jacket and kilt, when yer buggy rolled up, me heart leapt."

"Uncle Hugh was ready to walk me down the aisle and a felt radiant, anticipatin' the moment ye would lift me veil."

Remembering the moment, he reached over and hugged her.

"A'll never ferget me shivers when the organist pounded the keys to *Here Comes the Bride,* but then everythin' stopped!"

"Because there, at the back door, me bedraggled parents stood after weeks of travel. A beamed with joy when Uncle Hugh made way for me father to take me arm."

"And Vi hurried yer mother to the front seat. When the processional began, a could feel yer eyes fixed on me. All a needed was yer smile to make me heart sing!"

"Did ye notice when the priest asked people to 'speak now or ferever hold their peace', 'twas only met with a little shufflin' and throat clearin'?"

"Were ye expectin' somethin' else?"

"Nae!" she snickered and quickly reached for his hand to admire the rings, "The $1.75 gold bands were worth it!"

"A loved when he pronounced us man and wife!" and with that, McLaren made his move, starting slow but with her response, it developed into the deepest kiss he had ever attempted.

Despite her body tingling, she disentangled herself, "A need to relieve meself," she said, and jumped up, heading for the outhouse.

"A'll come too and watch fer wolves," he wasn't kidding.

There was no toilet paper and he volunteered to run for more. Doing her business, was not the best time to think of food but the meal they'd prepared that day was a hit. A slow-roasted pig on a spit complemented wild turkey, potatoes and gravy, stuffing, turnips, and coleslaw. Dessert was cake and homemade ice cream.

After grace, her usually proper father, George, had spouted, "Amen! And pass the gizzard!" even more surprising, her mother jumped up to find it.

When the speeches started, McLaren went first to do the thanking. Rose-petal wine, and an assortment of inebriants swished in goblets. Glasses clinked, and the guests imbibed long and hard.

Hugh stood up to toast Tessa but roasted McLaren while Lizzy said, "We're parched from our trip and this wine is decadent!"

"Aye!" a woman beside her said. "try the spiced rum!"

The fiddler's tender first waltz was for her and her father, the second for the wedding couple alone. Finally, the crowd of dancers formed a large circle. Ladies wore hats and frock-like ball gowns with trains. Young girls wore shorter frocks with pantaloons and tall boots while men sported argyle jackets, kilts, and hose. After each dance, whether reel, jig, haymaker, or lilt, people caught their breath and clamoured for more.

Tessa's thoughts returned to the present. By this time, the couple were back in the bunkhouse and Tessa's parents snored loudly in the bed opposite.

The new bridegroom stretched out his hand, "Me darling wife, 'tis bedtime."

Even though it felt improper, there was no getting out of the wedding gown alone, and she allowed him to follow her behind the screened-off corner. Glorying in his touch, she giggled as they got down to her undergarments but then she shooed him away.

"But," he protested, "we're merrit now!"

A few moments later, draped in flannel, she tiptoed barefoot across the cold floorboards where he waited under the covers. Slipping into the icy bed, their own buttery warmth caused an instinctive closeness.

Shivering, he teased, "Me darlin', in future, what say we remember to use a hot water bottle?"

She burst out laughing.

Despite the bizarreness of the evening and worries about their progress, with no roadmap to follow, the newlyweds gave it their best shot. He rolled towards her and she felt his hands searching under her nightgown for bare skin. When he found it, to her alarm, there was a warm sensation in her nether regions not unlike peeing. When he took liberties, she tingled, riding an unfamiliar wave, having to bite her lip to keep silent. All else was forgotten when the passion between them crested a ridge, smooth as silk. The young-girl-turned-woman had received the bull by the horns. The two performed gallantly and the intruders beside them snored like the Lord.

Fast forward eight and a half months to Tessa's first birthing experience. With settling into their home and clearing the land, Confederation had come and gone on 1 July 1867. Now, it was January 1868, and her water broke too soon but nothing happened for a full hour.

"Let's hope the bairn isnae premature!" she thought, "a bet McLaren takes back everythin' he thought about me parents." To her, he had tried to cover his impatience. The Reverend George and Lizzie had stayed all that first summer but were long gone by fall.

"Me long-sufferin' in-laws," he had groused to Hugh, unaware the women were listening around the corner.

McLaren fetched Vi. The talented woman went straight to the helm, then emerged to say, "'Twilt be hours with a first baby, so get the midwife, then try to relax."

After seven hours of contractions that had Tessa doubled over and sweating profusely, McLaren was beside himself when a baby wailed. Vi opened the bedroom door and the midwife held up a squalling baby and spoke proudly, "Ye have a beautiful baby girl!"

All butter fingers, they gave him a pillow and laid the infant down. An exhausted Tessa saw Vi try not to chuckle but McLaren looked like he'd gone through the wringer. He moved to his wife's side and looking adoringly from his baby to her, he cooed, "And now a have two people to love."

When the beaming couple named her Emma, Tessa officially felt like a mother.

Twenty-three years later, crying, teething, and diapers were almost a thing of the past because by 1890, eight growing children graced their household. Pregnancies, births, and childhood may have sounded run of the mill but were far from it, being their greatest accomplishments.

"There could have been a few more but a listened to old wives' tales and nursed the bairns in between," Tessa said.

"Childbirth is supposed to be good fer the heart," McLaren said. "Like if ye exercised fer seven years!"

"And the 73¢ safety syringe douche from Sears & Roebuck might help if a woman didn't feel like exercisin' fer seven years in one fell swoop!" she said under her breath.

Birth control was a touchy subject. After all, the Roman Catholics said conceiving a child was a gift from God and part of His grand plan. Any woman took care to guard themselves during pregnancy for fear of miscarrying. Nobody wanted to be accused of the criminal offence of abortion.

Over time, McLaren cleared the land, built up the farm, and in winter, worked in the bush logging. In due course, their log home graduated to a larger, two-storey frame house. It was amazing but aside from a little sciatica, neither Tessa nor McLaren were much the worse for wear. The devout members of the Anglican Church thanked God for their thriving family.

In five years since 1885, however, Tessa had lost both her parents and her aunt and uncle. The Reverend George, from liver failure, then Uncle Hugh from a stroke. Auntie Vi, stooped and crippled over time, and in the end,

Lizzie, from a heart attack. Most devastating was that Tessa missed her parents' funerals.

By 1892, McLaren, at 51, and Tessa 41, felt fortunate that she was through menopause and their brood was large. Emma was 24, Jake—23, Clarice—19, Sean—16, Barbara—13, Bessie—11, David—8, and Anna, a toddler of 2.

"At this stage of life, we want to grow auld together and play with our grandchildren."

"Farmin' means never endin' work, but we've all these extra sets of hands now to help." Tessa laughed.

The summer before, Emma, a serious-minded girl, had married Jock, a strapping young fellow from the Purbrook area. A healthy baby granddaughter, Eliza May arrived, May 1892 and was named for her birth month.

"We're overjoyed!" Tessa gushed. "Our own sweet Anna will be happier and far less spoiled with a playmate."

Anna was technically Eliza May's aunt, and the toddler gloried in holding the new bairn every chance she got. The two little girls were a delight and the older children kept them entertained.

2

Sweden

June 1891–1902

Across the world in Sweden, in the middle of mixing dough, a tentative knock sounded at the door. At the slight noise, the old dog let out a roar, followed by a round of barking sure to wake the dead. Racing in circles, he jumped up and down, panting hard, trying to see out the window. The frightened kitten skittered under a chair and Lasse gave a soft Swedish curse. She wiped her hands and wondered who could be so thoughtless to call at nap time.

Five-year old, Little Bjorn, reached the door first, so she wrestled the misbehaving dog back. If he hadn't already, the beast would wake the little girls and then there would be hell to pay.

She asked herself in Swedish, "Is it a delivery?" but no, there in the cool Stockholm air stood her father, and behind him, the pastor, along with her husband's boss, the train station manager, whom she barely knew. Out front stood a uniformed member of the Swedish Police. Shadows crossed their faces and she froze. Her heart thudded, and her legs grew weak as she struggled not to lose her grip on the dog.

The little boy sensed the ominous mood and clung to his mother's leg. Speaking Swedish, he asked, "What's wrong, Mama?"

She couldn't answer.

"I'm sorry but there was an accident," the policeman cleared his throat and hung his head. "There's no easy way to tell you this but your husband was killed." The dire words came at her like a steam roller, opening the portal to hell.

Clamping both hands over her mouth, she felt her father close in, unaware she had pitched forward into a blackened world. Mercifully, the little girls slept.

For the next minutes, a paralysis set in but bit by bit her consciousness returned. Was this a nightmare? Her mother sat in the chair opposite. The beautiful woman's face was puffy and her eyes red-rimmed. Her father didn't look much better. Heavy grief blanketed the room, weighing them all down. Her breath left her and the feeling of drowning returned. Bjorn was gone. For a moment, she couldn't speak.

"Where are the children?" Lasse gasped between anguished sobs.

"They're fine." Her father strode to her side and took her hand.

There was a long moment of silence before he began, "When the train went over the Birs River bridge, the trestle faltered and broke. Tragically, Bjorn was in one of the central cars that plunged into the river below."

Her mother interjected, "They said he died instantly."

Lasse felt a wave of nausea but imagined the headline, "June 14, 1891, rail disaster claims life of train konduktor leaving 21-year-old widow and three pre-school children."

"Bjorn's parents are on their way," and a painful wave consumed her at the thought.

Thank God, none of them knew the details of the horror that had transpired the evening before. At Munchenstein, over 70 were killed. The one simple truth was that Bjorn was never coming home again.

In time, she wondered how to stop reeling from the devastation when most of the community was affected. Bjorn's funeral fell on Midsummer's Eve, June 24, 1891, and all her usual baking orders fell by the wayside. Receiving the friends and neighbours who crowded around the mourners meant they had the best of intentions at heart but still, it meant no end of reminders.

Wherever she went, they wept, wrung their hands, and beseeched God, "Why would He let such a tragedy happen?"

Gossips placed blame, "They say the bridge was faulty, designed by the same engineer as the Eiffel Tower!"

Allowances for the mourner's grief showed in faces at the market, at church, and inside their own homes. The majority would give the shirt off their back and tripped over themselves pouring coffee and performing staggering acts of goodwill. It was much more than appreciated and at times, Lasse felt overwhelmed.

One outlet for her was Bjorn's father, Farfar, *Grandfather.* He was heartbroken right alongside his wife, Farmor, *Grandmother,* and had stopped by Lasse's cottage.

When she poured the coffee, he said, "Farmor has taken to her bed and won't eat. Nothing I do consoles her."

"Please," she motioned him to sit on a kitchen chair and sat beside him.

"I would like to lay down beside her myself and sob my heart out but I don't dare," Farfar said, tears spilling down his cheeks.

Lasse gulped, "I feel every bit as bad but if we give in, we're done for."

"And nobody can bring Bjorn back," Farfar was convincing himself.

There was a moment of silence and then he said, "I'm trying to think of ways to make the children understand how their father can be here one day and gone the next."

"You have helped more than you know with your angel stories," Lasse reassured.

"I think that's a good start."

She reached over and took his hands in hers. "I so appreciate you bringing light to their sad little worlds. You're a one-of-a-kind man and Bjorn lives on in you." She couldn't help but put her arms around him.

It took a long time but strengthened by his selflessness, Lasse pulled herself together and trudged to her in-laws' house.

Farfar greeted her at his door, then spoke with fondness to his bed-bound wife, "Lasse is here and made your favourite, tomato soup!"

He looked thrilled that Lasse had perked up and he affectionately spooned the soup into his wife. Farmor tasted the first spoonful, then slurped with a half-smile. Just maybe, she would rally.

"How about a cup of coffee?" Lasse offered and her mother-in-law nodded.

Lasse knew with all the grandparents at their sides, life would improve. In fact, her own parents, Mormor, *Grandma*, and Morfar, *Grandpa* were hands-on helpers for the children. Their incredible input eased the burden to support them on the long road to healing.

Over time, anywhere Lasse went, people asked, "How are you?"

Her answer went from a pinched, "fine," to an optimistic, "very well, thank you!"

Throughout, she pushed back the lurking bitterness. Various people thought she got the short end of the stick and even months later might break down crying in front of her, which didn't help.

Others said things like, "He was a prince of a man," which did.

To discuss the worse misfortunes of others hurt.

"Yes, there are people worse off," she admitted, ashamed of the vicious cycle of guilt and praying for forgiveness.

More helpful was, "Your husband was a man of merit who would want you to succeed."

Those words she appreciated. "I will," she replied.

Unexpectedly, at the one-year mark, Lasse awoke with a feeling of lightness. Undoubtedly, she felt a shift within her on the anniversary of his death.

That morning, she said to her children, "No more feeling sorry for ourselves. We will never be okay with your father's death, but we have to live with it and go on with our lives."

From here, things improved and Lasse, more than ever, returned to filling baking orders. She kneaded a batch of dough and told her mother, "I think we may have all reached a turning point."

Starting at 10 years old, in 1896, Little Bjorn did odd jobs for neighbours but now at 15, worked as a hired hand on a local farm. His sisters helped wherever they could. Little by little, Lasse was pleased her household's meagre savings grew, and Bjorn's railroad death benefit remained untouched. Over time, Lasse's mother-in-law, Farmor, returned to her old self.

A full decade after the accident, the two grandmothers threw a small 30th birthday party for Lasse, at her parents' house.

After coffee, cake, blowing out candles, and singing happy birthday, Lasse raised her cup of glogge in a toast, "To the new decade. May our insight be great and our lives filled with sunshine! Skål!" They clinked their cups and took a swig of her father's homemade concoction.

About a week later, Lasse let her guard down for a moment and widower, Anders, a wealthy landowner breezed into her life. They had bumped into each other at the market, and he seemed the perfect package. A gem at fixing things, all fall, he showed up daily at her cottage to help. At first, she was curious and appreciative but before long, she sensed something was off. The biggest complaint she had was how he monopolised her time.

"Good grief," she thought. "He's elbowed his way past my work again, to force me to pay attention to him."

When Mormor asked how things were, Lasse admitted, "Mother, I have an urge to reclose the door I opened."

"My dear, don't you know? Shutting the barn door after the horse leaves is a waste of time."

"Well, if there was a prize for trying too hard, he'd win."

Even her father, Morfar commented, "His capacity for drumming up make-work projects around your house is astounding!"

"Yes, and never is it leisurely but always with such intensity that I'm expected to drop everything to help. I do appreciate his time and efforts but why does my work have to take a back seat?"

"Well, he is doing it for you, after all," her father reminded.

"Yes, I know." Conflicted, she worked around her instincts because his attentions felt better than nothing.

When she asked, "Can I pay you for your work?" he wouldn't hear of it.

"I will accept an occasional meal," he said, then showered her with praise, "you are a fabulous cook!"

Flattery didn't sway her, but she loved feeding people and for this he scored points. Interactions with this attractive man and his endearing smile were easy at first. He even alluded to a sister no one had met.

On the other hand, he made a point of ribbing her at the supper table, "Where's she hiding that red-headed temper?"

When her throat reddened, the kids exchanged looks, spotting her discomfort.

Then he did the unforgiveable in front of everyone. "You know I love you," and it made her freeze.

She refused to respond. To her, that talk was private.

When alone, he put his arms around her and pressed, "I love you and you love me, we should marry."

She remained silent and thought, "Maybe it's me. I don't find those loaded expressions easy to say." At the same time, she stepped back and muttered, "I don't think so."

But he ignored her response, sweeping forward again.

"You're beautiful, and we're so in love. It's time."

She stepped away again, thinking. "No, we're not! This has to stop. He makes the pronouncement like it's an established fact!"

Instead, she joked, "I'm well past the first bloom. How could you think you know my feelings when I don't?" What she felt around him was closer to embarrassment.

Still, she tried to reduce the tension and look past his goading, "It's too soon."

"It's not like men are lined up at your door," he scoffed. "You can't keep comparing me to your husband!"

It was a low blow but she was guilty every time she thought of her husband, Bjorn. Nothing sent shivers through her like his touch, and when they said, "I love you," they meant it.

With Anders, it was like kissing the wall. It wasn't love, and she didn't want to lead him on. The children didn't outright hate him but rolled their eyes. The first time he asked where to sit at their kitchen table, they had his number.

"We aren't stupid. We know manipulation when we see it," Little Bjorn said. "What a clever way to reassure us he wasn't trying to replace our father."

Lasse noticed Anders sidling up to her girls and chastised herself for being suspicious, but negatives were piling up. Actions spoke louder than words and his actions were odd. Entertaining marriage the day after meeting? Talking to himself? And not just a little bit. Alarming patterns formed, despite her giving him the benefit of the doubt. Perhaps he was eccentric or had an invisible friend?

The one time he had enticed her to visit his home and toured her around, two things stood out. First, the place was impeccable, cleaner than hers. Second, was the box of saws and an empty, over-sized trunk. At the time, it gave her goose bumps.

Christmas came, and awkwardly, he invited himself to join the grand affair.

"Thank you for the sweets," the children were polite.

Come New Year's eve, on the brink of 1902, everything changed. That afternoon, in the shimmering midday haze, once the youngsters went sledding, Lasse felt torn between her workload and entertaining Anders. She'd made coffee admitting to herself she needed him to go home.

"You've already cleaned the lantern and trimmed the wick, then fixed the bucket's slow leak. Last time was chinking a wall. I feel bad for taking up your time. Thank you very much but don't you deserve a break?"

Still, he dug in his heels, having no intention of missing the New Year's celebrations.

During the evening meal preparations, she tried broaching the subject again. "Perhaps I should take time to work on my baking orders tomorrow. I can't leave them, and I'm sure you have things to do at home," she wasn't rude but direct.

"After all," she thought, "without you underfoot, I could accomplish so much more. You can't get blood out of a stone when it comes to love."

Either her words or body language touched a nerve, and he reacted like a lit fuse. His face darkened, and he stood up fuming, then spun away, clenching his fists.

Caught off guard, she asked, "What's wrong?"

When he turned back, his eyes flashed and he spat in a menacing tone, "How do you think I feel?"

She hadn't asked the question and he said it again. It was like he was reliving an old argument.

"I'm sorry," she ventured.

"Your life would be in shambles without me," he accused.

"What?" she faltered, dumbfounded and a little afraid.

He paced, making fists, swinging into thin air while her throat went dry.

"Don't be upset," she tried but he gave her the cold shoulder.

"Well," she thought, "catching the fly with sugar didn't work."

Questions whirled in her mind. "Is he hungry? Possessed? Or a Mr. Hyde?" and the hair stood up on the back of her neck.

"I guess he can't take rejection. If such insignificance triggers him," she thought, "how long before the real explosion?" How had she hurt his feelings? His fixing was appreciated and according to him, no trouble. She had politely asked for time to herself.

"Does he have two personalities?" she wondered. "Because I don't recognise him." Deciding his mood wasn't about to lighten, she edged towards the fireplace.

He continued the insanity with, "I feel so used."

Making her sound like a gold-digging shrew was a low blow. He'd thrown himself at her! If he kept it up, he might get a taste of her red-headed temper.

"I think you'd better leave," she said in measured tones.

In that perilous moment, he stepped forward, grabbed her by both wrists, and tried to heave her across the room. Stumbling but with temper fuelled, she wrenched away, grabbing the fireplace poker. While clawing a fistful of her hair with one hand, he ripped her bodice with the other. White flesh and delicate underthings sprang forth. Armed and on the offensive, she jabbed, missing his flesh by mere inches.

Done being polite, she shouted, "Get out of my house!"

Slowing, his eyes and body twitched like a cat's, ready to pounce. He could get the poker away if he wanted but instead, he backed up.

She spoke in stilted tones, "Leave me alone!" If ever there was a time to sic her old dog on something, it was now but he was long gone.

Whether Anders had a moment of clarity, she would never know but he turned on his heel and stalked out, scowling all the way.

"Don't come near us again!" she growled. Putting a curse on him was called for if she only knew how.

Complacency was no longer an option and Lasse chastised herself for ever letting him into her life. No need to find out what else lurked beneath his façade. At once, she feared for her children. Within moments, she pushed one arm through her coat sleeve, ready to go searching, but heard banging at the door. Expecting Anders, she grabbed the poker but her heart lurched when her two icicle-covered daughters appeared.

"Thank God! Come in quickly! Where's Little Bjorn?"

"There!" they pointed at their older brother bounding towards them raining streams of ice fog with every breath.

None of them could believe the sight of their mother with ripped dress, crumpled hair, and red and bruising wrists. Once all three were safely inside, Lasse turned the iron skeleton key in the door behind them.

Without attempting to remove coats and boots, Little Bjorn begged to know, "Mother, what happened?"

"Look at your dress!" Mikaila echoed in alarm.

"Cross your hearts and hope to die, to never go near Anders again," Lasse commanded, "he's a monster."

With no room for argument, all three promised, feeling her fear.

"Help me bar the doors and windows."

Little Bjorn barred the front door with its heavy plank, while the girls pushed a cabinet to block the back. Lasse wedged broom sticks and mops across the windows. The girls fussed around their mother trying to pin her dress back in place.

"All I suggested was I work on my baking and he flew into a rage. When he grabbed me, I threatened him with the poker and told him to leave and never return, and he did. I don't trust that he won't come back. We have to be extra careful."

Little Bjorn said, "Let me tell you what I heard. Just now, I saw him trudging past the skating square. He was talking to himself and the music masked what he said but I did hear the words, 'run-in with the law', and 'stays buried with her'."

Lasse shuddered. *Who was the buried woman?*

Sleep eluded them that night. Fearing he might return, Lasse sat up in the dark with the fireplace poker across her lap, waiting, listening, and watching. With eyes accustomed to the darkness, she hoped for the advantage.

Her son, soon a grown man, was restless and kept getting up to check on her. "He was never worth it, Mother."

"I was a fool to trust him but how do you get to know someone otherwise?"

Towards dawn, Lasse prayed Anders had disappeared for good. After another tense 24 hours with no sign of him, she relaxed somewhat and over time, the barricades came down.

Morfar, asked daily, "Any sign of that coward?"

"After weeks, Father," Lasse said, "he seems to have faded from sight but we'll keep looking over our shoulders!"

"Best to be wary but it's good he's gone. I never liked him."

Not long after, one morning when cleaning, Lasse uncovered a forgotten pamphlet stuffed at the back of her dresser drawer. Periodically, immigration literature flooded the European countryside, offering whole new lives across the ocean. The idea had seemed remote to start with but now was taking hold.

One line caught her eye, 'Scandinavians are some of the most desirable settlers for the Canadian prairies'. Seated on the bed, she read the description of the Carrot River Valley in the Northwest Territories as a fertile belt for homesteading. Was that the place for her? Rebuilding her life wouldn't be easy but women heads of households were eligible, and she could be one of them. Hundreds of thousands had already left Sweden and why not her? After all, something had to change.

Rearranging the drawer, she thought, "My life will unravel with or without a man. If I stay here, sooner or later, the kids will leave home and there I'll be, living on the edge of poverty, all alone, like so many others."

Back in the kitchen, finishing her baking orders, she daydreamed, "With hard work in the new country, anything is possible and poverty is no disgrace. I've discovered men are a touchy business so any new partner will need references!" That night a dream captured her fancy.

Waving for her to come along, a young blond fellow stood on a ship's deck. His Scottish brogue was foreign, but they understood each other, Like an old friend, he toured her around and she could smell the salt sea spray. When he showed a trunk filled with strange possessions, she awoke.

The trunk stuck in her mind but so did the urge to travel. Resistance from her parents and in-laws would be a given but they could come along.

For the first time in a very long time, she allowed herself to think back to when her husband, Bjorn, had died and dream-like, she remembered it all…

The old border collie and his newly adopted kitten had soaked up the sun beside the wood stove. In the other room, Little Bjorn shouted, "95, 100!" and his younger sisters, Mikaila and Lovisa, scrambled to hide.

"Here, I come, ready or not!" Lasse heard, wiping her fingers on her apron.

Two-year old Lovisa, attempted to hide her face under a cushion but her brother swooped in to catch her up in his arms.

Mikaila, much wiser at three, made a break for it, and cried, "Home free!"

Lasse couldn't help but laugh. She and Big Bjorn loved children but were not rich and hesitated to have more.

"Come and have your stew and längfil," Lasse called, knowing it might take coaxing for noon leftovers. Most times, they didn't fuss but today, Mikaila turned up her nose and Lovisa copied.

"I don't yike ogurt," the littlest one whined, "I want ganola."

Little Bjorn, on cue, launched into his fire-breathing dragon routine. "I'll burn up your food," he whooshed in.

The girls squealed and ducked but took the bait, gobbling their stew and yogurt, never realising they'd been had.

Lasse winked at her son, "You're a dragon magician!"

With their poor sleep, the girls wouldn't be up much longer. Mikaila had awoken in the night crying, "I want Papa!" and of course that woke everyone.

"I know you're Papa's girl, but Mama's here," Lasse hushed, trying to let her husband sleep before leaving for work.

Something in the little girl's dream took rocking and soothing and Mama fantasised about an afternoon nap for herself.

After dishes, Lasse motioned, "Come, let's put your dollies to sleep," and with reluctance, the girls snuggled under their favourite quilts.

Cradling her precious rag doll, Lovisa cried, "No, I don't want to."

Even so, they were sleeping before their heads hit the feather pillows. Little Bjorn kept a low profile, keeping to the shadows, slaying dragons on the straw broom pony Papa made. The little Viking was five, going on 12.

In 1891 Stockholm, Lasse did custom baking and had orders for the upcoming Midsommarafton *Midsummer's Eve* on June 24. Today was June 14, so over a week away. Payment was seldom in cash, often eggs, meat, or vegetables, all welcomed in her larder. Her dreaming reverted to when she and Big Bjorn had met.

She told her parents, "He may be six years older than me, but he's already promoted from brakeman to konductor! And he looks grand in his uniform!"

His love notes were for her eyes only but his invitations for bird watching or sight-seeing included both sets of parents and she loved that about him.

"Bundling sealed our deal," she thought. The not-so-secret practice had her waiting as a teen for him to show up at bedtime to lay on her bed and talk.

Little Bjorn was born 9 months after the wedding but other bundlers were less fortunate. Lasse remembered that her light-hearted Big Bjorn seemed troubled. The last bedtime story he told, revealed it.

"A konduktor hated fining poor people," he started.

"What did he do, Papa? the littlest ones, sitting on his knee asked."

"Well, a wizened old lady, and a struggling young mother had no money. The konduktor was at his wit's end and looked to the Heavens for help. The answer came, 'start off with a warning'."

"Good idea!" Little Bjorn said, cuddling with his mother.

Papa went on, "After three warnings, it was their third strike, like when you play ball, what happens then?"

Mikaila spun around to look up at him, "You're out!"

"Does that mean they couldn't ride the train again?" Little Bjorn sat up a little straighter.

"The konduktor knew free rides were against the rules yet, the poor people needed to get to the market for food! What was he to do?"

Lasse felt his pain.

"Couldn't he just let them ride for free, Papa?"

"He was about to when the young woman held out a fistful of Krona, enough to pay all the fares! The konduktor was amazed but oh, so curious!"

"Where did she get the money?"

"Well, the two turned out to be special Nordic fairies who blessed him with their magic."

"How?"

"By sprinkling him with their enchanting dust and promising him a happy life!" With stars in their eyes, the children said their prayers, and were tucked into bed.

Working overtime seemed non-negotiable for Bjorn, and at bedtime, he wore a hangdog expression about missing a Sunday with the family.

Lasse remembered him saying, "It's a large music festival in *Schweitz* Switzerland so it's all hands-on deck. Hundreds of performers and their audiences, from all over the continent, will travel by train."

"Well, there's still plenty of summer left," she consoled, "and time to go blueberry picking."

"Our parents will jump at the chance. They love seeing those stained little fingers and purple mouths."

"In mid-August, we can still go for lingonberries, with only one jar of jelly left in the cellar."

Lasse and Bjorn loved nature and fresh air and watching the children scrunch their faces after tasting the sour lingon from the tree. Adding sugar made it better to go with delicacies like pickled herring and lutefisk. It was an acquired taste for children.

Now, a decade later was a new ache to leave Sweden and Lasse made up her mind. Secretly, she mailed letters to Gothenburg to investigate passenger ships leaving via Hull and departing Liverpool but that was an English-speaking ship. Knowing few English words, she would have to give this careful thought and pray to God for guidance. Her prayers were answered when, without warning, two old friends, Kirsten and Greta sat at her kitchen table, sharing their news, and revelling in their decision.

"We're boarding a cattle ship departing Hamburg for Halifax the beginning of May," Greta babbled. "My brother, Hans, is a stockman on that ship, and he says for reduced fares we can work jobs on board."

"We are jumping at the chance and want you to join us," Kirsten urged. "Meeting future husbands on the prairies has many single maids giddy, not just us."

Kirsten coaxed, "Those other girls have written that, 'Western Canada has far more bachelors than anyone can count, and most are looking for wives, housekeepers, and cooks.'"

"Be careful!" Lasse warned. "You don't want to run across another Anders!" Everyone sobered having already heard her story.

"Don't you think conversing with a European crew on a cattle ship would be easier for us than floundering around on an English one?" Kirsten changed the subject. She had read Lasse's mind.

Not waiting for an answer, Greta went on, "And with the cheaper fare and the protection of Hans and his mates, we're set! Nobody minds cattle, but so you know, Lasse, the vessel is a 'tramp', and it makes stops, so isn't a direct trip."

At Lasse's nods and questioning look, Kirsten filled in the blanks. "It makes drop-offs and pick-ups, so the voyage could take a bit longer. What do you think Lasse? Will you come with us?"

Enticed, Lasse imagined her own dynasty in a whole new land. The image was alluring and addicting. Surely her other loved ones would follow. The only thing stopping her was herself.

Greta and Kirsten were convincing, and Lasse found herself nodding in agreement, filled with promise but wondering if all three had lost their minds. She thanked God for Bjorn who was most assuredly watching over her from on high.

3

Scourge

Muskoka *1892–1894*

Back on the Muskokan farm, no one noticed the chill that crept into the farmhouse air by late August 1892, so no one expected Barbara to get sick. When McLaren and Tessa's 13-year-old daughter developed a mild fever, sore throat, and difficulty swallowing, the household waited and watched.

"'Tis a good sign we've had nae word of others growing ill around Muskoka," Tessa said.

Forty-eight hours later, the teen got worse.

McLaren's eyes clouded when he looked at his wife, "'Tis time to send Jake fer the doctor." On horseback, their eldest at 23, could ride like the wind.

While the physician examined Barbara, the kin held their breath.

In a grave voice, he whispered, "I'm afraid it's diphtheria. As you know, a markedly contagious disease."

He had confirmed their worst nightmare.

"My hands are tied without tools to prevent or treat it, and there's no cure. Word will circulate fast for people to stay away. The rest is up to God."

With his head in his hands, McLaren anguished, "But where did she get it?"

The middle-aged, former army surgeon, explained, "With an incubation period of one to 10 days, it's impossible to trace the source."

Tessa and McLaren knew the professional man had returned east after serving as a medic in the Riel Rebellion at Batoche.

He was known to say, "War wounds to grown men are horrific but I will never get used to standing by, watching contagious disease ravage innocent children."

Shortly, the circles under Barbara's eyes darkened and indeed, 11-year-old Bessie grew ill next. Tessa wept seeing Bessie watch Barbara's symptoms unfold until it was clear what was in store for her. For the family, pretending everything would be all right was hard but when there was little time left, the girls clung together in terror. Happy little Anna played alongside, oblivious to her own fate.

Throughout the ordeal, the Anglican priest at every service, begged for prayers, and lit candles. "Dear God, Please save these children," he prayed, inviting the congregation to, "Beg the Divine Healer to intervene."

The doctor offered a microcosm of hope, "Word of a promising anti-toxin has come out of Germany,"

When the household's bewildered eyes fluttered open, Tessa sensed his guard go up.

He explained, "The serum is harvested from horses." and promised, "I will do whatever I can to lay hands on it."

It wasn't that he didn't try. To his credit, even burning the midnight oil was of no use, and in the end, he confirmed, "Being an ocean away, my efforts were futile."

Deep down, Tessa already knew what he would say. "A medicine in the trial stages without mass production, is almost impossible to obtain."

The symptoms raged and the brood took turns sponging, moistening lips, and wiping brows.

"The girls are not to get a draft," Tessa reminded. "We must keep the fires burnin', indoors and out." She knew the boys were doing their best.

McLaren didn't have to remind them, "Chores still have to be done twice a day, but the large livestock go out to pasture. We have to ignore the ripenin' grain on the other side of the hedge fer now. Jake, Sean, and David, we'll keep firewood chopped, to boil water fer the dirty linens."

Tessa appreciated that her daughter, Emma, living at Purbrook, reluctantly stayed away to protect little Eliza May. If her sons worked hard, so did her youngest daughter, Clarice.

"Clarice," Tessa hugged her, "a see ye cookin', cleanin' and doin' the laundry to spell me off. A know scrubbin' is back breakin' work. We pray hangin' the beddin' and nightclothes out in the sun will kill the germs."

All were desperate for answers to their prayers, and crooned lullabies to the girls. In fact, eight-year-old David tried to heal his ailing sisters with kisses.

He slipped to their bedsides every chance he got, kissing them on the hands and foreheads and saying, "All better now!"

Jake told 19-year-old Clarice, "A kiss has always done the trick fer him. A dinnae have the heart nor the energy to shoo him away, do ye?"

With tears streaming down their faces, his younger sister shook her head.

"David, yer such a good wee lad." Tessa tousled her darling's hair. "Playing noughts and crosses makes yer sisters smile," she stifled a sob, because she knew at times the ailing girls were well beyond playing.

David had no idea what was to come except that it was bad. No neighbour had gone near them but mornings at the end of the lane was evidence of their generosity. They left anything from fresh baking to cooked chickens, or hams.

Grateful, the family's hearts almost burst, "Thank ye God fer the tender mercies shown!"

For six weeks, overwrought and sleep deprived, any of them would collapse whenever they could go no more. When that happened, it was a short stress-riddled sleep. At one point, Tessa's slumber was crowded by a dream.

A young boy of about eight was laden with schoolbooks and trudged across a rainy moor in Scotland. His distressed mother found him at the door, soaked to the skin. Tessa heard his hacking cough while she crawled under his bed looking for his lost shoes.

She heard him say, 'Here they are', and pulled two big, croaking bull frogs from under his pillow.

At the mischief, the boy's caramel eyes flashed, and a teasing smile covered his face. Despair turned to joy on his mother's face.

The false sense of security vanished when Tessa awoke and her own truth flooded back. There was croaking but it was Barbara's breathing. A lethal grey pseudo-membrane was fast growing across the girl's throat and to see it, broke Tessa's heart.

On 10 September, Barbara took her last breath. Bessie and the bairn, Anna, were both sick by this time but so was brother Sean. Another month took them to 10 October, and Bessie met Barbara's fate. Within 10 days, so had baby Anna.

Tessa replayed it over and over in her mind. "First came the laboured breathin', then the crowin' and gaspin' with full consciousness until the deafenin' silence. A death by strangulation is just that, a stranglin' death." She felt like vomiting.

"Our hearts are shattered," Jake said, crowding together with his traumatised loved ones.

"Our one glimmer of hope is our sweet sixteen, Sean," McLaren said holding his wife. "He's a strong lad and 'tis God's will that he's recoverin'."

Being thankful, all Tessa could see in her mind's eye was the funeral cortège, painstakingly making its way to the isolated cemetery. Down the tree-lined lane and through flickering rays of sunlight the hearse rolled. Over time, she hoped to appreciate the eternal home her daughters would share with a young lad who died unjamming river logs. Near to him rested Auntie Vi and Uncle Hugh. Stoically, Tessa imagined herself and McLaren standing at the graveside with the priest and undertaker.

The priest would end his benediction with, "Dear God, please bless and care for these young souls who will never grow old. In Jesus' name we pray, Amen."

Lowering the wooden caskets would cause her to sob and fall to her knees and McLaren would console her. Both would remember their daughters' bodies laid to rest facing east to meet Christ upon His second coming. The image of them and the girls watching the same sun rises, for an eternity to come would be a comfort.

***

When Tessa told McLaren her thoughts, he said, "The imagination is a wonderful thing, and a too envisioned the whole ritual but when reason returned, me comfortin' fantasy faded."

"In reality," he said, "as ye know, 'twas me, all alone there in the cemetery, burying them, in the black of night."

Tessa heard him say, "Fer the third time, because 'twas a contagious disease, there was no funeral and no others attendin' at all."

She went on, "Instead, ye had the grim task of transportin' their dear bodies to the cemetery after dark, and buryin' them, one after the other. Ye alone built their wooden caskets, and 'twas an open wagon they travelled in, not a grand hearse. 'twas ye doin' the prayin' not the priest."

"Tessa, ye might have come along," and they both wept, "but ye were physically and emotionally bankrupt yerself." His anguish was no worse than hers. "Wantin' to prolong me lovin' goodbyes, it took the whole night to bury them."

"And thank ye God fer sparin' Sean."

***

After the burials, despite stumbling like rag dolls and having no tears left, the siblings and parents stared stonily at the bonfire raging out in the yard. The flames licked up everything their girls once possessed from clothing to straw mattresses, bedding, feather pillows, and toys.

If that wasn't enough, McLaren had stood by helpless, watching his neighbours work his land. "Bless them!" he cried. "They've brought in our whole harvest, cut it with a binder, stooked, and threshed it. Now there's piles of straw and feed fer our animals, and grain in our bins!"

When the neighbour ladies delivered the garden bounty, the crowd assembled a good distance away.

"Here's yer potatoes in gunny sacks and all yer vegetables dug and picked. We canned and pickled what we could to see ye through the winter!"

"We will never be able to repay ye," the humbled parents repeated.

"Ye folks would do it fer us in a heartbeat."

No one wanted to tell them but eventually they heard the rumours. "In this same outbreak, others lost all their children to diphtheria and had their homes burned to the ground."

Truly, others were worse off but McLaren and Tessa were not out of the woods yet. It was a mere two years later, in January 1894 when Emma and Jock's little Eliza May developed a severe hacking cough.

The doctor said, "There is no mistaking the high-pitched whoop."

To everyone's utter devastation, the 20-month-old girl became a fatality of whooping cough, destined to join her three young aunts in the Matthiasville cemetery. At that point, it was more than anyone could bear. This time, for moral support, McLaren tried to soften the blow by accompanying his son-in-law, Jock, to the cemetery after dark.

Tessa's mood seemed to drum up a thunderstorm, and her mind was crowded with questioning thoughts of God's power. "The crashes of thunder and lightning show His power and fury, yet the gift of a refreshing rain shows His mercy."

She thought of Eve's sin, and how God punished women with the pain of childbirth but tempered their suffering with a blessed bairn. "Where is the mercy in taking away four children?" she cried. Her one consolation was that Heaven would be a better place. The family would persist and she would see to it as a mother.

Over a quarter of a century would pass before the scientific community developed and enabled distribution worldwide of a diphtheria vaccine. For whooping cough, it wouldn't be until the 1930s, well past McLaren and Tessa's time but available to protect future generations should they deign to accept it.

4

Draft Horse, Owl, and Sawmill

Iowa *1893–1902*

Knut whistled as he walked past his father, Nils, and the neighbour, Mr. Johnson, rocking on the veranda.

"He's a confident young man!" Mr. Johnson complimented, "and it's decent of you to share your libations!"

"Ja," Nils answered. "It was the least I could do for you delivering our new Clydesdale!"

The unsuspecting Knut was destined to become a branch of a new family tree, unaware of the others from Muskoka and Stockholm. The scenario was unfolding at the Winnebago County farm where the men had already fawned over the new horse.

Inside the house, the young Norwegian American lamented, "It's nearly the turn of the century, and I'll be middle-aged soon if this keeps up." The yearning was written all over Knut's face.

"He wants to homestead in Canada," his mother, Astrid, said to the neighbour lady. "He turned 21 last August."

Knut was on his way back outside.

"Uffdah! It's a cold November," Mrs. Johnson said from across the kitchen table. "Has little yurggin been looking at ads and poster maps again?"

Astrid put another log in her wood-burning cook stove. "Ja! Maps, and drawings, and whatever else he can find."

They sipped their steaming hot coffee, "The ones from the Canadian Pacific Railroad and Ministry of the Interior?"

"Ja, for the Northwest Territories," Knut filled in.

The neighbour smiled. "Our own son already left this beautiful Mount Valley Township and you'll go too, Knut! Yumpin' lutefisk! The Canadians sure know how to attract them! These young men of ours are intelligent and shrewd! I'm only sad to lose them but we are over 2,000,000 in Iowa, so it's getting crowded."

There was a moment of silence before Mrs. Johnson reminisced, "Astrid, do you remember the thrill of coming from Norway?"

"Ja, your people sailed with ours," Astrid remembered. "Nils and I landed in Minnesota with our parents, the year after the Civil War ended in 1865. But then both families ended up here, so we go back a long way!"

"It's funny how we exchanged our farming and logging birth right in Glemmen, Østfold, for the same thing in America!" The older woman was pensive but had them all smiling.

"It doesn't matter where you live, there's no end of work," Knut reminded.

"Ja, luckily, it's a close-knit community here and makes us happy but it was hard to say goodbye to that beautiful old country," Astrid remembered.

"Are you ready for Thanksgiving?" the neighbour asked. "We've rendered the lard, butchered the turkey and baked the pumpkin."

As Astrid nodded, Mrs. Johnson winked. "Time to go before our men get too far into the home brew."

"Not the gopher poison already?" Astrid sighed.

"Thanks for the visit," the woman drained her coffee to lead her protesting husband away.

Knut and Nils strode out to the corral to admire the new draft horse. The majestic stallion drank from the water trough, safely fenced off from the other horses.

"Some might consider our family a little unorthodox," Knut pondered.

Nils cocked his head.

"Well, Mother is seven years your senior and brought her son, Wil, from Norway."

"Age is unimportant and I accepted him with open arms. She told me, 'My parents raised him, and theirs is the only home, he's ever known.'"

"Then came all five of us kids, and the years we helped Grandpa Svend on his Minnesota farm." Knut remembered living there and the mound under the tree where his infant sister was buried.

The father and son leaned on the fence and watched the sublime creature throw his head and prance. Cisco was glorious and statuesque with a distinctive

Roman nose and white, well-feathered lower legs. When Knut held out an apple, the proud horse bobbed his head and trotted over to take a nibble.

"He's used to being spoiled," Nils gave him a scratch behind the ear.

"We could've used him long ago."

"Like in '79 when we bought this place and started logging. Or when your mother's brother got caught in that blinding snowstorm and froze to death back in Minnesota."

"All of us waited and watched all night, but he never showed."

Both knew by heart what happened next, but it helped to talk about it.

"It's hard to erase the springtime image of his rig at the bottom of that ravine," Nils admitted.

"And now Uncle Lars's widow is remarried, unable to survive on her own."

"They had it rough," Nils continued, pulling long grass for Cisco to nibble. "They emigrated ahead of us in 1861. She gave birth mid-Atlantic but the baby died and was given an ocean burial. They still had to make it overland from Quebec. By the time Lars died, they'd already lost six children of their nine, all under three years old. Sad for him to die so tragically after all their losses."

The horse nuzzled the men and then sauntered off, curious to meet the inquisitive herd on the other side of the fence, who had wandered in from the paddock.

The men meandered down the length of the pole fence. "Let's see how they take to him." The resident horses were placid except one, who had his ears pinned back and tried to bite. The lumbering newcomer jerked away, faster than he looked.

"Hmm, might take a while." Knut predicted.

"Ja."

After a moment, Nils returned to their previous conversation. "Depression had reigned in Lars's household for years."

"Ja, as a kid, I had multiple hiding spots and big ears. I heard Mother and Grandma Helene talk about it when they thought no one was listening."

"Astrid said they wondered if Lars intentionally drove off the trail that wintry night."

"I heard them make a pact not to breathe a word of that to anyone," Knut felt a little disillusioned that the secret was out.

Nils made a face. "Helene vetoed the idea because she and Svend also lost four of their seven children and suicide never came up. I agree with her, I don't think that ever entered Lars's mind."

Knut counted, "And, before Lars, there was their brother, Swen."

A couple of pigs rooted along the fence and just then a gelding turned his back and kicked hard through the fence. Cisco wasn't having it and punted back as good as he got. The fence was taking a beating so both Knut and Nils let out roars for the animals to stop. Not that it helped and when a post went flying, they knew something different was in order.

"We'll have to make reinforcements because Cisco has to stay quarantined for three weeks. By then, the deworming medicine should work and we'll see if he has any other signs of disease. Maybe that'll be enough time for the others to warm up," Knut said.

"I guess Cisco was a top dog at his old home," Nils revealed. "He'll have to work hard to carve out a spot in the pecking order here."

"About Swen," Knut went on prompting his father who knew the story well.

"Your mother's younger brother was barely legal age when he sailed from Norway to enlist in the Union's cavalry. The family was distraught until he used his enlistment bonus to help fund their voyages to join him."

"Swen was long gone before I was ever born," Knut said, "but I learned his stories. He was brave to stand up against slavery. Uffdah! What a shame he died from malaria two years after the war ended!"

"At least, he was at peace. You learned, along with the rest of us, to hate everything about war. Then, you were only five when your Grandma Helene passed away, the year after Lars. You saw first-hand how someone can die from a broken heart."

The pigs were grubbing and wallowing in the dirt and Knut continued, "When we lost Hans, to a burst appendix, I was only 12. My brother was my best friend you know."

"You were pretty broken up. We all were."

"And that's when I realised life is short and started mapping out my future."

That night, after being awoken by a strange dream, Knut couldn't sleep so got up and went out into the yard. A hoot owl perched in the barn window staring and blinking at him a little too long, making him feel strange. At breakfast, he told his parents about his dream.

There was a young, Scottish man about my age wearing a highlander's kilt. He offered me haggis and in the background a bagpipe played a bonnie tune. He talked of Nessie, the Loch Ness monster, then his lord and lady parents came. The father said, "Get away son and avoid the war," then he turned to me and said, "You go too."

Nils grunted.

After that, we were in a fog, him leading me onto a Pullman train with parlour coaches and sleeping cars.

"Remember, we heard about them?"

Both parents nodded.

"Not sure we'll ever get to see one," Astrid frowned, "eat your bacon and eggs before they get cold!"

She sighed, "Did you have too much lutefisk last night? Or was the idea already rolling around in your brain?"

Regardless, now Knut was dying to see a real Pullman, "One day, I will," he promised. His parents exchanged looks, resistant to the idea of him leaving.

Grandpa Svend, and Knut's half-brother, Wil, visited every so often from Minnesota and were his perfect co-conspirators. The elder's wisdom and experience from having emigrated himself, was lost when he died in 1894 but Knut still counted on Wil.

"Your last sketches showed a farmyard with log house, barn, pig pen, and chicken coop, what else?" Wil asked. "Close your eyes and look around, what else do you see?"

"Rain barrel beside the house, water trough for the animals, a well, maybe a cistern under the house for drinking," Knut imagined. "Oh, and enough trees for a shelter belt."

Out on the veranda after supper, his parents teased, "You make our backs hurt just thinking about it."

As brother, Eli, married and three years older, left on horseback, he joked, "The first building better be the outhouse!" Knut and Jens, his younger brother, snorted.

Older sister, Marion, stepped off the porch and defended, "What about stoking a fire with an attractive wife and children?" Knut's blush surprised even him because deep down that's what he wanted. He was glad his brothers weren't close enough to see.

In bed that night, he overheard Nils chuckling to Astrid, "The older he gets, you can see those eagle eyes for quality, grain, livestock, and lumber, fuelling his entrepreneurial twitch."

She smiled, "He tries hard not to let us see how homesick he is, even before he's left."

Knut understood that his mother knew him well and that his father didn't want to coddle him. Bit by bit, he hoped they were convincing themselves it was okay. It weighed heavily that the rich, loamy soil of the Carrot River Valley called to him, yet his own country pushed him away.

Stepbrother, Wil visited, and carrying loose hay from the barn, Knut defended his decision to emigrate, "Wil, you know why I can't buy farmland here. It's hard to come by and expensive."

"And it cycles rain with drought."

Wil was easy to talk to, so Knut admitted, "I should have met a wife by now."

Wil had married Penny and watched Knut's love life falter. "It's tough to break free from the family businesses. You did have a couple sweet girls over time."

"Ja, but they fizzled out. It was too little too late."

"Wait 'til Canada!"

"With so many others leaving, it's exciting to strike out on my own but I hope I'm not jumping from the frying pan into the fire."

Indeed, history repeated itself for another five years when something always came up to prevent his leaving. Like the spring of 1897, with hat in hand, Nils apologised, "Son, I need your help to get through seeding."

Harvest and some really hard winters came and went.

"Son, we need help to run the lumber camps."

The new responsibilities enticed Knut like any young man and gaining mastery of the farming and logging operations was challenging. Still, he couldn't drown out the sound of his own destiny. His father's crew was dependable but season after season, someone fell victim to accident or illness and was part of the reason Knut stayed.

Sitting in the logging camp kitchen, Nils spoke of some of his absentee workers. "They're sent off to quarantine in a pest house on the outskirts of nowhere for anything from smallpox to tuberculosis."

The cook spoke from his work behind a pail of potato peelings, "Yes, and the others scatter at the sight of fevers and pustules. Good thing the new smallpox strains are weaker and there's the cowpox vaccine."

Knut walked in and sat down across from the other two, "But so many won't touch it with a 10-foot pole."

"The die-hards have mouths to feed or think if they haven't caught it by now, they never will," the cook said.

"So, when a hole needs filling, someone has to step up. As usual, that's Knut," his father jested but to Knut it wasn't all that funny.

"Yea, and it's become a bad habit."

Life in a lumber camp toughened most men because felling and skidding trees or driving logs down a river called for strength and skill and left little room for error.

Knut was adept at making the crosscut saw sing on the oaks and cedars but the sudden and horrific news at times of, "A tree fell on so and so and broke his back," came whether anyone was ready for it or not.

That kind of horror could have destroyed him but instead, like the others, he learned to keep his emotions in check and to distract himself. Pulling out the tobacco tin and rolling a cigarette or chewing snoose, helped pass the time. Saturday nights brought any combination of riotous gambling, raucous singing, dancing, or fist fights. Alongside the moonshine floating into camp was white lightning that burned on a spoon. Both were rotting gut foul but better than meet-your-maker wood alcohol. Often, violent puking, sheepish green faces, and wild headaches predominated on Sunday.

Knut heard the cook tell his father, one time, "Good thing this line of work has little down time, so the drinking is hard and fast one night a week. Some of the obnoxious drunks pass out and others go at it so hard, you hope they don't go blind!"

The cook turned to Knut and Nils asking, "How come you never do?"

"What? Go blind?"

"Pass out or get into a fight. You're both jolly but annoying when you repeat yourselves over and over. When you sober up, there's not even a hangover."

Knut answered as deadpan as could be, "We're pacifists not masochists."

No one knew but Knut, for one, felt the dregs of remorse but hid them well behind a genuine smile and twinkling blue eyes.

"You've got comical natures and big hearts."

"Like father, like son."

Nights at the sawmill, Knut listened for the call of the Great Horned and Snowy Owls.

"Their mournful cries likely tell us something," Nils said.

Knut said, "Surely that we're encroaching on their habitats, it's their piercing eyes that touch my soul!"

"With every stand we cut, we're working our way out of a job," Nils hit the nail on the head.

In fact, time marched on in the world of timber, and the owls' foreboding came true because the wood supply diminished and sawmills started shuttering. Although Iowans had looked to the pine forests of Minnesota, their lumber was threatened too. By the summer of 1901, the industry was so bleak that Knut and his co-workers dismantled several of his father's lumber camps.

Knut said, "In the Northwest Territories, there will be more than enough lumber with so much pristine forest close by. From my homestead, I'll have less than 50 miles in almost any direction for all the wood I can use."

Knut heard Astrid lay down the law to Nils. She towered over her short husband, pointing a finger, "If his brothers get the farm, then Knut gets equipment and machinery."

Nils could have escaped by walking underneath her outstretched arm, but he enjoyed the sparring and the chance to interact up close.

"And what do you think about the makings of a sawmill? Would that work?" He teased, jumping up on a stool, sneaking a smooch, and patting her bottom. It wasn't hard to miss her trying to hide a smile as she turned back to the wood stove.

Displays of affection discomfited Knut, but this time, he was over the moon. "Is this proof that you're finally resigned to my leaving?" Noncommittal as ever, they ignored him.

Astrid may have seemed abrupt but Knut knew she always had a soft spot for his father. Nils's own mother had died when he was only two, trying to give birth to a second baby sister who didn't make it. Then Nils's older brother died at five.

"I never understood what happened to my brother," Nils said. "My father couldn't seem to talk about it. It had something to do with a distressed cow birthing a breech calf. My father was left a widower with one small child, me. I can presume that was at least part of the reason we emigrated to America."

Another reason Knut knew his parents hemmed and hawed about him leaving was worrying about the Indians in the Northwest Territories.

"Uffdah!" Astrid joked, hanging up her apron, "we don't want him to get scalped but maybe the practice fell by the wayside?"

"Ja! The place has a history," Nils warned. They all headed for the barn, "For one, the North-West Rebellion in 1885."

"How many battles were there again?" Knut asked while he and Jens mucked out the stalls.

"Well, four between March and May. The Battle of Duck Lake, the Massacre at Frog Lake, and the Battles of Cut Knife and Batoche," Nils knew the history well because Astrid saved the newspaper clippings.

"At the time, I was 10 and can still remember," Knut rendered. "But you know how the details either blow out of proportion or fall off with each telling."

The father and sons scattered clean straw around the stalls, put fresh hay and chop in the mangers, and let the two milk cows back inside the barn.

"The battle sites are a little too close to your new homestead for comfort," Nils said with fascination but not meaning to frighten. "In reality, it might be about 75 miles as the crow flies."

Knut saw Astrid's hackles rise as she took her stool and pail to sit down and start milking the Holstein.

Nils reassured, "With Louis Riel tried for treason and hung in Regina and Gabriel Dumont run off to Montana, life should be safer."

Nils remembered aloud as he sat down to milk the Jersey. "During Louis Riel's trial, they said the situation was so volatile that certain farmers called for jury duty, couldn't go, out of fear."

"After the Battle of the Little Bighorn in Montana, Sitting Bull, Chief of the Sioux, and his triumphant band sought asylum in Canada but got coaxed home after four years," Nils said squirting milk towards the hungry, caterwauling cats.

It occurred to Knut that his parents relived activities on both sides of the border. The incident had happened when he was barely a year old.

"Not that returning home was any better for them," Astrid pulled long draws of milk from the Holstein to fill her pail.

Nils needed a strong hand to get a skinny stream out of the Jersey, whose teats were half the size of the Holstein's. His cow was not coping well with flies and kept switching him in the face. Almost on cue, she picked up her foot, knocked over the pail, and spilt the milk, landing Nils on his backside.

"Uffdah!" Nils blasted. Being a wiry fellow, he got up unhurt but cursed the spilt contents, even if it was only a quarter pail. Nothing was wasted because the barn cats lapped up every drop.

"Whoa Bossie!" Nils soothed and plunked back down to try again.

The others tried not to laugh.

Settled in place, he spoke. "We all know the proud American Sioux were reduced to virtual refugee status."

Knut put his pitchfork back in the corner where it belonged and took the filled milk pail from his mother.

"I guess many Sioux moved near Brandon, Manitoba and south of Saskatoon and being peaceful, did well," she said.

Jens had climbed up into the hayloft in the meantime and was pitching out more fresh hay. "Then came the slaying of Almighty Voice five years ago, in 1897," he interjected. The boys had a soft spot for the Cree-leader-turned-outlaw, who was close to their own ages.

Knut said, "It was tragic miscommunication, with his people starving. Almighty Voice was arrested for butchering a steer that happened to belong to the government."

"It's obvious he was trying to feed his people."

Knut put the pail of milk inside the milk house, where the cream separator was. Now, he moved to the chop bin, to get chop for the pigs and chickens.

"The Duck Lake jail cell was no bigger than a hut and the jailer joked that the punishment for cattle rustling was hanging," Nils said.

"That was no joke to Almighty Voice," Jens defended. "He panicked, escaped, and was hunted a good 70 miles to the Carrot River Settlement. There, he killed his pursuer, a North-West Mounted Police sergeant."

Astrid left the milk house door open and pouring the milk into the separator, called, "Do you realise that settlement is close to where you want to settle, Knut?"

"Yes, less than 20 miles away."

"Can I take over the cranking?" Knut asked.

She nodded and stepped away.

"Almighty Voice was at large for two years, and on the final two days, six people were killed. Two travelling with him, two police officers, and the Duck Lake postmaster."

Knut finished the cranking, then took another pail of chop to the pigs.

Nils warned, "The Saskatchewan district has had its fair share of drama, you'll need to watch your back."

Knut thought, "Duck Lake is only 50 miles south of Prince Albert but things are settled or we'd have heard rumblings by now."

Astrid poured off the cream and gave half the remaining skimmed milk to the pigs and cats. When the men moved to the well to draw water for the water trough, she made for the kitchen. Hauling water was heavy work but kept them lean and muscular.

Knut knew that his parents, like others, had reservations about train travel. There was a common suspicion that the new immigrants pouring into the Americas carried disease.

In fact, he'd heard his mother say, "Some people think the germs are reproducing in the passenger cars."

Nils and Astrid knew it was time for Knut to go but Astrid pondered, "I wonder who you'll meet in your travels, and if you'll marry?"

Nils joked, "The way your life goes, you might not have time."

"I'll make time," Knut reassured.

"Well, let's hope she's a nice Lutheran Scandinavian. She'll have to be a real go-getter to keep up."

Knut said, "Think about it, this last decade I was eligible to file for a homestead at 18 but not old enough to vote. Then at 21 came the suffocating expectation to volunteer with the militia."

"They're evolving into the National Guard," Nils said, "and expect eligible males between 20 and 46 to volunteer. Plus, there's ludicrous talk of prohibition."

Jens wisecracked, "Service is not compulsory, just expected."

The country's military flavour was palpable even after the majority of Civil War veterans had long passed away. In fact, Iowa alone had over 25,000 members of the group advocating for soldiers' widows and children, including those in their own community. That was commendable but certain members weren't shy in their disgust for the newest generation's 'lack of patriotism'.

Knut figured he was counted as one of that new generation and questioned, "Is it patriotism or insanity?"

Jens came home one afternoon, disgusted, "I was in the livery stable, and all I heard was the rhetoric about the 'boys in blue'. Fighting slavery decades ago and fighting overseas today are two different kettles of fish."

"You said it!" Knut thought of the stories about the underground organisation that helped blacks escape to freedom in Canada.

"They said the first militia call for overseas volunteers for the Spanish-American War four years ago was a fiasco, totally disorganised," Jens interrupted Knut's thoughts.

Knut quipped, "Thank God the farm and sawmills are as essential to keep me home as they are for you and Eli."

From 1898 to 1901, the wars overseas, and the unwritten commitment to join, hung over Knut's head like a dark cloud. Anguished, he had watched his childhood friends get swallowed up. The numbers of dead, wounded, or court martialled put a foul taste in his mouth. He had heard of the Presidio training facility and brutal atrocities by soldiers on both sides. He shuddered at the thought of lynchings, burning villages, torturing, or terrorising civilians.

One night at the supper table, Nils posited, "With the Filipino American War dragging on, volunteer numbers soon won't be enough. Mark my words, they'll be legislating service soon."

Knut knew it was a very real possibility and worried aloud, "There are too many males farming this farm for us not to be singled out. Losing one soldier in a lifetime is enough."

Astrid urged, "Before you go, I want you to put on your Sunday best, and go and have your photograph taken. If you're leaving, I want to at least be able to look at your picture!"

Knut did and with all the talk, he firmed up plans for his long-awaited 1,000-mile trip. He planned to walk the first 700 to the border, then take a train 400 miles north, deep into the Northwest Territories to Prince Albert. Another 50 miles east overland by horse and wagon would get him to his homestead.

After a telegram inquiry, Knut decided to ship his household effects by freight car to Prince Albert.

"The train portion should be easy," he thought, "with the first and last legs of the journey the most challenging."

The thought of navigating the frontier alone made him a little nervous but still, all he could do was grin. He would have nothing but time once he got there.

Regardless of all the fears and impediments, by spring of 1902, Knut's life in Iowa came to an abrupt halt. At 26, the most pressing reason to leave was avoiding the militia's recruitment to fight overseas. First the Spanish-American war and the ensuing Filipino American war had employed 125,000 volunteer soldiers but they were looking for 35,000 more. The handwriting was on the wall.

In fact, his father, Nils, came home from town in a frenzy, "Uffdah! They're saying certain states are offering up whole militia units for the federal army to send overseas. The National Guard members are protesting but getting ignored."

"It's only a matter of time before they come knocking," Astrid edged.

Indeed, the dreaded news arrived.

"If volunteer quotas aren't met, soldiers may be drafted under special statutes." The manure had hit the belt-driven fan.

For Knut, to face off against that tangled mess would go against everything he held dear. "No question. It's time," he rationalised, "and, all the best land might be gone if I dally."

Spring seeding or not, short-handed, or not, without reservation, his people reluctantly pushed him to be off, all fearing the dangers and great loss his leaving would have.

His parents helped him pack and Nils reached into his own pocket. "We want you to have Grandpa Svend's pocket watch."

Knut was floored. The coveted watch was windable, and smooth, fourteen karat gold with a hinged case. He felt his father's warmth as the watch slid into his pants pocket, making him somehow feel distinguished. He made steadfast promises to return and his father agreed to ship the sawmill equipment by rail after freeze-up. Astrid and Marion grew teary and the men swallowed hard. Knut planned to walk to the Minnesota border. After covering the full length of that state, he would swing across North Dakota to the wide-open Canada/United States border at Portal and North Portal.

Thirty years before Knut was ever born, Canada had issued the *Dominion Lands Act* which meant that for a mere $10.00 registration fee, any man and his family could have 160 acres of land…with strings attached, of course. The Canadians were waiting, and if the parents could have foreseen what was to come, they would have tied him to the bedpost.

5

Crop Failures

Muskoka *1897,* **Neepawa** *1898,* **Stoney Creek Settlement** *1902*

Tessa and daughter, Clarice, waited as McLaren and the boys came in from their Muskokan field with another limping mare. It was summer, 1897, and five years after the epidemic.

"Bess is lame from steppin' on a sharp rock in the field. The frost heaves up those cursed stones every year," McLaren moaned as he sat down for supper.

"A do me best!" 13-year-old David feigned innocence. His squeaky voice embarrassed him but they all hoped it was a passing phase. McLaren affectionately ruffled his son's dark hair.

"Every time we turn around, some piece of equipment breaks," Sean had survived diphtheria and maybe that's why his voice still squeaked like a small animal caught in a foot trap. At 21, he towered over his father and his lean muscles attested to the farm's demanding work. Forever hungry, he swallowed mouthfuls of mashed potatoes, one after the other.

Clarice poked him in the ribs, "Dinnae eat like a pig!"

"So many years of fightin' stones," Tessa interrupted, ignoring their banter.

"There has to be somethin' better," Sean concluded, "and dinnae get me started on the hours it takes to find wood."

"Things are gettin' tougher, all right," McLaren admitted.

Tessa saw her husband reach for a second helping, then put it back.

Looking at her maturing children, the mother decided she would have to start making bigger meals at dinner if she wanted enough leftovers for supper.

Tessa walked over to scour a cupboard drawer, "Remember, Jake brought us this homesteadin' pamphlet about the Northwest Territories?" Their son,

Jake, had married Martha three years earlier and they farmed on their own place.

"I wonder if the claims are true." McLaren eyed the paper while the youngsters crowded around. "Homesteader grants to a land of fertile, loamy soil with virgin stands of timber are invitin'." The father became pensive, "'Tis somethin' to think about."

Unnerved yet excited, at the back of Tessa's mind were the four little girls out in the cemetery. They would be the hardest to leave. Life had gone on and five grandchildren followed, all nicknamed by Grandda McLaren. With a growing brood and dwindling returns, the family had to consider how to improve their lot.

Emma and Jock had three more children. Freckle-faced Bunny was already four. Tadpole, at two, rose early and talked a blue streak. Peanut was a babe in arms, still nursing. Jake and Martha had two, Toot, at two, sneezed if he looked at the sun. Fleck, a happy baby boy, still nursed and had flecks of hazel in his eyes.

After supper, to get their minds off it, Tessa said to Clarice, "Let's make lye soap!"

"But the wind is gettin' up," her daughter protested.

Tessa stepped outside. She knew the many faces of the wind, sometimes friend, sometimes foe, suddenly rushing forward, ebbing backwards or falling into a mysterious hush.

"Dinnae worry," she said, "smell the stagnant slough wafting by. The breeze will carry our lye odour away too. The boys can light the fire and haul the water."

"I hate makin' soap! It burns if ye splash it on yer skin!" the girl pouted but knew how to be careful.

"Well, think of how we can make it like a rich perfumed French soap," Tessa challenged.

Tessa snickered thinking of how she had rendered lard and thrown scraps of pork, fat, and rinds into a barrel with lye that was leached from hardwood ashes. The ashes were boiled with rainwater for half an hour, then allowed to settle. The caustic liquid skimmed off was lye.

The iron kettle hung over the outside fire and Tessa stirred turpentine and handfuls of salt into the already boiling mixture. The smell was atrocious but they knew the aroma of rot would evaporate while curing. Once the bubbles started and the potion thickened, it was time to add a scent like lemon, or citrus, and pour it into soap moulds.

Clarice said, "Ye look like a witch stirrin' a cauldron."

Tessa ignored her, "Aw pish! Clarice, what do you want the scent to be?"

"What about the lilacs dryin' off the veranda?"

"Should be luxurious and fragrant!"

Towels covered the soaps to set overnight before cutting into bars come morning. The soap took weeks to cure, but they already had a good stockpile. Letting it get too old never seemed a problem but they knew to discard anything with orange spots.

"If some of our men would join a harvest excursion west," Tessa broached McLaren later, "they could see what the land and crops are like out there. If things are better, then our brood might have a brighter future."

"A agree," McLaren looked optimistic. "Maybe we could become wealthy landowners one day," he teased before ducking out to the barn.

The next day, McLaren mentioned the idea of joining a harvest excursion to Jake and Jock, who agreed to think about it.

Afterwards, Jake winked at his parents, and excited the others when he announced, "Jock and me are joinin' a harvest excursion to Manitoba fer a dollar a day's pay."

Amid stooking and threshing, these two married men would size up the stones, crops, and wood situation. Come August, they left their wives, Emma and Martha alone with the children. The harvesting at home then had fewer hands, so took a bit longer.

Upon their return at the end of October, the adventurers couldn't stop raving. "The glorious golden grain rippled in the fields with few stones and ye could see stands of available timber. This year was a grand harvest!"

"'Tis apparently even better further west. With land at $10.00 a quarter in the Northwest Territories, this is somethin' worth considerin'," McLaren concluded.

Jake, now all in for a move, folded his hands. "What would ye think of rentin' instead? There's a farmer at Neepawa, Manitoba, and the place has enough buildin's to accommodate all of us. The owner might even be interested in sellin' one day."

Tessa and McLaren looked at each other, minds whirling, "Maybe we could get ahead there. Here we're sluggin' it out year after year."

Jake grinned and turned to enfold his wife in his arms. "How did ye make out without us?"

"We're strong, independent women!" Martha teased, "we dinnae have to ask fer help once, did we, Emma?"

Emma and Tessa both raised their eyebrows. Emma winked at Sean and David, then whispered, "That's because the boys continually checked up on us, right?"

"Yup, and helped haul water, split wood and do yer chores!" Sean didn't seem to mind.

David buzzed with laughter, "These three," he looked down at Bunny, Tadpole, and Toot, "always taggin' along or climbin' all over everythin'." The affection ran both ways.

With stars in their eyes and growing disillusionment about life in Muskoka then, McLaren sent a letter of interest to the Neepawa landlord. It would be a good test of the land one province west. With subsequent agreement, the momentum built. McLaren rejoiced when his friend, Philip, asked to join them. He too had found a farm to rent close to them.

The Muskoka and Purbrook farms were advertised, offers made, contracts signed, and hands shook. Though chaotic on the nerves, the stars had aligned and all four places sold. Tourism speculators were eyeing up the Muskokan Lakes area, but no one realised how lucrative that pushed the offers. At Easter, 10 April 1898, the deals were sealed and it was too late to turn back. Not that anyone wanted to.

Hovering on the brink of departure, McLaren said, "A'm proud of us thinkin' ahead and makin' such an unconventional decision. The farm sales mean money in the bank, and our collection of farm equipment will serve us well."

By the following Tuesday, they were packed and ready. It was the eve of departure and feeling deep emotional pain, they stumbled through fog to the cemetery to say their last goodbyes. Everyone gathered around the headstones and graves of the young, deceased girls, three daughters and a granddaughter. All present bowed their heads showing the greatest deference.

McLaren prayed, "Dear God, please console us that these four girls will always be together. Bless and protect their souls in Heaven. Please God, give us the strength to continue. We ask in Jesus' name. Amen."

Each took a moment of individual silence where no one moved. Then, without faltering, Tessa took the lead to turn around and leave. No one dared look back.

On Wednesday, 20 April 1898, the throng ascended the steam engine locomotive for the 1,300-mile, five-day journey. Tessa checked her bag again for the special memory box she'd filled with timeless keepsakes of her precious girls. Pictures, lockets, locks of hair, hair pins, and Bibles were all she could salvage, memories that could never be lost. Anything cloth, like their dolls, ribbons, and clothing were burned long ago.

The six men travelled in the box cars to tend the livestock, bringing water, hay, oats, and straw. The Grand Trunk Railroad would take them north to Parry Sound, then angle west to Sudbury, Sault Ste. Marie, Thunder Bay, Winnipeg, Kenora, and finally, Neepawa. In the passenger car rode the four women, five children, their luggage, boxes of foodstuffs, and cooking utensils.

Martha rolled her eyes, "'Tis like goin' on a long picnic with no ants."

The train whistle blew and the steam engine rhythmically chuffed forward keeping time with their heart beats. Emma and Martha still nursed Peanut and Fleck but the sealers of cow's milk reserved for the other three, Tadpole, Toot, and Bunny, had to be drunk before it went sour. A small stove at the back accommodated their meals which they coordinated with the stops. Freight cars weren't connected like passenger cars so they took advantage of the 20-minute stopping window to eat with the men while the train workers restocked wood and water.

It was the week of the full moon. With jostling and lack of a meaningful, tranquil rest, at least the women and children could still see the outline of the landscape passing by day or night. It was a job and a half to make sure the little ones didn't roll off the seats. With all the shaking, the mothers wedged them behind bags and blankets but somehow, things jiggled loose. Three-year old, Toot, was one casualty who landed on his elbow and was inconsolable until his mother, Martha came to the rescue.

"'Tis only swollen and bruised," she soothed. "Everyone's cranky and overtired, and at times, giggles turn to tears and that's just us mothers!"

Tessa laughed but saw that the adventure was far more taxing than anyone dreamt. She wondered if the ringing in her ears would ever stop.

At first, they tried to ignore the food vendors who waited at the stops. On the last day of the trip, Tessa said to McLaren, "our rations are gettin' slim. Fer the comin' stop, let's sample the vendors' food."

He agreed. But the first sips of coffee were bitter and it was hard not to spit.

"The food will taste better," the grandfather promised but the stale bread and tough ham barely filled a hole. The children started whimpering.

In the end, Tessa said, "We'll buy apples and sweetmeats from the newsies next time they board."

When they rolled into Neepawa on day five, their tensions eased to discover a sizeable regional railway hub with lumber and agricultural opportunities. It was noon on Sunday, 24 April 1898, and here, they read that according to the fire code, all new buildings had to be brick. Their destination was farmland north of the Stoney Creek, a branch of the White Mud River, only a short distance away. Once the train stopped, they took the time to stop vibrating.

When they stepped off the train, it was the height of a spring day, with crisp, fresh air and blooming lavender crocuses. McLaren squeezed Tessa in a one-armed hug, saying, "The lush countryside and rollin' hills takes me breath away!" She leaned into him, smiling with satisfaction.

The baggage handlers assisted to unload and their new landlord, the delightful Mr. Aspen, came forward with outstretched hand.

"My wife and I are getting on in years," the seasoned farmer, dressed in overalls and straw hat, said. "We weren't quite ready to give up our land in light of a loss of partners. Our three sons moved west so instead of selling, we're taking a gradual path to retirement, renting it out. In time, we may sell."

McLaren replied, "Thank you, sir, that's good to hear."

At Mr. Aspen's urging, bigger items were stored in a station shed for later retrieval. After what seemed forever, the challenge of unloading the animals, harnessing the horses, and loading the wagons was met. Off they went, with Mr. Aspen leading the way.

At the new farm, four miles later, they breathed in the wide-open spaces. After pointing out key structures and doing a walk around, McLaren and Mr. Aspen signed the rental agreement.

In the meantime, the younger men settled the animals. Jake and Jock turned horses, steers and heifers, out into the pasture, Sean took the milk cows to the barn and David herded the chickens to their coop. Philip guided the pigs to the pig pen with a stick and a pail of feed. Bunny, Tadpole, and Toot carried the mother cat and her two kittens up into the loft.

The sun streamed through the sparkling, glass windows of Martha's new house and she laughed, "A almost feel like a fish out of water. It seems funny not to be hemmed in by forest. The housin's good though, enough to maintain privacy."

"Yes, and there's well water fit fer humans," said Emma. At the same time, she eyed an outhouse set off in a small bluff.

"What more could we ask fer with wood piles waitin' to be split, and an icehouse ready to fill?" Martha wondered.

"The place is more than expected," Tessa paid homage.

Once Mr. Aspen left, the real unloading began. The men carried in the furniture, boxes, kegs, trunks, and barrels, and the women tirelessly unpacked at each of the three houses. Heaviest were the canned sealers filled with fruit, vegetables, and meat and only one jar broke.

Tessa sensed that her youngest daughter, Clarice, was self-conscious around their friend, Philip. How awkward they had planned for him to bunk in with them that first night because no one had the heart to send him to his new place alone.

Clarice avoided eye contact with Philip, and Tessa thought, "The poor fellow has to get the message but cannae the girl see he's a good match?"

"Why is Philip lookin' at me all the time?" Clarice scowled at her mother. "Don't make me sleep near him!"

"Of course not! Dinnae worry, he's too much of a gentleman to bother ye."

At bedtime, Tessa herded the men to another room. "'Tis fer one night, in the name of decency," she pointed to the floor and rationalised, "until we get the beds set up and sort out the sleepin' arrangements."

In private, she told McLaren, "I have never discussed the birds and the bees with any of the children and am not about to start now. 'tis just not done." She went on, "Philip's a good catch and she's playin' hard to get!"

McLaren grunted, "Say nothin'. Whatever will be, will be. Tomorrow, we'll get him settled at his own place."

Still, while using the scrub board the next day, Tessa overheard Clarice lamenting to Martha, "He's old enough to be me Father! Not much younger than me parents!"

Her wise sister-in-law, at a year older, said, "Age is only a number, I dinnae think he means ye any harm. He's a good-lookin' man and seems to have a soft spot fer ye."

Tessa hoped the talk would help because there was no decent way, she knew of, to make a young girl savvy in this department.

By May 24, 1898, settled in, the women planted a communal garden. The children helped by using their bare feet to push dirt over the planted seeds, leaving crooked rows of little footprints. The men laboured in the fields with horses and ploughs to sow wheat, barley, and oats. At the close of the month, they shifted gears from worry to amusement with neither lame horses nor broken equipment. They fixed fences and nailed down shingles on houses and outbuildings instead. Further, the Heavens co-operated and a gentle rain nourished the seedlings. The first week of June, it was delightful to see the tiny sprouts poke through the soil.

When McLaren watched the plants reach toward the sunlight, he remarked, "See how strong and uniform they are? 'tis this rich loamy soil with no stones nor stumps and we can look forward to real bumper crops!"

"I cannae believe the difference!" Sean echoed. "Wait 'til harvest!"

Squeaky Sean poked David in the ribs, "With so few stones to pick, ye might grow soft, brother!"

Tessa never thought twice to thank God for them opting for a crop share rental agreement. Mr. Aspen provided the land and a portion of the input expenses while the Scottish families provided the labour, and everything else.

By the setting sun in mid-June, a thunderstorm roared through with hail that pummelled the tender stalks. The plants were hardy, however, and patches revived. Over the month of August, there was fussing with every threat of frost overnight. Covering the garden with blankets became onerous but there would never be enough blankets to cover the crops.

By late August, their optimism was dashed when a bright morning fell into darkness. At dawn, Philip rode up, and they all walked out to the field. "A hard, killin' frost has paralysed everythin'," McLaren moaned.

"The feeble stalks on their second growth dinnae stand a chance but the healthy ones are destroyed too," Philip shook his head in disbelief.

Within the hour, the landlord was there to reassure, "It's a freak year and one bad one out of many!"

Jake and Jock too, attested to the bounty of the previous year. "At least, we can use the frozen grain fer animal feed." The two were masters at seeing the bright side.

The men were alone with Philip getting water. While sending the roped bucket down into the well, Jake broached another subject, "Philip, ye've done yer best all summer not to force Clarice's attentions."

Philip gave an embarrassed cough as he held out a pail for Jake to fill. "A first saw her in a dream, did ye know that? A thought nothin' of it, 'til a saw her in person at church. Then a knew fer sure she was the one, but a couldnae tell her or she would've called me crazy."

"A never knew any of that but yer smart, makin' her think ye werenae interested, and focusin' yer attentions on the bairns," Jock said.

"Sometimes ye have to take a step back in these matters," Jake complimented.

"At least, the bairns like me. If that helped to win her over, then good."

"Well, somethin' worked! I think ye've caught her eye," McLaren smiled.

At the clothesline, an eavesdropping Tessa smiled too. When she told Martha and Emma, Martha winked, "Maybe Clarice softened when she danced with him to Jake's harmonica the other night."

"The day she saw him shirtless probably dinnae hurt either!" Emma chuckled.

"The man does have a good build!" Martha added.

"Looks like she let go of the fact he's 40," Tessa sighed.

"She can always take the knittin' needle to bed with her if she has to fend him off!" Martha had all the women giggling.

"We willnae tell her that!" Tessa wondered what kind of bedtime ritual her son and daughter-in-law had.

By October 1898, then, Clarice admitted to her mother as they washed dishes, "A guess Philip is a gentle soul after all, and not bad lookin'."

On the sly, Tessa reported to the others, "'Tis done, he's in her good graces," and they breathed a sigh of relief. For Clarice, maybe she wouldn't be an old maid after all.

There were few secrets in their close-knit lives, so no one was surprised when Clarice announced, "To offset the harvest losses, and to keep up everyone's spirits, on November 29, Philip and a plan to be merrit." The young woman blushed and turned to face her betrothed.

"The weddin's to be a simple affair," he teased, "fer the special, youngest daughter!"

Clarice trembled when Philip swept her up in his arms and planted a kiss squarely on her lips. They all sensed if the girl wasn't already spoiled, he was about to do it. Neighbours came to the small wedding supper, along with Mr. and Mrs. Aspen.

McLaren rationalised, "Philip may be 23 years her senior but he's kind and considerate. As far as a'm concerned, he's a good catch. The one drawback is she's leavin' the nest."

In 1899, their second year in Neepawa, the Scottish family thrilled to their first bumper crop. But the third year, at the turn of the century, it was as disastrous as the first, with crops pummelled by hail.

During the four years in Neepawa, five more grandchildren were born, and all at home. The families got to know the midwife like an old friend. Two for Jake and Martha gave them four with Toot and Fleck. Dot, a little girl, appeared in January 1899 and October 1900 was Blue, named for his bright blue eyes. Two for Emma and Jock made five for them with Bunny, Tadpole, and Peanut. Bud came one frigid night in January 1900, so the midwife missed him but Tessa and Martha did the honours. By March of 1901, the midwife delivered a bald-headed girl, named Boo. Clarice and Philip had their first boy, Birdie, in April 1900. Spring thaw was starting and the females clucked over her. Now Tessa and McLaren had 10 grandchildren. It was hoped the three turn-of-the-century babies Bud, Birdie, and Blue, would grow up to be best friends.

Disheartened weather-wise, McLaren called a family meeting in January of 1901. With a furrowed brow, he said gravely, "'Tis time fer us to decide if this is our last year in Neepawa. Even with a good crop this year, our battin' average is poor. Should we look further west fer opportunities?"

Jock ventured, "A'm playin' the devil's advocate but maybe we should try cattle ranchin' in Alberta? There's no guarantee of crop success in Saskatchewan, is there?"

No one answered because he had a point. The situation was complex and Tessa mopped her brow. She could see no benefit to giving up on mixed farming. Out of courtesy, she waited for the men to weigh in.

McLaren, rationalised, "The Carrot River Valley is said to have fertile soil and a good climate."

Jake and Martha nodded. "Aye. They say there's been no crop failures there since the 18th century."

Tessa spoke, "The truth is, grain farmin' is what we know and what we're set up fer."

Philip nodded, "'Twould be expensive to try to get into a new business now."

Jock laughed and winked at Emma. "Yer right and cattle can be trouble."

Sean piped in, "I heard of a rancher who tried to move a herd of longhorns in a snowstorm and lost most of them."

"Two things nobody can tolerate in this country is stupidity or laziness. That was pure stupidity," Jock muttered.

"Or maybe desperation."

"Me position is we've come this far so let's choose the best of two evils. 'Tis a mere 300 miles northwest to the Saskatchewan district, so let's go," McLaren, the patriarch, had spoken. "All in favour?"

It was ayes all around.

"We want to make money, not break even," Tessa echoed.

"We need to get to the land office and start lookin' at maps showin' the land available."

"And we should give Mr. Aspen our notice."

Even though this year wasn't a dud weather-wise, the decision was made. Instead of worry, there was excitement and chatter in the air. The $10.00 quarters were all anyone could talk about, and Tessa dreamt of their new home. When she awoke, the pull was stronger than ever. She pushed aside her morning duties and walked outside to clear her head. When rounding the corner, a large snowy owl with wings splayed, sat in the middle of her path. Although startled, when the owl's stare caused a warm sensation in her, she took it as a good omen.

"But how are we goin' to get there?" David, the youngest at 17, asked.

Jake spoke as he and the other men poured over a map, "The train only goes as far as Erwood but this route, by Yorkton, angles north," McLaren said. "Are we up fer a wagon train adventure?"

The excited children cheered, "Aye!" and everybody laughed.

Jake said, "I guess so then!"

"We could ship our implements to Erwood, then travel across country for them later."

Tessa watched the children play wagon train by the hour, and it was a zoo in every sense of the word. Bunny was an officious little leader and the one old enough to wear pastel colours, a pinafore apron, and knickerbocker drawers. Everybody under four had to wear white clothes from diapers up.

Bunny organised where the others would sit inside the imaginary wagon, "A'm the driver, and a get to say, 'wagons ho'!"

To stop Tadpole and Toot's constant hounding, she let them pretend to drive the horses. The two boys, at six, did what she told them. For their penchant of digging and playing in the dirt, they graduated to clothes of jersey, in darker colours like their fathers. They played so hard, got so dirty, and slept so well; they were a joy to have around. Tessa loved Tadpole's toothless grin and cute pug nose and Toot had lost one bottom tooth and was wiggling the other, working around the gap to manage his lisp. They were big enough to help carry a bucket to feed chickens. Toot was going to be an astronaut when he grew up but Tadpole saw himself as a circus clown.

The two four-year-olds, a girl and boy, Peanut, and Fleck, were cousins who shared with each other and tried to copy their older siblings. Peanut's favourite colour was purple and she mostly collected purple stones and flowers but made an exception for moths, and fat caterpillars. Fleck would rather carry frogs and mice in his pockets. These two were often dressed in hand-me-downs from their older siblings. In summer, they could walk to the pasture calling "Come Boss!" to get the cows home for milking. As middle children, if ever they got heck, they might pack a knapsack to run away. This time, it was over snitching cookies.

David told Tessa later, he caught up to them heading out the gate, and called, "Hey, ye two, where're ye goin'?"

"We're runnin' away," Peanut pouted.

"How come?"

"Cause our mothers are mad at us," said Fleck with tears in his eyes.

"Oh, no! I'm gonna miss ye! What will ye do when winter comes, and ye only have yer summer clothes on?"

The two stopped, blinked, and looked up at him, ready to cry.

"It's okay, ye can come with me." They turned around and followed him like he knew they would. Uncle David always had something special for them to do like letting them hammer nails or sit on his horse.

The five eldest, Bunny, Tadpole, Toot, Fleck, and Peanut no longer took afternoon naps, but they enjoyed the break from their younger siblings when nap time came around.

Two-year-old, Dot, Martha had trained for over a year and like most toddlers, she provided entertainment by mispronouncing words.

"I hab the hippicks," she tried to tell Jake she was hiccupping and all he could do was laugh and tease, "you mean the hippups?" And she would hiccup and say it again.

Kittens were fair game for her to drag around by the scruff of the neck if she got a chance. At times, she amazed everyone by how fast she could move.

"Oh you! What's that in yer mouth? That's not a safety pin I hope?" Martha called. It was a race to catch her, and the toddler would fight tooth and nail to keep it.

The three, one-year-old boys, Birdie, Bud, and Blue, were saying words and either crawling or walking but getting into everything.

"Ba'woon," Bud cried to Emma as he tried to swat a balloon that kept bouncing away.

When anybody asked, "What does the kitty say?" all three would meow.

"What does the cow say?" got three moos or four if Dot was within earshot.

It was because of them that rubber sealer rings locked all the cupboard doors. All except Clarice's Birdie were easy to train but all still wore diapers at night. Birdie had a mind of his own and had no interest in training. Emma's Bud wouldn't crawl but did a crab-like movement on his seat then went straight to walking. Martha's Blue crawled and walked at 9 months but spoke late. When he did talk, he started out with the most difficult words like 'unfazed and claustrophobic'. If any of the imps could get to a cupboard and open it, they would have it emptied faster than a frenzied squirrel.

The three littlest boys and Dot were masters at crib scaling, so this was a game that kept the families running. All four teethed unmercifully and wore bibs to absorb the drool. The crankiness, and runny noses drove everyone crazy. Little tooth smiles, however, did the opposite.

The wagon trek was at the front of everyone's minds and Tessa wondered how they would fare with all these little ones. As grandparents, she and McLaren would guide, and they set about planning. Rough sketches, maps, and lists came together. When Mr. Aspen received notice the spring of 1901, it was a full year before departure and he was genuinely disappointed.

"I'm sorry to see you go, but I can understand your predicament. We've never seen weather like these past few years," he apologised.

"'Tis not yer fault!"

Before long, the men clamoured for the local land agent who was the agricultural implement dealer. His map showed the available land they sought.

"In fact," the agent said, "a good chunk of two townships are open for you to homestead near one another." McLaren filled Tessa in and they marvelled at how their dreams were coming true.

The agent suggested, "It's wise to take a reconnaissance trip to avoid surprises," then rattled off the requirements. "You will have three years to prove up your homesteads before applying for a patent recommendation. If approved, the Letters Patent will transfer official title to you from the Crown. Proof of fulfilment such as acres broke, planted, and six-month annual residency, must be given by sworn affidavit."

The land agent went on, "A Homestead Inspector visits to complete the process. Neighbours can swear that you're an upstanding individual and how you met your conditions."

They chose their quarters and McLaren paid the $10.00 owing for each, $40.00 dollars in total. Come July 1901, the women and children kissed their men goodbye. Leaving for the reconnaissance trip were McLaren, Jake, Jock, and Philip taking a team and wagon to head west. Sean and David stayed home to help. For Tessa and McLaren, it was their first significant time apart since marrying, 34 years ago, and they would have to get used to it. For Emma and Martha, they had done it for the harvest excursion and could do it again. Clarice however, left alone with Birdie, seemed quite bereft. Tessa decided, of all of them, this youngest daughter would need the extra attention. She started with suggesting an ice cream-making day and Bunny, the eldest grandchild, led the others in jumping for joy. It was almost deafening.

The travelling men, in the meantime, took a walking plough, a scythe, bedding and enough food for the long trek. It was a hot, dry summer, and they made good time. It was hard to be homesick on such an arduous adventure, but each had their moments. They missed their wives, and children. After short weeks of navigating the dusty country trails, they arrived. Using a township map, corner posts, and section posts, they found the promised quarter sections. At all four sites, the men set about stacking loads of wild, sweet hay and ploughing fire guards to protect against prairie fires.

The land agent had said, "Not every quarter is open for homesteading. Only even-numbered sections are available because the Canadian Pacific Railway owns the odd-numbered ones. In every township, the Hudson's Bay Company owns section eight and three-quarters of section 26. Schools get sections 11 and 29."

Philip and Clarice's land was furthest north near Lenvale, about 16 miles from the original Stoney Creek Settlement. They shared a section in Township 46 with McLaren and Tessa, them on the northwest quarter and the elders on the southwest. Jake and Martha were closest to the settlement and situated on the northwest quarter of a section in Township 45. Jock and Emma shared Jake and Martha's section but on the northeast quarter. The future Stoney Creek school would be built soon, south of Jake's, while the Clapton school wouldn't be built across the road from McLaren's until 1909.

At 25, Sean was of age but single and chose to help the others instead of going it alone on his own place. David, at 18 could have moved in with his brother, but both boys appreciated their mother's cooking.

After a time at their homesteads Jake and Jock headed back to Neepawa and their young families. McLaren and Philip stayed on for the summer and Philip worked for a neighbouring homesteader. In the meantime, the younger men reassured the older two, they would see to Tessa, Clarice, and Birdie. Over the summer, Philip helped McLaren construct a windowless log shanty of poles plus a log stable and roofed the buildings with hay. It was good summer accommodation and come fall, the two older men made their way home. They faced a major problem of timing for the actual wagon trek that the land agent needed to help them work through.

During the men's absence, aside from gardening, preserving, and doing household and barnyard chores, the women and children took a day to make ice cream. It meant mixing sugar, egg, and vanilla into a milk custard for churning and cooling. Cream was set in a tin pail inside a large wooden pot packed with ice and salt. Bunny, Tadpole, Toot, and Fleck, who hid a baby mouse in his pocket, and Peanut wearing a bright purple ribbon in her long ringlets, kept the handle turning. Occasionally, one of the mothers stepped in to add new ice and salt. Sean and David kept checking the progress amidst their outside chores. At the same time, the women worked from their own recipes to craft concoctions of tooth powder, lotion, and shampoo.

When the ice cream was ready and the babies had awoken, the women, 10 children, and two young men, were ready to sit down. The delicious ice cream, Martha scooped into new-fangled cones invented overseas by an Italian.

Uncle Squeaky lined up the bigger children, Bunny, Toot, Tadpole, Fleck, and Peanut, on the braided floor mat. Dot climbed onto Uncle David's lap. The one-year-olds, Birdie, Bud, and Blue went into highchairs to hold their own cones with Grandma Tessa, Martha, and Clarice sitting knee to highchair to help. Boo at five months sat on her mother, Emma's lap, and was given licks. All were sticky eaters and the women's generous aprons came in handy to wipe dribbles from chins.

The mothers hoped the treat wouldn't spoil their potluck supper, a group effort of leftovers. Afterwards, the older children helped clean up the mess and took charge of play time. By then, the mothers tackled their more serious recipes for silver polish, and rat poison. The latter sounded dangerous but was a simple solution of sugar, cocoa, and baking soda. The chocolate attracted the vermin that led to the deadly ingestion of baking soda. Uncle David saw a mouse's tail sticking out of Fleck's pocket and helped him turn it loose outside before the little creature became an unintentional victim.

Upon McLaren's return, Tessa was never so happy to see anyone and they talked and daydreamed late into the night. In a short while, he spoke to the land agent, "We cannae make the six-month deadline and survive wagon travel in January at 40 below zero."

The agent understood. "It's possible to petition the Ottawa Department of the Interior for six months' grace. I can swear a declaration of facts and send a request letter on your behalf."

They waited and when the approved letter said occupation of the land could begin the coming 1 June 1902, it sounded much better than January.

The spring of 1902, Martha found herself expecting again for the fifth time. The women talked among themselves, "Pregnancies and deliveries are no picnic but everyone agrees we have to strive for big families to offset losses."

If the women's difficult lives of kitchen, cradle, and arduous work weren't enough, they were about to expand to include the adventure of a lifetime.

6

Crown of Myrtle

Sweden—*January—April 1902*

Did she have the guts to emigrate? Lasse wondered as she hung up her apron and threw on her woollens. Stopping now wasn't an option but still, she dragged her feet across the cobblestone foot bridge. The misgivings were mounting. What made her think she was clever enough or had enough energy to pull it off? Why did she feel like she was letting everyone down?

It was mid-January 1902, and at 31, she felt torn and suddenly teetering off her high horse. Her biggest fear was losing the family's closeness but now with her rashness, she dared not fail or face humiliation. The sun was sinking on the horizon, and it had taken her all day to find the courage to share her decision.

At her in-laws' airy and well-lit cottage, they gathered and chatty Lovisa was telling a story. The two sets of grandparents were all ears, but Mikaila and Little Bjorn rolled their eyes having heard it all before. Lasse removed her kerchief and declined a biscuit. She held her breath, steadied her nerves, and tried to focus on the detailed table edge carvings.

When the chit chat dwindled, she began, "Thank you for coming, I have an announcement."

Trying to remain calm but attempting to read their minds, she looked each in the eye, "You've all heard the stories of good fortune with emigrating."

Flickers of foreboding flashed across their faces but she went on, "The children and I have a chance to go to Canada in May with Greta and Kirsten. We'll work for our fares on a cattle ship out of Hamburg."

"What?" her father-in-law, Farfar demanded, staring at her in disbelief.

"So many others are going, and you know as well as I, it might be the best chance to improve our lives."

The kids looked like they'd taken a knock to the head. Her mother, Mormor, started to cry but her mother-in-law looked fit to burst the stays of her homespun dress.

Her father, Morfar, got very red in the face and sputtered, "Have you not seen the anti-emigration pamphlets? The foreigner thinks he's getting an ideal life, but the reality is wilderness, wild animals, grizzlies, and Indians!"

At that, her father-in-law's lit pipe dropped from his mouth and almost burnt his beard.

"You know that's all propaganda!" Lasse pooh poohed.

"Maybe but you'll be headed to the ends of the earth!"

The worst reaction came from Little Bjorn, now only answering to Bjorn, and a head taller than her. Alarmingly, he raised his voice, "I, for one, will not be going!"

He jumped up and hissed, "I'm not leaving Sweden!" Shaking his head in disgust, the door slammed behind him.

Lasse couldn't believe the reaction of her sensible, soft-spoken first-born. His 'Stub Bjorn' nickname was no longer funny. Surely, he would change his mind.

The ensuing day, she walked to her parents' house and asked, "Am I being selfish to want a better life?"

"Oh no," her mother busied herself with dirty dishes as her father made for the door. She smiled. True to form, her parents were experts at evading conflict and the conversation was over. At home, she spoke to her teenaged daughters as they swept and dusted.

Mikaila said, "Wherever you go, I'll follow."

"Me too," Lovisa echoed.

"Thank you, but I can't imagine going without Little Bjorn," Lasse stewed.

Mikaila said, "You can find cooking work in Canada and us kids can do odd jobs. With Papa's death benefit and our scrimping and saving, maybe one day we can afford a homestead."

"The $10.00 fee isn't the problem, it's the equipment that costs the money," Lasse pondered. "Surely we can do it, even without him."

Even so, she went at Bjorn again at supper that night.

"Sorry, Mother, I'm not budging, come hell or high water!" He took another forkful of pie, digging in his heels and using a full mouth like a shield.

Seeing the hurt look on her face, he softened, "Somebody has to keep an eye on the grandparents and the land we love so much."

She didn't remember such fierce loyalty and patriotism from him and narrowed her eyes.

"OK," he admitted putting down his fork. "In truth, with Olaf's death, I have a golden opportunity to become a landowner."

"Poor Inga," Lasse sympathised, "left a widow, alone with young Ava."

"I'm more than a mere farm hand, I think you know I've developed feelings for Ava," he blushed.

Lasse was well aware that he secretly mooned over the blonde fifteen-year-old. "Your marriage to her had already crossed my mind, but in a future sense, like a year or two from now. You're only 16!"

"You know that Inga needs security in her old age and I need security too," he pleaded.

"True, except you need to be 18," Lasse was obviously stalling because with parental permission most things could happen.

"Regardless, you know I'm mature enough, plus I'm a very hard worker and a prime candidate."

She couldn't argue.

"A marriage for love and security does look appealing. At least, neither of you would be forced and it's better than the so-called Stockholm marriages."

He smiled. "I know we're both young, but with a steadfast mother-in-law like Inga, our grandparents, and all our other relatives…"

"You'll be in good hands," Lasse finished, already feeling the sting of not being there.

"Morfar has offered to make the betrothal approach to Inga as Ava's guardian," Bjorn admitted, then picked up a tea towel and started drying dishes.

"Already?" Lasse was a little hurt that in mere days, her father and son were colluding behind her back, even if it was the best solution.

"At church this Sunday, Morfar will make the traditional approach to Inga, according to custom, and with your approval, of course."

Lasse ventured a smile because in truth, she already imagined the process. The idea really was wonderful, and she could already see how the two families would do the customary exchange of refreshments and baking at church over the coming Sundays.

And it would happen that after church, Morfar, with a hip flask of schnapps and twinkle in his eye would chirp, "Farfar, to represent Big Bjorn, will you join Inga and I for a drink?"

Her father-in-law would bow graciously to accept.

Lasse calculated, "Even with the three Sundays needed to post the marriage banns, there's enough time to pull off a wedding before planting crops and us setting sail." By this time, Mikaila and Lovisa were listening.

"The publishing of the banns prevents bigamy. The three weeks allows the pastor to see if the couple's catechism knowledge is satisfactory."

"What's bigamy?" Lovisa asked.

"Somebody already married to someone else," Bjorn had done his homework.

Lasse marvelled, "A week ago, if you'd told me this was to happen, I would have said you were joking."

Later that night, however, she bawled her eyes out at the immensity of the situation. When Bjorn saw her tears, he crossed the room to kneel by her armchair and took her hands in his.

He was gentle, "It will be all right, you'll see. Someone has to stay behind as a guardian of this homeland and our people."

"It's true," she sniffled, "our stake in this country will never be lost as long as you live here." She blew her nose and wiped her tears. "I can't dwell on you remaining behind, but the way you frame it is better than the abandonment picture I had in my mind! Whether you realise it or not, you have unwittingly pledged yourself to care for Papa's grave and our ancestors. The image both comforts and disturbs me because that responsibility should be mine."

"I hadn't thought of it that way," he sobered.

"I can see you're wise beyond your years and have a brighter future in this ancient country than your sisters or I. It was unrealistic to think you'd follow me anywhere. You're soon a grown man and there's no promising a better life in Canada."

Their intentions were genuine, promising to see each other again someday. Either she would return, or he would visit Canada and until then, there was always letters. Somehow both knew they were on shaky ground because they might wait forever. Still, Bjorn had chosen love and security, and she had chosen a whole new life.

During subsequent days, Lasse persisted. "Bjorn, you and Ava should come to Canada with us." She made similar invitations to the grandparents.

"Ava can't leave Inga, who will never leave the farm, and the grandparents won't leave either," His words were painfully true because they did nothing but resist.

Wedding planning commenced for two separate spaces at Inga's farm. One was out in the yard; the other, indoors. In addition, the groom's home would host the betrothal meeting.

Inga said, "The outdoor ceremony needs chairs and an altar set up."

"If it rains, we'll have to move indoors," Lasse mused.

"Yes. For the supper, the mice have scampered away from the emptied hay barn. The red barn is out. It reeks of manure and has rats."

"Ugh!" Lasse shivered.

"We'll need to borrow tables and chairs from everybody we know."

Lasse asked Bjorn, "Will you live at the farm with Inga, or do you and Ava want to take over my cottage?"

"We'll live with Inga," he said. "Please sell your place so you can have a nest egg for Canada."

"Bjorn, you'll get a share of the proceeds as your inheritance and to help with betrothal commitments."

He didn't argue.

When buyers for the cottage came forward, Lasse said, "Tonight is the betrothal meeting, the last function in the home my children grew up in."

With a handful of relatives attending from both sides, the place was bursting. Of course, Morfar *Grandpa* led Bjorn's betrothal proposal and reached an agreement on the finances.

Morfar handed Inga the sealed document, "The friendship gift, decreed by law, is what Bjorn provides to you and Ava, and is necessary for a valid marriage. It's part of the purchase price Bjorn pays for Ava."

Morfar began the dowry discussion, "Normally the bride's parents provide the dowry, but because Inga and Ava already bring land and a home to the union, the groom and his people will take that responsibility."

Lasse finished with, "Both families have saved for a lifetime. Land and home from Ava. Money, bits of silver, a feather bed, and chests of bedding and linen from Bjorn to make the wedding legal. The betrothal ensures that any child born to this union is eligible for inheritance."

With the added financial burden, Lasse said to her mother, "It was touch and go but through the sale of the cottage, part of Bjorn's death benefit, and the combined donations of our loved ones, the commitments were met. Thank you!"

"It was our pleasure. We keep a running list of who donated, so in future, we can return the favour," Mormor, her mother, said. "In fact, we have donated to countless other marriages, so in some cases we're being paid back."

Inga brought out the retirement institution document. "This ensures my care, including a place for me to live, and food for me to eat." Both she and Bjorn signed.

Morfar said, "This concludes the betrothal agreement and is confirmed with the bride and groom's handshake. Those of you present are witnesses."

Bjorn and Ava stood up, shook hands, and placed the engagement gold bands on each other's ring fingers. Everyone clapped. Now it was time for the refreshments.

The short days flew with wedding preparations and packing and the eve of the wedding was soon upon them. It was the tail end of April Fool's Day and Lasse thanked God it was too late in the day for pranks.

Bjorn's stag party was at a local tavern. The tankards of ale, song, and dance would have the young unmarried men dancing with him, to signify his changing marital status. Lasse knew he had her sense of rhythm, and it would serve him well. Ava's female friends and relatives kidnapped her for the hen party, and God only knew what they were up to. Mikaila and Lovisa were too young and needed to help their mother with last-minute preparations.

At the marketplace on the morning of the wedding, 2 April 1902, Lasse was paying for fresh produce when the vendor inquired, "I saw you and that fellow, Anders, together last fall. What's he doing these days?"

She was taken aback and blurted, "I have no idea. I haven't seen him for months."

The man lowered his voice, "That's good. His wife died mysteriously, you know, and her body was never recovered."

Lasse's hand flew to her mouth. The two exchanged looks of dread, and she backed away, speechless. The merchant had no idea how his words impacted her. With suspicions about Anders confirmed, Lasse felt like she'd had her bell rung. The nail was in his coffin, so to speak. At the moment, though, the biggest danger was being late for a wedding.

According to old tradition, the morning was for Bjorn and his retinue to visit the bridal home to ask the widow to see the bride. Inga met them at the door wearing a gold-ornamented, forest green Edwardian suit with matching jewellery to set off her silver hair.

"Welcome to our home," she said. "Please come in."

It was a moment before Ava entered the room but when she did, Inga began the marriage rite speech. "I am delighted to gain such a reputable son. This ceremony is to hand Ava over to you, Bjorn…"

Lasse in her pale blue homespun woollen suit with her husband's wedding gift of a pearl necklace and earrings saw that her son, Bjorn, dressed in his dapper finery, had stopped listening. All he could do was smile at the sight of Ava, adorned in her delicate champagne gown with a long train. He obviously didn't hear the Swiss clock cuckooing 12:00 noon, nor did he notice the fresh paint or the electric blue attic ladder gracing the middle of the room. Ava and Inga's hours of fashioning paper flowers and ribbon bows were lost on him.

As Lasse hoped, Ava smiled back at the love of her life.

At Inga's final, "Welcome to our family," Bjorn did remember his manners and thanked his new mother-in-law. As was etiquette, she thanked him back.

In a gesture of fika, Inga daintily poured coffee from a silver coffee service. Then she motioned to the delicacies spread out on the table. They were to choose to their liking. At that moment, Lasse realised Inga held the key to her son's future. Either she would make or break his happiness. Would the widow remain as sweet as she appeared?

After the light lunch, the group proceeded outdoors for the two o'clock ceremony. The guests seated themselves on the rows of available chairs and the Lutheran officiant stood waiting at the altar. According to the egalitarian society's custom, the couple walked arm in arm from the house through the pergola to the garden. The winding wooden walkway was flanked by shrubs. The processional was accompanied by music from a key harp, and the couple were led by two little flower girls distributing flower petals and stealing the show. Ava's innocence was demonstrated with a crown of myrtle leaves and for luck, she had coins in both shoes, one from her mother and one from the spirit of her father. The conscientious Inga winked at Lasse.

As Bjorn and Ava stood before the pastor, he began, "Dearly beloved, we are gathered here in the sight of God and these witnesses, to join this man and this woman together in holy matrimony…"

Again, Lasse noticed Bjorn trying to pay attention but distracted by the whole affair.

The solemnisation ended with, "I now pronounce you husband and wife; you may kiss the bride!"

Those words were an open invitation for the crowd to line up to kiss the couple too, which took time. In due course, the guests moved indoors to the fully decorated hay barn. Over 100 guests crowded into the space. Bjorn and Ava were seated in places of honour at the front, with mothers beside them, surrounded by special guests. The huge smorgasbord was contributed to by the visitors, farmers, and members of the working class. Baked ham, salted beef, goose, suckling pigs, hens, ducks, and veal were topped off with sponge cake, crullers, and almond wafers.

Homemade spirits from malt to brandy and wines, were donated and Bjorn's grandparents proudly supplied their homemade glogge. Neither the bride nor the groom was of legal drinking age but that didn't matter.

Since Morfar had been so involved with the betrothal arrangements, Bjorn asked Farfar to be the master of ceremonies, and he invited the pastor to get the meal started with a prayer.

The cleric waited for the bowing of heads, "Bless us, O Lord, and these, thy gifts, which we are about to receive. In Jesus' name we pray, Amen."

One by one the table groupings lined up and heaped their plates making their way back to their seats. In the jolly atmosphere, people were happy to pour each other's drinks.

"What's in this old-fashioned glogge?" one asked.

"My father combines port wine, bourbon whiskey, white rum, cardamom, cinnamon, and cloves."

"You can feel the heat!" the woman drained her goblet and looked around for the jug.

Mikaila and Lovisa, both under aged, rationalised, "It's our brother's wedding and we should be entitled to lift our glasses and say 'Skål' for the toasts too!" No one argued.

Games were threaded throughout the festivities. If Bjorn rang his bell, the males jumped up and ran to kiss Ava on the cheek. When she rang her bell, the females raced for Bjorn. Once fed, everyone pushed back from the tables, stuffed to the hilt. The jostling and spillage began, and the air bordered on riotous.

Farfar calmed the masses with invitations to make good will speeches.

The groom went first. "Thank you all for the spectacular meal, your presence and gifts will never be forgotten!"

Applause came, goblets clanged, along with a round of 'Skåls'. Lasse watched Mikaila and Lovisa take a big swig.

Ava jumped up to add her words, "Thank you! We love you all!"

People cheered, shouted Skål and drank up. The young sisters kept up.

The speakers were either heart-wrenching, long-winded or hilarious.

"To the bride, no longer a little girl!" her uncle toasted, "Skål!"

"To the bride and groom! May they live long, healthy lives, and be blessed with a houseful of children who don't take after their father!" It was one of Bjorn's lifelong friends, "Skål!" he chuckled.

At this point, Mikaila and Lovisa made a beeline for the door and Lasse could only imagine they had made themselves sick. It was a hard lesson.

The other speeches were poignant and gut-wrenching as they wished the couple well but slipped in their heartfelt goodbyes to Lasse, Mikaila, and Lovisa.

Farfar changed the mood by introducing the entertainers, "Please welcome Johan Johnson on the fiddle, and his brother, Adam, on the nyckelharpa."

The musicians started with a slow waltz for the wedding couple. Then came a series of lively Nordic dances, sets, rings, and turns. At every break, the bride and groom games of guess and toss resumed.

The children marvelled at the nyckelharpa, and allowing them to hold it, Adam explained, "It looks like a fiddle but has strings and keys."

After the break, came a polska to work the dancers into a lather but a waltz afterwards let them catch their breath. At the stroke of midnight, Farfar made a production of calling Lasse and family to the front of the room.

A neighbour took over, saying, "On behalf of all of us, we wish to honour your decision to emigrate. From the bottom of our hearts, please accept this purse of money as a small token of our affection."

Lasse gasped, then burst into tears with Mikaila, Lovisa, Bjorn, and the grandparents following suit. It didn't seem there was a dry eye among them.

"Thank you," Lasse cried, clasping the bulging purse to her bosom. "We will miss you all and will keep you in our hearts forever."

The crowd shouted "Skål!" clapped, cheered, then went back to celebrating. The light-hearted toasting, dancing, and games continued until well after midnight but the musicians were beginning to tire.

"Well," Farfar announced as emcee, "As usual, it was determined that the new household's boss is the bride." Bjorn tried to feign disappointment but couldn't wipe the smile off his face.

"May your harvests be bountiful and your troubles few!" An ancient gentleman, dressed in his finest hand-embroidered outfit, made a final toast but toppled over, too plastered to finish.

A final feeble, "Skål!" echoed throughout the room.

The night wound down and guests felt no pain but anxiously awaited the highlight event.

Mormor said to Lassie and Farmor, "Not mentioning any names but for some of the youngsters who thought toasting was a good idea, they've discovered otherwise."

"Yes," Farmor agreed. "Retching around the corner isn't much fun. Time to wake them from sleeping it off on a pile of coats."

At last, it was time. The whole troupe, including slightly green girls, left the hay barn and proceeded to the house. Ava and Bjorn were led by the pastor and parish clerk to the bedroom for the 'conducting to the bed' ceremony. Per custom, a roomful of spectators watched them lay down, fully clothed, side by side on the bed. Ava tried not to giggle but the pastor shushed her and started the prayer ritual. After the guests sang a psalm, it was pure silence, as the symbolic covers were pulled up to their chins. The crowd gleefully clapped and cheered, ready to head home. The sensuality of medieval times with full-on nakedness was missing, but who cared, the deed was done!

7

Broken Pottery and Stone Axes

Iowa to North Portal—*March 31–1 May 1902*

Could a grand plan have any credence starting on April Fool's Day? Perhaps not. By leaving on Monday, March 31, 1902, Knut shook off the superstition and sped as fast as his legs would carry him on the adventure of a lifetime. He'd said his goodbyes the night before, knowing full well his parents would be up wishing him well before he left at dawn. It was 6:00 a.m., and brimming darkness, when he walked out the gate of the Winnebago County farm in Iowa. He had hugged them all for dear life.

His mother Astrid murmured, "Don't worry about us, we'll be fine."

She turned to Nils, "His first stop is a little far for the first day."

"At least, he'll get to see Wil."

"A 14-hour plus day of walking is long but other days, might be shorter."

"He'll need to keep moving to stay warm. It's 37 degrees Fahrenheit this morning," his father said. Astrid pulled her coat a little tighter.

Knut hoped to reach Wil's before midnight and felt into his pocket, reassured by the feel of his grandfather's watch. Today, he would travel over Iowa's border to his birthplace at the Freeborn County farm in Minnesota. Invigorated, he cycled through walking then running and finally, well after the nocturnal creatures emerged, he dragged himself up the farmhouse steps. Wil still lived in his grandparents' home and waited on the veranda.

Rubbing his eyes and yawning, the half-brother jumped up and pulled Knut to him in a bear hug, "Welcome, little brother! How are you faring? You look pretty good!"

"Uffdah!" Knut sighed. "So far, so good," he dropped to the veranda floor and laid down flat on his back, waiting for his heart to slow. All he saw were reminders of his grandparents, their rocking chairs and wind chimes.

"Here's a drink!" Wil thrust a dipper to Knut's lips who drank gustily.

After a rest, Wil said, "Looks like we need to get you fed, watered, and tucked into bed!"

"Ja and thank you! That's exactly what I need."

Penny, Wil's wife, had waited up too and welcomed Knut with open arms. Moving the lantern closer to cast a better light, she served a plate of chicken and dumplings with tea, and apple pie.

Wil said, "How does it feel to make your dream come true?"

"Hard to believe! Penny, you're an excellent cook!"

Wil got to the heart of the matter. "The volunteer troops are flowing overseas like a river. It's beyond alarming and I hope you know we've got your back."

"Ja, I appreciate it," Knut sighed blinking back tears. In truth, Wil had always been a good friend to him and he hated to leave his loved ones behind. When they went to bed, he slept like the dead.

The next day was April Fools' and he woke up stiff and sore. Saying his goodbyes, he saw 6:00 a.m. on his grandfather's pocket watch. Angling northwest, he followed old bush trails, crossing the country as the crow flies. After another long day, he had worked his way to the rich land beside the town of Waseca in Waseca County. He found a barn and threw down his bedroll in the loft.

Two more 10-hour days of angling westward got him to Belle Plaine in Scott County, a place bordered by the Minnesota River. The weather warmed up past 48 degrees. On the shorter days, he hunted game and journalled.

Pain first thing in the mornings but better once moving. Playing game of finding icy well water to slurp as a treat. Campfires in remote areas for trappings of rabbit and fish. Growing lean and willowy but trying to make jerky, dried fruit, and nuts last. Finding out-of-the-way places to sleep is not always easy, but body heat from animals and enough space for a bedroll works. Grandfather's pocket watch has been a Godsend!

Two 12-hour days later, he came near Annandale, called the Heart of the Lakes, in Wright County. Here he could avoid the cities of Minneapolis and St. Paul. After one full week, it was Monday, April 7 and he was standing adjacent to a place called St. Joseph in Stearns County. He stole across to the

Mississippi River and avoided the city of St. Cloud. Here, three towns surrounded two deep ravines that joined the Mississippi.

His blistered heels were killing him so he sat down and rubbed in his mother's camphor. He put on his socks then shoved the fleece he'd snagged from a sheep inside the back of his boots. The padding helped.

Warmer weather made the snow melt and turned things to mud, which could be bad. Seeing distant campfire had him creeping past out of an abundance of caution. He stole along, not wanting to be side-tracked or snared into any unwanted situation.

Following the majestic Mississippi, for one 12-hour day, he made it to Little Falls in Morrison County and wrote in his journal.

Feet are improving! At Little Falls, an 11-foot drop in the river is used for power. Here the river curves east, and on Tuesday, April 8, I leave for Motley, also in Morrison County. Motley has lumbering and fur-bearing animal farms.

At sunset, on Friday, he neared Menahga, in Wadena County. The days grew brighter and the temperature hovered in the 50s and 60s, dipping to half that overnight. The sign said 'Gateway to the Pines', since it bordered the Huntersville Forest. The place was renowned for blueberries but not this time of year.

Knut sat down beside a creek to rest. He was about to take his boots off and slather his blisters with ointment when a rugged-looking, bearded trapper stepped out into the open. The whiskery white man wore buck skin clothes with a raccoon fur hat.

"Hello stranger," he called.

The huntsman's easy manner had Knut smiling back. "Hello!"

With sore feet, he didn't get up but kept loosening his boot laces. Trappers had a reputation for thriving on isolation, so Knut didn't figure the interaction would go much further.

"I'm Gus. What brings you to these parts?"

After they got the pleasantries out of the way, the man asked, "Can I offer you my hospitality? I'm cooking venison stew for supper and I have an extra cot if you care to stay the night."

"Well, thank you," Knut replied somewhat startled. He envisioned a seedy old hermit's dwelling but the man himself seemed genuine enough. "You read my mind."

Knut took it as a good sign when there were no weeds sprouting up through the trapper's bed springs. In turn, Gus didn't seem concerned about Knut either or his reason for travelling but instead wanted someone to talk to.

After a substantial meal, Gus said, "I've been through Indian country time and again and sign language comes in handy. Let me demonstrate," he offered. "Bring your index fingers together in a cone shape and that means tipi."

Knut tented his index fingers together.

"The sign for a woman is a hand sweeping down from the top of the head to show long hair."

"Makes sense."

"An index finger with the palm towards the speaker shows an erect animal, the sign for a male."

"Uffdah! That one's crude but effective."

"The sign for a white man is moving the fingers across the forehead to show a hat."

Knut chuckled, "Are white men that obvious?"

The trapper smirked.

Knut figured one day, he might just need this information and the man was a fountain of sage advice.

Seated outside smoking, Gus went on, "The Indians believe in the power of the Creator and that creation is a living process." He explained how kinship exists between all things in a living universe like Mother Earth, the waters, and the sun. "Everything in nature is considered a gift and a state of sacred reciprocity needs maintaining."

"Give me an example."

"Anyone drinking from a spring needs to show gratitude."

"You mean give back and be thankful?"

"Exactly. The worldview is that we are all one with nature and everything is alive, even the rocks." He explained, "The fathers are above, the grandmothers are underneath, and all around are relations. The trees, rocks, plants, and animals are sisters, brothers, uncles, and grandfathers. The older relatives, like buffalo, sturgeon, bear, and wolves came before and taught the people how to live."

The words would take time to process but Knut thought to ask, "How does a person give thanks?"

"An offering of tobacco shows respect and gratitude."

After smoking, they pouched a plug of snoose inside their bottom lips, needing to suck and spit for a time, more than to talk. Gus had moved the spittoon in between their chairs at just the right angle.

"If you want a bath, we can warm some water."

Even though it was the day before Saturday, Knut laughed, "You trying to tell me something? A bath would be a dream!"

The galvanised bathtub hung on the outside cabin wall and the warmed water made for a glorious soak. Knut scrubbed himself raw with lye soap and emerged from behind the cabin, fully dressed. Gus offered cloth bandages for doctoring his feet. When he went to put his shabby boots back on, Gus stopped him. "They look pretty rough."

Knut sighed, embarrassed at the soles of his feet showing through.

The host got up and retrieved a pair of deer-hide moccasins from a basket, "Here, try these," he offered.

Knut found they fit, even over his bandages. "Comfortable!" he exclaimed.

"They're warm in the winter and cool in the summer and you'll leave no footprints."

"Thank you! I've still got thousands of steps to go."

As a parting gift, Knut couldn't resist leaving Gus the one thing he had that might mean something, a plug of tobacco. His parting steps felt lighter but when he reached into his pocket to check the time, the gold piece was missing. Sick at heart, he wondered if he'd lost it when he took a bath? Then his heart sunk thinking Gus could have stolen it out from under his nose. He didn't know what to do but couldn't risking losing the precious object, so circled back. Thinking Gus was a thief didn't sit well, the man was far too generous and kind and it didn't make sense. Why give him moccasins only to steal his watch?

Knut snuck up the backside of the cabin and looked through the window. Be damned if Gus didn't have the watch in his hand, looking at it. What? Now Knut was miffed. He marched around and through the front door without knocking.

Gus looked up and said, "Did you forget something?" and held out his arm, dangling the pocket watch.

Knut breathed a huge sigh of relief. "I found this out by the bathtub. You better be more careful in future! I think it's worth money."

"It's worth more than money to me, thank you!"

Feeling sheepish, Knut was off again. This time, if too near civilisation, he adjusted to travelling by the light of the silvery moon. Nights with an overcast sky, it took fancy footwork to navigate the tangled undergrowth and rotten-iced sloughs.

He wrote in his journal.

One night, negotiating the bluffs and terrace of a creek, I stumbled over the mounds of a Native American burial site with hidden resting places beneath vines and tall grass. Glowing eerily in the moonlight were old artifacts and relics of broken pottery, knives, and stone axes. I had no intention of messing with this eternal resting place, disturbing the skeletal remains or their lingering spirits. Despite chills running up and down my spine, I thought of Gus's words and scooped out earth near the base of a tamarack and replaced it with tobacco. With a prayer, I offered thanks to the Creator and hoped it was enough.

When he reached Lake Itasca in Itasca County, on Sunday, April 13, he took a second look at his map and realised his error. Inadvertently, he had ventured onto the Leech Lake Indian Reservation. Instead of trespassing and cutting kitty corner across the northeast portion of the reserve, he held steady northward then made a sharp left turn to Bagley. Further west was Fosston in Clearwater and Polk Counties. He journalled,

The sign says Fosston has ties to Paul Bunyan. I made it all the way to Mentor in two days. Canada's Manitoba border was close but I didn't want to cross there and kept angling west. After two more days, came Grand Forks. It is Friday, April 18 and here sits the Minnesota and North Dakota border. Temperature is holding in the high 60s and dipping to the high 30s overnight. Much better.

The state of North Dakota took 13 days to cross, but on the 11th day, Tuesday, 29 April, something interrupted him between the communities of Norma and Bowbells.

He had gone hard that night until dawn when roosters crowed, and cows bawled for milking. With the first morning stirrings, he found a barn and waited in the shadows for completion of chores, before curling up. Too large for a manger, he capitalised on the animals' heat rising into the hay loft.

He awoke to a little girl, about four, standing over him. She had crept up the inside barn ladder rungs and crawled up into the loft through the trapdoor. Unafraid, and innocent, she whispered in Norwegian, "Have you seen any kittens?"

He almost laughed at her boldness but instead, with wide eyes, held his index finger to his lips, and pointed to exactly where they were. She was delighted and edged over on tippy toes. The two held and adored the kittens until without warning, a woman roared up through the hatch, armed with a pitchfork.

In a shrill voice, she demanded, "What are you doing here?"

"So sorry ma'am!" he apologised, "I'm just a weary traveller, who needed to lay his head down. I'm on foot to Canada and mean no harm!"

An older white-haired man was right behind her and poked his head through the trapdoor. Knut moved forward to offer him a hand up, which the old man had no qualms accepting. Once they determined the stranger wasn't an immediate threat, the family took the time to listen to his story.

Knut ended with, "And my grandparents came from Oppland and Østfold, Norway after the Civil War."

"My mother was from Oppland," the elder's scowl turned to a grin. He motioned to his daughter and the situation took a turn for the better.

The old man introduced himself, "I'm Leif. This is my daughter, Anna, and my granddaughter, Marta."

"All Marta's known since birth is hired men coming and going, so she has little fear of strangers." Anna and Leif invited Knut into the house where they seemed happy for the company.

Leif said, "When it comes to this current call to patriotism, overall, we aren't too impressed either."

"Sometimes it's for the better," Anna said, getting a little red in the face.

"Anna's husband is a volunteer, away serving," Leif explained. The look he gave Anna made Knut wonder what was up. Anna stepped out of the room for a moment to check on Marta.

Leif took the opportunity to say, "Like you, we worry about the militia. Fighting goes against the grain," Then he lowered his voice, "The husband here holds the power, and he's an angry man. For all of our sakes, it was best he signed up. The one thing standing between him and my daughter is me, but I'm an old man, and all I can do is my best."

Knut nodded but kept quiet. It wasn't his place to delve into the situation and the grandfather needed to get it off his chest, even to a total stranger.

The family, including Marta, plied him with freshly baked ham, biscuits, jam, a big wedge of cheese, and hot coffee. "You can catch a train in North Portal," they advised, sending a grateful Knut on his way.

It took two more heavy days of walking for him to reach Portal. It and North Portal on the Canadian side shared a 24-hour border crossing between North Dakota and the District of Assiniboia in Canada. No records were kept of entries or exits, so anyone could walk across unfettered.

On Thursday, 1 May 1902, Knut stood looking up at a slightly tattered and fluttering Star-Spangled Banner, plus a wooden sign that said United States-Canada Border—49th Parallel. Across the line was a similarly tattered Union Jack, and another sign saying 'Welcome to Canada'. Given all the trouble his home country had getting out from under British rule with the War of 1812, he wondered what it would be like to live under British Monarchy rule. He would soon find out and proudly strolled out of the United States into Canada, without the hint of a lightning strike.

8

Wagon Trek and Pow Wow

Neepawa *1898* to Stoney Creek Settlement *1902*

The first question was, how to transport all their possessions? The Scottish family leaving Neepawa by wagon train for the Carrot River Valley, decided they had to reduce the weight on the wagons. Tessa remembered how it all went down.

McLaren spoke, "We'll haul a load of machinery and furniture to the Glenella train station fer shippin' to Erwood. It's about a 75-mile return trip from here. Once established at our homesteads, we can travel cross-country to Glenella to retrieve everything."

Philip and Clarice volunteered and left in the rain, 10 days before the wagon train departed, giving them ample time to get there and back.

The short trip took over three days and they were met by an exasperated train agent. "The weather's thrown a wrench into things! The tracks are washed out in places with all the rain."

Philip's face fell. "We want to be back in Neepawa before May 8 when the wagon train leaves. Could we get help to unload, then have the items shipped to Erwood once the track is repaired?"

"Normally, yes. But unfortunately, with the railroaders out making repairs, we don't have enough manpower to unload you. I'm all alone here and you and I can't do it by ourselves. God knows when they'll be back."

Philip took the agent's words to Clarice, "When the north line is fixed, they'll ship our load to Erwood. In the meantime, he suggests we pitch a tent and wait. We can leave our rig and horses behind and catch the train to Yorkton as soon as one shows up. The wagon train shouldn't reach Yorkton before the third week of May and surely there will be a train by then. We can take a few smaller things with us in a freight car."

And that's exactly what they did. Mercifully, the rain stopped so the repairs could be made. Little Birdie at two, was his usual curious self and kept his parents hopping.

Even though the north line was repaired, more bad news came. "There's another delay, the Red Deer River near Erwood is impassible and the ice took out a couple of bridge timbers."

Meanwhile, back in Neepawa, come Thursday, 8 May 1902, the wagon trekkers were ready to say goodbye to their temporary home of four years. A big 'For Sale' sign stood at the entrance gate since the landlord had thrown in the towel. They were relieved to receive a telegram from Philip and Clarice, saying they would meet up in Yorkton.

McLaren and Tessa's whole family, plus Jock's brother, Timothy, and Martha's brother, Angus, Effie Mae, and six children, plus three single men, set out for the Carrot River Valley. Fired up and confident, Willy, Wyatt, and Charlie, all strangers to the family, jumped at the chance to join the travellers.

The three young men assured the kin group, "We cannae pay ye, but we'll work hard, and share our food, if that's okay?" They lined up to shake hands and seal the gentlemen's agreement.

McLaren was grateful to have them. "Yer extra hands are a Godsend."

Before departure day, the bachelors helped soak the canvas bonnets in linseed oil for rain proofing, then applied them to the wagons' framework bows.

"Packin' too needs extra hands because 'tis a tricky thing to offset the top-heavy wagons," Tessa was playing out and brushed a wisp of hair away from her face.

The wagon box space was only 4 x 10 feet, no bigger than a bed but two of the covered wagons didn't have children and could take more supplies. Emma and Martha made sure the heavier trunks of tin dishes and pots, along with chests of clothing and bedding went on the floor. Anything that could make an excessive rattle or bang together had to be secured or risk startling the horses.

Toot suggested on behalf of the other children, "If we put hooks on the inside of the bows, we can hang up our raincoats."

Martha smiled, "That's brilliant, me darlin'! Sometimes believin' children should be seen and not heard is a bad thing!"

Tessa stood with hands on hips and directed, "Now comes the butter churn, washtub, and kegs and crates fer staples."

"Let's hope everythin' stays snug, and doesnae turn into a can of worms!" Emma declared.

McLaren had summed it up at the outset, "We've a herd of 30 cattle, and just as many horses. Then half a dozen dogs and milk cows, a flock of hens, Ike, the rooster, and Dunbar, the turkey tom. There are four covered wagons, two farm wagons, one caboose, and a buggy. Our pregnant mare, Briney, we'll hitch to pull the cart fer crates of layin' hens."

"The farm wagons," Jake said, "'are loaded with bags of seed to plant', then oats, hay, and barrels of water fer the animals. The horses work hard and need to eat and drink often."

He went on, "Two men on horseback, can help direct the wagon drivers and help herd the cattle. The third has to drive a farm wagon."

Jock cautioned, "Drivers! Keep a gun and ammunition under yer seats and away from the children."

"Ye'll notice a box of tools hangin' on the outer front left of each wagon box," Jake pointed, "'Tis beside the barrel of water strapped atop the shelf."

McLaren clarified, "To lift the wagon fer wheel repairs or axle greasin', ye'll find a wagon jack hangin' beneath the undercarriage. All the wagons have wooden brakes to hold the unit steady fer workin' underneath."

"Or to stop from rollin' downhill!" that was Emma's biggest fear, "well, rollin' backwards downhill!"

Prior to 7:00 a.m., on 8 May 1902, before thundering off, McLaren, the elected wagon master, proclaimed, "In total, we're a party of 32 men, women, and a whole bunch of little bairns!"

They all laughed, and the children cheered.

"When Clarice gets here, she needs to keep a record of all this in her diary." Martha said. "Remember, we are five families, 11 men, five women, and 16 children under the age of 10."

The couples didn't realise that each other lay awake nights worrying. Tessa figured she and McLaren were the worst. "Will our wagons and horses hold up? Will we have enough food? Will everyone come through the other end safely? Can we meet this incredible challenge?"

She prayed, "Dear God, please give Dad and me sound judgement, the wise old elders of the group! Keep us strong, capable, and full of confidence!"

The ensemble had few regrets and listened to McLaren recap their winter discussions. He started with a prayer, a chuckle, and a review of the group's list.

"'Tis me job to lead all of you. Both men and women will follow routines. Each unit is responsible fer their own meal preparation, but we'll eat together in a communal settin. Teamsters will tend the horses, and the men are responsible to keep the wood and water stocked and to manage the tents. Fer campin', we'll pull the wagons in a circle at night, with men beddin' down in the tents and women and children sleepin' in the wagons. Certain wagons even have boards that pull out fer beds," he raised his eyebrows at the invention.

McLaren went on, "The plan is fer everyone to be up by 4:00 a.m., rollin' by 7:00, and stopped fer the day at 4:00 p.m." There were audible groans, but no one could argue the early bird and worm theory.

The elder laughed. "Sometimes, we'll pack a lunch and eat it on the fly. Cattle herders, Jake and Jock, on foot, will leave first in the mornin' and likely straggle in behind us at night. We need to camp where the animals can graze and find water. Come mornin', each person will know what their job is to take up the camp and get on the road."

"Be prepared to change wagon positions every day because 'tisnae fair to always be first or last. Those in the rear cannae eat dust all the time, but with the wet spring, 'tisnae much of a concern."

Departure morning, a light drizzle put a damper on things. David tethered his team and jogged forward from rig to rig to check on the others. "Hold yer horses!" he warned.

The horses could sense the excitement. They ground their bits, tossed their heads, pranced, pawed the ground, and strained in their traces. The drivers did their best to hang on.

With the gang loaded and in their rightful places, at 7:00 a.m., McLaren roared, "Wagons ho!" and the entire assembly rumbled off down the good road, inching southwest between Neepawa and Yorkton. The string of nine outfits and horseback riders wended their way, despite being a curious spectacle.

When the earth-shattering noise broke the sound barrier, Jake ahead, walking behind the cattle, waved across to Jock, "Here they come!"

Wood, leather, and metal creaked and groaned, unmistakable even over the pounding hooves of the cattle and horses. Worse was the staggering rattle of the wagons' undercarriages.

As Martha's wagon gained on, then passed the herd, Toot exclaimed, "It dinnae take us long to beat them cows!"

All the passengers, including the children made a big deal of waving to Jake and Jock. The slow-moving animals needed a good head-start and the single men, Willy, and Wyatt, rode back and forth acting as go-betweens. The border collies were either keeping the animals in a group at the front or heelers at the back to keep them moving forward.

Six-year-old Toot said to his four-year-old brother, Fleck, "The cattle get the message after the first few heel nips!"

"Nobody likes gettin' bit by a dog!" Fleck retorted.

Everyone was to walk as much as possible to save the horses and at the start it was exciting. The children soon discovered, if they didn't work hard to keep up, they might get left behind. With mothers driving and shorter legs playing out, eight-year-old Bunny was the runner. Keeping track of her siblings and cousins was a full-time job. She ran to lift the four-year-olds, Peanut and Fleck in and out of the wagons. Once back on board, they stopped crying but then before she knew it, they wanted to try walking again. After a while, Willy or Wyatt had to do the rescuing when Bunny played out.

The men on horseback relayed messages between wagons. If something was wrong, each wagon had a bell to clang. In Bunny's spare time, she rode with her mother, Emma, who was alone with four other children. In their caboose, Bunny helped siblings, six-year-old Tadpole, and four-year-old Peanut to entertain the babies. Padded dresser drawers came in handy for Bud, and Boo. In the meantime, in Tessa and Martha's covered wagon, Toot and Fleck kept track of their siblings, Dot and Blue. The older children knew they might be in trouble if one of the little ones got hurt on their watch.

The caboose was unique in that it had oilcloth on the sides that could be rolled up. Further, the floor was removeable leaving seats all around the edges. With babies crawling around, however, they kept the floor intact. Still, this vehicle was the children's favourite.

Martha's brother, Angus and his wife, Effie Mae, tried to keep their six children, also under 10, accounted for. One child at a time could ride with their mother as she drove the cart horse. Otherwise, their father was in charge of the other five in the covered wagon. As usual, the older ones were in charge of their little siblings.

Tessa was proud of all her brood, like 34-year-old Emma, who still nursed a bairn. Starting the journey six months pregnant, Martha too, despite threatening morning sickness, took control of the reins, and tolerated the bone jarring travel. The children faced the expedition with innocence, marvelling at all the new sights and sounds. Their stubby fists filled with wildflower bouquets of crocuses and dandelions, showered Tessa most days.

"Here Grandma," they would say.

Sometimes it was caterpillars, ladybugs, or frogs, but she was always careful to praise their kindness. The free hugs that came with their generosity kept the grandmother joyful. When nightfall came, the little troopers ran and played, giving the horses treats of sugar cubes or apple wedges.

"Pay special attention to the horses' ears. If they're laid back, they might kick!" every adult seemed to say the same thing.

The two-week mark of Thursday, May 22 drummed up darkening skies and brisk temperatures. The wind, their constant companion, blew raw and snow swirled until before long, a blinding snowstorm raged.

McLaren spoke to the men on horseback. "Take a message to the herders and other wagons that we'll stop and make camp now. We've made good time and the storm shouldnae last too long."

"I cannae believe we've covered 175 miles!" David shouted.

"Two miles an hour gets you 10 miles a day!" Charlie answered.

Spring snowstorms were enough to frazzle the nerves. The temperature wasn't bitterly cold but with wetness, it chilled to the bone and was hard on the animals.

"Jake and Jock found a bluff to shelter the herd," Willy and Wyatt rode up with the news.

"Thank goodness we havenae lost any animals sae far. The coyotes and wolves howlin' every night are a constant reminder of predators," Sean said.

Tessa awoke in the wee hours to see the clouds melted away revealing a brilliant full moon. Dawn was around 4:00 a.m., and time to get up. The sun peeked over the horizon introducing brilliant hues of yellows, oranges, and reds. A much more forgiving day.

"Red sky in the mornin', sailor take warnin'," McLaren rhymed as he finished his campfire coffee and set out to check the caravan.

He returned more quickly than expected, "The carthorse foaled overnight!" he said excitedly, "the filly's weak but a fighter, and the boys got her all warmed up and nursin'."

The exhausted mare, Briney, and her foal, however, proved too weak to continue the trip.

At Yorkton, Sean reported, "We found a farmer who bought the whole kit and kaboodle, mare, foal, and cart. Fer the layin' hens he paid 25 cents apiece."

Martha lamented, "No fresh eggs already on day 15? 'tis a loss, not to mention Dunbar and Ike!" She assumed the tom and rooster went for more and worried about her brother. With the cart horse gone, Effie Mae and their entire brood would squish in with Angus.

The men topped up the drinking water at the Yorkton pump because when the barrels ran dry, creek water or the insect-infested waters from a stagnant slough weren't appealing.

"If ye drink slough water with tadpoles in it, ye'll get frogs growin' in yer tummy!" Tessa heard her eldest grandson, Tadpole, proclaim to his sister Peanut, and their cousins, Toot and Fleck. "A should know cause that's me nickname!" Tessa elbowed Bunny and they were quick to the rescue.

"See how ye pour the water through a clean cloth to block the little bugs and make it safer to drink?" Bunny held the handkerchief while Grandma poured the water through. They could see the dark bugs wiggling on top of the cloth.

"Ye willnae grow tadpoles in yer tummies!" Grandma reassured.

With relief, the two little ones, Fleck and Peanut, wiped their tears because they had drunk water straight from the slough and could already feel the squiggles.

At the general store, a Babushka-wearing senior with a thick Ukrainian accent, spoke to the women, "This is a wery vet spring and rapid thaw. You vould be vise to vait until it dries up a bit."

Tessa answered, "That sounds temptin', but we have a government deadline and would risk too much to hold off now."

The woman's husband suggested, "You better find yourselwes an Indian guide then."

"But where?" Tessa asked.

The old-timer shrugged, "Good kvuestion, but maybe you'll come across one on the trail."

The women took the suggestions back to camp.

"We've already lost time waitin' fer the Glenella group," McLaren reasoned.

When their train arrived, Philip slid the box car door open to reveal another stack belongings. "If ye think packin' the wagons was challengin' before, just wait," he said.

By Tuesday, 27 May, and day 20, the topped-up wagons were far too heavy, and they all knew it. Even so, with a 1st June deadline, they could do nothing but keep going.

Emma remarked, "Now we're headin' into no man's land down settler's trails, and surveyors' cut lines!"

"'Tis true," Tessa answered.

The creaky wagons ventured off with cattle bawling, and dogs barking. At least, the overhead strings of migrating geese and cranes were drowned out. They hoped the noise might keep the bears and wolves away but the horses were another story. They could be gentle enough for a child to manage or with a sudden noise be stomping everything in their path. With blinders on, at least they didn't go into a full panic at the sight of their own shadows!

Soon, the soft trails got softer until the wagons were cutting into the mud up to their axles. With Clarice and Philip returned, at least there were more drivers. Clarice and Birdie rode with Emma while Philip took over for Tessa and Martha.

Bad thunderstorms didn't help. At the first bridge, water ran across the trail at either end to cause a gaping hole at the bridge's entrance. The men decided to tow each other across. On the first attempt, the wagon tongue broke. While the rest of the excursion waited, Timothy, Jock's brother, took the buggy back to Yorkton for a new tongue. When he got back that night, McLaren made the repair.

They all agreed, "First thing tomorrow, we have to lighten our load."

At the nearest farm, with the farmer's permission, they set up a tent, and left a portion of their goods behind for later retrieval.

The courageous trekkers continued their offensive through the mud to reach the community of Theodore. They were 25 miles from Yorkton. 'Little Denmark' had a post office and store and they camped on a small hill. It rained, so bedtime came early.

The following day when a slough wasn't too wide, McLaren, via Willy and Wyatt, explained the situation. "There are remnants of a corduroy road ahead that we can reinforce with more cut-down trees and branches."

The men got to work cutting and dragging brush. The herd crossed the bumpy makeshift road first and the wagons followed. They skirted the deeper sloughs, the ones up to the men's necks or well over their heads. Travelling miles out of the way threw another wrench into their timeline.

"One thing about it," McLaren said, "we're gettin' to explore the prairies!"

With 140 miles still to go on their six-month deadline day, they weren't even close. It was Sunday, 1 June, day 25, and it rained the entire day. The deluge continued until Wednesday, 4 June when they rolled again. At Insinger, 10 miles from Theodore, there was a store and post office but another creek with bridge washed out from rushing waters.

McLaren shouted over the rapid current, "Let the herd, herders, and dogs swim across first. Men! Each of you find a dry log to keep yerselves afloat."

Everyone held their breath watching. It was amazing how the dogs continued to herd the animals even when faced with drowning themselves but they all made it across without incident.

Now it was the horses' turn. The men unhitched them from the wagons and everyone stood and watched four of the men lead a horse each into the roiling water, enticing the animals to swim across. All the men had to do was hang on.

Tessa said, "Horses are funny creatures. If the lead horse will do it, the rest might gain the self-confidence to follow."

Four other men waited on the opposite shore, crossing earlier by raft, ready to catch the horses by the halters. The dry men brought the raft back, then it would be their turn to swim across with more horses. With almost 30 to cross, it took multiple attempts.

Charlie and Wyatt got wet first but their two horses tried to circle towards each other in the water, and McLaren roared, "Keep the horses movin' straight across! Don't let them circle! Splash water in their faces if ye have to!"

The women, children, and small calves were next and twittered, riding the tipsy raft secured by ropes to trees on either side. The wagons were last with a rope through their tongues acting as a block and tackle to pull them through. These eight crossings were dramatic, despite being oiled and waxed specifically to float. Midway across, the wagon beds disappeared from sight, dragged down to the bottom of the creek bed. At the first vanishing, the crowd gulped and clamoured closer but five or six heartbeats later, the whole rig safely bounced back to the surface.

The crossings took all day and with almost everything and everyone soaked, the banks were littered with supplies and possessions laid out to dry. Drivers without children, scrambled to help those with. By lantern light, and a waning crescent moon, they reloaded their rigs.

An onlooker walked by and said, "Some travellers upend their wagons and cross that way."

An exhilarated but tired McLaren sighed, "Even so, a think this major event has given us a boost, no matter how we did it. Me stomach, fer one, has unknotted, now 'tis over."

At Sheho, they encountered a new kind of storm. Swarming black flies, hungry for blood, had every warm-blooded creature flicking, swatting, or on the run. The cattle suffered the worst, bitten relentlessly around the eyes and horn roots. Smouldering smudges helped.

The older children snipped, slapped, or squished the biting insects off the babies, and kept rhyming, "Steady as she goes! Only forty kazillion to go!"

On Monday, 9 June, on day 33, they reached Foam Lake and found the perfect spot to camp near fresh water. It was 23 miles past Insinger.

At the centre of the journey, were these memorable encounters with washed out bridges and water running freely over trails. Countless creeks and small rivers had the wagons floating across or nothing but stuck. During these episodes, wagon occupants waded back to shore awaiting a complex rig extraction.

More joyous occasions were mealtimes, the highlight of the day. Tessa and the other women fought the all-consuming feelings of desperation with food.

"At least our bread, biscuits, and butter are hits," Tessa said.

"With all the wagons shakin' and rollin', the pails of skimmed cream we hang underneath turn to butter and buttermilk by day's end." Emma said. "A love dolin' out the buttermilk fer a treat because everybody's sick of drinkin' creek and slough water! Buttermilk is somethin' even Martha can tolerate."

At noon, they made yeast and at night set the sponge and mixed it up before leaving in the morning. By afternoon, the dough was formed into pans, then once stopped for evening the stoves were lit and the bread was baked.

Tessa eyed McLaren, "Bein' in charge of breaks and builds, he still cannae believe how well the reconnaissance trip went compared to this one."

Emma worried, "A wonder if they'll penalise us fer bein' late?"

"Dinnae worry, me dear, we'll make up fer lost time."

In the meantime, after the first newborn calf arrived enroute, the mother cow hid it, and the search was on.

Eventually, Wyatt came riding up. "Look what a found," he said, cradling the new calf.

Afterwards, the calves took to resting under the wagons. Thinking their babies were left behind, two mother cows went back on their own to search. Again, the hunt was on for the cows, this time, caught by a farmer. The mother cows were happily reunited with their calves, but it made sense to build a special rack to house the little critters.

On Tuesday, 10 June, and day 34, the trekkers camped near a store past Foam Lake. The path to the Nut Lake Trail over the succeeding two days was terrible and constantly pulling wagons through, meant hard days on the men and horses.

On Friday, 13 June, day 37, they were 52 miles past Foam Lake. When they passed Quill Lake, the trekkers hit clay. Even the cows got stuck, and the men, trying not to curse a blue streak, had to sweet talk them to yank them free. They met a man on horseback who confirmed they had made it a mere 16 miles from the last store. Travel was pitifully slow.

The men reported, "When the wheels were fully caked, teams hurried to pull the wagons loose, but in the rush, one hit a rock so hard it separated from the box and back wheels!"

That wagon had children in it and they were never so surprised as when it went thump and they were all thrown forward in a heap.

McLaren told Tessa, "No one was hurt," but she saw his frustration.

Finally, he admitted, "Son-of-a-gun, a've almost had it."

"No wonder, when we have to do a total unload every time somethin' breaks down."

After Quill Plains, tricky sod over mud had to be raced over. Come Gull Lake, it was Monday, 16 June, day 40. Here, it took four teams per stuck wagon to get through. One horse fell and got dragged.

"Ye lily-livered pot lickers!"

Once again, the group decided to offload more items and left them covered by canvas behind a willow bluff for retrieval at a later date.

On Wednesday, 18 June, when two teams were pulling a wagon across a creek, the lead team didn't stop when a horse at the back fell and was dragged across. It was like déjà vu. Although no horse was seriously hurt, they were sweated up and panting, and it put them in a skittish frame of mind.

By 20 June, a worn out, McLaren sighed, "Will we even make it by 1 July?"

Tessa lamented, "It tells ye somethin' when the cattle are stayin' ahead of the wagons. Plus, our food supply is dwindlin'."

The day clouded over, and a light drizzle fell as a wash of wind came up to rustle the tree leaves. A disgusted McLaren cursed, "Ye dirty rotten son of a," then stopped, admitting, "A've been cursin' and swearin' at anythin' that moves!"

"Does it help?"

He only glared.

With mounting problems, Tessa ramped up her prayers.

That afternoon, they came upon a survey crew happy to sell them flour, beans, and coffee. The surveyors seemed to understand their predicament and had an ideal solution.

The survey boss sidled up to one of his Cree-speaking, Métis drivers, "Please go and ask the Indians about guiding these folks. Otherwise, the poor beggars won't stand a chance!"

"There's an Indian encampment over the ridge," he reassured the trekkers. For the first time in three weeks, the waggoneers, held a glimmer of hope.

The survey boss spoke pointedly to the men, warning, "Try not to insult the Indians. The Cree dislike profanity and don't even have swear words in their vocabulary."

Dumbstruck, there was complete silence for a moment, then everyone laughed. Something else to worry about.

The driver brought the chief back, and said, "This is Chief Eagle Feather." The stately Indian male sat astride a bareback pony.

"Wa-chea," the chief greeted, and the others nodded their heads in deference.

Medium height, the Indian man wore buckskins to offset his dark skin, and jet-black braids dangling to his waist. Over an ornamented porcupine quill sheath, and across one shoulder, he wore a bow and quiver of arrows. Chillingly, no one missed the broad, animal-hide belt and scalping knife. The chief threw his right leg over the pony's neck and slid down the side to walk over and shake McLaren's hand.

"A handshake is a gesture of great respect," the survey boss shared.

Before long, the men sat in a circle passing around a peace pipe. The coughing and sputtering by the white men had the chief concealing a smile but he agreed to guiding them.

The survey boss said, "Chief Eagle Feather knows all the dry spots and can get you across country on high ground."

"Our original plan was to go north through the Barrier Valley," Jake interjected.

The chief looked startled, when the Mètis man interpreted, they laughed aloud, "Too many lakes and swamps!"

"Thank God, ye stopped us!"

Relief washed over the wayfarers who got into place behind the chief, waiting for him to take the lead. Squeezing in behind him though, came his entire tribe, making their way on foot. Even Tessa was thunderstruck. There were four families of parents, elders, teens, and small children. One crippled child bumped along in a small wooden cart. Their ponies pulled contraptions of two poles lashed on either side with animal skins laced behind, heaped with robes, dried meat, and pemmican. The Métis man called them travois. A multitude of dogs and ponies followed along.

McLaren winked at Tessa, "We must be quite a sight, this string of wagons following a tribe of nomads who think we're deluded!"

The chief and his people stayed well ahead. When it was time to camp, the sojourners could see the Indian women erecting the tipis, cutting wood, and making fires while the men hunted. For the newcomers, the experience was spellbinding, especially the children who had only ever read about *Hiawatha*. It was a breath of fresh air from juggling dangerous waterways.

On Saturday, 21 June, day 45, there was a full moon to match hearts and minds. McLaren was grateful, "With the chief's guidance, the trip has improved substantially! Suddenly, the world is a much rosier place!"

"'Tis delightful to watch the Indians make use of every wild creature and plant," Emma observed.

"They use everything from duck eggs to prairie chickens fer food," her brother, Jake, added, and when Martha almost gagged, the grandparents snickered.

Tessa said, "'Tis everythin' from gophers, to badgers, and rabbits. Poor Martha, 'tis too much fer her, after slough water."

Martha remembered, "A've eaten wild duck and rainbow trout from a pond and they both tasted like mud."

In fact, a day later, the chief almost came unravelled, signing about a bear ahead, and begging to borrow McLaren's Winchester. He galloped off, shot the bear, and generously shared the meat all around. The Indian women acted out the bear scratching at an anthill and it brought tears of laughter.

When the caravan rested on Sunday, 22 June, day 46, they camped at Wolverine Creek. At dawn, drumming, chanting, and dancing began and the settlers were flabbergasted to discover they were in for an all-day pow wow. The costumes were bright and decorated with feathers, beads, and quills. The festivities lasted until sunset but come late afternoon, the chief, in full regalia and feathered head dress, invited the married men, to his tipi.

The older children clamoured to go too, but their mothers shushed them, warning, "No children or women are allowed."

As a result, Bunny, Tadpole, Toot, Peanut, and Fleck spent time pouting until the festivities ended and they could hear the stories from their fathers. All they knew was that the drumbeat signified the heartbeat of Mother Earth.

Upon Jock's return, he shared his amazement. "Inside the tipi, we sat on blankets, heard prayers and songs in Cree, and were given a bowl of sweet bear soup. In reality, me head ached with the chanting."

McLaren grinned, "We're getting better at smokin' the peace pipe. Too bad we're not smokers."

Jake who was suffering with all his walking, hadn't felt well when he left for the tipi, but said, "Me stomach is no longer grindin' but a'm still stiff and sore. The awful pain a had in me right heel was relieved when the chief's wife massaged it and put on a salve that smells like spruce."

The children loved the stories. They began to pretend they were doing all the things their fathers had experienced, including smoking the peace pipe. No matter what age or race, that night the star constellations shone a little brighter across the midnight sky.

On Tuesday, 24 June, day 48, when they got to Lake Lenore, they had logged almost 50 miles since Quill Lake. They thought it would be smooth sailing to get the 30 miles to Flett Springs on their own. On that note, McLaren paid off the chief, who seemed a little dismayed and reluctant to leave.

Indeed, the trail looked easy enough but soon turned into treacherous hills and narrowed to a trail that dead-ended at a slough. At that point, the ensemble camped and contemplated how to proceed. When they were at their wits end, to their astonishment, the chief reappeared. Concerned for their safety, he had come and found them. They had a good laugh at their poor judgment and he was rehired.

Day 52 was Saturday, 28 June and amid faint streaks of daylight they set out. Now the hills and valleys were panoramic, and they travelled 11 miles to St. Briéux, a French settlement on the Carrot River. Here the local pioneers showered them with new potatoes as a treat. The caravan travelled further than usual that day, so by Wednesday morning, 2 July 1902, day 56, their destination was a heartbeat away.

With a blue sky overhead and the sun baking their faces, they were a little weather-beaten, but happy and feeling a great sense of accomplishment. Luxuriating in these last few hours they took their time, seeing everything with fresh eyes waiting to have their destination come into view.

And there it was, Vaughn school, at the Stoney Creek Settlement, about six miles south of Jake's and Emma's quarters. Chief Eagle Feather accepted his cash payment and shook the men's hands. He disappeared, then returned carrying an armful of furs. In return, McLaren held out a spare rifle and shells, thinking of the chief's hunting. Tessa produced household items like a kettle, and bolt of cotton cloth for the women. With warm feelings, the parties waved goodbye, and in the distance, the trekkers saw a gathering of welcoming pioneers.

9

Tramping the Atlantic

Sweden to Hamburg *April 30—May 1, 1902*

Before the train rolled from the Stockholm station, what had been upbeat, turned sombre. Lasse's mother presented her daughter with an heirloom Bible, and Lasse sobbed feeling the pull of her heart strings. The five females, herself, her daughters, Mikaila and Lovisa, and friends, Kirsten, and Greta, embraced the well-wishers, trying to crystallise their final moments. Were they ready? Yes, mentally but maybe not emotionally. Bjorn, Ava, and the four grandparents, wore hangdog expressions.

Once boarded, Lasse saw Bjorn murmur something to Ava, who put her arm through his. Lasse sighed deeply but knew there was no turning back. Once the train edged forward, the whistle blew, and the engine's loud chuffing drowned out the shouts of "Goodbye and bon voyage!" It was exactly 4:30 p.m.

With tears dripping down her face, Lasse realised she hadn't cried this hard since her husband died. Hoping her family's strength would carry her, she wasn't prepared for the thought of never seeing them again. Her son motioned the grandparents off the platform. At least, they had each other.

Lasse could hear the conversation in her mind. Her mother, ever positive, would wipe her tears and say, "We wish them every success. It's for the best."

Her mother-in-law, meaning no harm, would worry, "Let's hope the grass is greener on the other side."

Farfar, would cluck over his wife, ever fearful she might take to her bed again. He and Morfar would drown their sorrows in a shot of glogge.

The overnight trip was 17 hours through Copenhagen and the novelty soon wore off. Grappling with stiff bodies and bleary eyes, the females arrived in Hamburg by 6:00 a.m. A horse-drawn omnibus took them to the famous

Hochbahn Port of Hamburg through a booming city, boasting new residential quarters. Reaching the port, Lasse cringed upon spying their upcoming mode of transport, an old, converted tanker ship.

"Is the second leg of our journey to be on this floating monstrosity?" Kirsten whispered tongue-in-cheek. "Indeed, it was red and white but paint-chipped with a rusty undercoat."

Lasse stared in dismay, "She's not pretty but maybe she's sturdy?"

The lonely creaking structure had cows bellowing in the background.

Young Mikaila snorted, "Don't tell me we're getting on that thing!"

"Life with a teenager," Lasse sighed at the girl who was the spitting image of her father. Raising a stink was part of growing up and she had a penchant for stating the obvious.

"That cold hard reality is the key to our futures!" Lasse quipped.

"Of course, we're getting on!" saucy Lovisa was unafraid. She was more like Morfar, her grandfather, "It'll be fun!"

The temperature held at a respectable 17 degrees Celsius. With the last steers herded up the ramp, Hans, in work clothes and boots, strode forward to hug his sister, Greta.

She introduced him, then a sailor appeared at his side, "This is First Officer, Piper."

The shiny-faced young man winked, and seeing the looks of trepidation, announced in German, "Don't worry, we're almost loaded."

Lasse prayed in silence, "Whatever he said, please keep us safe!" If there was a cover-up, she'd smell it a mile away.

Hans was serious, shaking his head, "No storms are forecast," and Greta's eyes widened.

"You look like you've swallowed rancid lard, Sister!" He pointed to the passel of life rafts and buoys, "we're well prepared."

"I hope your will is written, Mother!" Mikaila was indignant.

Lasse asked in earnest, "I bet the wind whips up pretty quick, but can you even predict storms at sea?"

The moment was awkward and Hans translated as Piper spoke, "Yes, out of the stillness of the doldrums, Mother Nature can change fast. The smallest refreshing puff of wind can turn into the harshest roar but never fear, the ole girl noses into a storm like a vixen."

The officious German captain strode over in his crisp uniform and got right to the point.

Hans translated, "Captain John Galen here. Welcome aboard *The Helmut*!"

Lasse wondered, "Is he straight out of Deutschland? Better watch for goose stepping."

"Hans has already negotiated your passage," the captain said, "and we sail tonight, Thursday, 1 May 1902, with the tide."

"Otherwise, a sea voyage starting on a Friday is doomed," Hans interpreted.

"Oh, Lord!" Kirsten threw her head back.

The captain raised his eyebrows, "Since the cattle are moved in and out of different countries, our first port of call is less than 24 hours away at Amsterdam in the Netherlands."

He went on, "Kirsten, and Greta will work with the stewards as domestics."

They nodded once Hans interpreted. Lovisa seemed mesmerised by the captain's bushy eyebrows and fleshy nose and couldn't stop staring. Since she had a contagious smile, he grinned back and that's when Lasse noticed the twinkle in his eye.

The commander turned to her, "Lasse! Last night our scallywag cook's helper ran off and Hans says you cook. Can you help?"

She brightened and extended her hand. "Yes, I can. Thank you!"

"Otto, our cook, will be miserable because you're a woman, but…" the captain chuckled, "he'll get used to it."

Lasse shrugged.

"What's wrong with women?" Mikaila asked.

The captain spoke like it was God's own truth, "Well, women in general, especially red heads, are considered bad luck on a ship."

The females groaned but at least they knew where they stood.

"Otto is a cantankerous old fart and women in his kitchen are an abomination. But he'll warm up."

Lasse said in Swedish, "Half the battle is knowing that up front. I hope the meals are plain and easy to master."

The captain, with a puzzled look continued, "Mikaila and Lovisa can assist as domestics or with anything the cooks ask, like caring for the kitchen animals."

Lovisa whooped, excited to meet the creatures. Mikaila smiled too but was embarrassed by outright displays of emotion.

"Girls, you may go below deck to the cattle to watch and learn," the captain continued, "but stay out of the stockmen's way. Never trust cattle because they are unpredictable."

Lasse winced and hoped they wouldn't do anything stupid. The captain was blunt and in charge, so surely, they would listen.

"One duty I am assigning all is to check the pen gate locks whenever you go by. If you find one open, lock it. Otherwise, it's alarm schlagen!"

They all knew what that meant.

"Extra sets of eyes never hurt," he added.

"These girls will be busy," Lasse raised an eyebrow. They still had school studies. Sweden's Lagom lifestyle meant not working oneself to death. She would stand up to him if she had to, but sensed he got the message.

"Take them to stow their gear below," the captain directed Hans.

One cabin housed all five females which they didn't mind because it felt safer. They'd already heard Kirsten's foghorn snoring on the train, sound asleep sitting up.

Mikaila had whispered, "Soon she'll start whinnying like a horse," and Lovisa giggled.

Lasse said to Greta, "It might take everything we've got not to shove a sock in her mouth."

Their sleeping quarters were grand compared to the workers'. Hans pointed to the cattlemen's berths, down low in a stinky, hell hole.

The noise was deafening, and he shouted, "They can't hear themselves think for the pounding of the ship's engines. Nobody blames them for dragging a hay bale up higher to sleep in the fresh air."

A fog rolled in and the Captain shouted, "Muster the men! All hands-on deck!"

Once they assembled, he directed, "We've already charted a course. Get ready to make full sail!"

The men scrambled to their rightful places and the captain shouted, "Full sail. Course North."

When the ship moved out of the harbour, the captain called, "Stow the anchor and cable marker."

At bedtime, came Lasse's first chance to open her Bible, and a note on old, floral stationery floated out like a leaf. On it, in her mother's best Swedish handwriting, said:

My dearest Lasse,

A pale blue flower from the shepherd's cot, silently breathes forget-me-not.

Love Mother.

Lasse sniffed back tears and clutched the note to her heart. She allowed the scriptures to fall open and *The Book of Job* appeared. When the words narrowed to a leviathan sea monster, she slammed it shut and reached for the cotton to stuff her ears.

Once they left port and reached the North Sea, it didn't take long for the seasickness to make its appearance. Most were over the worst after the first few days, but the nausea could rise up at any time. The wretchedness came and went with wind severity and rough waters. Other times, cattle manure, slop pails, or chamber pots did the trick. Seeing someone run to heave over the rail was common.

Lasse lay awake, marvelling at their situation. Within cramped quarters, there was much to overcome. For the most part, the air they breathed was a fresh salty sea spray but often mixed with unforgettable stinky manure. Still, besides the ship sounds and smells, she was lulled to sleep by its rhythmic creaking and baying cattle. From somewhere, she heard men singing.

When the ship veered off the North Sea to enter a canal, the fog cleared. The Swedish females wondered what lay ahead but sometime later, they saw a labyrinth of canals revealing the enchanting architecture of Amsterdam.

"Look low down on the horizon, it's the Royal Palace built in 1648," Captain Galen said via Hans translating, then commanded the helmsman, "Not too close to the shoreline!"

The Swedish females leaned against the ship's railing. The captain pointed out, "It's a Dutch 'cradle of creativity'. See the timeless curved gables? They're from the Renaissance."

Indeed, there were countless grand buildings and the captain explained, "The Canal Belt is from the 17th century. It's a system of concentric semicircles formed by four major canals around the old city centre."

Greta breathed, "So far, at least that short jaunt gave us a taste of our sea legs. Stopping here gives us another chance to gain our equilibrium."

By Saturday, 3 May, they were back on the North Sea. After another three days on the water, the captain announced, "Welcome to the Port of the Flemish Oostende, Belgium."

Piper bowed with a flare as Hans translated, "This West Flanders port town is on the Ghent-Brugge Canal. The fishing village is from the ninth century and important for mussels, but the community was founded in 1584."

"Impressive!" Lasse commented, "but Sweden's first town, Sigtuna, was founded in AD 980 during the final century of the Vikings."

Kirsten added, "And our university city, Uppsala, was established in the 1400s."

The captain continued, "Leopold II, King of the Belgians, made use of this long beach and promenade. See the city's neo-Gothic architecture with the soaring church spires, and vibrant, stained-glass windows?"

Lasse exclaimed, "I want stained-glass in Canada if it's the last thing I do!" The sight made her tingle with anticipation.

When ready to leave, the Captain shouted, "Sail ho! West by north!"

Another three days would pass before they reached their final stop on the North Sea.

"This is Le Havre, France, on the Normandy coast where the Seine River meets the English Channel. It's considered the gateway to the Atlantic and the port is tops for freight."

Just then it began to rain. Umbrellas were opened but some popped in the fierce wind.

Hans pointed, "Through the mist, do you see the Shipowner's House? It's a mansion from the 18th century, and there's a museum full of art works by impressionist artists."

"Who?" the girls asked.

Hans laughed, "Monet, Pissarro, and Renoir."

Amazed, Mikaila said, "If I don't meet my Prince Charming in Canada, I will consider you, Hans."

He blushed.

Around 9:00 p.m., the tide went out and the ship wedged itself on a sand bar. They were stuck five hours until the tide returned. Once the sailing resumed, the ship's rocking lulled them to sleep. Even the cattle quieted. On Monday, 12 May, the sun shone and a gentle breeze nudged the ship along. This voyage excluded Liverpool but the English Channel behind them was a beehive of activity. Looking ahead, they faced the lonely, empty expanse of the Atlantic Ocean.

Hans chuckled, "We have over 2,000 miles to travel, and on average the water is 1,800 fathoms deep or over 11,000 feet!"

Audible gasps showed an inability to comprehend such staggering details. An image of falling overboard and sinking down, down, flashed through Lasse's mind and by the looks on the others' faces, she wasn't alone.

After a time, routines established and Lasse tried to improve upon the menu.

One evening, at bedtime, she said, "I take back my initial thoughts of Otto. He's a magician with what he's had to work with. If it's the captain buying the groceries, it's obvious rations aren't his priority."

"And no buying bananas," Kirsten laughed. "bad luck, you know?"

The females rolled their eyes.

"I sprouted the shrivelled potatoes and sifted the beans and rice from the weevils and worms."

Greta gagged.

"The rock-hard peas, I boiled, mashed, and sieved for pea soup and mushy peas. Even fresh water is too skimpy to wash dishes in."

Greta said, "Hans hopes you can improve on the salt junk and unleavened bread."

Lasse said, "Well, I am out to live down the curse of women on a ship."

Indeed, once her recipes had the crew's mouths watering, they appreciated having her around. With a half day's work each day, the stockmen played cards in the galley and included the young girls like little sisters. Growing up in a household of loving men, the girls weren't shy.

Otto warned, "Aboard a ship, you must never say goodbye, nor utter a breath that someone has drowned."

"How can we keep all these superstitions straight?" Greta asked.

"Oh, we'll remind you!" the men chimed in.

Mikaila and Lovisa were helpful above and below deck and weren't afraid to get dirty. It turned out they had a new purpose on board.

Mikaila told her mother, "We found a simple cure for those antsy steers!"

"We sing or tell them stories and they listen," her sister admitted.

An African stockman within earshot winked at his shipmates and spoke with a thick Afrikaans accent, "The livestock is their captive audience."

"A new auctioneer could have a real shot with those beasties."

"Well, at least they wouldn't be whistling," one cackled.

The females knew whistling could drum up a storm.

The captain's favourite word, "Verboten", they heard so often, they began to say it themselves.

Hans impressed upon the girls, "Steers can kick, gore, or trample. Stay out of the pens, understand?"

"Are you saying it's verboten?" Mikaila giggled.

Hans told Lasse, "You can be proud. The girls listen and give the men room. It's all about timing to feed and do the muck out."

One day, Lovisa reported, "Alarm schlagen! A gate was unlocked and we saved the day! What if they had stampeded?"

Hans answered, "Cattle know how to swim, but they aren't the smartest. They'll jump overboard thinking they can make it to shore."

"Secondly, lack of fresh air can spell death. The animals must be well cared for."

"Who would buy sick cattle?" Lovisa wondered.

He went on, "Finally, we watch for crowding and disease. You'll see coughing, limping from broken bones, goopy eyes, or weeping and bloody sores."

The girls' interactions with man and beast saw them gaining a certain measure of self-confidence and they learned tidbits of the other languages. Most men seemed content with their presence, except for one. Carl was a big growly Norwegian who seldom smiled.

On one occasion, he snarled and Lovisa apologised but Mikaila retorted, "We wanted to show you a hurt steer, he's limping."

The girls told Lasse, "Carl found the poor creature and tenderly fixed its leg! His bark is worse than his bite! After that he almost smiled and started calling us, Mac, and Lou."

Most mornings, the girls helped the maids make beds and tidy rooms. By nightfall, if they could get to sleep before Kirsten's snoring, they would sleep but cotton in their ears didn't always survive the night. Since they also helped tend the kitchen animals, their days were full.

Otto offered, "The girls can gather the eggs."

The cranky laying hens pecked and Lasse knew the girls would get rapped without exception. "It's treachery," she thought, "but the girls have to learn for themselves."

When they carried in a basket of eggs, Mikaila smiled, "the hens like our voices just like the steers." They had a way about them but then so did their mother.

Piper said, "We think the world of you ladies, and Lasse has worked her way into our hearts through our stomachs. Any one of us would offer his hand in marriage to any one of you but it's easy to see you're bound for land lubber husbands. Forever, we have to live down our infamous sailor reputations."

Otto slyly added, "Woe is me but it's bad luck to utter the word pig on a ship, don't you know?"

The females gave him a wry look.

Usually, from the kitchen, Lasse kept her eye on the galley. For instance, Otto liked to win at cards. If not, the men might see his wrath at the dinner table. With Lasse around, they started letting him lose now and again.

"No more worrying about dishwater soup if he doesn't win," Hans joked. "Potato sprouts, and old boot tongues leave us with an echoing case of the bloat!"

Piper said to Lasse, "I like your fried potatoes with cabbage and onion."

The African added, "I like the biscuits boiled in fat and molasses."

The plot to keep Otto away from the kitchen had Otto winking at her. Aha! He knew about it all along, so maybe he liked her cooking too.

There was a tumultuous storm about 10 days in, Tuesday, 22 May. By sunrise, the galley flooded and starting the stove's fire and keeping it going for Lasse and Otto was a chore. The temperature dropped and their fingers stiffened.

Over the crashing noise, she yelled, "Unsteady footing on good days is one thing but wading through water?"

"Could be worse." Otto was blunt.

The frightened teenagers stayed close to their mother and helped when a fireman was brought in with burnt hands. Otto doubled as the ship's first aider and sprang into action, plunging the man's hands into a bucket of cold water.

"Make room," he shouted, "and help him lay down with his head lower than his heart, and his feet elevated."

Although awkward, his hands cooling in water stemmed the burning and the position warded off shock. The girls found a blanket to cover him.

One of the rescuers said, "The coal in the bunker spontaneously combusted so this man risked his life to put the fire out."

He went on, "To find the seat of the fire, he smothered the flames and hot spots with water way down deep in the coal reserves. If he hadn't, a full-blown fire could have sunk the ship."

By this time, others gathered and heard the captain admit, "That the fireman endured the gases and didn't cause a steam explosion from the water itself is a wonder."

There was real reason to rejoice because they had a true hero in their midst and the storm was subsiding.

The moments ticked by, and Lasse ventured her mother's words, "There's enough blue sky to sew a sailor's pair of pants."

Otto cooled the man's burns again, then wrapped them in clean bandages. They would watch for signs of infection and the patient would have to find a doctor upon docking.

As things settled, the teenagers prayed aloud, "Please don't ever make us evacuate into those wretched little lifeboats."

Trying to distract them, an African with a mat of hair, described how ancient sailors soothed vexed sea gods when a woman was on board. With a straight face, he said, "There was only one way the gods could shame nature into backing down."

"What was that?" the girls were curious.

"Do you really want to know?" He lowered his head and looked at them out of the corner of his eye.

"Yes!" the girls cried. Lasse figured something was fishy.

"They strapped the woman to the prow, stripped naked from the waist up."

"What?" Mikaila and Lovisa's jaws dropped.

"In the olden days, a clothed woman wasn't even allowed on a ship," his white eyes flashed against his dark skin.

Greta jumped to the girls' defence, "all you're missing is an eye patch and a peg leg," then she gave him a little shove.

He and his cronies cackled but the teens were embarrassed. With red faces, they fled the galley under the guise of checking the steers.

"Let's never again complain about lifeboats!" the two promised each other.

Lasse scolded the African, "OK, your tale of lore worked even if rough-around-the-edges."

"But their fear disappeared!" he argued, and he gave her an 'I told you so' look.

With the storm ended, the crew went to work making repairs and Lasse marvelled at the many sides to Otto. She had certainly misjudged him. At the same time, her mind drifted to Canada, and homesteading as the sole head of a household. If she could survive storms and superstitions at sea, surely she could manage.

Hans reported to the captain on the state of the animals, "Pens will dry and they still have glossy coats. There's a bit of bruising but on the whole, their feet and legs look good. Now we'll watch for eye infections or the like."

In the meantime, the stockmen's stories of seafaring cruelty to animals poured forth.

"In hot tropical climates, animals die enroute and they either throw them into the sea or leave them on-board to rot," Carl said.

Hans nodded.

"On some hellish excursions, cattle are so crowded, they can't move for weeks. If they go down, they're prodded and stomped on," one of the Africans spoke. "Inhumane stockmen give them shots to the eye, belly, or genitals to make them move!"

"No animal deserves that!"

"Some get so covered in manure, they can't breathe," the African finished, "and that's the truth."

After this, on the cloudless twilight of a full moon, Piper thought he would get back at Otto for his remark about pigs. Not breathing a word, he set six loose. The high jinks caught everyone's attention when the cook raced around, diving to catch them, but came up empty-handed.

"They're slipperier than eels," he blurted, red faced and puffing. It was funny in any language.

The pigs' squeals had the cattle bellowing in sympathy, so the girls tried to corner them too. Thrilled to run around, the beasts had no intention of being caught. When it got dark, Hans and Piper stopped laughing and grabbed lassos. Even Carl grabbed a fish net and caught two. Lasse's bucket of slop was the final straw that worked. The next day, a cry went up that the vessel needed to steer clear of a pod of whales.

Hans explained, "They're pregnant females spending time resting at the surface."

Congregated at the rail, everyone watched the massive mammals roll and spray. Dipping in and out of the water, the amazing creatures stayed alongside the ship for a long time and it was thrilling to watch.

After that, the days dragged on and most grew tired of the monotony at sea. Hair and beards needed trimming and when Greta offered to cut Hans's, he shook his head, "Not at sea, it's bad luck!"

The women couldn't help but burst out laughing at the insanity and it made him blush.

The travellers expected it would be weeks before their trip concluded but in reality, the estimate of a month or two was spot on. On 15 June, a sea gull circled overhead heralding land, and before long, a welcoming light house beckoned on the Canadian shore!

10

Fertiliser and Death Chant

That Thursday afternoon, Knut's pace relaxed once across the United States/Canada border. To officially become a Canadian citizen, a person petitioned for naturalisation papers but that was for another day.

At the North Portal train station, the apologetic agent said, "Sorry but the train to Prince Albert doesn't leave until tomorrow afternoon."

With time to spare, Knut washed, shaved, and changed clothes in the station's bathroom. That evening, after wiring a telegram to his parents, he poured over the wall map showing where the Soo Line and the Canadian Pacific Railway met.

"It's about 450 miles to Prince Albert," the agent showed. "From here to Moose Jaw, you take the CPR straight west past Estevan and Weyburn. At Moose Jaw, the line backtracks northeast to Belle Plaine and Grand Coulee, then to Regina. I know, it's the long way around. From there, it's now the CPR but three years ago, it was the QLLS line or Qu'Appelle Long Lake and Saskatchewan, since 1886. After that, it's Lumsden, Craik, Saskatoon, Hague, Osler, Rosthern and Duck Lake."

Knut purchased a first-class ticket for sleeping car and meals. Although expensive, after his passage on foot, and last night spent parked on a hard wooden bench, it was well worth the $12.00.

Being young and naïve, Knut ignored worries about train travel and its occasional bad accidents. To him, last October's North Carolina incident where part of Buffalo Bill's Wild West Show collided with a fertiliser train was a freak accident. Annie Oakley was hurt, and famous exotic show animals and over 100 horses died.

The train departed at five minutes after 2:00 p.m., Friday, May 2, 1902, and he had a dèjá vu when peering inside the Pullman car. Black porters carried luggage and seated people, and Knut was reminded of family stories about the Underground Railroad. The seats were plush mulberry velvet and placed so one side faced forward and the other back towards the caboose, with a table in between. Overhead berths were folded up for daytime and Knut shoved his satchel and gun under his seat. Bathrooms and a smoking area were at the rear.

After the whistle sounded and the train chugged huge plumes of steam, the porter did his best to make everyone comfortable.

The conductor moving down the aisle called, "Tickets!"

The countryside slipped past and passengers gawked out the smudged windows. Spring was late. Pussy willows blossomed and wagon trains in the distance transported hordes of settlers. In fact, groupings of 30 or 40 men, women, and children walked or rode in wagons pulled by horses and oxen. He was amazed at all the small children and the obviously pregnant mothers driving the teams. Men rode horseback or herded livestock on foot and led the rigs through the waterways.

In less than an hour was the first village of Estevan, which had a coal mine at Roche Percee. The porter assisted a senior lady to disembark and made a quick round of the coach to remove garbage. He offered beverages and seemed happy to serve them.

Knut didn't take long to find his footing and explore the car ahead. No longer a matter of timing and risking life and limb jumping couplers, the access was simple, through a couple of doors. The deluxe parlour car had parents and children gathered around, looking out the windows. The coach had small tables for card playing and a substantial library.

Out the window, because of washed out bridges and trails, wagons floated across creeks and rivers with horses, cattle, and men swimming. Anything that shouldn't get soaked like women, children and calves got floated across on a raft. The wagons followed old settlers' trails but at times, stacked high with household contraptions, sat mired in the muck. One or more teams would pull them out using a block and tackle.

"The water has to be frigid," Knut used his best English and an infectious laugh to note the ice chunks floating downstream. Passengers seemed at ease and turned to nod.

The wagon crossings were long, drawn-out affairs because, once across, it meant unloading and laying all the contents out on the banks to dry. For the train travellers, riding at 35 miles per hour, it was a little too fast for the children's running game of I spy. The littlest boy lisped out his win and the oldest boy gave over his turn.

Long freighting wagon processions called 'swings' also traversed the prairie trails. Although unable to hear over the roar of the train, Knut imagined they creaked and groaned, loaded to the hilt with supplies. They would be crucial for isolated settlers and communities in this virgin territory. He walked back to the smoking area to sit and roll a smoke. His pocket watch said 4:00 p.m., once he puffed through two more.

At Weyburn, a sign said, Signal Hill, and Ralph, a stylish gentleman explained. "The Blackfoot and Assiniboine sent messages great distances from the crest."

The porter came along with a shoe-shining kit and certain men, stuck out their black patent leathers for a shine. Knut saw them reach into their pockets and jingle change to indicate there would be a tip. The children made a game of what the smoke signals meant.

"Buffalo here!" one guessed.

"We've arrived!" suggested another.

The Weyburn stop was short. He heard passengers refer to the honkers winging northward overhead as Canada Geese and chuckled because it seemed both countries claimed the birds. A little further along, a herd of deer fled south. Along the way, he had already seen wayward rabbits, foxes, and coyotes ducking in and out of thickets. In two more hours, they were halfway to Moose Jaw at Milestone.

Ralph said, "Original settlers thought Milestone might be part of Palliser's Dry Belt, until they found thick wild grass and good rich soil for farming."

Knut replied, "I imagine the settlers' relief when the place wasn't a desert!"

"Oh George!" Ralph signalled the porter. "I need a shirt pressed." The porter took the wrinkled shirt and within minutes, returned it anew. When others made use of the same service and also called him George, Knut realised the significance of status.

At Rouleau, supper in the dining car was brilliant with crystal chandeliers, white linens, and china dishes. Formally attired waiters brought dinner rolls and vegetable soup to start, followed by entrées of baked salmon. The chocolate cake and whipped cream for dessert Knut topped off with brandy.

"Rouleau is an oasis of trees," the waiter said, "surrounded by crops and named after a French judge."

He pointed through the window, "That hole in the ground is one of the first settler's dwellings in the area. It's roofed with poplar poles, then covered with sod." He went on, "At night, from here, you can see the lights of Moose Jaw and Regina."

After the meal, the sunset blazed so that people shielded their eyes.

Knut heard one young boy ask his mother, "Why do the geese fly north?"

"Well Son," she winked, "because they're harbingers of spring."

The little boy had stopped in his tracks, spying the tipis on the outskirts of Moose Jaw. Ralph said they were Sioux and Knut remembered the Sitting Bull story. Knut's watch said 7:30 p.m. and the brakeman lit the interior coach lamps. Outside lights blinked in the distance through evening's murky twilight showing the place was a good size.

The conductor shared, "There's plenty of businesses here, from farm implement dealers to a bank, and law office. The new town hall bell for curfews and fires has never been rung."

Knut stepped out onto the platform to stretch his legs, then spied a bulletin board. One poster read, 'Spring Stallion Fair' and another advertised 'Syndicate Threshers'.

Although intrigued, he hurried back at the call of, "All aboard!"

When the whistle blew, the locomotive chugged again, backtracking past Belle Plain and Grand Coulee.

Ralph said, "If it was daylight, you could see a round barn with vertical siding."

By 8:30 p.m., the porter busied himself letting down upper berths. Using a small step ladder, he applied bed linens and closed window drapes, and privacy curtains. By the time the youngest children were in bed, the train slowed to a stop for Regina.

One mother declared, "Regina is named for Queen Victoria but 20 years ago, it was called Pile o' Bones Creek. It's the capital of the Northwest Territories, the Assiniboin District, and the headquarters of the North-West Mounted Police."

"So, this is the capital of the NWT," Knut breathed.

Ralph scoffed, "It may sound grand, built along the rail line, but the settlement started out as a disappointment with one petty stream and few trees or wildlife."

"In the dark, who can tell?" Knut thought.

"Even so, now there's a territorial administration building, a supreme court, and a government house. It's a population of over 3,000 and the Romanians are building an orthodox church," the woman protested.

An old-timer who got on at Moose Jaw, had sat beside Knut in his forward-facing seat and introduced himself as Stub. "The pile of bones were bison, gathered from old hunts and placed on a small hill just west of town."

The children' s ears perked up. An old couple sat across from Knut and Stub, and the woman, Georgia, said, "the run-off channel rises a mile or so away."

Her husband, Walter, motioned with his arm and said in a scratchy voice, "Then reaches the Qu'Appelle Valley to the north."

"The Cree piled the bones in a circle to honour the herds and keep them coming." Stub described, "they believed the bison wouldn't leave where their ancestors lay."

"Where's the bones now?" a boy heading to bed asked.

"The bones started getting shipped east to make fertiliser sometime about 20 years ago, Stub scratched his balding head."

"There was good money in it," Ralph added, "for the railroad hauling them and for homesteaders and natives. The bones were the first true crop of the prairies, they say."

The boy wrinkled his nose.

Walter, startled everyone when he growled, "I'll grind yer bones to make me bread!"

The bigger kids played along but it frightened the littler ones who scattered back to bed. Knut figured *Jack and the Beanstalk* was all they knew about bone grinding.

He thought of Stub's words and wondered, "Did the loss of the bones contribute somehow to the disappearance of the buffalo? Amid all the finger pointing, hunting to extinction was blamed, but what of the spiritual connection lost with their removal?"

Not only that but "Was killing the bison done for survival, greed or both?"

The complexities were well beyond his comprehension. One day, perhaps the answers would come to light.

Stub brought him back to reality, "In an apparent show of retribution, the settlers named the creek using the Cree word *Wascana* which means inspiration."

Knut was startled to hear a woman across the way hiss a controversial, "Savages!"

Just then, the porter announced, "Lights out at 10:00 p.m."

It didn't take long before they entered Lumsden's deep valley. Knut's watch said 10:00 p.m. on the nose, and as promised, the lights were put out. For the scenic views of the Qu'Appelle Valley, he wished it weren't so dark. Not ready to turn in yet, he veered back into the smoking area and doctored another roll-your-own. Inhaling each drag and blowing smoke rings, he heard a cough. Sitting in the shadows was a striking lady wearing a forest green hat with ostrich feather and matching silk-gloves.

"Sorry ma'am, I didn't mean to bother you," he apologised, "I'm Knut."

Ralph had walked in and introduced her, "Meet Mrs. Edwina Smith."

"Why did she sit in the smoking area if she wasn't smoking," he wondered but said, "Nice to meet you."

"I'm returning from my aunt's funeral in Regina," she explained. "My husband already went back to Prince Albert early to tend our clothing store."

"I'm sorry for your loss ma'am," Knut offered, tipping his hat, "I'm going through P.A. myself."

"Edwina and I are acquaintances from way back," Ralph explained.

"I wasn't feeling up to the parlour car," Edwina lamented, "and I'm not sleepy."

When Stub walked in and lit his pipe, Knut gave them a mini run-down of his long walk into Canada. He described stumbling onto an ancient Indian burial ground and getting caught sleeping in a hay loft.

He ended with, "And thank God for the trapper's moccasins."

"Be careful or they'll think you're one of them," Ralph taunted.

"I, for one, can't even fathom how you could walk so far!" Edwina changed the subject.

"Lots of people do it," Stub reminded, "but not for long, someday, there's supposed to be rail lines no further than 13 miles from any town. By the way,

I'm going as far as Duck Lake. My brother and I have farmed our whole lives near the Beardy's reserve so we know almost everyone."

Ralph said, "I'm off at Saskatoon."

Outside, the brilliant crescent moon stood stark against a twinkling star-filled sky. Once Stub heard that Knut would be living in the Carrot River Valley, he had to fill him in.

"Almost 30 years ago, when I was a much younger man, they signed the treaties. Over 2,000 Cree, Assiniboine, and Ojibwa travelled to Fort Carlton for negotiations. It was 1876 to be exact."

Knut remarked, "That's significant, even if I was only a year old," he laughed. "Fort Carlton is between Duck Lake and Prince Albert, right?"

Stub nodded, and they all padded back to the sleeper car where a small child let out an ear-piercing wail. Through his tearful blubbering, his mother found he had bitten his tongue. Despite being in trouble for eating candy in bed, she tried to calm him down.

Knut was sympathetic but Stub went on, "The Indians agreed to maintain peace in exchange for necessities. You know, to farm, have their children go to school, receive medical aid, and get enough food not to starve."

"For as long as the sun shines and the rivers flow," Mrs. Smith, the refinement evident in her voice, contributed. Knut had her pegged at about 30.

He half listened to Stub, hearing the little boy whimper, "Time to go to sleep," he thought.

"But within four years, people told of Indians starving," Stub finished.

Edwina agreed.

"Well, if you won't work, and sit around waiting for hand-outs from the government, what else can you expect?" Ralph's critical voice had a cruel edge.

The image set Knut's teeth on edge, and he challenged, "With the bison gone, being put on reserves, and told to farm, couldn't have helped."

"Then there's the Métis," Georgia swiftly changed the subject. "After Manitoba's 1883 Red River Rebellion, they came here in their squealing wooden carts, leaving their river lot farms. God knows maybe the South Saskatchewan River lots reminded them of home."

Edwina added, "The Indians and Métis were allies but the Indians had their own troubles. Their gatherings like pot laches and pow wows were outlawed."

"A trapper told me pow wows are still held in secret," Knut lowered his voice.

"Probably."

Once again, a disparaging male voice from not far off spat, "Dirty Indians!"

Knut decided to ignore such negativity.

"Dear, don't eat those!" Georgia grabbed a pill bottle out of Walter's hand and Knut saw it was a box of Allen Cocaine tablets.

"You only get one a day!"

"No!" he protested, his ire rising.

Instead, she produced an oatmeal cookie and when he settled, she mouthed to the others, "He's worse after sundown."

Acting like nothing happened, Knut continued, "The ole Mississippi has outcroppings with tunnels, and ice caves beneath. How would you describe a river lot here?"

"A river lot is not necessarily square," Stub answered, "It borders the water and goes backwards up the riverbank."

Ralph interjected, "It seems the Métis couldn't create a land base in Manitoba but did already have their own government, constitution, and legal code."

Edwina questioned, "Maybe those virgin lots were sitting there ready for the taking, maybe first come, first served?"

"Think about it," Stub ventured, "the John Smith Reserve people already inhabited the river lots further downstream. I'm not sure there was much of a rule book to follow."

"Well, it was a question and the Dominion land surveyors sent it to their higher ups in Ottawa," Ralph said.

Stub explained, "With no response, the Métis were forced to ask Ottawa again and again but it took years to get an answer."

By 11:30 p.m., shrouded in darkness, they were about to pass Chamberlain. Without warning, a singular flash of fork lightning lit up the night sky and silhouetted the hamlet. Ear-splitting thunder and countless crashing lightning strikes followed. The storm hit so hard; Knut wondered if they were in the eye. Rain drops pelted the metal cars but soon became a slashing, torrential downpour. The smell of the wet earth was heavenly but Knut, who had started to yawn, got his second wind. In fact, so did Stub and he wasn't done talking by a long shot.

"Gabriel Dumont was the ferry man at Gabriel's Crossing, an essential ferry between Batoche and Fort Carlton," the old-timer said.

Edwina offered, "Living right there, Dumont was one petitioning for the river parcels. You can imagine, certain people sympathised but others thought the Métis should jump through the same hoops as the settlers."

"To confound matters," Ralph said, "white squatters were taking up some of the land the Mètis had already chosen."

"Sounds like a kettle of fish! Did they ever get an answer from the federal government?" Knut asked.

Stub raised his voice above the storm. "It seems they were told to apply for square lots like everyone else. You have to understand, during the mid-1880s, from Fort Garry to the Rockies the CPR's monopoly meant high freight rates and that no other roads could enter the country. Proving up a homestead took three years but then another three years for the patent. Tensions ran high, and tempers flared because petitions to Ottawa were ignored so talk of annexation to the states was rampant."

Knut was glad it hadn't come to that.

"Riel in the meantime, defended the new Métis provisional government and attempted to settle the land claims with the Dominion."

Nearing 1:00 a.m., the storm subsided and they came to Craik. Knut eyed his upper birth.

Shuffling off to bed, the demented Walter was co-operating but asked Georgia, "Did you feed Father?"

"Yes, dear," she played along.

"The year of the rebellion was 1885 and only 17 years after the treaties were signed," Georgia smiled.

Stub took over, "Dumont was Riel's military commander and the river lot fiasco, they say, was the major reason for the rebellion."

Edwina said, "Did you know? During the fighting, regular Métis folk sought shelter at a hidden grotto between Duck Lake and Batoche. The place of miracles is Our Lady of Lourdes, St. Laurent Shrine. It's a sacred place of pilgrimage to this day."

"Yes," Stub turned to look, then went on, "and Dumont wasn't without his own manoeuvres like lowering a ferry cable to shear off the smokestack of

General Middleton's gussied up steamboat turned battleship, the S.S. Northcote."

Knut's jaw dropped. "Well, being a ferry man, he would know all about the cabling!"

A couple of older children gathered around. This wasn't stuff they learned in school or on the street. The mothers cast furtive glances.

"At the Rebellion's trial, where Riel was hung, 42 Natives and Métis were charged with treason. At Regina, James Prendergast, was their defence counsel and he had them plead guilty to petty treason. Two were released and the rest received short prison terms."

"Chiefs Pound maker, One Arrow, and Big Bear, on the other hand, were found guilty of treason felony and sent to Manitoba's Stony Mountain Penitentiary."

"What's a penutenshuree?" asked the little fellow who bit his tongue.

"It's a prison, silly," his sister chastised.

Stub went on, "Pound maker, considered a great leader to his people, was imprisoned because a young, militant faction of his band had joined the resistance."

The little guy whispered, "What's a miltan fackshun?" They could hear his sister shushing him.

Knut laughed out loud. The kids didn't know how funny they were.

Edwina whispered, "Don't forget the Massacre at Frog Lake in April that triggered the rebellion. Nine settlers died, and others were taken prisoner. The communities were terrified."

"The Plains Cree were fired up but the Woods Cree joined them and ensured the prisoners' survival," Ralph claimed.

Edwina confided, "A grandmother of one of the young white girls taken hostage told us that, 'friendly Indian women hid the young girls in their tipis away from the more hot-blooded warriors!'"

Georgia and Knut both stifled yawns. Although fascinating, it was 2:00 a.m. and he'd been making an obvious show of his pocket watch for some time.

At Davidson, even with more story to tell, people were tired and had to lay their heads down. Knut climbed up to his bunk and slept soundly through Kenaston, Hanley, and Dundurn. His sleep elixir was interrupted when the train slowed at 5:30 a.m.

The conductor announced, "Saskatoon has an outbreak of scarlet fever."

Passengers moved to windows for a better view. The water tower was nothing new but the solitary train bridge was. Knut assisted Georgia to get the unsteady Walter to his seat while the train's metal wheels clickety-clacked across the bridge's timbers.

Georgia patted her husband's arm, "This is the South Saskatchewan River, dear."

She spoke for Knut's benefit. "The name, Saskatchewan, is a Cree word meaning big swift flowing river. Saskatoon means red berry."

Knut nodded in thanks and took a gander at the shimmering waters below. He wondered when there would be another bridge built.

Edwina said, "The QLLS built the train bridge but it keeps collapsing during spring breakup."

The porter told them, "Thank goodness this year the only damage was the beams closest to shore and they're already fixed."

A little boy pointed, "Look, the ferry's making a crossing!"

Sure enough, the barge was already busy, taking horses, a wagon, and passengers across to the west side.

"Sometimes it breaks free of the cable lines," the porter said. "then the passengers have to help recapture it!"

"People do cross train bridges on foot," the porter said, "but they don't want to get caught by an oncoming train!"

Knut knew the feeling.

"See the stone schoolhouse, and post office?" an older boy showed his little sister.

"Yes, and I see stores, houses, and shacks too."

Edwina explained, "The east side is a Temperance Colony and three of those houses were converted to military hospitals during the rebellion. One is the Marr Residence then there's the stone schoolhouse. The central part of the village is called Nutana."

"It's a good-sized place," Knut observed, "maybe 300 people or so?"

Across the bridge, they pulled into the 1st Avenue and 20th Street station and a hush fell watching the porter assist people off. Ralph was one who said his goodbyes.

"There's the North-West Mounted Police barracks."

A young boy said, "I can't wait to meet a Mountie one day!"

Knut grinned, "Me too!"

"Last year, the west settlement became the village of Saskatoon. A third settlement is developing further west called Riversdale."

Once the train rolled again, a mother breathed a sigh of relief, "Thank God no one got on. Nobody needs another epidemic."

At breakfast, Knut enjoyed porridge and after a smoke, back in the parlour car, Stub continued his story.

"They said Chief One Arrow was in mourning for a grandchild and wanted no part of the resistance. After the farm instructor ordered the reserve's cattle slaughtered, the entire band was sent to join the Mètis at Batoche. Dumont's men took the chief hostage and, in the end, General Middleton arrested him."

Edwina and others edged closer and Stub beamed at his audience.

"Despite Chief Big Bear seeing Treaty Six as unjust, he refused to spill blood by joining the uprising. Yet, hot bloods in his own band, the Warrior Society, had other ideas. Regardless, the trial deemed he could have mutinied when things turned violent."

"Were the chiefs lucky? Couldn't they have been hung like Riel?" Georgia asked.

"That wasn't luck," Stub argued. "The jail sentences broke them."

"Don't forget about Chief White Cap, the Dakota leader," Edwina prodded.

"Yes, he was acquitted. A Saskatoon merchant testified that he talked his angry warriors out of ransacking Saskatoon on their way to Batoche."

At this, the mothers herded their children back to their seats and Georgia whispered to Walter, "Dear, that ointment is not for your lips."

Knut and the others stifled laughs when they saw it was haemorrhoid cream.

Stub shook his head, "Today, Indians can't leave the reserve without a pass from the agent and the children must go to residential schools. Duck Lake has one, built 12 years ago and it's run by the Roman Catholics."

"The Anglicans run the ones at Prince Albert and Battleford," Edwina said.

A sour lady across the way said, "At least the children get rescued from their squalid living conditions!"

Stub gave the woman a hard look and lowered his voice, "Not necessarily", and went on, "the kids get food and medical care but it's not like they haven't used traditional medicines at home for centuries. With tuberculosis running rampant, the worried parents set up tipis outside the gate. At one time, my brother and I helped fix the school's furnace."

Edwina said, "Sadly, their family life takes a beating. If not for the Indians and Métis, settlers might not survive this harsh country."

The small group agreed but audible 'tsks' came from across the way, even with the eavesdroppers' heads turned away. Knut had no quarrel with Indian or white and the whole situation seemed tragic. He tried to swallow the hard history but realised the situation was bigger than him.

A traditionally dressed Mennonite family had boarded at Regina. The husband changed the subject, "North of Saskatoon, Mennonites inhabit an entire belt of farmland, all the way to Rosthern. These places sprung up with the arrival of the QLLS rail line after 1890 and prosper with dairy and grain farms."

Fifteen miles later, the Mennonites got off at Osler where Knut saw his first Mennonite house-barn. The two buildings, attached by a covered passageway, had a fenced yard and horses mingling outside with Holsteins.

It was also Walter and Georgia's stop and she said, "We enjoyed the stories and it was nice to meet you all!"

The porter assisted them off and a bearded young man stepped forward to greet them. They saw a school and general store.

In 12 miles, came Hague and it was almost 8:00 a.m. Here, another Mennonite gent got on. He pointed, "That tall four storey building is Klassen's Flour Mill. The railroad's water tower holds 40,000 gallons and is pumped from an old spring-fed well east of town."

"Has to be a God send."

"And what about you and your homestead?" Stub ventured to Knut.

Knut stifled a laugh. "I have to live there six months every year for three years so, I'll farm in the summer and do bush work in the winters. Give or take, depending on the weather. I hope to break 15 acres and crop 10 in the first year."

"Balancing harvest and bush work is tricky. Come spring, you'll have to head back to the farm while the ground's still frozen."

"When do you get a break?" asked Edwina.

"Well, bad weather does have its advantages, I do love snowstorms."

In 30 miles, it was 9:00 a.m. when the train lurched to a stop in Rosthern. They said the population was about 400 and well over village size. The new station had an attached freight shed's hip roof and overhanging eaves, to protect passengers and luggage. Knut saw a post office, flour mill, and hotel called *The National*, under construction. A young reverend with white collar, was among the newest to board.

Passengers stretching their legs returned to their seats and the cleric said, "If you travel east about nine miles, you'll come across the Gabriel's Crossing ferry on the South Saskatchewan. Gabriel Dumont ran it for about 10 years in the 1870s and 80s. The ferry was a 23 x 12-foot scow."

He had no way of knowing how interested Knut was.

In another 15 miles, came the Duck Lake boarding school with tipis set up outside the gate.

"With the coming of the railway, the original lakeside settlement moved here, a half mile east of their original site, to be closer to the railway," Stub said.

"How do you like Duck Lake?" Knut prodded before Stub left.

"Well, there's great trails all through the forest, along the river, and to Fort Carlton. They're sheltered from the wind and you get to see lodges, hawk's nests, evergreens, tall willows, and open meadow. Over the boggy marshes, you have to hopscotch logs and be on the lookout for wildlife."

Stub reached for his bag beneath the seat. "Duck Lake boomed since the 1860s with Doukhobors, English, French, and Métis. As you can see, there's Roman Catholic and Anglican churches, a grist mill, trading post, school, and post office. During the rebellion, Duck Lake was the halfway point between Batoche's Métis headquarters and the North-West Mounted Police at Fort Carlton."

Stub said his goodbyes and was met by a man, obviously his bewhiskered bachelor brother.

As the train moved again, the reverend suggested, "Look over there, and you'll see the jail that housed Almighty Voice!"

Knut and others jumped up to get a better look.

"It was the North-West Mounted Police's temporary jail," the cleric said.

They could see a one-room stuccoed log building with a single barred window.

"Wasn't he providing food for his hungry family?" a teen asked.

"Apparently, he thought the animal was part of a herd given to his father. It was 12 years after the rebellion," the reverend said.

"Was he from Duck Lake?" the teen asked.

"There's conflicting stories. Some say he was from the One Arrow Reserve and that Chief One Arrow was his grandfather. Others say he was Salteaux from the Duck Lake Band. Regardless, he was well known and liked as a runner, a hunter, and a man of courage."

Edwina leaned in, "Of course, to the white settlers, he was foreboding but he had won running events at Prince Albert Field Days over the years."

The reverend went on, "On the day he died, surrounded, he and his wounded friend hunkered down in a dug-out rifle pit in the middle of a green bluff. His mother sat high on a hill nearby, wailing his death chant."

Knut got goose bumps. "Chilling."

He imagined Almighty Voice's ghost running along the forested trails. If his soul hadn't crossed over to the Happy Hunting Grounds, he could still roam the earth. With those thoughts in mind, the north-bound locomotive's rattling box cars shattered the silence of the Nisbet forest.

The tongue-biting child whined, "How much further?"

"About 35 miles."

"Which tribes live around here?" Knut asked.

The reverend remarked, "First, the Indians refer to themselves as nations and not tribes. Around Prince Albert there are over half a dozen, Plains Cree, Saulteaux, Nakota or Assiniboine, Dakota and Lakota or Sioux, and Denesuline or Dene/Chipewyan."

"And what about the treaties?"

"This is Treaty Six territory and around Regina is Treaty Four. Chiefs Mistawasis and Ahtahkakoop negotiated Treaty Six at Fort Carlton through an interpreter, Peter Erasmus. Treaty Six had terms not incorporated into Treaties One to Five."

Pulling into Prince Albert, they saw more tipis on the outskirts, and the clergyman hurried to finish, "Treaty Six has a medicine chest clause, protection from famine and pestilence, more agricultural implements, and on-reserve education. A Red Pheasant headman Poundmaker, and later chief, demanded the famine clause."

11
Bridging a Gap

The history fascinated Knut but the train ground to a halt at Prince Albert. It was 10:35 a.m., Saturday, 3 May 1902. He broadcast his goodbyes, then helped the baggage handlers unload for a time, while inquiring about his own shipment from Iowa. The workers pointed to the freight shed so he could return later for the carload.

Conscious of his winter clothes, he walked to Central Avenue and gawked in amazement. Folks inter-mingled on the street like home with one exception, the large numbers of Indian families.

Picking up his jaw, he thought, "With all the Indian nations around, it shouldn't be a surprise, but do they live together peacefully?"

Eyeing the foreboding prison overshadowing everything, gave him an inkling, "A big hoosegow, eh? I wish my family could see this!"

Besides the unsettling jail, further down the street sat a North-West Mounted Policeman astride a horse. The Mountie's pill box hat, held on with chin strap, was tipped to the side.

"No wonder they're called Red Coats," Knut thought. "The flaming scarlet jackets must create quite a stir."

To offset the jacket, the Mountie wore steel-grey trousers with tall brown boots and a holstered revolver. Knut reached his hand out to shake hands but the officer gave him a white-gloved salute instead. Knut tipped his cap in return.

Walking along with rifle slung over his shoulder, Knut noticed people still wore winter garb like him. Indian men wore buckskins and beaded moccasins, long braids, with or without hats. Women had heavy shawls or furs, colourful long, cotton chequered skirts and blouses with multiple long, beaded necklaces.

White people dressed similar to home with children resembling miniature adults. Little girls showed frilly edges to white dresses and dark stockings beneath coats and bonnets. Ladies wore solid dark ankle-length skirts and stylish hats, often with ostrich feathers. Men dressed in dark suits with hats and canes, like him. The difference was they wore boots, not moccasins. Typically, Knut wore a heavy chequered work shirt with the sleeves rolled up to show forearms covered by long underwear, wide suspenders held up heavy woollen winter trousers.

Horses, buggies, and wagons lined the dirt streets, flanked by wooden sidewalks. Happy it wasn't much different from home he didn't need reminding it was a whole new world. Out of the corner of his eye, he saw an elderly Indian man stop beside him. His flowing grey hair was tied with a beaded head band. His tanned and wrinkled face erupted into a smile and Knut was awestruck. When the man pointed to Knut's moccasins, both men grinned, acknowledging the footwear. The elder offered his hand and the warmth of the clasp was unexpected. They moved along having bridged a gap without saying a word.

Knut saw that Prince Albert sat on the banks of a river, at the edge of the northern forest. The town had its own Dominion Land Office, where he headed.

To his comment on the size of the place, the agent admitted, "Prince Albert is a town of 800 and is the capital of the Saskatchewan District. It marks the treeline point where the aspen parkland meets the boreal forest."

Knut was thrilled when granted the very quarter section in the Carrot River Valley he had seen on a map back in Iowa.

"It's about seven miles northwest of the Stoney Creek Settlement," the agent confirmed.

"Excellent! It's not always easy to scout it out beforehand."

"That could backfire if you filed on a slough!"

"I chose that quarter for its closeness to the settlement but it's not too easy to find, so fairly private. It's near a creek, not barren but with rolling hills. It's close to other Scandinavians but not too close. Here's hoping it meets my expectations!"

The agent described, "In three years, you can apply for a patent to transfer the land into your name. You give six months' written notice, then produce evidence of how you met the requirements. At that point, you're eligible to purchase the adjacent 80 acres for $3.00 an acre."

"I've heard there can be a delay to getting the patent?" Knut said.

The clerk cleared his throat and changed the subject, "That will be $10.00."

Knut handed over his American money and grinned like a Cheshire Cat. At the Bank of Ottawa, he set up an account, made a deposit, and exchanged American money for Canadian. By nearly 27, living at home and working for his father, he had accumulated a small bankroll.

Outside was a young dog, a border collie cross with black and white markings and one floppy ear. Knut absently patted him on the head and continued down the street. Whistling away, he was quite aware that the dog was not far behind, and soon realised that the male was a female.

Leaving the crush of the street, he wandered into the stables and discovered a fellow with two good-looking bay mares for sale, Topsy and Nell.

Knut was sold and paid cash when the livery man said, "This big four-wheeled farm wagon can convert to a sleigh for winter."

Picking up his freight, the baggage handlers assisted to load his new wagon with the walking plough, scythe, disc, and harrows, along with the rolled-up tent of household goods.

"I'm expecting an entire sawmill after freeze-up but it'll be hard to transport overland."

"It will take brute force and ignorance," one handler said. "Your steam engines and carriage will be the worst."

"Well, we're strong but I don't know about ignorant!" one joked.

"Don't worry, there'll be help when the time comes. Leave it until the river freezes good so you can slide it across country on sleighs. Be careful of the snow because if it's too deep, it'll be hard on the horses."

Another mused, "Four steam engines will be dicey. Maybe hook up with a freight swing. Freighters do get ingenious."

"Like putting a snowplough on the lead horse and wrapping the horses' legs in gunny sacks to protect from sharp ice."

"A rail line is supposed to come west from Erwood to P.A. in the next year or two, if you can wait," the man offered.

"I can't wait," Knut replied, "the shortened season will give me time to find a crew. I'm hoping to get a solid couple of months' bush work in."

The men understood.

Knut worried aloud. "With the South Saskatchewan high and swift this time of year, how difficult will it be to move my farm equipment across?"

"The ferries got started last month as soon as the ice was off. If the Adams ferry at Fenton isn't running, there's the Cecil further downstream, or you could backtrack to St. Laurent or the Gabriel," the workers reassured.

"Hopefully not the St. Laurent or Gabriel, they're too far."

"If ever the Adams isn't running, the Cecil might be best. You should connect with Ned; he leads the freight swing east of town."

As it turned out, Ned was easy to find, and said, "You're welcome to join us but we leave tomorrow morning, first thing."

"Experienced drivers leading the way would make it much easier, thank you!"

"We leave no later than six," Ned was a stickler.

"Ja! I'll be there. How about after freeze-up, transporting my sawmill equipment? There'll be four steam engines, various saws, and a big carriage, so it'll be a gigantic load. What do you think?"

"Sounds huge, but we love a challenge!"

Relieved at having sorted out his biggest concerns, Knut headed back downtown.

At the general store, he asked the merchant, "How bad is crime around here with such a big jail?"

"Well," the merchant half-joked, "it does hold lots of offenders, plus houses the warden but this is a huge territory for the police. Travel takes forever by horse or rail but if it's by dog sled, sometimes well over a month and the prisoner is held until the trial comes around."

Knut said, "I hope I won't need their services where I'm going!"

The merchant laughed. "You might! Say, I caught wind you're a new settler heading east. Would you consider freighting for me off and on? I'll even sweeten the deal with a crock for your homemade wine!"

Knut thought for a moment. "Ja! I could. I don't have freight racks for a big load but I see no reason why not."

A faint awareness crept over him that the birth of a freighting side-line was happening. He would add racks to his wagon. If already making the trip, carrying goods back and forth seemed reasonable and lucrative.

"I bet you sell work boots." Changing the subject, Knut scanned the store. "Since I've almost walked out of all my footwear, I could use a new pair."

"That'll be $1.25, but you might want to consider a pair of rubbers to wear over top and I'll throw them in for an extra 50¢."

"That's highway robbery," Knut joked, good-naturedly handing over the money.

Knut's arms were loaded and he jammed items into every free corner of the wagon. The shopkeeper's boxes were small and destined for Birch Hills. In exchange for the favour, the merchant directed Knut where to buy livestock. The heifer, Meg, was a young black and white Holstein, bred to deliver in July. She would follow along tied to the wagon. The stock owner threw in cages for the chickens and weanling piglets.

Knut drove down the main drag and saw a sign, 'Meals At All Hours', in the Klondyke Hotel's window. His stomach growled and he yearned for a warm bath and comfortable bed. Returning his horses and loaded rig to the livery, he fed the animals, then walked back to the hotel to rent a room.

On the hotel's veranda, he enjoyed a mug of beer with Ollie, an old-timer waiting for supper. The 50¢ roast pork meal drew them in with dessert of strawberry shortcake.

"It was one of the best meals I've had since leaving home. Small mercies mean so much!"

"We eat plenty of pork here because it's easy to cure and keeps good," Ollie said.

Feeling full, Knut asked, "Do you want to join me for a walk down River Street?"

Ollie agreed, but so did the spotted dog waiting on the boardwalk. Knut gave her another pat on the head at the same time noticing vagrants and drunks reclining along the riverbank.

"Is this river part of the South Saskatchewan?" Knut looked at the water flowing east.

"No, it's the North Saskatchewan."

"Looks about half a mile across," Knut observed, strolling along the banks, the dog at his heels.

"Yup, it's glacier-fed, coming straight out of the Rockies and it's about to become a beehive of activity with the steamship season."

"Back home," Knut remarked, "the Mississippi is over 10 miles wide in places. The log booms on it are the size of a football field and guided by a steamboat in the front and one at the rear."

Ollie reminisced, "In my day, men and boys straddled those logs and tried not to fall in. Too many lost their lives," he lamented.

Knut noticed the river was high and still had a bit of ice. He saw a ferry called *The Battleford* crossing to the north shore.

Ollie paused, "This is 'last ice' but not long ago, it was spring breakup, a deafening roar that gains momentum crashing downstream. The breakup happens without warning and is magical to witness. You're dumbstruck and rooted to the spot but it's a powerful force that destroys everything in its path."

Knut remembered talk of the damaged train bridge timbers in Saskatoon.

"I could count on one hand the number of times I witnessed it," Ollie said, "it's not funny for animals crossing when it happens."

Knut shuddered. "The best place to see it might be at the Forks, about 30 miles east, where the North and South river branches converge."

"Oh!"

"Soon, the passenger steamships and riverboats will be moored along the south bank, behind the windmill."

"We're hoping one day for the rail to extend north but that would mean the train bridge would have to swing open to let the steamships through. The steamships take passengers back and forth to Saskatoon and nobody wants to hinder that lucrative business!"

At the sawmill on the south bank, they heard buzzing saws and steam engines shutting down as dusk approached. The noisy place went eerily silent with the overpowering scent of sawdust in the air. Within mere heartbeats though, the men whooped, jubilant for week's end.

Knut said, "I forgot, it's Saturday night!"

"Yup, and there'll be lots of drunk and disorderly arrests before morning."

A quieter flour mill standing against the forest on the river's side, pumped out smoke from its chimney. The river water in front was littered with wayward floating logs.

Ollie explained, "Scads of bush workers harvest spruce and jack pine but they leave the tamarack and poplar alone. The jack pine gets cut into cordwood."

Knut looked around to see telegraph poles and wires.

"The local brick yards built the land titles building and the town hall/opera house," Ollie added, "the red brick buildings had their brick shipped from the east. The salmon brick is made here. To top it off, P.A. has enough sand and limestone for a glass factory."

The Hudson's Bay Company store stood on the south side of River Street facing north. There was a fur wagon parked out front and one sign in the window read, 'Exporters and Importers of Northern Furs'. Another was, 'Highest Prices for Raw Furs'.

The men walked inside but a rank smell hit them in the face.

Knut gasped, "Phew!" and Ollie chuckled.

"I'm used to it," the greasy-looking clerk snickered. "It's from rancid unscraped fat left on the pelt. Of course, each animal has their own peculiar odour."

"Would you happen to have a bison robe to buy?"

"Are you kidding?" the clerk jeered, "I'd like one too. Maybe there's one for sale in the community or maybe the Mounties have one but otherwise, no."

Knut felt stupid because he knew there were no more bison.

The clerk pointed, "There's raw pelts of muskrat, beaver, and bear, though. Then there's badger, skunk, marten, or ermine. Take your pick. If you want a coat ready-made, there's these on the back wall or you could buy the furs and take them to the tailor."

The clerk had red, watery, owl eyes and pointed, "Rabbit, fox, raccoon, or dark sable mink."

Knut was fascinated and decided on the fox. "And a racoon hat."

He'd always liked the look of Davey Crockett. The clerk took his money and swiped his sleeve across his nose for the umpteenth time.

At the tailor shop, the tailor showed him deer-skin leggings to cover his woollen trousers, moose hide moccasins, and woollen mitts with mule hide pullovers.

"Even though it's spring, nights still get cold and winter is never far off."

Afterwards, Knut made for the train station to send a telegram.

The telegraph operator said, "Want to hear something funny? When the telegraph poles were first erected, people revolted and dug them all out!"

"What?" Knut snorted, unable to believe his ears.

That night, he took a bath, emptied his pockets, and washed his clothes in the same water. The hotel's bed was decent but he couldn't sleep so sat in the chair by the window and wrote in his journal.

Can't sleep. My body must be used to the ground because the bed is too soft. The hooting and hollering from the bar below doesn't help. The Big Dipper sparkles in the northern sky and the three stars of Orion's Belt are shifting from east to west. Knowing my family is back home watching the same sky makes me lonesome.

By morning, when he went to leave, the spotted dog bounded up and plunked herself beside him on the wagon seat.

"Uffdah! Don't you have a home?" he frowned. "Go home!"

He tried to shoo her off but she put her head down and thumped her tail, planting herself into his life no matter what.

Knut gave up and petted her. "I guess I've inherited a dog! How come you're grinning from ear to ear?" she had turned to show him her belly.

"It's okay. I don't mind, I can use the company. What shall we name you? Luna?"

The dog gave him a glib look.

"Bella?"

No reaction again.

"Lady?"

The dog cocked her head to one side.

"Lady it is!" his countenance brightened, "you're one self-confident, pretty lady!"

Turning to leave, Knut figured the 50-mile trip to the Carrot River Valley might take at least five days. Now, travelling with a freight swing on an established freight haul route, he didn't know.

Ned, the swing boss explained, "Stopping at every little port of call, it takes longer and our overnight places are pre-determined. The first is on the other side of the river at Fenton. Past that is a stop in Birch Hills but the second overnight is at Brancepeth. Next, we go to Weldon, and our third overnight is at the Carrot River Settlement. The last 20 miles goes past one tiny community and then it's your Stoney Creek Settlement."

Knut flashed a smile and hoped there wasn't a catch. It sounded too easy.

This morning, the sun shone, and a good drying wind blew. Knut followed behind the freight swing wagons leading the way on the trail east out of town. He enjoyed the crisp cool air and the smell of the forest. The noise of the wheels and the groaning loads, along with the sound of the horses' hooves pounding the earth, broke the morning silence. They were six wagons with racks, and each was pulled by four horses, with a driver and another worker. The remarkable booming town disappeared from sight.

"This convoy is a lifesaver," he absently spoke to the dog.

It was about 15 miles to the river, and they would be doing good to get there by afternoon. With the ferry operating, Knut felt lucky. They wouldn't have to float the wagons across the river, and it wouldn't take hours to dry things out. He had watched these crossings from a train window and hoped he wouldn't look like too much of a greenhorn. At home, there were bridges and even multiple ferries at a given crossing. As it was, with a single ferry, it would take more than one trip to move them all across.

"Two wagons, eight horses, and their riders cross per ferry trip, so four crossings in all, including your rig," Ned said.

Knut hoped daylight and the weather held. A mile or so out of town, the well-packed trail was interrupted by a large slough with established corduroy road. Substantial layers of poles and branches lay before them. Instead of jumping down to cut more bushes, the men pushed through, and Knut realised this was his first test.

12
Carpet of Dreams

Prince Albert to Stoney Creek Settlement—*May-October 1902*

Knut was exhilarated with Canada and his overland journey from Prince Albert to the Stoney Creek Settlement. Accompanying a freight swing, they faced the turbulent South Saskatchewan River, knowing the crossing would take an enormous chunk of the afternoon and evening. Indeed, it took multiple ferry trips for all six rigs, 22 horses, and a dozen men to reach the eastern shore. Knut went last. It was long past dark when he, his livestock, and wagon made for the 55-foot cabled ferry. Pulling the wagon, stubborn Topsy balked at the first step, but alongside her, Nell, the older mare, navigated the barge like a pro. Topsy was forced to go along, harnessed together with pole and traces. As the scow moved across the water, Knut revelled in the cool breeze, it was Sunday, 4 May 1902.

As Ned promised, their first overnight was at Fenton. With horses tended, after the campfire communal supper one man played harmonica while the others spewed a little bull.

"I knew a man, who knew a man, who rode with Jessie James!" one said.

Eyes rolled having heard it before.

"What about me and the grizzly trapped inside my hunting shack?" an Irishman started. "The ole bore was easy 700 pounds, in a rage, and his dish face and hump were just a shakin'. I lay on my cot and every time I went for my rifle, he roared and spewed drool everywhere. Eventually, I shot him dead but my horse, Ole Billie, bolted at the first musky smell of him. Gettin' the beast outta the cabin was no easy feat!"

When the crew threw bedrolls under their wagons to sleep, Knut followed suit. Laying there, the fireflies winked in and out of the darkness but turning on his side, he realised his pocket watch was missing. In desperation, he tried other pockets, then sat up and bumped his head on the undercarriage before getting up to rifle through the wagon box. No luck. Sick at heart, he wracked his brain trying to remember the last time he used it.

The next day, down the line seven miles to Birch Hills, a crowd gathered and it was amazing to see their enthusiasm. Many hands pitched in for the unloading and reloading of lumber, hardware, furniture, groceries, and confections.

Knut walked his one lone delivery to the storekeeper who was most appreciative, and said, "Did you know? In the days of the fur-traders, they used our birch tree bark to build canoes."

"Makes sense!"

On they went for eight more miles to Brancepeth, their second overnight stop. After unloading and setting up camp, Knut rolled a cigarette.

Ned sat down beside him and said, "This place has connections to the Brancepeth Castle in England."

"I didn't know there was one. A castle, I mean."

A man in business attire meandered over. "I'm John, the postmaster."

They shook hands and Knut said, "So, tell us about this place."

"Well," he laughed, sitting down. "We're east of the Forks where the North and South Saskatchewan rivers merge into one river, the Saskatchewan. There's an old fort there and it's where the Red River cart and Kelsey trails join. It's a traditional Indian gathering place and renowned for turtle fossils on the riverbanks. In the 1770s, independent fur-traders held the fort but by the turn of the century, the competing Northwest and Hudson's Bay Companies operated it together. Once that ended, it sat abandoned until the Hudson's Bay Company reopened it as Fort à la Corne."

"An old-timer in P.A. told me the Forks might be a good place to see the ice go out in the spring," Knut said.

"If a person had time to sit around waiting for it!"

"Maybe one day."

Tuesday, 6 May, the freighters delivered items seven miles further east to Weldon where Knut learned there was another ferry north of it to cross the Saskatchewan. The Carrot River Settlement with its rich soil was their third overnight.

"Another 20 miles east is my homestead," Knut beamed to have chosen land in the fertile Carrot River Valley.

"There's even a doctor. He's black and a teacher who came six years ago. Seeing the need for medical services, he went back to Ontario to get his medical degree. Two years later, he set up practice, and has been here ever since," Ned said.

"That's good news!"

"Our next stop is about 16 miles south of the James Smith Reserve and just so you know, James Smith and John Smith, from the reserve east of Prince Albert, are brothers."

When Knut saw a party of Indians on horseback, waiting for the freighters, he was intrigued and decided this was a highlight of his trip. They retrieved sacks, boxes, and kegs like the others. Very few words were exchanged, even when they handed over furs to Ned.

Late Wednesday afternoon, the freight swing rolled into the Stoney Creek Settlement. Like the other stops, a crowd gathered, eager to receive their wares. Here, Knut was pleased to see a general store, post office, hardware, and blacksmith shop. The men fed, watered, and groomed their horses then settled in for a late evening meal.

Knut told Ned, "With the days getting longer, I could strike out for my homestead right now but I'll wait for morning to get my bearings."

"Good idea. Tomorrow, the freight swing will head straight east to the end of the line at Erwood. For us, it'll be hard slogging through the forest after Eldersley."

After a restful night, the freighters waved farewell as they found the trail east to Star City. Knut mailed a postcard home, then set out on his solo mission north. After navigating creeks and hills for about seven miles, he stopped at the crest of a hill and couldn't believe his eyes. There lay the magnificence of his beloved quarter section and shivers of joy coursed through him.

By tickling the reins, the horses moved slow enough for Knut to watch for the property's corner stake. Every mile the markers were set in the centre of four pits, three feet square, and 18 inches deep.

When he saw the wooden post in the centre, he muttered, "A dab of red paint would help."

Then the realisation hit, and jumping down from the wagon, he fell backwards shouting, "I've made it in 45 days! Six weeks since I left home!"

Realising his dream felt incredible but he wished his family could be there. Scrutinising his long-awaited parcel, he saw a hilly kingdom all his own in an aspen parkland untouched by time. Sloughs and creeks meandered through trees, some that would need clearing. A large, flooded area in a low spot along the east side, scores of acres in size, hosted a spectacular concentration of migratory waterfowl. Flocks congregated en masse looking like a moving carpet of white.

The flood made his path impassable so he backtracked to detour, a few extra miles west. Once around, he could get so much closer to the water's edge. Dancing and sparkling in the sun's rays was a symphony of swans, pelicans, snow geese, whooping cranes, and gulls. The dark markings of the Canada Geese, loons, mallards, and wood ducks enhanced the blend. Smaller birds flitted in and out like red-winged black birds, mud hens, and cow birds, texturizing the sight, not to mention adding to the thrumming cacophony.

Majestic swans and pelicans floated, and others splashed and bathed their own plumage or dove into the water for food. Others were relegated to the sidelines, in groups, or standing one-legged. In an irregular cycle, huge flocks arrived, and others took flight. Thrilled with his unwitting purchase, Knut vowed to preserve Mother Nature's glorious spectacle forever.

As much as his joy soared, Lady was done lapping the water and wanted to hunt and chase the prey. "Go leg da hound!" he shouted in Norwegian.

The 'go lay down dog!' command didn't work, so he caught her, held her tight, and scolded her for the first time. She was smart and shaking his finger in her face, he saw she got the message. The alluring birds were hypnotising and hard to tear himself away from but eventually he ambled back to the highest point of land.

"I'll pitch the tent here, in the place where I intend to build a house."

With no one else to hear, he spoke to the dog, "Now close your eyes and imagine fields filled with bumper crops," he splayed his arms across thin air, and Lady cocked her head, listening to every word.

He felled, limbed, and strung small diameter trees for a pole fence as a makeshift animal pen. Unleashing their tethers, the animals ran around and settled in to find food. He shook his head, "That was like inciting a small riot!"

At supper, he spoke to his animals, "Oats and creek water for you lot but Lady and I get fried side pork and beans." Watching the lard pail bubble, slung over the fire, he thought, "It makes the best coffee."

As darkness rolled in, the Norwegian American lay beside his campfire watching the flames snake towards the sky. As the wood snapped and popped, he was thankful for the warmth of the fur robe; confident the fresh air would one day trump the odour. The waterfowl quietening in the distance, soothed him like a mother's lullaby.

A night owl hooted and Knut imagined she and her mate waiting in the crystal-clear night ready to pounce. Lady pushed her head under his hand, and he fell into a sound slumber. She gave a low growl when a fox slunk past, then a skunk, both investigating the roosting chickens. Coyotes may have howled but Knut missed even their mournful cries. Overhead, the Northern Lights danced and upon awakening, all he could smell was pungent skunk.

"We've had a visitor, headed for the buffet at the flood, no doubt. This time."

He knew once summer came and the water dried up, the birds would go, and his animals would be fair game.

To the chickens, he whispered, "I'll build you a hen house before a weasel finds you."

His to-do list kept growing but like his mother said, "You've only got two hands!"

On May 10, Lady barked at a man on horseback.

"Hei! Hei! Welcome to the neighbourhood! I'm Halvor and live a mile and a half southwest."

Knut recognised a fellow Norwegian when he saw one, and smiled, speaking their native tongue, "Nice to meet you. I'm Knut."

Halvor jumped down and they shook hands. Maybe the same age, he was tall, lanky, and a little funny looking with big ears. "I'm from Minot. Can I give you a hand?"

Knut grinned. "Are you kidding? Where do I begin?"

They hit it off instantly.

"What do you think with the short growing season here?" Knut asked, "is it too late to sow in the open patches now for harvesting this fall?"

"Ja! Should be fine. With Red Fife wheat, we pray for a late fall. Maybe try oats."

They walked down to the flood, and Halvor explained, "With the ice jams, the Stoney Creek backs up into the Thatch Creek."

It wasn't long before Knut took the time to see Halvor's farm. They stood on the banks of his creek, the Stoney, and Halvor said, "the animals can just walk down here for a drink. Plus, I've got a well."

"A well, a log house, barn, sheds, and granaries. Your cattle look healthy too," Knut was impressed.

"Ja! But this is my third year here. This wet spring, my seeding is late."

Halvor was always eager to help but seemed anxious.

"Uffdah!" he said. "You might as well know, this month, my mail-order bride comes by train, and I'll fetch her from Prince Albert. Technically, she's not mail-order but she did answer my ad."

From what Knut could tell, the anticipation was killing him. Knut found himself listening and even giving advice about women on occasion. This was amazing because he had no idea what he was talking about, but then, neither did Halvor.

Halvor asked, "What if she doesn't like me?"

Knut kept a straight face. He guessed anybody knew more than Halvor when it came to women.

Thinking of his sister, Marion, Knut reassured him, "Don't worry. Before long, she won't be able to live without you."

That did the trick. The soon-to-be groom beamed and Knut knew he'd made a lifelong friend. Knut wondered. If it worked for Halvor, maybe he should place an ad too. For the time being, he would hold off.

Halvor brought over a jug of his homemade wine one rainy afternoon and through the mist offered, "If it's gonna rain, we might as well have a drink and play some Whist."

"Why not?"

Sitting outside, shuffling cards, the beet wine was foul and yeasty in the tin cups and sent zingers through the teeth. It was almost bad enough to pour out, but of course, they didn't. Overhead, dark, saturated clouds drizzled. When the clouds burst, the two made a nosedive into Knut's tent, and almost pulled it down on top of them.

"The fact is," Halvor said with embarrassment, "the wine's shy of the cure by a few weeks."

"Really?" Knut screwed up his face, shaking the rain off.

Knut sat on his fur coat and Halvor perched on the bedroll.

"What's all this talk about prohibition?" Knut was dealing a new hand.

"I say it'll never happen. Somebody will always brew it, sell it by the light of the moon, or smuggle it," Halvor predicted.

The overturned card showed diamonds were trump.

"On the train, men spoke of hiding liquor under their women's skirts if they have to. Of course, I have no proof." Knut chuckled, a little embarrassed. "It sounds worse than I meant."

"We'll never know," Halvor hooted. "They say the Northwest Territories is so full of stills, they'll never sniff them all out."

The cards were played and Halvor won the hand. His five of diamonds beat Knut's Ace of Spades. The wine's taste improved by the second drink, and anything, however absurd or humdrum, made the two crow like a pair of old hens.

"Speaking of lawbreakers," Halvor's tone clouded, "about five years ago, a pair of horse thieves shot and killed a homesteader near Qu'Appelle."

"Ugh…"

It was Halvor's deal and he went on, "Don't ever think any place is safe. Even here, two sets of brothers try to terrorise anything that moves." The card overturned meant clubs were trump.

Alarmed, Knut asked, "Who are they?"

"Bullies you do not want to cross. The Blacks and Swallows. They take what they want. Kill or steal livestock or ransack for liquor and cash, even if you're there. They show up out of the blue and don't care who they hurt."

"You'd think they'd be caught," Knut said. He didn't like this news one bit and could tell Halvor gave them a wide berth.

"Enough said," Halvor, feeling no pain, seemed satisfied to have apprised his new friend. "At least, forewarned is forearmed."

The hand was won by Knut this time and he was feeling festive, "Let's finish this bottle. Out here, we can get as drunk and disorderly as we want!"

In the days to come, felling trees and pulling stumps was slow and tedious work.

"Good job girls," Knut praised Topsy and Nell, while walking behind his single furrow plough. Strength-wise, it took both, straining hard, to remove the stumps.

"Someday I might get a gang plough. I have to build a granary first unless I want to leave grain on the ground. With the garden sown, I can start on a house next."

Knut took the time to visit the Stoney Creek Settlement for food, supplies, and to use the post office, then found his way to the clapboard buildings of

Flett Springs. Everywhere, the settlers were welcoming and happy to greet a new homesteader.

Reginald Beatty, the Stoney Creek postmaster explained, "I worked for the Hudson's Bay Company and settled here on the advice of Indian friends at Birch Hills. Turns out I was the first white man to settle here but the Indians weren't keen on having me. They tried to get me to leave until I helped heal the Saulteaux chief, Kinistin's wound," he chuckled.

Knut said, "To start a place must be an honour!"

Beatty was a rather humble character and didn't want to take much credit.

A postcard came from Iowa but had taken weeks to arrive. His mother wrote,

Dear Knut,

We are thrilled to hear you made it safely and in good time! We are dying to hear every detail. At the moment, your father is limping around with a case of the gout. The rest of us are healthy and miss you. Looking forward to your letters! Thinking of you always.

All our love, Your family.
PS. In case you haven't heard, the Filipino American War ended on 4 July, after you left!

During July and August of 1902, Canadian Northern Railway surveyors came from Portage la Prairie, Manitoba. To everyone's dismay, the route they chose for the tracks would run a mile and a half north of the existing Stoney Creek Settlement. With transportation and shipping vital, the entire community, buildings, and all, was forced to pick up and move to the new location.

In the meantime, Meg was a good 1,200 pounds and went into labour one evening in mid-July. Knut was on the alert, knowing her time was close and when she disappeared, he went looking. Instinct had her hiding behind a willow bluff at the far reaches of the enclosure.

She dripped sweat and moaned when seized with each painful contraction. Knut soothed and checked her internally to find the calf turned the wrong way. A foot was coming first. With no veterinarian, he grasped and secured both legs with ropes. But even pulling with all his strength, was no use. The calf would not budge. Knut felt stressed, the poor mother was suffering and his miserly help was all she had.

He tied a rope to Topsy and tried to use her strength but really needed two people. Just as he was at his wit's end, footsteps pounded his way.

"Halvor! Thank God!"

The two heaved for all they were worth and it was the boost needed to save the calf and its mother. Meg lay gasping after delivering the afterbirth but within minutes, she struggled to get up and walked over to the newborn to lick and nuzzle it, bringing the newborn to life. In the end, the tiny heifer stood up and wobbled over to suckle like a champion.

Both men were filled with relief and pride and Knut said, "Daisy sounds better than Blackie for a girl, don't you think?"

Halvor didn't hesitate, "Ja. Sweet and black like the ace of spades, with that single white forehead tuft."

The wind picked up but the two men sprawled on the grass to rest. Knut told Halvor of his earlier horseback ride.

"I went northwest through the pines and met an Indian man. We greeted with sign language, then I found out he speaks English."

"Smith?" Halvor cleared his throat, "I know him too."

Smith, Knut, and Halvor were to become lifelong friends or 'nîcîwakân' as Smith said, and their conversations would be a mixture of Cree, Norwegian, English, and sign language.

Halvor said, "Smith knows all the best places for berries and fishing."

"He says he's from the James Smith Reserve," Knut stood up and asked, "What about a hit of my chokecherry wine?"

"Not a bad idea."

The two walked back to Knut's unfinished log house.

"We spoke of the government and how it isn't in tune with his people." Knut sighed.

"Two different ideals. Like no longer returning grandmother fish."

Knut went straight to his crock of brewing chokecherries, raisins, water, sugar, and yeast and poured a dipperful into each tin cup.

"And trying to force a block system for trapping instead of their tried-and-true kinship system to let the animals recover. Their families share traplines and licences and don't hunt for sport."

"I look forward to learning from him and maybe he'll be interested in learning from us."

Knut was thrilled that his wish to meet an Indian had come true and it gave him a good feeling. He was ready to exchange gifts like tools for fresh venison or bannock.

Indeed, at Smith and Knut's next meeting, Knut found himself talking about farming, "There's ploughing, discing, and harrowing, then seeding. Over summer, there's roots to pick, haying to do, and repairs to wheels, harness, and fences. Breakdowns throw a wrench into everything."

Knut snickered, "If the animals could talk, they'd tell you of the occasional tantrum I throw. My cussing might be heard miles away."

"It is!" Smith joked. "But swearing is something my people don't do."

"Life is never boring. I'm either sprinkling lime to kill outhouse odour or standing on the ladder's top rung to skim a mouse or bat from the rain barrel. I fight weeds and do my best to preserve fruit and vegetables."

"You need a wife!" Smith pronounced as he and Pond Lily waved goodbye. "She could forage in the bush for all sorts of food and medicines!"

Saturday night was bath night and Knut pailed water into his tub after heating over a fire. Afterwards, he scrubbed his clothes on a washboard with lye soap, appreciating cleanliness and sponging daily otherwise. At times, his laundry took a backseat but if he was going to town, he took the extra time. Interaction with humans became rare because travel ate up too much of his day.

Knut kept liquor on hand from habit and living a hard life on the frontier. He was hard-wired for drinking, like his father and an extensive line before him, especially during bouts of brooding and loneliness. One of the first things Smith said when Knut offered him wine, was that he didn't drink.

Smith warned, "Don't share alcohol with my people or you're asking for trouble."

Knut respected his wishes. "I think I understand."

"Supplying Natives with liquor is a crime against the Indian Act," Smith said, "possession or having liquor on the reserve are both crimes, as is holding a dance."

"Sheesh!"

That summer and fall of 1902, Knut handpicked a sawmill crew from the settlement. Not the cream of the crop but enough weren't entirely green. The good ethnic mix of farmers and strongmen were hungry for work. His father would have barely raised an eyebrow understanding men wanting to keep their farms afloat. Income from bush work was good money.

13

Pier 2 and Traveller's Aid

Land was in sight, and a chorus of seagulls greeted the cattle ship. Lasse, her daughters, and two friends were joyous, "Canada! I can't believe we made it!"

"The Atlantic coast looks like sailing into a postcard!" Lovisa gushed. They saw a lighthouse, islands, and fishing villages far off.

A colony of squawking sea birds escorted their entry into Halifax's Pier 2 Harbour. The racket drowned out Hans who yelled something about, "commercial and public marina," but all anyone could do was lip read.

It was almost noon on Sunday, 15 June 1902, and the ship's occupants were eager to feel dry land under their feet. Before disembarking, however, came the border inspections for both humans and cattle. Watching the officials board, including veterinarians, and out of the girls' earshot, Greta whispered, "Sadly, the creatures go to market."

When the 'all clear' came, to avoid the sailors' bad luck, no goodbyes were said. Even siblings, Hans and Greta embraced in silence. The strangers, both crew and passengers, now friends, had few illusions of ever crossing paths again.

"Apart from lying face down and hugging the cold plank walkway, does the spring in our wobbly steps give us away?" Lasse laughed, very happy to reach land. The mother, cook extraordinaire, and voice of reason couldn't believe their good fortune.

When it was time to herd the cattle down the ship's ramp, the stockmen used panels, flags, and rattles to get them safely to a corral.

"Poor creatures," Kirsten mused. "They're happy to be on shore too. Mikaila and Lovisa should have sung them one last song!"

After the ship's exodus, the females had a taste of how the cattle felt, herded down a walkway to two stadium-like buildings, the immigration processing facilities. Pier 2 people handed them off step by step. First, their carry-on luggage went under lock and key inside a chain-link cage. They shuffled down the rows of seating, for paperwork and medical inspections. A uniformed customs agent, seated at a separate table, and an interpreter, helped with their meagre English.

"Receiving the 'Landed Immigrant' status is incredible!" Lasse laughed.

Once through, with hand luggage retrieved, a Mrs. Peterson, also an interpreter, guided them to the showers and rest room.

"After a month at sea, we are beyond ready!" Kirsten sighed.

Lasse caught sight of herself in a mirror, "I look like the wrath of God!"

"We all do!" Greta snickered.

Mikaila and Lovisa were shy about the communal facilities but the group held up towels for privacy. When clean and refreshed, the interpreter reappeared, pointing to a sign on the wall.

She read,

'Attention Young Women Travelling Alone. Avoid strangers and look for women wearing a Travellers Aid badge. Do not start for a strange town, even for a night, without knowing where to stay in advance. No advice or directions are to be sought from anyone except railway or Travellers Aid personnel. Do not enter any house, restaurant, or place of amusement upon invitation from any new acquaintance. Travellers Aid can help with lodging, boarding, and offered positions.'

"Thank you," Lasse promised, "we will be careful!"

In the meantime, an enticing aroma wafting from the food area made them hungry.

Greta said, "Time to try Canadian food!"

After the wait staff served them and their first few bites, Lasse gushed, "This fried chicken is scrumptious! Someone else's cooking always tastes better!"

"The cranberry sauce, and potatoes and gravy are delicious!" Mikaila was impressed.

"The white bun is a little gummy though, not like ours," Lovisa made a face.

"Try putting butter on it!" Kirsten suggested.

The next bite was slathered with butter and Lovisa said, "Much better!"

Finishing their main course, Lasse murmured, "The pumpkin pie looks good with a dollop of whipped cream!"

After supper, the interpreter spoke of their upcoming train trip, "For safety's sake, a matron will accompany you to your destination and the charitable organisations give you snacks for the train ride. The Canadian government wants you to have a good experience."

Mrs. Peterson spoke of church connections and introduced them to church volunteers.

"Did you know they call Winnipeg the 'Swedish Capital of Canada'? It has a wonderful Lutheran church on the corner of Ellen Street and Logan Avenue."

This was the information Lasse needed. "It sounds tailor-made for us. Being around people speaking our own language would make life much easier. What do you say girls? Should we make Winnipeg our first landing point?"

"Why not?" Mikaila and Lovisa grinned.

"I can find a job and we'll join the church and meet other Swedes."

Greta and Kirsten still had to decide their own fates.

At the ticket counter, no one looked forward to sleeping on the seats, but beggars couldn't be choosers. The sleeper car price was out of reach. "Sorry, but we have to save our money."

Mikaila and Lovisa made faces but nodded.

"We'll be right beside you," Kirsten and Greta agreed.

They spent the evening playing with babies at the Red Cross nursery then slept in the rest area. When it was time, they got in line to wait for the train.

"This heavy baggage already burns my shoulders," Lasse winced but baggage handlers came to the rescue and manhandled the heavy trunks.

It was 1:00 p.m., Atlantic Time, Monday, June 16, when they boarded the Intercolonial train.

Finding their seats, Greta pointed to a small stove at the back for cooking. The multilingual matron, accompanying them, Madame Agnew, said, "Be thankful at least none of you were sick on arrival and had to quarantine on an island somewhere."

"All we got was seasick," Lovisa joked.

"Good, because isolating tears families apart. They can't afford to wait around for weeks."

The conductor collected tickets, "Settle in for a long ride. It should take about thirty-six hours to make it to Montreal."

The train rolled northwest across Nova Scotia, and the rugged coastal scenery took them inland to their first stop at Truro, the hub of the province.

Madame, as self-assigned tour guide said, "At Five Islands not far off, is a lighthouse and whether low or high tide, the sight of the Bay of Fundy is incredible. Truro is home to Mi'kmaq's, Blacks, French Acadians, and Presbyterians."

Amherst, sitting on a height of land, came next with the Bay of Fundy to the south and the vast Northumberland Strait to the north.

"Amherst is a centre for shipbuilding. Eighty miles across the strait is Charlottetown, Prince Edward Island's capital."

They could see the grand Victorian and Edwardian homes, prompting their chaperone to say, "An Amherst female was afflicted by a great poltergeist mystery here in the 1870s."

"Oh no!" Mikaila uttered, "are you superstitious?"

"Oh yes."

"Like the bad luck of Friday the 13th?"

"More like covered bridges. One was built for a promised community that never materialised, 'The Bridge to Nowhere'. Another collapsed and sent a herd of cattle plunging into the river."

The topic of bridges touched a nerve with Lasse and her daughters, giving them goosebumps. The matron had no idea that Bjorn had died in a train trestle accident. The females exchanged looks but said nothing, sojourning into the evening's twilight, through New Brunswick's forests.

The matron went on, unfettered, "Then, there's the covered 'Kissing and Wishing Bridges' where a wagon master must slow his team to a walk or risk causing a tidal wave that could collapse the bridge."

"Is it dark inside a covered bridge?" Mikaila asked.

"Well, at night, maybe one small window let's in the moonlight. With the slowed passage, lovers have time to steal a kiss."

"But what if you're all alone and a black cat crosses your path?" Lovisa entreated.

"Well, if you're alone, walking through the dark, meeting creatures of the night, I think you'd be wishing you could run!"

Those thoughts took them to the largest central town of Moncton, where torches showed wild roses and lupins surrounding the head of a deep-water inlet. The travellers were met with lit fisherman's cottages, a wharf, and bleached whale bones. The flocks of sea birds had quieted for the night.

"Moncton's Magnetic Hill has a tidal bore," the matron said, "that rises up to six feet a day, surging into the murky waters of the Petitcodiac River. A shipbuilding industry came and went but when named headquarters for the Intercolonial Railway, Moncton thrived."

It turned dark and foggy at Miramachi.

"Fishing, mining, and forestry support Mi'kmaq's, Acadians, Scots, and Irish alike here," Madame Agnew yawned. "Oh, and by the way, at times, they say the valley is haunted by the ghost of a headless nun. Pirates beheaded her over treasure, centuries ago."

Despite the bright waxing full moon, with the hair standing up on the backs of their necks, her story was enough to keep them awake but they were dog tired. In the meantime, the train angled west and a small sprinkle of rain freshened the air. According to the map, they would miss the Jaquet River along the shores of the Baie des Chaleurs, off the Gulf of St. Lawrence. There, Madame had told them to watch for a flaming ghost ship, but they could no longer keep their eyes open.

Lasse stirred as they crossed the New Brunswick and Quebec border onto the vast Gaspè Peninsula. Once Madame slipped onto her back, no one could miss her trying to out snore Kirsten. The others kept their eyes squeezed shut.

"The two are louder than roaring freight trains," Mikaila rued.

The first Quebec stop was Matapédia on the southern tip of the peninsula, Tuesday morning, June 17. Lasse opened her eyes and saw the others trying to squeeze in a few more minutes of sleep.

Madame Agnew rubbed her eyes, then whispered, "Here comes Amqui, the base, then Mont-Joli, the gateway to the Gaspésie."

"It's 7:30 a.m., how on earth did we lose a whole hour?" Lasse was confused looking at Bjorn's pocket watch from her dress pocket.

"Time zones. There's about five as you cross-country. The Maritimes were Atlantic Time and Quebec and Ontario are Eastern Time."

"Sweden has Central European Time, one standard and one summer."

When the train swung southwest at the St. Lawrence River, it jarred everyone fully awake. Over the next few stops, they drank coffee and ate boxed cereal. Flanking bedrock and forest, the bubbling river beside them raced towards the ocean.

"This is the Great Canadian Shield," the matron said.

Birds flocked in massive groupings on lush islands along the way.

"Heaven smiles on the furry creatures," Madame went on, "they're finally increasing in numbers after the fur trade era."

"There's a beaver dam!" Lovisa pointed, "and the kits."

At Montmagny, Quebec, it was early afternoon and they could see dairy farms and market gardeners tending their plots.

"Canada's Snow Goose Capital is a former haunt of mine," Madame said, "there are pulp and grist mills here and foundries for rolling and carding. Factories make things like furniture and brooms."

Levis, Quebec was an hour later, across the river from Quebec City and the massive Hotel Frontenac. "During the 1500s and the days of Jacques Cartier, the place was called Stadacona."

Levis was where the Intercolonial Railroad ended and the Grand Trunk began. It took seven more hours and four more stops, including a night crossing of the St. Lawrence River to reach the Montreal archipelago.

At twilight, Madame said, "Those lights on the river are canallers. They're rebuilt cargo ships, sturdy enough to navigate the river, and to haul grain and ore."

She went on, "The island of Montreal is Canada's largest city. Back in the 16th century it was called Hochelaga, a French colonial city, started by missionaries and fur-traders."

"The architecture is stunning!" Lasse gasped.

"We should climb Mont Royal!" Lovisa suggested enthusiastically.

Madame lowered her voice, "Know that at dusk, the heart of Montreal is filled with wandering ghosts, like Algonquin warriors. They're from its four cemeteries in Mount Royal, also known as the 'City of the Dead'."

"OK, maybe not," Lasse exchanged worried looks with her girls.

When the Montreal Central Station appeared, it was 8:30 p.m. and they disembarked and walked around the station stretching their legs, finding snacks at a canteen. The next major stop would be Union Station in Toronto,

Ontario, on the banks of Lake Ontario, one of the five Great Lakes. It was a closer lap at 300 plus miles so less than a 20-hour stint.

"I'm getting so I could lay my head down anywhere and sleep through a hurricane," Lasse admitted.

"The snoring doesn't even bother me anymore," Greta agreed, too tired to laugh.

This time they placidly slept through Dorval, a borough of Montreal, still on the island, inhabited by Montreal's wealthiest residents. Then they crossed the border into Ontario with Brockville, Kingston, and Belleville the main in-between stops.

When Lasse awoke, Madame said, "You missed a whole playground for ghosts! The tunnel at Brockville, Kingston's penitentiary, and the prosperous Belleville where they manufacture everything from carriages to candles!"

Lovisa admitted to her mother, "I guess I don't like ghosts or crossing bridges."

Lasse reassured her, "I'm scared too but look how brave we were to cross the Atlantic! God will help us cross all the bridges we have to. Ghosts? I'm not so sure of."

At the stops, young boys called 'newsies' got on with newspapers and snacks for sale. Greta and Kirsten bought newspapers whenever they could. The food at the food stops was awful so after a while, the girls lost interest.

The girls found rummy partners through Madame interpreting for two young boys from Austria. Kirsten and Greta scanned the bachelor ads and Lasse searched for cooking jobs. Madame railed against the two maids about the dangers of meeting strangers but they only laughed.

Toronto arrived in the late afternoon of day three, Wednesday, June 18 and once again they got off and strolled around the station.

Madame filled them in. "See the tall skyline? Isn't Toronto big and modern? The streets are even asphalt and they have a Board of Trade and Eaton's factory."

The final leg of their journey was gruelling but beautiful and took another four and a half days. They went north to Sudbury, and two more Great Lakes, Lake Huron and Lake Superior. At Kenora, they crossed the border into Manitoba. By early morning on Monday, 23 June 1902, the train rolled into the Winnipeg station.

The Swedish Immigration Hall was the midway point for train travellers and the bathing facilities were welcomed after so many days of dirt and grime. Afterwards, Lasse spied a poster board beside a canteen where a local hotel's café advertised for a cook. With map in hand, the small group set out to find the place and upon presenting herself, the Italian owners hired Lasse on the spot. Seeing the girls, the owners pointed her in the direction of a respectable rooming house. In the meantime, Madame Agnew left to visit relatives and Kirsten, and Greta, came upon what they thought were the perfect ads for bachelor situations. Throwing caution to the wind, the maids sent telegrams.

Their wires simply read, "Interested in your newspaper ad."

By the next day, Greta's potential husband replied back, "Accepted. Please take train to Prince Albert for pick up on Saturday."

Kirsten's reply came later, "I will meet you in Prince Albert on Monday."

Having never laid eyes on the men or the place, the women clapped with joy, thinking they had the world by the tail.

Lasse gasped, "Oh my God, I think you're both crazy!"

The two maids winked, "Why do you think we've come all this way?"

"Good thing Madame Agnew's gone!" Lasse said, "she'd have a stroke!"

By July 1902 then, both Greta and Kirsten had reached their new destinations and sent telegrams back to Lasse in Winnipeg. Greta was with a farmer close to the Stoney Creek Settlement and Kirsten was with a farmer further north at Brockington.

14
Whitewash, Bears and Prairie Fires

Stoney Creek Settlement—*July-December 1902*

At their new homestead north of the Stoney Creek Settlement, McLaren and Tessa's greatest wish had come true. It was early Wednesday afternoon, 2 July 1902, and the families' four new homesteads all fell within a 20-mile radius. The friends and shirt-tail relatives who accompanied them on the wagon trek departed for their respective properties. Martha's brother, Angus, and brood headed 15 miles east to Campbellville near Star City. The three single men, Willy, Wyatt, and Charlie and Timothy, Jock's brother, struck out northwest for Bagley, Thaxted, and Fairy Glen.

The first stop for the Scottish clan was son, Jake and Martha's northwest quarter on Township 45 where they divvied up enough supplies for them to set up camp. Next, it was on to daughter, Emma and Jock's northeast quarter. Awestruck by the lush aspen parkland, the children scattered to climb trees and plan forts. No one could stop sifting the black loamy soil through their fingers. By 3:00 p.m., they stopped for a break and afterwards, the seniors, along with Sean, David, Clarice, Philip and Birdie, struck out for their own places on Township 46. McLaren had ploughed a fireguard the summer before and thinking he could drive right through it, got stuck midway. It took some fancy manoeuvring to get out. If that wasn't bad enough, the hay roof on the log shanty had caved in, as had the stable's. Inside each building stood a foot of stagnant water.

"We'll set up camp now, and dung them out tomorrow," Tessa said, "we've shorted ourselves a whole month, so let's get to work."

Philip and Clarice took their supplies and headed to set up camp at their own northwest quarter. McLaren, Sean, and David had more than enough to do so Tessa said, "Tomorrow, I will plant potatoes anywhere there's an open space!"

McLaren sounded optimistic as he got the scythe going to cut the long grass, "Just think, in three years, we'll be applyin' fer Letters Patent!"

That night, tired but happy, Tessa and McLaren talked of their anticipated harvest and realised maybe they needed help. Both commented on how quiet it was without the grandchildren. She wrote her sister, back in Muskoka.

Dear Mary Ann,

We have arrived and the air is electric with anticipation but it is still mayhem living out of the wagon. The men remembered where the property stakes were and everyone is now camping at their own homesteads. The parkland has poplar and willow to clear, but nothing like the heavy timber back home. Wild grass and pea vine is lush, and the livestock are in their glory. Would you ask Ronnie if he's interested in coming out here this fall to help us with harvest? Thank you and God Bless one and all.

Love always,
McLaren, Tessa, and family.

That first Sunday, the elders hosted a family church service in their yard. They took turns reading Bible verses, leading prayers of thanks, and singing hymns like *The Old Rugged Cross* and *Jesus Loves Me*. With utmost respect for the sabbath, the families rested but chose to explore the countryside.

To the west, after the wagons crossed a shallow creek, came a small hill but on the other side, their driving trail was flooded over. They saw a large body of water crowded with waterfowl and it gave Tessa a sense of dèjá vu.

Across the water, and well back from the bank, a tent was pitched on a hilltop beside a small corral for livestock and a wagon.

"Looks like more new homesteaders!"

"Well, without a boat, we'll have to wait to meet them," McLaren said.

Erecting dwellings before winter was critical. Philip had a log structure half built for Clarice and family but siblings, Jake and Emma, would share a structure. Jake and Martha's fifth child was due in August, so they needed something soon. Forty miles southeast of the settlement, the men found a sawmill run by a Métis family. It was between the west end of Kipabiskau

Lake and the Salteaux Kinistin Reserve near Chagoness. On the way by the settlement, they saw Canadian Northern Railway surveyors taking measurements.

"That's a little too far north of the existing settlement," Jake remarked with concern.

The plan for the temporary dwelling to build, had Jock and Emma's family at one end and Jake and Martha's, at the other. With nine children and a new baby, it would be interesting. McLaren knew how to build and got them measuring, sawing and hammering. Earlier, he had put Sean, and David to work reinforcing his shanty's roof and given Philip a hand.

Once McLaren's roof was repaired, to Sean's joke of, "Now, it only leaks when it rains," the father showed his son how to tack up oilcloth.

After the first good rain, David complained, "The oilcloth doesnae hold and all we get is an ice-cold shower!"

"Dinnae worry, these cramped quarters are fer one winter only. You climb up and try to seal the leak."

Trees needed felling and bucked to make way for open fields and McLaren helped keep the others pointed in the right direction. It was a massive job but even before the land was collared, a crop of feed oats was planted in all the open spaces. It was too late in the season for anything else.

The general store manager told Jake, "You could plant winter wheat."

"Seein's believin'. I cannae feature a seed germinatin' and maturin' when 'tis minus 40 degrees!"

"Strangely, freezing triggers its growth and this is next-year country!" the businessman replied.

When August came, the shared house was complete and Martha produced their fifth child, a healthy girl, with Emma attending. After all the hard months of morning sickness, her labour went well. They named the sweet bundle, Barbara, after Jake's eldest deceased sister but Grandda McLaren, as usual, suggested a nickname.

"Let's call her Aggie!"

Neighbours to the south, Milly and Harley, relatives of the folks from the general store, showed up at Jake and Martha's one day when all the family visited. They brought freshly baked buns and seemed thrilled with all the children.

"Welcome to the community!"

"Thank ye!" Martha said, inviting Milly in while the men hovered outside.

"Your new home looks comfortable!" Milly complimented.

Martha laughed, "At least it's a roof over our heads. Me father-in-law oversaw the work."

"Good job."

"He built a big barn back in Muskoka, is a blacksmith, and has a lime kiln fer whitewash."

"Whitewash helps. Otherwise, ice will crack the logs for insects to nest."

"The bairns call it pancake batter," Martha laughed, pouring coffee while Tessa held Aggie.

When the men came in, Jake said, "We're lookin' forward to the bumper crops!"

"It's all about the weather but generally they're good."

"We've heard there were no huge crop failures since the 1700s and the days of Chevalier de La Corne."

Harley smiled.

Tessa said, "Our garden is coming along and we've been fillin' milk pails with wild berries just there fer the takin'. Choke cherries and cranberries hang in great clusters."

"If you drive up to the pines," Milly said, "there's blueberries carpeting the forest floor."

"What are those sweet, dark blue berries on the taller bushes," Martha asked.

"They're saskatoons. For centuries, the Indians used them in teas and medicines."

"We'll preserve everything we can to survive the winter," Tessa said.

Martha added, "Our stores must be overflowin' before the snow flies."

Milly added, "Oh, they will but the other things bulking up are the black bears. Have you seen any?"

Martha admitted, "At first, we felt skittish but after a time, grew a little careless. One day, it caught up to us seein' a dark movement on the other side of the bush. Me blood ran cold. 'twas all a could do to calm meself and get us all quietly backing up. Even inside, the bairns and a couldnae stop shakin'. Bein heavily pregnant, 'twas almost enough to put me into labour! From then on, we make plenty of noise. That's how singin' at the top of our lungs got started!"

Everyone laughed but they were glad she hadn't had the baby right there and then.

Milly said, "If you can, try to stay downwind, so it blows from him to you."

"Be in the wind that's blowing from him?" Martha asked.

"Yes. They have poor eyesight, but a keen sense of smell."

"Thanks, I expect he'll smell us before we ever figure out he's there."

"Maybe."

"Even the dreaded wolves have kept their distance, but coyotes and foxes are already stealin' chickens," Clarice piped in.

Harley explained, "Most one-room country schools are coming along and a grain elevator is supposed to be built every seven miles. There's even talk of a hospital."

Jake said, "We're happy our places are close to the schools' quarters. Education is a big priority when yer family's bigger than a baseball team!"

Indeed, along with the neighbours, Jake and Jock instigated a one-room country school called Stoney Creek school. They formed a school board and with application accepted, the local carpenter began, paid by the ratepayers. Jake and Jock became trustees and Jake stepped in as the first president.

At the same time, McLaren asked Reginald Beatty at the post office, "What about roads and bridges?"

The postmaster smiled, "The government's Department of Public Works, through its local improvement districts, will take care of that, plus drainage and dams."

The first settler to the area went on, "They operate ferries, test water for drinking, and build fire guards."

"It all costs money," McLaren knew from Muskoka, and thought to himself, "and could take ages."

"All the ratepayers are invited to the first meeting."

"We'll be there! Thank ye!" McLaren answered proudly.

"By the way," Beatty remarked, "it's official, the entire Stoney Creek Settlement is picking up and moving to be closer to the rail line."

McLaren didn't know what to say.

In fact, the Canadian Northern Railway's general manager honoured the first European woman in the area, Mrs. Reginald Beatty, by asking her to name the newly moved community. She chose Melfort in honour of her family home in Scotland. Her husband too was honoured as Melfort's first settler and the nearest community west, was named Beatty.

In September that first year of 1902, conditions were dry and word came of runaway grass fires a couple 100 miles to the southwest near Saskatoon and Dundurn. People had hoped it would never happen in their area.

On the dreaded day, the homesteaders fought that awful fire, then gathered together, walking away from it. Jake jumped down from his wagon and spoke to McLaren and Martha, "You heard the thunder crashin' and rollin' last night too?"

"Yes, and all that lightnin' struck way too close!"

"There was hardly a spit of rain, but the entire sky lit up," Martha lamented. "A almost cried when we saw the smoke. Thankfully, it wasn't just us that saw it."

They caught up to Emma and Jock, "Nobody would deliberately light hay or brush when it's so dry, would they? With no fire brigade, we dropped everythin' and ran, knowin' the land is tinder dry."

"Good thing. We prayed fer anyone seein' the smoke to come help," Martha added.

"Yes," quipped McLaren looking over at the other volunteers. "'Twas amazin' how everyone got here so fast."

"Even Indians on their ponies, and a man with his wagon from Gronlid," Jake said.

After a moment of silence, Martha wailed, "Aw! The poor wild animals!"

"Seein' them terrorised and leapin' out of the smoke was heartbreakin'," Emma sympathised.

"'Twas worse fer the ones that didn't make it," McLaren still carried a bucket and shovel. "A guess we're all a little naïve about prairie fires."

"'Twas surreal to watch," Jake said, loosening the handkerchief from around his neck. "That thick and mushroomin' smoke had us coverin' our faces with whatever we had," He reached for his father's tools and threw them into the back of his rig.

"There we were," Philip, who had also driven over, added, "ploughin' fire guards and drivin' to the creek, fillin' barrels and buckets, and shovellin' dirt."

"And usin' wet gunny sacks," Philip's wife, Clarice, rued. "Me back is killin' me!"

"Mine too," in unison, Milly, Martha, and Emma chimed in.

"When the tempestuous wind gusted, and it jumped the guards, ye could hear cursin' a mile away," McLaren admitted. "'Twas a stark moment, and everyone prayed fer the hellfire to play out before it reached the creek."

"But it didn't take long to get there," Jock said, "and heading fer Harley and Milly's yard! A, fer one, thought all was lost."

"Me too," Harley sighed. "Except for the creek, the blaze was comin' full bore, straight for our place."

"That was a few tense moments but fer no good reason, the wind died down," Jake rejoiced, "and everythin' stalled."

"Now, we have to pay attention to the hot spots," Jake continued. "Don't leave anythin' smoulderin'."

"Given a little oxygen," piped in Knut.

He was walking beside Halvor, Smith, and Ivar so Sean introduced him first.

"Meet Knut! He's our new neighbour, the one who's still tenting'." Sean introduced.

"A log cabin is in the works," Knut said extending his hand, then he introduced Halvor and Smith and his men. Lastly, Halvor introduced Ivar from Gronlid.

At that moment, the sooty fire-fighters, including the women, reached a stretch of green grass and dropped to the ground for a much-deserved rest. All kept a vigilant watch but once the ladies regained their strength, they went to fetch nourishment and the children. Even surrounded by the sight and smell of black, burnt char, they drank lemonade and ate sandwiches, trying to stay out of the line of smoke.

The nearest farm to the east was Jake and Martha's and at the first hint of wildfire, Grandmother Tessa had taken all the grandchildren and run for safety.

Tessa said, "A took all the bairns to the centre of the furthest ploughed field. The bigger children carried the wee ones and we ran hard. Better than bein' near somethin' that might catch fire, like the house."

The oldest grandchild, nine-year-old Bunny smiled, "'Twas not easy, Grandma carried Birdie and laid Aggie and Blue in a little wagon with a bucket of water. A carried Bud, Toot had Blue, and Tadpole carried Dot."

"Fleck, and Peanut held my skirt," Tessa said, "and stayed close but got there on their own steam. All a could do was pray. Me heart broke listenin' to the wee one's cry."

Bunny used a funny voice to imitate her siblings and cousins, "'Me eyes hurt', they said, because all we could see was smoke and fallin' ashes."

Tadpole, her brother at seven, said, "'Twas dark and the sun turned orange!"

Tessa nodded, "Yes, 'twas awful. A told them to dip their wee socks into the bucket of water, then hold them over their faces."

Bunny added, "Me, Toot, and Tadpole, helped the little ones."

"Ye sound like such good children!" Martha praised, then turned to Tessa when she said, "those sets of bare feet sitting in a circle were a sight!"

Toot piped in, "We couldnae even watch the firefightin' but Grandma said, 'our parents were like mice slayin' a dragon'."

The adults shook hands and welcomed each other to the prairies. They rehashed the day's events in their respective accents, mostly in broken English.

"I got here May 14," Knut smiled.

Then Halvor, Ivar, and Harley compared notes about who had homesteaded the earliest.

Soft-spoken Smith and his men approached in a teasing manner, "But remember, my people were here ahead of all of you," and the others, who couldn't argue, snickered and tipped their hats or nodded their heads.

"We got here on July 1st," Jake replied. "But how ironic that Mother Nature brought us together like this to meet fer the first time?"

Emma started, "A hope ye all realise how lucky we were that the wind came from the north."

"Oh, yes!" Milly agreed.

"And with the homesteads distributed such as they are, we all came from different directions to fight it," Jock added.

"The wind abating saved us today," Smith said, "but be warned, fires like this happen every year."

"Ja," breathed Halvor, "we do everything in our power but don't always emerge the victor."

Walking around the burn afterwards, the children traipsed along getting covered in soot. Smith was the first to find the seat of the fire, a large old poplar tree.

He pointed, "See where the lightning burnt it black? And where the flames jumped across the treetops, only scorching the bottoms? That's crowning."

McLaren said, "The forest fires back home tore communities apart."

"Ja! At least this time there was no loss of life or buildings." Knut was grateful.

"On a positive note, this burnt land vill be easier to break," Ivar chimed in.

What Tessa noticed was that when the sun began to set, and the group walked away, Halvor, Knut, Smith, and Ivar lagged behind. They were looking at something off to the west and there sat four men on horseback.

The matriarch felt goosebumps just as Knut's expression clouded and Halvor cautioned, "I don't have to tell you who they are. If not for the lightning, I would guess they lit it. Notice how they didn't lift a finger?"

"They're slippery," Ivar spoke, turning for home. "Ve call them the Blacks and Swallows, or the BS boys for short. Ve give them a vide berth. They'll do vhatever they feel like vhenever they want."

Tessa was surprised that people as far away as Gronlid knew about the troublesome men.

Halvor sighed, "Ja! And us immigrants are some of their biggest targets."

Knut growled, "I've already met them."

No one mentioned the sordid brothers after that. Weariness abounded and Tessa knew nobody wanted to be a fear monger. Why frighten everyone? Today was neither the time nor the place. Another day, when there weren't so many sets of little ears around, they could hash it out. Still, no one was blind.

It was well after dark before everyone went home and only then that David wondered aloud, "Why didn't the four riders pitch in to fight fire?"

Jake admitted, "The general store owner warned me about those two sets of brothers, the other day. Keepin' them at a distance is fer everyone's benefit."

It was then that Tessa revealed the earlier conversation she'd heard from their new neighbours, "As Jake has said, steer clear of them!"

By late October, Melfort's Main Street had furrows ploughed to run north and south. In the meantime, the entire settlement picked up and moved but not overnight. The original stores were followed by so many other businesses springing up that by 1903, Melfort was officially proclaimed a village with a population of over 300.

It was a similar story 15 miles west. The rail line was placed north of the Carrot River Settlement, so that the community was forced to move closer. The new site was renamed Kinistino in honour of the Saulteaux chief, Kinistin.

After harvest ended and the terrain froze, the Scottish men took the over 200-mile round trip east to Erwood. The station master at Glenella had shipped their large equipment once the bridge and rail repairs were made. Travelling with the empty wagon, ready to convert to a sled if it snowed, was easy up to Crooked River. Here sawmills were erecting and crews scrambled to get operations underway.

The Scottish men navigated heavy black spruce close to 50 miles one-way. They dared not traverse the partly frozen Mistatim Bog yet even though there was ice water in the bucket at home most mornings. The muskeg was full of peat moss and smoking ground fires, so instead, they detoured by Bjork Lake. Communities of Peesane, Mistatim ('Big Dog' in Cree), Bannock, Prairie River, Greenbush, White Poplar, and Etoimami were along the route. It would take a week and a half to travel the stretch one-way in the midst of howling wolves, rutting moose, bugling elk, honking waterfowl, and bears bulking up for hibernation. Watching the bull moose or bull elk spar to gain the favour of a cow was a real highlight.

Hidden further off the beaten path were hunters and their hunting shacks. The Scottish travellers were warned to wear white suits and red or orange caps during hunting season, to avoid becoming targets and they didn't need to be told twice. A quick darting movement and a trigger-happy novice might not mix.

The closer they got to Erwood; the more evidence came of the Canadian Northern Railway Branch Line making inroads. Predicted to be complete by 1904, the line was coming from Dauphin, Manitoba through Erwood, Etoimami, and over to Melfort, then Prince Albert. Eventually, Mistatim would be considered Mile 436 between Bannock and Peesane with passenger service.

15

Logging and Criminals

Melfort—*November 1902* and **Prince Albert Court Room**—*October 1903*

At his new homestead, Knut spoke to Meg and her calf that first November 1902. "Uffdah! Meg! It's time you weaned Daisy! She's gotta be over 300 pounds and soon as big as you. It's been four months and she needs weaning before you go to Halvor's for the winter." The cow stood chewing her cud and listening like she knew what he said.

Knut warned, "If I'm forced to use the 17¢ calf weaners from the general store, I will."

After freeze-up, with a weaned calf, and livestock tucked in safely at Halvor's, Knut left for Prince Albert to retrieve his sawmill shipment. He booked into the same hotel and for some reason, found himself in the same room. His grandfather's pocket watch was on his mind and he got down on his hands and knees to hunt. Searching under the bed and chair, behind the curtains, and in every nook and cranny was a lost cause. The next morning, he paid his bill and asked the time. The clerk pulled out a pocket watch and lo and behold, there it was.

Knut yelped with delight.

"Sorry!" the embarrassed clerk protested, "I found it!"

Knut reclaimed his prized possession without song or dance, doubly happy because the countdown to his invasion of the Crooked River forest had begun.

Freight workers helped load the four steam engines and long bulky carriage onto his wagon and those of the freight swing. Heavy and awkward, the whole process, from the time he left home to loading and unloading in Crooked River, took almost two weeks. The trip was not without its backbreaking challenges.

At the sawmill, the assembly of lumberjacks gathered and waiting at the camp site was impressive. Dressed in parkas, bush boots, and winter garb for -40 weather, they had their own canvas tents set up.

Their new boss, Knut, gave an introduction of what was to come. "We have to build the camp from the ground up and clear the roads. I won't lie, harvesting lumber is not easy. It's rough and tumble work and puts a big strain on the body. We work from sunup to sundown every day of the week except Sunday."

The young Norwegian American went on, "These tents are our homes until we build a bunk house so let's make it quick! Don't expect a palace, it'll be more like a sardine shack," and that got hoots.

"We'll build a mess hall and Sully and Li Ping will keep us well fed."

Greyed and moustached Sully nodded his head before yanking off his toque. Li Ping, the China man, bowed. From what Knut could tell, the two were already working wonders slinging hash over a campfire.

Knut went on, "Sully's two daughters, Minnie and Mel, will keep the buildings clean and keep us men on the straight and narrow."

Sully snatched the toques off his blushing daughters' heads and mussed their long sun-streaked tresses. Both girls dressed like tomboys since dresses weren't practical in the bush. Still, Knut expected them to be better house-trained than the men by far, even if they were freckle-faced teenagers.

According to Sully, "They can work rings around any man!"

The girls weren't hard to look at either which might be a drawback in an isolated bush camp. Sully warned in plain language, "None of you young bucks are good enough in any way, shape, or form, for my girls, so bugger off and keep your paws to yourself."

When the men whistled, Knut went on, "You'll get paid at the end of every two weeks by the cord and not by the hour. Twice a month, the scaler will measure the wood cut, and I'll pay you accordingly. A cord is 4' x 8' x 4'."

"I'm looking for volunteers," Knut said having met with all of them but doing this for the group, "who will be the scaler to do the count?"

Ross put up his hand, "I can." He was middle-aged, tall, and his Roman nose gave him a cranky look. Surely, he could hold his own for count discrepancies.

"Logging can be deadly," Knut went on. "Watch for trees falling, men falling out of trees, logs rolling, and axe and saw accidents. Protect your fingertips against slams with frozen logs!"

Sully added, "We cooks provide first aid."

"Still, you'll be well paid," Knut promised. "I'll assess the timber rights and map the logging roads. The loggers will fell selected trees, then buck them to length, limb, scale, and debark. Loaders skid the logs to the sleighs, then lift them up onto the sleigh with a jammer."

Knut hardly stopped for a breath, "The top-loader oversees the loading. A load is about 20 logs or up to 6,000 board feet. His job is the most dangerous, do I have any volunteers?"

A handsome and well-muscled youth put up his hand, "I will. My name is Percy."

Nobody missed Mel and him locking eyes. Knut decided she must like a little danger in her life, but then obviously so did Percy.

Knut gave Percy, who was the image of confidence, a solemn nod. "So be it. I appreciate you stepping up."

"Roadmen use a rutter to rut the roads, then run water into the ruts to make ice, so it's easier for the teams."

Knut went on, "We need teamsters."

Two, young, red-headed Irish brothers, Bill and Ed raised their hands. "We're teamsters and know how to sharp shod horses to work on ice roads."

Knut said, "It's a long day for teamsters. You'll be up by 5:00 a.m. to feed them and do it again at 6:00. You'll work 'til 8:00 p.m., grooming and tending their needs."

Ed added, "Horses don't take a break."

"Neither do cooks," Sully piped in and got smiles all around.

"The horses are yours then," Knut looked at the red heads.

"We still need roadmen!" and more hands shot up. "You're on!" Knut said.

A similar process happened for the loggers, loaders, and landers. Each time, men waited to fill the void.

"When we're ready to start work inside the mill," Knut said, "we light lanterns before dawn and the steam engines are fuelled, fired, and ready by first light. The fuel is leftover wood and sawdust from the milling process. The gauge shows when the steam builds to the right level, then the operator calls 'stand clear' and the sawing operation commences. The noise is deafening!"

With Knut's experience, serving as the sawyer himself for the first few runs would give him the opportunity to train someone else. Key was a sawyer with precision and a trained eye.

The men were at various stages of knowing, so he explained, "The main engine runs the line shaft that drives the log carriage. The head rig circular saws consist of a lower main saw and a top saw, plus adjustable edger saws. A skagit winch brings the logs to the log deck. A third engine runs the conveyor belt and empties sawdust from the top saw. The fourth engine is the cut off saw."

He went on, "Frenchie will run the canter that twirls a hook and spins the logs." The young man had a thick accent and a hearty laugh.

"The sawyer is me for the time being. Bruce as carriage setter, will load a log onto the carriage, then secure and position it." Bruce was a stocky Ukrainian with a bulbous nose. He wore a fur-lined aviator hat with the flaps tied up because as he put it, "I sveat like a pig."

"Even your ears?" someone razzed.

Knut went on, "The sawyer directs the cutting pattern, signalling the carriage setter for the next cut. The carriage moves the log, and the head saw slices it clear through. It breaks each log into cants or unfinished logs, and unfinished planks called flitches."

"Any volunteers?"

Blond-haired, slender, Keith stepped forward looking keen and about Knut's age.

"I've done it before," he offered.

"You know your most important job is to know when to rotate the log to look for a clear face?"

"Yes, a half-turn is the second face and you turn it again for the top and bottom faces."

"Don't saw too long on any one face or risk losing value. It makes the edger's workload less and produces flatter lumber for drying."

Einar, dressed like a snowman, was an older, bald-headed Dane. He wore a fur aviator hat tied at his throat.

He spoke up, "Edging takes the flitch, and trims off irregular edges, marked knots, and defects, leaving four-sided lumber. I have experience."

Knut described the trim saw man position, "Trimming squares the ends at accurate board lengths for air-drying."

Danny at 20 something, had a hair lip but his good looks made up for it. He volunteered but his words revealed a slight speech impediment. Knut could see him checking out Sully's daughters, and hoped he wasn't girl crazy.

Alf had experience as a planer and was slightly bent with age. He said, "Planing smooths to uniform width and thickness, then the eight-foot lengths are stacked in the air-drying building."

Knut went on, "A green chain man is this big Swede, Olaf, who can polish off a tin of snoose before breakfast. Olaf will load the trimmed lumber onto a cart and sort the outgoing lumber according to quality and size. Stack it by grade, even if we say for now, they're good, better, and best, it's a start. If we charge the same price for everything, regardless of quality, we'll lose money. Make no mistake, our expertise doesn't come for free! When the rail line gets built, we'll load the finished product onto boxcars for shipping to market. Parts of the US and Upper Canada are prime markets with their own wood depleted."

The men got to work and by New Year's eve, they had transformed their timber world into a rudimentary mill with appropriate shelters. The log buildings were simple but effective, including a barn for the horses. One of the biggest thrills was for them to stand back and admire their 12-foot-high loads where the stakes were spread wider at the top to span up to 17 feet.

Knut was a man with a dream and there was nothing quite so appealing for a crew to follow. When the day came to stoke up the steam engines, the men were stoked too. The first go-around was rocky, but in time, the rough edges smoothed and after a while, the sounds coming from the forest were more like a melody.

"Do you hear that?" Olaf asked.

"What?" Keith answered.

"That's the sound of money!"

Once folks discovered the sawmill was up and running, Knut was surprised at the demand. Saturday morning was sale day and customers from miles around showed up to buy boards and haul them home.

"Measure the board feet as you load," Knut told the men, "so the customer knows what he's buying. Also, the receipt needs to say the customer inspected the lumber and found it satisfactory. If you can't read and write, tell me now!"

No one said a word.

When profits rolled in, it made Knut and his crew proud to earn an honest living. Like cogs of a wheel, their routines shifted into place and with that came motivation and inspiration. Daily, the gang worked like dogs filled with determination and passion but come Saturday nights, all hell broke loose. Drinking, dancing, gambling, and singing filled the air. Sometimes fights broke out. Percy and Danny were friends but fought often, over the girls. Percy didn't like Danny's attitude about taking liberties. After a long week's work, neither the fresh pine scent of sawdust nor the beauty of the sudden quiet with the sawmill shut down could pacify them. By Sunday morning, they were ready for a day to sleep in and count their money.

In the meantime, Knut received a letter from Halvor.

Valentine's night, Greta and I awoke to a noise outside. Instantly, I wondered why Shep hadn't barked. Without words, I placed a hand on Greta's pregnant tummy so she'd stay still. I had a gut feeling the noise wasn't coming from the animals. In pitch blackness, I felt for my rifle and crept to the window to see the outlines of two men, on either side of the barn. When two others came around the corner, each leading a steer, I ran to the door, and started shooting into the air. They ran off but one winced and fell, dragging himself off and firing return shots. Horses galloped off, so I knew they were gone. My heart almost beat out of my chest and my hands shook but I threw on clothes over my long johns and raced outside.

Coming face to face with Smith and his man stepping out of the shadows was a shock, especially seeing the war paint. You had to be there! Smith admitted that his man nailed one of the intruders in the leg with an arrow. Smith said the brothers had stolen their ponies and been to your place. I guess they rooted through your buildings, smashed things, and helped themselves but nothing was burned. I don't trust that they won't be back.

We searched my yard and found tracks in the snow leading to a scuffle. I stifled a sob seeing my faithful old dog left mangled behind a bush. A set of reins was around his neck and I realised they'd wrung his neck. I knelt down to cradle him and all of us shared grief and confusion over the senseless act and motivations of evil people. Shep was innocent.

Greta tried to comfort me but I know she's wondering what she's gotten herself into, living here. I didn't have to tell her this wasn't our first run-in with the brothers. She made a 'No Trespassing' sign that I posted but those idiots likely can't read. We don't want to put Swift Arrow in harm's way, for the arrow to the leg, but the police need to know. Smith has agreed because it's obvious the brutes won't let up. I am notifying both you and the Prince Albert police by mail but I hope this issue resolves by your return. Sorry to be the bearer of bad news.

By spring breakup at the end of March 1903, Knut was past ready to get back home. For the sawmill's first season, he felt they had done very well and all sawmill hands went home with money in their pockets. Now everyone suffered from cabin fever and thank God there was no bad injuries. The worst thing was Sully's youngest daughter, Minnie had fallen in with Danny.

Li Ping shared with Knut, "Percy was right. I listened to her secret retching for at least the past 10 mornings without fail."

"It seems our trim saw man, has hidden talents."

At his homestead, even though Halvor had forewarned Knut about the vandalism, what Knut encountered left him angry and questioning the human race. When picking up his livestock, Halvor gave the rest of the details and was disappointed that the brothers had eluded capture by the police.

"After the incident, within the hour, I was on my way into Melfort to send a letter to the North-West Mounted Police in Prince Albert. Something has to change because now we don't dare leave our properties unattended. About 10 days later, two constables interviewed Smith, Swift Arrow, and I. They searched the area but turned up nothing. Working against time restraints, short-staffing, and serving a huge district, they returned to Prince Albert, promising not to give up."

Knut's first chance then, he too went into Melfort and sent a letter to report his own vandalism and theft. He wrote,

Dear Sirs,

Please refer to previous report from my neighbour, Halvor. At my homestead, the snow and howling winds have whipped the snowbanks smooth, so there's no tracks left. A host of my tools and supplies are missing, plus lanterns and harness. Evidence of vandalism is all around.

Sincerely, Knut.

In the meantime, spring 1903 progressed and Knut's flood and the annual waterfowl convention amassed. The usual trails leading out of Knut's farm to the south and east became impassable. To go into the village then, unless he built a boat or ferry, he had to go the long way around by the west. One afternoon, when coming home from town, he heard gunshots. When his team and wagon crested the hill, he saw four hunters sitting astride horses, shooting waterfowl from the flood's shoreline.

Instantly provoked, he cursed, "Geese are one thing but who would kill swans and cranes?" As far as he was concerned, migratory birds needed protecting at all costs. His ire swelled and the well-trained horses needed no coaxing. He hollered gruffly but the strangers ignored him. They were armed with rifles but so was Knut. The four men turned towards him, laughing in his face, and Knut recognised them from Smith and Halvor's descriptions. He wondered why an illegal market for migratory birds hadn't dawned on him and how long they'd been getting away with it. Along with his own risen hackles, he could see Lady's fur spiked all the way down her back.

The snub-nosed, short one, Owen Swallow, goon that he was, shouted, "Who the hell are you?"

The smooth-talking, greasy-haired, Jeb Black, chided, "Now, now, it's all copacetic. No one owns these bodacious birds."

Knut cursed under his breath, "Scum of the earth," but shouted, "I own this property and you are trespassing. These birds are protected by law!"

"At least they are in the US," Knut thought. "But what these men don't know won't hurt them."

Lady growled as Knut declared, "I don't want any more birds harmed," then carefully articulated each word, "Please…leave…my…property."

When nobody moved, Knut lost all patience and hissed, "Sic 'em!"

Lady lunged at Owen, who was walking menacingly towards Knut. Amos was right behind, and that's when Knut saw the limp.

"Ha!" he thought, "the arrow recipient."

While Knut wondered which one had strangled Halvor's dog, Lady didn't care and snapped Owen's hand and ground down. The earth spattered red with blood and Owen yelped like Armageddon was upon him.

Jeb had his rifle cocked and pointed towards the dog who may very well have interrupted the stand-off. Now, she faced lethal consequences. Instead, the crooked nosed, Gib already twirled his lasso in her direction. When horses and a wagon approached fast from behind, Gib's hat fell off. A frenzied Halvor raced forward, and seeing him, the heinous men mounted their horses and galloped off.

"Thank God!" Knut exhaled and cradled his dog. "Those ignorant sons of bitches aren't worth the powder to blow them to hell."

"I saw your wagon fly by and figured it was suspicious."

"Now they're poaching. Don't they know when to quit?" They'd left the dead birds scattered along the shoreline as a gruesome reminder.

"That goon will have a sore hand." Halvor observed.

"Yeah? Well, he asked for it," Knut spat. Lady, on the other hand, smiled from ear to ear as she carried Gib's hat to her master.

In Knut's second letter to the police, he wrote:

Dear Sirs,

Is it against the law to kill migratory birds in Canada? The two sets of brothers are at it again. I've never been introduced but of the Blacks, Jeb has dark greasy hair, and Amos walks with a limp. My dog bit Owen Swallow's hand, and his brother Gib is just a plain goon. They travel together, so aren't hard to miss. I can't mail you a sample of the dead birds but they are majestic swans, cranes, and pelicans. I did retrieve Gib's cowboy hat as evidence.

Sincerely, Knut.

By return mail from 50 miles away in Prince Albert, Constable Len Grieves replied:

Dear Knut,

You describe the brothers to a tee. My partner, Constable Alfred West and I are getting tired of hearing about their shenanigans. Yes, there is a black market for migratory birds around the world. Shooting them isn't against the law here, although it should be. You'll find there are wrongs of this nature running unchecked, like killing bears for their gall bladders. I'm here to tell you to take precautions because now that these men are foiled, they'll be out for blood. Don't worry, this time, we'll find them. Hang onto that cowboy hat!

Yours respectfully,
Constable Len Grieves.

Indeed, within two weeks, the two constables formed a posse and with Smith's help, uncovered the fugitives shacked up at Eagle Lake about 25 miles south of Melfort. In a night raid at their den of iniquity, the searchers surprised the offenders who awoke to a display of guns and handcuffs. The villains were spitting mad and made vehement denials but were still arrested.

"You have the right to remain silent, anything you say can and will be used against you in a court of law. You are charged with multiple counts; discharging a firearm with the intent to harm, break and enter, vandalism and theft including horses; and attempted armed robbery of cattle. Further, you are charged with trespassing, and cruelty to animals."

The four suspects were hand-cuffed and hauled away for incarceration in the Prince Albert Gaol to await sentencing.

On the court date, which was 1 September 1903, Halvor, Smith, Swift Arrow, and Knut, attended as witnesses. Greta, and two of Smith's men, accompanied them and the men sat one row behind Greta in the courtroom gallery as spectators. When the puffed-up defendants entered the room, they skewered the white woman with their gazes and sneered at the other men.

Swedish Greta toting her baby, was unfazed and turning her head, whispered so Smith's men could hear, "They're not quite so intimidating in chains, are they?"

Knut overheard the two constables whispering, "Prosecutors seem a little less willing to indict these days, but it's obvious these brothers knew what the consequences of their actions were,"

"The police officers had put Gib's cowboy hat and the set of reins that strangled the dog, into evidence."

Sadly, when presented for Knut to identify, all he could do was hang his head and admit, "Yes, I recognise both. The reins are the ones stolen from my property." He felt like someone punched him in the stomach.

Throughout the proceedings, the court listened to the accused men spout not even one kernel of truth. Their bald-faced lies denied everything including being anywhere in the vicinity. After hearing the evidence and contemplating his decision, the police magistrate said, "Will the defendants please rise."

He went on, "Gentlemen, your actions are repugnant and morally reprehensible. It is obvious that you have acted knowingly and with forethought and malice."

Knut knew the burden of proof in the theft of horses and cattle was onerous but the police magistrate said, "In 1901, British courts used fingerprints as evidence, but that hasn't happened in this part of the world yet. One day, perhaps. Regardless, given the evidence, eyewitness statements, your reputations, lack of remorse, and continued destructive display of behaviour today, I find you guilty."

As a result, when bringing the verdict home, the magistrate's judgment was, "In the matter of the Crown vs. Jeb Black, Amos Black, Gib Swallow, and Owen Swallow, you are hereby found guilty as charged. The court will adjourn and reconvene for sentencing in one month's time."

Sentencing followed in October and all the players returned.

The magistrate said, "You are sentenced to two years for discharging a firearm with the intent to harm. Two years for horse theft. Two years for break, enter, vandalism, and theft under $5,000. For the attempted armed robbery of cattle, you are sentenced to one additional year. Two hundred dollars plus costs each for trespassing and three months hard labour for animal cruelty. Total incarceration time is seven years and nine months."

The magistrate surveyed the room. "Is there any reason why the sentences should not be imposed at this time?" he asked. There was a moment of silence.

"Finding none," he went on, "the guilty parties will be sent to the Stony Mountain Penitentiary in Manitoba."

He pounded his gavel and said, "Court is adjourned!"

The leg-shackled prisoners were booed as the guards escorted them out, hissing and cursing. The culprits claimed injustice and after the fact, tried to charge the police with unlawful arrest but got nowhere. At least they would remain locked up until 1910 and society could feel relieved for a time.

Knut, Halvor, Smith, and supporters stood outside the courthouse afterwards feeling a little stunned but relieved.

"Congratulations everyone. I for one, am satisfied with the outcome," said Halvor.

"Me too, except too bad they didn't get 20 lashes for killing migratory birds," for Knut that was a stickler.

"And 20 more for killing Shep," Halvor said.

Smith and his men chuckled. "The arrow injury was considered an act of self-defence and Swift Arrow was shown leniency and not charged."

The two constables walked over, "Congratulations," they said.

"We thought you might like to know they're talking about opening a barracks in Melfort once the railway gets there!"

At the time, Melfort was booming with more settlers coming by train. Men arrived to build a Canadian Pacific Railway bridge between Melfort and Kinistino. The train bridge at Fenton across the South Saskatchewan River would follow.

16

Trappers, Brawls and Muskeg

Winnipeg—*June 1902* **to Melfort** *June 1903*

It was the last week of June 1902 and the Swedish mother and daughters had arrived at an old Winnipeg hotel-turned-rooming house. Ebba, the stocky Hungarian proprietor, invited them into the parlour and tried to steady her voice. Looking at her husband in the other room, she said. "War has turned my spirited Isak into a vacant sort of man."

"The Boer War?" Lasse asked. Indeed, the man looked sad and beaten down.

"Yes, the Second Boer War. He was with the Winnipeg Strathcona Horses in southern Africa and returned three weeks ago. I guess it was a doozie."

"Give him time," Lasse encouraged.

Ebba changed the subject, "I hope you'll enjoy your stay with us. If the girls helped me do housework, I could reduce your board and room costs."

Mikaila, more than willing, said, "We know how to pitch in," and Lovisa nodded.

Over the following summer's heat, the lodging house was quiet, aside from a neighbourhood lout named Larry. He was a teenager who prowled around, getting into things, and it drove Ebba crazy.

"He's harmless but dances to a different drum," she told the girls.

Lasse worked five days a week in a hotel café on Main Street. Her Swedish flair, combined with the new Italian and Canadian cuisine soon produced mouth-watering antipastos, cheeseburgers, and Swedish meatballs.

Her daughters were never far from her mind and at day's end, the first thing she did was check in with them about their day.

"We're exploring the city but never straying too far," Mikaila assured. "Ebba and Isak look out for us."

"We're steering clear of that fellow down the street, too," Lovisa promised. "If he comes near, he talks non-stop, so I think he's lonely."

Once school started, Ebba and the girls encouraged Isak to walk them to school. The walk went through a park and they noticed Larry trailing behind. Isak never said a word but he and Larry stayed to feed the pigeons. On Sunday, it happened again on the way home from church.

Over that year, Larry and Isak seemed to bond and the young fellow became somewhat of a fixture, helping do odd jobs. Isak's mood slowly improved and it was him who took them all to see their very first motor car downtown. In winter, it was Isak who scrounged around for skates so they could glide the trails of the Red and Assiniboine Rivers. And finally, it was Isak who took everyone to a hockey game. The Winnipeg Victoria's, outfitted in red and yellow jerseys, played their hearts out but lost the Stanley Cup. Even so, the game left smiles all around and that's all that mattered.

"They will always be champions in my eyes!" Isak said.

Ebba agreed, "Absolutely! While you were away, Isak, they won two years running."

When the weather warmed in March, a newspaper ad appeared for a cook in a new Melfort hotel.

"I'm sorry," Lasse apologised to her landlords and employers, "but the time has come," torn between happiness and regret, she admitted, "this might be the chance of a lifetime."

Listing off the reasons to leave wasn't necessary because they understood and expected it. Goodbyes were always hard and their dear friends, were disappointed but happy for the blessed opportunity.

Lassie's telegram to The Hotel owner in Melfort was affirmed and the question of how to get there arose. Fortunately, an opportunity presented itself through an older couple from church. Hilda and John were heading for Brockington, an area north of Melfort, and were going via the Erwood route.

"Doesn't the railroad end at Erwood? What about the forest after that to go through?" Lasse questioned.

"Yes. After Erwood, we plan to continue by horse and covered wagon and it should take about a week. We're only taking that route to visit my sister in Prairie River," Hilda admitted.

Lasse said, "It couldn't be better than to travel with people we know who speak English and Swedish."

Lasse promised to contribute food for the trip and packed a substantial box of staples. The day they left Winnipeg, it was Saturday, 20 June 1903, at 4:00 p.m., and the weather was mild.

The conductor said, "You'll find Erwood feels quite modern with their new wooden bridge across the Red Deer River. The Red Deer Lumber Company built it."

The man, in his uniform, couldn't help but remind Lasse of her husband, Bjorn and her life in Sweden. She wondered how Little Bjorn was making out. His letters were few and far between and she tried not to read anything into it.

Travelling north, the train pumped thick black smoke and the travellers knew to keep the windows closed. The trip was breathtaking through forest and past clear lakes. After three hours, Neepawa was the first stop. Dauphin appeared by 9:30 p.m., and by Swan River it was midnight and coach lights were out.

They dozed and by 3:30 a.m., Sunday, it was the end of the line at Erwood. The travellers hastily unloaded, and dawn's first light peeked over the horizon, A covered wagon sat waiting for them courtesy the livery man, and Lasse and the girls slept under it, while Hilda and John slept inside.

About three hours later, they discovered that Erwood, although remote, was a going concern with settlers arriving, and the Canadian Northern rail line extending. Amid the hustle and bustle was the overpowering fragrance of sawdust and woodsmoke and friendly people were in a hearty mood. The group made their way to the livery stable to get the horses.

The bright-eyed livery man stuttered, "It's a g-g-good 60 miles to Crooked River. You've m-m-missed the winter's logging season but can expect to see sawmills. You'll s-s-see trapping and hunting cabins, and maybe wild game."

"How many people do you think this section of bush houses in a winter?" Hilda asked.

"Maybe t-t-two or three thousand if you go all the w-w-way to Crooked River," he answered, and her jaw dropped at the number.

"Does that include big game hunters and rail crews?"

"Nope."

At the general store, the storekeeper pointed out, "At this time of year, the bears have awoken from hibernation with their cubs. The cow moose have calves, and the bulls are morose, nibbling new growth. It's the circle of life and predators lurk in the shadows waiting to prey on the weak."

After striking out nine miles, the noisy wagon made it to the first community of Etoimami. Here, they were directed to 'the Springs', at the bend of the Fir River. When their rig rolled downhill to the riverside spring, people were crowded around, watching something.

"See the mother bear, and her cubs on the opposite bank?" a man said.

Lovisa and Mikaila were thrilled, "The babies look adorable running and playing alongside their mother!"

"Could they swim across to us?" Hilda's voice got high-pitched.

"If you don't bother them, generally, they won't bother you," the man answered.

The wagon travellers waited their turn to fill their water jugs from the spring. To people here, bears were old hat and listening to the rushing water amid wildflowers and pine trees seemed idyllic. The locals spoke of little else except the arrival of the new rail line.

"With the expansion, Etoimami is to become a major junction one day," they vowed.

"Remarkable!"

Back up the hill, they camped. While tending the horses, crickets chirped in the setting sun, and John helped erect the tent. Long after bedtime, close to 2:00 a.m., the ponies fussed and roused them from a deep sleep, Lasse poked her head outside to see the backside of a ringed tailed creature rifling through their foodstuffs. She froze but the masked thief lost interest and sauntered off.

"Thankfully, it was only a raccoon and not a bear!" she said.

Hilda nodded but John said, "From now on girls, we hang our food up high, and away from camp!"

On Monday morning, June 22, they travelled west but met the Fir River again and crossed at a shallow pebbly spot. Straight west, a community called White Poplar came first, where the homesteaders had built log homes behind clumps of bush. Not too long after, came an area walled by timber, dubbed Greenbush. The tall jack pine and spruce evergreens were dark and foreboding. Here a young Irishman, herding two piglets had set up camp.

"Nice to meet you," Troy said, "I'm heading to the Carrot River Valley to homestead." Looking at his pigs, he explained, "To ride a freight car, you need livestock. We rode the train as far as Erwood but now, it's hitching a ride or walking."

He shared his kindling and campfire that night and, in the morning, hitched a ride. Surprisingly, lulled by the wagon's movement, the pigs fell asleep. From Lasse's perspective, another male's presence came in handy, especially when he led the team across the next creek.

When they saw two log cabins crowded together, decorated with racks of sun-bleached antlers, Hilda said, "My sister says the dense forest leaves no room for homesteaders but there are plenty of hunters and trappers."

Only the second cabin had smoke coming from the chimney and off to the side, under a large evergreen stood a solitary weathered wooden cross. Was it the trapper, his wife, or his child? Whomever it was, for the newcomers, it was a stark reminder of life on the frontier. As they looked around, a tall, thin trapper stepped out from behind the second cabin leading a milk cow but his movements seemed odd, like he'd moved sideways through the bush too long.

He laughed, "I apologise for the aroma. A skunk and a badger had a fight under my original shack, so I moved to the other."

They laughed and John raised both hands, "We're only passing through but nice to meet you. Seen any wildlife?"

"Oh yes, lots of black bears," and at the women's obvious disdain, he said, "but I'd be far more afraid of a moose in the rut. One stalked me through the bush one fall and I was never so terrified in my life." The bearded man offered them a drink of rum with cream but they politely declined. Content with his solitary lifestyle, he puffed on his pipe, and wished them well.

The noisy forested world of crying whiskey jacks and screeching squirrels went on until they saw smoke from another cabin. Here a greyed and bewhiskered white man lived with a young Indian woman and baby. When the travellers were invited in, Troy politely declined and he and his pigs pressed onward.

"Guess we're moving too slow for him," John said.

"I'm Jim," the trapper said. "Please meet my wife, Fanny, and our six-month old baby, Nora," he said.

The Cree woman served bannock and tea and couldn't miss the guests admiring her papoose strapped to her back.

She spoke shyly in English, "It's a *Tikinagan* moss bag and cradleboard."

Lasse smiled, "I've never seen one."

Truly, the baby seemed contented in the hide-laced contraption. The mother undid the strap across her chest and propped baby and board against the wall for closer inspection.

An intricately beaded floral design graced the front along with tiny bone trinkets that hung from the frame as playthings.

"Did you make it yourself?" Lovisa asked with Hilda interpreting.

"My parents made it according to our culture's tradition. My father prepared the frame, hoop, and footrest from tamarack."

"What's the hoop about?" Mikaila wondered.

"To protect in case the backboard falls over and to attach netting against bugs, or a screen from the sun," Jim answered.

The young Cree woman went on, "While singing ancient songs, my mother beaded the deer-hide covering and lined it with rabbit fur and sphagnum moss."

"The contraption leaves her free to do her chores. In summer, she ties it to a tree or in winter to a sled," Jim said.

"Looks like Nora has a wonderful vantage point!" Lasse exclaimed.

Out the back window, the trapper pointed, "See the jumpers?" A small herd of white-tailed deer tasted oats scattered on the ground.

Mikaila and Lovisa were enthralled but Lasse thought, "Poor creatures," thinking of when next the family would need meat.

By Wednesday, 24 June, they had covered over 35 miles from Erwood. At Prairie River under mainly clear skies, there was evidence of sawmills with piles of sawdust, tree stumps, and rutted dirt roads. Scouring the handful of shanties for Hilda's sister's home, a local man finally directed them. The dwelling made Lasse shuddered, because the chilling winds could blow right through it.

When the sister was nowhere to be found, the disappointed group set up camp and could hear the music of a wedding dance in the distance. Men, hopped up on moonshine, brawled outside, fists first. The Swedes kept their distance, but a couple half-drunk partiers wandered over.

"Tough guys from around, tried to make names for themselves, roughing up us locals," one said.

What the men really wanted was sympathy and because the music was so lively, to dance. For the adventurous migrants, it was too good to pass up.

"If you can't beat 'em, you might as well join 'em," John said, and there in the dirt and grass, they whirled and twirled to jigs and reels.

At last, Hilda's sister, Beth, arrived and the two were overjoyed. Dancing was Beth's favourite but despite her husband Ray being hurt long before in a logging accident, he watched the others frolick as a bystander. The music ended in the wee hours to let the haunting night sounds take over.

In the morning, tired and bleary-eyed, the rejuvenated Hilda and Beth said their goodbyes and poor as he was, Ray offered the travellers a cooked ham. Not wishing to offend, they accepted, seeing the man would give the shirt off his back. Again, the wagon rolled, and within several miles, had they blinked, they might have missed the community of Bannock, announced by a simple, hand-painted, weathered sign. At one time, it was said ancient native peoples congregated here to hunt.

After another day's travel, Mistatim was a good place to camp. Towering aspen, spruce, and jack pine surrounded them but looking up, they saw a massive fire lookout tower. A middle-aged man in denim overalls and straw hat, stepped out from within a weathered barn.

He tipped his hat in greeting then looked at the tower, "She's sixty feet tall and a Godsend for wildfires and storms."

The girls begged, "Can we climb up?"

"As long as you hang on tight and don't look down," he warned, "but it's up to your mother!"

Lasse hemmed and hawed for a moment but eventually went too. It was arduous work, and after the first 20 feet, Mikaila, breathing hard, prompted the trio to rest.

"My legs turned to jelly!"

"Look at the view!" Lovisa gushed then continued scrambling up, mindless of her long skirt and pantaloons.

High up, the wind whistled, and pushing open the floor hatch, they climbed through, into the cab. The room was solid windows, and the vast canopy of greens and greys set against a sky-blue horizon was breathtaking.

"There's a mother bear and her cubs!" Lasse pointed to the north. Not far away was a moose cow and calf running with a wolf not far behind. On the ground, they hadn't seen much wildlife but knew the animals were around and staying concealed. The most alarming sight was a muskeg with smoke in their path, to the west.

After clamouring down, they overheard the man telling John, "You'll have to veer south around by Bjork Lake to skirt the muskeg. It's about 15 miles out of your way but then you angle back northwest to Crooked River."

"You're kidding!" John was indignant. "We've only just come 50 miles and by the time we're done, the detour will be another 25 or 30."

"If it were winter, you could cross on the ice, but not now."

"We saw smoke when we were in the tower," Lasse worried.

"The smoke is from ground fires smouldering in the peat moss. Nothing to worry about unless the wind really picks up."

He went on, "Every Tom, Dick, and Harry has tried to figure a way to cross the muskeg in the summer. Even surveyors tried building corduroy roads but were stumped. If they can't do it, neither should you. And legend says its bottomless."

"Why do they say that?" John and company looked dumbfounded.

"Because whole herds of cattle and broods of pigs have strayed onto it during wildfires, never to be seen again."

With that chilling news, the Swedes spent an unsettled night. In the morning, they followed the man's directives to the letter. The trail kept them out of the muskeg but in Lasse's imagination, it was like a giant cauldron, bubbling, boiling, and threatening to their right. With the stagnant water layered with stunted and dead jack pines laying askew, the ambiance unsettled not only the females, but John, the driver. Even the horses seemed skittish.

John said, "I wish I'd climbed the tower to get a better lay of the land, but I'm scared of heights."

For the girls, they didn't have the heart to tell him the tower view made it worse.

"I'm waiting for a headless horseman to gallop out, surrounded by snapping wolves," Lovisa mused.

"I'm praying for no troubles with the wagon or horses this day," her mother looked skyward.

With nothing untoward happening, they camped beside Bjork Lake that night. In the early morning, it was delightful to see a cow moose and calf eating tender leaves off the aspen trees close by. However, something beyond the human senses alerted the cow. Her ears flicked forward and her head swung around, then she and the calf bolted. A predator was close.

It was Saturday, 27 June 1903, and the troupe hurriedly packed up, resigned to another detour day. The ground turned sandy and was difficult to navigate until the skies clouded over and it rained. Strangely enough, that helped. Indeed, the day went by without issue. The next day, they found that Crooked River as a hub community was a busy place. Here, they caught sight of Troy hitching a ride on another wagon. He had made good time.

The old male storekeeper joked, "Good thing you didn't go around by Yorkton."

"Why?" John asked.

"An eye-opening event, Doukhobors were protesting in the nude!"

When John interpreted, Lasse's jaw dropped and Hilda rolled her eyes.

The young girls, listening carefully, doubled over trying not to laugh.

"What's a Doukhobor?" Lovisa gasped.

"Russian dissenters come to Canada."

"What on earth provoked that behaviour?" John asked.

"They don't believe in government regulations. Some were jailed as vagrants, and others went to asylums."

"That sounds severe," John said. "It's not like they killed anybody!"

"It must have been bad for them to go to those extremes!" Lasse wondered if this was a bad omen. Would this be how they, as immigrants, could expect to be treated in the future?

The group bought flour and coffee then made their way the half day to Eldersley. To Lasse, it was freeing to finally be out of the heavy forest but after this were more creeks to navigate and they took turns leading the horses through. At the Doghide Creek settlement, they made camp, impressed with the surrounding aspen parkland and fields of grain. Before leaving on Monday, June 29, they became aware of how up-and-coming Doghide was, already producing honey and processing flour.

At the top of a hill where the sign said, 'Star City', they camped for the last time. In the late afternoon, of Tuesday, 30 June 1903, finally they could see Melfort, and summer was in full bloom.

"So, this is the heart of the Carrot River Valley!" Lasse exclaimed, "and the rich soil we've heard so much about."

The village of Melfort was becoming well established with construction evident everywhere. In fact, the sound of hammering met them. It wasn't hard to see the new businesses furiously preparing for the new settlers and what the harvest and promised train would bring.

The troupe saw two unfinished hotels, one where Lasse would work, called 'The Hotel'. Then they zeroed in on a rooming house a block and half down Burrows Avenue.

Their excitement deflated when the attendant said, "Sorry, we're full for another week with construction workers."

Hilda offered, "You're welcome to continue on and stay with us."

"You are kind but we can't," Lasse replied, knowing Brockington was 20 miles north and too far for her to try to work every day.

Leaving the little family alone without confirmed accommodations was obviously unsettling for the older couple. They hemmed and hawed at the public well, filling their water containers as slowly as possible.

"We'll be OK," Lasse reassured. After much coaxing, there was no choice but for the seniors to press on in the daylight.

When the wagon rumbled off Lasse heard Hilda say to John, "Those three could be at the mercy of all the construction workers in town! I don't like it one bit."

But he was anxious to get going and rationalised, "Lasse made it all the way from Sweden and she's nobody's fool. They'll be fine."

Lasse loved that man but she and her daughters sat on their trunks almost pouting. Though tired, the bustling atmosphere, filled them with anticipation. They'd seen a Chinese laundry two doors west on Saskatchewan Avenue called 'Hing Ching'. At least, they could wash their clothes. Further down was a blacksmith, a livery/veterinarian, and a barber. His window sign read, 'Shavings—Wednesdays and Saturdays'. It was then they saw Troy wandering by and felt consoled to see one familiar face.

"I'm heading to the land office for my homestead," he said with a smile from ear to ear.

Browsing around they saw on the north side of Burrows, a flour and feed store across from another hotel under construction called 'Humboldt House'. On the west side of Main was a harness shop. The 'Bank of Hamilton' sign said, 'Open in August'. There were a whole host of other businesses, including a furniture/undertaking shop.

"It's got almost everything as far as I can tell," uttered Mikaila.

"Except a church!" answered Lovisa.

Looking around, Lasse said, "I think you're right!"

It wasn't even 20 minutes and Lovisa reminded, "Remember the Traveller's Aid warning posters at Pier 2? This is why."

Lasse wondered how Greta and Kirsten had been so brave. "Well, they weren't responsible for two daughters," she consoled herself.

Within moments, a middle-aged man in a brown suit and derby hat approached them. They listened to his inquiry without understanding his English. To him, their exhausted looks, broken English, and travel garb must have been a dead giveaway. Soon, he returned with a portly and bespectacled gentleman dressed in business attire. The man had a ruddy face with a bushy moustache and salt and pepper-coloured hair.

Introducing himself in Danish, they could understand, "Pleased to meet you, I'm Harry, the hotelier, and this is Sammy, who owns the shoe store," he laughed. "Welcome to our humble oasis!"

When Lasse discovered this was her new boss, it seemed all their problems evaporated.

Harry insisted, "Until rooms become available, there is to be no argument because you three will be guests of my wife and I in our home."

Lasse could have kissed him and had to restrain both girls otherwise they might have. Ida, his wife, was Danish too.

"You're just in time," Ida said. "Tomorrow, Melfort is officially being incorporated as a village!"

"And we were witnesses to the rail line being built outside Erwood, so the train is definitely on its way!" Lasse said.

Tongue-in-cheek, Harry brooded, "And one of our two competition hotels is also opening July 1."

17

Getting Established and Falling into Place

Melfort—*June 1903–October 1904*

The week spent at Harry and Ida's gave Lasse an introduction to hotel planning. In fact, they walked over to the new structure for a quick review.

"There's a lot left to do for a January opening," Harry said, "we hired an architect, especially for the grand entrance and brick exterior."

"You built 'The Hotel' name right into the brick!" Mikaila exclaimed and Harry beamed.

Lovisa added, "And I love the Union Jack flying on the flagpole! We learned about it at school in Sweden."

Harry said, "We hope, built close to the train station, the architecture itself will attract people. We're committing to a five-star reputation."

"Aren't there a lot of hotels downtown though?" Mikaila asked bluntly.

Harry smiled patiently, "With all the travellers and single men, hotels ensure no one is lonely."

"There does seem to be a few bachelors!" Lasse agreed.

"Not just men," Ida interjected, "a hotel is a centre for anyone to relax, spend the night, and be fed and watered. Men can find the bar and with our reading and parlour rooms, women and children don't have to sit alone in their rooms."

The new hotel was redolent and balmy with fresh paint. "The outside walls are plaster, insulated with horsehair and wood shavings. We used a good lead paint that dries fast."

Ida pointed to one side of the entrance hall, "The barber shop, newspaper and cigar stands will go here. Plus, with no hospital, our beds are open to patients, in case of disaster."

Harry led them into the kitchen, "Not only that, but we're Americans. There, the trend is to get the ordinary Joe to step out of his comfort zone and learn to love immigrant food."

"Plain old Puritan meat and potatoes are too hum drum in this day and age," Ida added.

"Would Swedish and Italian dishes help the Canadian palate?" Lasse joked.

"You bet! Think of all that delectable food becoming a sensation!" Ida clapped. The more they talked, the more the momentum built, and Lasse was ready to get to work.

Despite the hoteliers' gracious hospitality, the first week of July, rooms opened at the rooming house and Lasse and the girls moved. About the same time, word came that because the quality of seafarers and food at sea was deteriorating, cooks would take over the purchasing of provisions from the captain.

"Otto will be in seventh heaven!" Lasse thought.

With their mother consumed by hotel work, a new self-confidence emerged in the daughters. The maturing Mikaila and Lovisa started a light housecleaning job with an elderly Norwegian couple, the Johnsons. With similar languages, and reminding them of Ebba and Isak, the easy-going elders helped with English and burning questions.

One evening at the rooming house, even though Mikaila's sat in plain view, Lovisa tried to kick her mud-stained shoes behind the door.

Mikaila cautioned, "We must remember, even though it's easier to speak to Scandinavians we do have to practice speaking English whenever we can."

"You're right," Lasse replied half-heartedly.

Regardless, Lovisa launched into Swedish, a little leery of getting into trouble about her shoes, "The streets are mud holes with the rain, and boards are strewn all over the place for sidewalks."

"I know," Lasse said, "are you taking a wide berth around the building construction sites?"

"Yes."

"What about school?" Lasse asked, "Harry says until a new school gets built, it's held at the back room of the town hall. Apparently, students are off on holidays now but go back shortly, until December. Usually, they close for the frigid months because it's too hard to heat the one-room schools."

"I could end my schooling now but I want to learn better English, even for one more year," Mikaila stated.

"How be if tomorrow, we go and sign you both up?" Lasse suggested.

The girls were ecstatic and hugged her hard.

The next mild summer afternoon, Harry produced fishing rods and tackle and the two girls made their way to the local fishing hole. It reminded Lasse of their life in Sweden. Upon their return, they couldn't stop talking about their new friends.

Mikaila was all smiles. "A couple of boys, Henry and Luke, showed us a jack hole and the best places to catch pickerel!"

"They shared their worms and showed us a secret path running beside the creek," Lovisa was impressed. "We had to use tree branches to swing over the water in places!"

Lasse imagined her tomboy daughters matching the boys' every move.

"We didn't catch anything but afterwards, they let us try their bicycles!"

Now their lives were all about bicycles.

All along, Lasse wanted to reward the girl somehow for moving to Canada but the new shoes they needed didn't exactly fit the bill. Instead, Harry produced two used bikes from his stash and the girls nearly bowled him over with gratitude.

"Now you can practise to your heart's content but don't let your skirts get caught in the chain!"

It was true. They were air-borne and free as birds. By mid-July when school reopened, they proudly showed off their practical mother's gift of new lace-up boots. With baskets overflowing with books, sweaters, and lunch pails, they pumped the few blocks back and forth to school.

The hoteliers continued to ready the hotel, awaiting the long-anticipated train and its platform teeming with travellers.

Harry confirmed, "The framing, shelving and cupboards are done, and the ice door is in place. No more running outside to the icehouse!"

Weekly, big appliances and furniture arrived by freight swing. In the meantime, Lasse developed menus with grocery lists that even Harry could shop from. After school, the girls picked up whatever equipment they could from the general store.

Ida sat at her treadle sewing machine saying, "That's the last uniform and with the kitchen pump and cast-iron sink, we are state of the art."

"The food staples are sto cked but fresh items we'll buy from local farmers," Harry mused.

"That's the key, simple and robust ingredients," Lasse agreed.

Harry's mahogany bar had a rapidly expanding liquor collection with everything from fermented liquors to hard whiskeys, and liqueurs. The cold storage room was stacked high with boxes, barrels, and kegs. Besides the kitchen and bar, a modest housekeeping department of chamber maids and housekeepers assisted Ida to bring her prairie colonial theme to life.

Porcelain bathroom fixtures and ornate furniture brought a stylish flair and a local wood carver did brilliant work.

"The bear statue is my favourite," Lasse said, admiring the owls and foxes.

By October, the hotel's construction neared completion. Harry hired local men plus the two young anglers, Henry and Luke. They worked hard to carry, position, and set up appliances and furniture. To stay competitive, when traffic appeared at the pub doors, the hoteliers opened the bar early with a limited menu. The demand was exciting but complicated their timeline. That was how Lasse met Knut, a local homesteader and fellow Scandinavian.

Melfort—*October 1903–February 1904*

Knut stopped at The Hotel's beer parlour in Melfort to get a meal before heading home. It was a sunny noon hour in early October 1903, and inside the pub was ornate, with a brand-new essence. With no women allowed, the serving staff were men. He sat at the mahogany bar, drank his coffee, then hungrily, started in on a plate of bacon and eggs. Tying up loose ends between harvest and bush work had him in town early running errands.

The cook poked her head out the kitchen's swinging doors and in broken English, asked, "Is it any goot?"

He smiled and nodded approvingly, "Ja, it's goot!"

Both recognised a fellow Scandinavian.

She spoke first in Swedish, "I'm Lasse."

His heart skipped a beat but he came back in Norwegian, "I'm Knut."

For him, the pretty face and unruly auburn hair escaping her chef's hat, caught him off guard and he tried not to stare.

He didn't see her again before leaving but thought, "I have to come to town a little oftener." On his next trip, he found himself back at the pub listening to Harry curse, "Damned potato beetles!"

Knut offered, "Do you need potatoes? I had a good haul."

"Really? Yes!"

"I could spare about four bags and will still have enough for winter at the sawmill."

"You're a lifesaver! How much would you charge me?"

"Is a meal now and then too much to ask?"

"It's a deal!"

The next visit, Knut, with a gunny sack of potatoes slung over his back, made a beeline for The Hotel's backdoor.

"Surely," he rationalised, "having another Scandinavian to talk to is doing her a favour." The truth was he couldn't get Lasse off his mind.

When he lugged the fourth gunnysack through the kitchen, and downstairs to the potato bin, she called out a thank you. He stood for a moment, but she had her hands in dough and kept working and he felt in the way, "Feels like winter's c-c-coming," he stuttered.

When she didn't answer immediately, he said, "Well, I'd better not keep you from your work."

Not that he had a lot of experience with women but he knew hanging around uninvited wouldn't win him any favours, and why was his mouth not working?

She turned around, wiping her hands off, and smiled, "You know, Harry and Ida do their best but having another Scandinavian like you to talk to is wonderful."

"Ja?" he felt relieved, "I usually talk Norwegian with my friend, Halvor but he's preoccupied with his new wife."

After the potato delivery, Harry told Knut, "Lasse's looking a little starry-eyed these days."

"Really?"

"The mere mention of you gives her quite a rosy blush."

Harry clapped Knut on the back. "She's even asked me what I think about you, and I said, 'That son-of-a-gun? I'll vouch for him any day of the week!'"

"I'll be damned!" Knut sputtered and his mind filled with unmentionable fantasies that he hoped were not apparent to the naked eye.

In fact, after a while, seeing Lasse made him feel worse because all he wanted was more. To complicate matters, were the men in town, working on temporary construction crews and train gangs. All women were fair game it seemed, and she was no exception. Overhearing wolf whistles and comments like, 'Nice redhead', made him fume In fact, one day, after meeting her on the street and tipping his hat, Knut watched her enter the post office for a tête à tête with a railroader. With steam blowing from his ears, he felt embarrassed, hoping no one noticed.

"You jealous idiot!" he scolded himself in the mirror at home, "those sapphire eyes have gotten under your skin!"

Disturbed by the truth, it became clear he'd better act soon, before someone else did. Had he gotten closer in the post office, he wouldn't have missed her body language telling the railroader to leave her alone.

It took a lot of savage courage but at the first opportunity, he posed the question, "This Sunday after church at the Johnson's, would you like to see the countryside in my buggy?"

"I would love to."

"Oh my God!" he wasn't expecting it to be so easy but then she blurted, "I'm not sure if you know but I was married once before, and have two daughters and a son?"

This surprised him, but contrary to being a deal-breaker, like a young ram, he looked forward to her experience with great anticipation.

When he showed up at the rooming house, the daughters politely stifled giggles. What did the eldest girl mean when she scolded her sister with, "Don't let Mother hear you say that!"

His questioning look had the landlady, Marj, whispering, "It's because their mother's about to date a younger man."

Knut laughed. First, how did they know how old he was? Second, were they talking about him? And third, where was their brother?

He shrugged it off and dove in, "Do you want to join your mother and I for a buggy ride?"

"No thanks!" the girls blurted, looking embarrassed, "we're bike riding this afternoon but thank you."

Being usurped by two teenagers wasn't bad, he decided, once he and Lasse were seated in the buggy. Topsy trotted off when he clicked his tongue and flicked the reins.

They rode in silence taking in the flaming autumn colours until Lasse spoke, "The fresh air! It's exactly what I needed! I wish I could paint these golds and rusts and put them into a prairie scene!"

"Do you paint?"

"Dabble."

"It's a beautiful fall but in summer," Knut said, "the countryside is filled with a kaleidoscope of lazy susans, purple thistles, and orange prairie lilies."

"We saw the incredible beauty on our journey here."

On the flat stretches, Topsy trotted, but for the hills and shallow creeks, Knut slowed her to a walk. The creek beds were shallow enough to see clear sediment and pebbles beneath the flowing water. Still, Lasse reached for his arm a time or two when the buggy shook, and that was an encouraging sign. While a hawk flew overhead, and cool breezes chilled the air, he fantasised that her actions were deliberate.

"Oh!" she exclaimed, watching the small birds flit in and out of the trees, "There's still sparrows and chickadees!"

"They stay all winter."

"The snow geese are plentiful too," she pointed to the mass of white birds eating grain in a harvested field.

"Yes," he shivered, "but doesn't that breeze feel like winter?"

"Makes me think of Sweden."

"I wish I could see those old countries. I've never been."

She joked, "Maybe, one day I'll take you!"

The trip took just over half an hour and Lasse looked relaxed. When they drove into his homestead, Lady bounded up and Lasse gave the dog a good rub behind the ears.

"She likes you," Knut said, happy his best friend wasn't jealous. He unharnessed the horses and they took a stroll around the yard, then east.

He pointed, "In the spring, there's an awesome flood for a migratory bird's paradise!"

"I can picture it!" she said looking at what seemed like any other harvested hay meadow. A chilling, north wind whipped, and he wanted to whisk her inside but hesitated, awaiting her lead.

She ventured, "Maybe we should go inside?"

As he reached around her to open the log cabin's door, her scent washed over him and his mind's eye saw the genesis of their life together. Instead, he said, "The place is rustic spruce and poplar logs but has all the basics."

"Seems homey," she complimented, looking around.

It was then he realised it was more than her looks that attracted him. Her voice and words felt like home. The handsome woman, a little shorter than him, stood back as he crouched down to strike a match and light the wood stove.

"Please have a seat and let me brew some coffee," he said.

The place filled with warmth and an incredible aroma as they sat across from each other nibbling cookies from her basket.

They had so much to learn, comparing notes of trials and tribulations coming to Saskatchewan. She shared the story of her first husband, and how she and the girls had come to Canada on a cattle ship.

With a catch in her voice she added, "Leaving my eldest son and parents behind was awful."

"I wondered about your son. That would be hard," he empathised.

"But I can't dwell on it."

"I've heard of people who cut off all ties with the old country because they can't stand the pain of never seeing their loved ones again."

"Oh, I have every intention of seeing mine!"

The two sat in silence for a moment, then he spoke with a sense of pride about his long walk into Canada. His voice quivered too, speaking of his family, the farm, and sawmills.

"Avoiding the militia was the worst for me," he admitted, "but they were on the verge of legislating overseas fighting and it's hard to go up against the war machine."

"I'm a pacifist too," she seemed delighted with his stories. "What you've been through is amazing!"

"You too but look at how worldly we've become," he laughed, then smiled sheepishly, admiring her beauty and reserve.

He sensed a spark between them and poured another cup of coffee.

"How can I tell you're Scandinavian?" she wisecracked, "this is the best coffee I've drank since coming to town!"

Praying the flicker in her eyes meant she was falling, just like him, he reached across to take her hands. To interrupt the blissful moment would be sacrosanct but Lady barked before a knock sounded at the door.

"Impeccable timing," Knut thought.

There stood Halvor. Once he stepped aside, his new wife appeared, holding a baby in her arms. She and Lasse screamed and ran to each other, hugging and laughing.

"Here's the woman who taught me everything I know," Greta made Lasse blush.

When they explained themselves, it was cause for celebration and Knut poured drinks of his finest attempt at last year's chokecherry wine.

"Would you like to hold baby Lizzie?" Greta asked.

"Oh, yes, please," Lasse relished the warmth of the tiny body against her own.

Knut could tell from Halvor's beaming face how proud his friend was of both his wife and baby. Knut was equally proud of Halvor, and whispered, "You figured out the woman thing after all!" and they both winked.

The visit came alive with stories from their travels and Greta and Lasse talked of antics at sea, squealing pigs, and bawling cattle. The men couldn't have been more entertained.

Greta brought news of their other friend, "Kirsten's match was not made in Heaven."

At that point, the baby fussed, and the new mother draped a shawl over her shoulder, to let the baby nurse.

"The brute got drunk and gave her bruises. The last time we spoke, Kirsten was making for Winnipeg with a broken wrist."

"Poor Kirsten! I hope she's okay!" Lasse sympathised. "How did she get to the train?"

"She caught a ride to Prince Albert with friends of yours, John and Hilda."

"Well bless their hearts!" Lasse lightened the moment with, "I hope the union didn't breakdown because of her snoring!"

They both snickered but Knut could tell they were sorry for Kirsten's hardships.

"I wonder if everyone named Anders is a brute?" The females snickered but it went right over the men's heads.

Freeze-up and bush work was coming too fast so Lasse and Knut's courting took off in a big way. One afternoon, he and Halvor leaned against the pole fence looking at the livestock.

Halvor shared some gossip, "Lasse told Greta what she thinks of you," and his voice turned singsong, "your even temper, your humour, and how easy you are to be with."

Knut lowered his head and got red at the teasing.

"Seriously," Halvor sobered, "she's happy you accept her daughters."

"We're a good match. I'm adding on to my house. Don't you think the girls will need a bedroom of their own?"

"Absolutely! I'll help! Have you asked her yet?" Halvor grinned.

"I'm working up to it."

On subsequent visits, the girls and their mother seemed to fall in love with the farm, the dog, and even him. He decided it must be love if they didn't mind swinging a hammer.

For Knut and Lasse, they couldn't get enough of each other. On Halloween night, they sat in the rooming house's vestibule, handing out popcorn balls and candied apples to ghosts and goblins.

Mikaila and Lovisa went trick or treating as pirates and when they returned, Knut promised, "We'll see each other again right at the end of January because I plan to come home early this year."

"How come?" Lasse asked nonchalantly, watching a pair of miniature witches walk away.

"Because I want to marry you," he caught his breath, going down on one knee.

In front of everyone, he pled his case, "Will you marry me, please?" he begged, "I love you and don't think I can live without you."

The girls looked dumbstruck but no more so than their mother.

Lasse didn't hesitate to accept with, "Yes. Yes. I love you too." Their embrace said everything, while all around cheers and laughter prevailed.

After dark at 7:00 p.m., the trick or treaters dwindled and the girls rooted through their pillowcases filled with candy. They shared their loot with Lasse and Knut who also enjoyed the popcorn balls, candied apples, chewing gum, and chocolate bars. Once the girls ate their fill and said good night, the couple sat together in the entryway and talked.

"How lucky was I to meet you," she said, "me being four years older."

"Just like my mother," he chuckled, putting his arm around her.

"And I come as a package deal with children," she reminded, snuggling closer.

"Just like my mother," he repeated. "The best part is you're not my mother and you can probably bake a better apple pie."

He was in a joking mood but bowled over by his good fortune and she seemed just as enamoured. "My parents thought I might catch a foreign disease from the likes of you!" he teased, and she punched him in the arm.

"My children spent years, pining for their own father, you know?" she said.

"I'll do my best," he pledged, "but I know I can never replace him."

The girls couldn't miss the couple's growing affection but seemed pleased. Being fall, he couldn't be romantic with fresh flowers so built a wreath from wire, stuffed it with moss then intertwined stalks of wheat, oats, bull rushes, and straw flowers.

"It's lovely and I can't wait to hang it on our front door," she gushed.

"After the rail line gets here, let's take a train trip to Iowa," he dreamt.

"I need horses and equipment and you and the girls can meet my family. What do you think? We could call it a honeymoon?"

She threw her arms around his neck. "Wonderful! That gives Harry and Ida time to find a substitute cook."

He kissed her soundly and groaned running his hands up the sides of her body, "I can hardly wait for you to move in with me at the farm."

"You have no idea how eager I am," she kissed him back as tenderly as possible.

He knew better than to push the subject but she would be so much more comfortable with him.

"Don't get me wrong, the rooming house is great," she said, "but it was never meant for long term."

On the ride home, he thought of the long letter he'd started to his family and had to reread it when he walked in the door. There were a few more things to add.

Dear family,

I can hardly believe it's my second year here! Now I'm adding on to the house and have a barn, and good shelters for the livestock. I dug a well but the water is only fit for animals. A rain barrel or melting snow and ice is for drinking. My cooling system is an icehouse filled with ice squares from the creek and packed with sawdust. I hang the milk and cream in buckets down the well, and you'll be happy to know I even churn butter! The system's not perfect and comes with occasional bouts of the backdoor trots. Please don't blame my bachelor cooking! I admit it, Eli and Jens, the outhouse did come first!

I've built a pumphouse over the well in the barnyard and the water trough sits up against it but needs filling twice a day, the animals drink so much. Luckily, Halvor, takes my livestock when I'm gone to the bush, and it's him worrying about colic in horses and chopping holes through the ice every chore time. Thank you for sending the sawmill unit. It was unwieldly but the freight swing did an admirable job of getting it across country to Crooked River.

In summer, it seems, the harder you sweat, the more the insects bite but I keep a smudge going. Thankfully, I turn the animals out to pasture often but the pitchfork and stone boat work fine for manure. Wish I had your conveyor and windmill. I save slops for the pigs and chickens and I've tried not to get attached because most will face the butcher's block. I had a runt piglet, smart as a dog, who followed me around the yard, like a goose. Weakling chickens would die a painful death if I left them to their hen-pecking sisters. I do my best to keep their backsides salved.

At home, he finished it,

Halloween, 1903

Harvest is over, I have done the butchering, and taken my livestock to Halvor's. I have met a beautiful Swedish woman named Lasse. She and her two teenaged daughters, Mikaila and Lovisa, came from Sweden about a year and a half ago. She left behind one grown son, Bjorn and his new wife, Ava. Lasse is a cook at The Hotel, and for the time being, lives at the rooming house. I asked her to marry me, and the wedding is in February. You will love her and be prepared; I plan to bring them all to meet you after the rail line gets here. One other thing, I want to buy a couple more teams of horses when I'm in Iowa. Would you look around for me? I hope this finds you all well.

Love, Knut.

The first week of November 1903, after some good heavy frosts, he was set to leave for the bush. He hated to say goodbye to the love of his life but made it a long, drawn-out one. Along with the dog and horses, Knut headed to Crooked River for his second winter of bush work. Waiting on tenterhooks, the crew convinced themselves they felt the vibrations of the hammered spikes coming west. The sawmill, near Murphy's Siding at Mile 63 near Eldersley, was beside the tracks, and meant his lumber would get to a bigger market.

All the same crew arrived except for Sully's one daughter, Minnie who now toted Danny's baby. At first, Sully was furious but once the baby came, he couldn't have loved it more. Day after day, the axes and saws sang, and the horses resumed working like mules, hauling the massive logs. With sleighs loaded high, it was amazing the tonnage the horses pulled. The crew were more than proud to supply the dimensional lumber for local buildings.

After 17 December 1903, the rugged bush workers learned ground-breaking news. A newspaper article told, "Two brothers, Orville and Wilbur Wright have flown a biplane through the air for 12 seconds and gone a distance of 120 feet. These amazing pioneers are from Kitty Hawk, North Carolina."

For a moment, the loggers were no longer isolated in a tall stand of virgin timber but like the rest of the world, daydreamed of flying through the air. Come Saturday night, they celebrated and unlike other times, there were no fist fights.

In the meantime, Knut received a letter from Lasse.

My darling Knut,

School is closed for the winter now, and being 14 and 15, the girls are getting too old to keep going. For the time being, they will help me at the hotel and continue doing their maid duties for the Johnsons.

The grand opening of The Hotel was a success. Come New Years Eve, Harry introduced the crowd with, "Our chef has prepared a feast fit for King Edward VII should he deign to attend!"

It seemed, despite the wintry cold, the entire community turned out and women were granted a one-time exemption to enter the bar. Ida pre-booked all the sleeping rooms and Harry's selection of alcoholic beverages was worth coveting. When the mayor cut the ribbon, people clapped and cheered. Melfort's newest hotel was brought to life with sufficient pomp and circumstance!

Keeping his word, Knut came home early from the bush. The trip by horse and sleigh took two full days and in the frigid cold, he avoided working the animals into a lather. He overnighted at Doghide Creek, making use of their livery. By day's end, the horses were exhausted, having ploughed snow all day, and he took great pains in their care. Inside the barn once home, he dried and curried them and placed more than the usual amount of dry straw bedding in their stalls.

"You might be thick and shaggy but you're soaked with sweat!" They needed time to cool down or could easily get sick.

"It's late. Tomorrow, you'll go to the open-air shed but if you start to shiver, you'll go right back into the barn."

Three days later, with no sick horses, came the afternoon of the wedding's eve. Halvor, Greta, and Lizzie arrived, toting a large box tied with purple ribbons and bows. Knut had retrieved Lasse and the girls from town.

"We hope you'll enjoy our wedding gift!" Halvor said.

The bridal couple unwrapped an elegant wash basin and pitcher; white with pink roses, set on a dark wooden stand.

"It's breathtaking!" Lasse gushed. "You are too generous!"

Knut agreed, "Thank you very much! What great friends!"

After the company left, Mikaila now 16, and Lovisa, 15, presented their gift, a set of cream-coloured cushions upon which they had embroidered colourful flowers.

"We love them!" Knut said gratefully.

Lasse adored Knut's gift to her of a crystal rhinestone necklace and earring set. To his delight, she gave him bubble glass cufflinks housing coloured photos of steam engines.

At the couple's marriage on 4 February 1904, the bride was radiant in a sea foam brocade suit and short, hand sewn veil. Knut, spit and polished, wore a dark navy suit and white shirt with his new cufflinks. Attendants, Mikaila and Lovisa, wore matching pale-yellow dresses as did maid of honour, Greta.

Halvor, the best man, held a squirming nine-month-old, Lizzie throughout while Harry gave Lasse away and he and Ida signed as witnesses.

When the organist pumped life into Wagner's *Here Comes the Bride*, arm in arm, Lasse and Harry walked down the manse's aisle towards Knut, followed by the attendants. Knut had a haunted but dreamy look, like he hungered to open the door to an unknown world.

When the pastor blessed the plain gold bands and said, "I now pronounce you man and wife," Knut kissed his bride and felt all remnants of uncertainty lift.

The organ bellowed again for Mendelssohn's *The Wedding March* and the guests clapped wildly as the newlyweds floated down the makeshift aisle.

An intimate reception followed at The Hotel's dining hall where Harry and Ida hired an alternate chef, Li Fong, for the occasion. The laundromat owner and his trusted friend. Li Ping, from Knut's camp, assisted. They felt mutually honoured to share their traditional cuisine.

When Harry gave the signal, the pastor asked the guests to bow their heads. Before they said, "Amen", the aroma of an unusual blend of spice and sauce wafted in. When the 12 dishes were presented on carts tableside, a pianist played quietly in the background. The guests were to point to what they wanted and Li Fong called it 'dim sum'.

"We start with egg roll and wonton soup," he said.

Next were chicken dishes with rice and sesame seeds, and chow mien noodles with sweet and sour sauce. More unusual was chop suey vegetables with bok choy, beef and broccoli, ginger beef, and deep-fried shrimp.

The guests thrilled to the savoury exotic faire and once sated, the servers provided tea in oriental tea pots with miniature teacups, along with fortune cookies.

Lasse snapped her cookie open and found a tiny scroll with inscription that read, "Look how far you've come."

Knut's was, "Success in life creates happiness."

The cake was rum carrot, decorated with cream cheese icing courtesy of Marj, the rooming house landlady. Orange Grand Marnier liqueurs over slivers of ice with orange wedges complemented the dessert. Knut and Lasse stood up and thanked the chefs for the outstanding meal and everyone clapped. Then they turned to their guests and gave thanks. The crystal wine glasses, filled with sparkling wine, shimmered in the chandelier light, and the toasting and clinking began.

"To the bride and groom!" Harry touted.

Greta followed with, "To the bride! Our dear friend, Lasse. May she always be as happy as she is today."

Halvor came after. "To the groom, Knut! Always a man of his word and one of the most genuine friends to have. Congratulations and success to the both of you."

Every so often, Mikaila and Lovisa took their butter knives and clanged on the crystal goblets, until others joined in. The bride and groom would then make a big show of kissing and the group would cheer.

Harry had words too, "I want to tell you how Ida and I met the bride and groom and what they mean to us but that would be a long story. It's safe to say that Ida and I are providing them an all-expense paid wedding night in the Presidential Suite!" He handed the room's skeleton key over but Knut and Lasse were speechless.

"Thank you!" they stammered. "We had reserved a room but not the finest suite in the hotel!"

The pianist and fiddler played the bridal couple's first dance, *The Wedding Dance Waltz* while the invitees gathered round waiting to join in for subsequent rhapsodies and reels. When the grandfather clock chimed midnight, Li Fong served a semblance of the evening meal, this time with coffee and Mrs. Johnson's oatmeal raisin cookies.

By 2:00 a.m., the celebration ended and Halvor and Greta offered to drop Mikaila, Lovisa, and Marj, at the rooming house.

"Thank you," Knut said, "we were going to walk them, even though it's not far."

Amid well wishes and good nights, the couple proceeded upstairs. Lasse waited for Knut to sweep her into his arms and carry her across the threshold which he did but it was no small feat. Their jaws dropped at the room's splendour.

"The marble and crystal is blinding!"

"But the king-sized bed beckons," Knut teased, awed by the forested wall tapestry.

Kicking off their shoes, they stepped onto the broadloom then ran their fingers across the intricate footboard mouldings. He came up from behind and pulled her to him into the reflection of the massive mirror atop the stone fireplace.

"What a handsome couple we make!" he complimented.

Between smouldering kisses and carefully stripping each other of clothing, the stunning library wall wasn't hard to ignore but when drawn to the luxurious dressing room and bath, they marvelled at the claw foot tub.

"With so much to accomplish in one night, how can we fit it all in?" he laughed.

"We have a whole lifetime ahead of us, my darling," she mewed alluringly.

Without a hint of shyness, she reached for him, taking the pent-up lead, to instigate a night filled with blissful passion. Her slow but much-anticipated seduction was tempered with tenderness, and left them both stunned, satisfied, and tingling. Lovemaking, bathing, sipping champagne and nibbling fresh strawberries and chocolates, took hours before they eventually slept in each other's arms. By morning, with bonds christened, they were exhausted but carried a distinct after glow, glassy eyed for a brilliant future.

Knut couldn't stop grinning and after breakfast and draining their coffee cups, the couple found Harry and Ida.

"We can't thank you enough!" they reiterated their appreciation.

"Now we're heading to the livery then picking up the girls on our way home," Knut felt incredibly proud to say.

"Not that we're excited!" Lasse laughed.

At the rooming house, goodbyes were bittersweet. They would miss the daily camaraderie but were happy to leave the cramped conditions. Sleigh travel was cold at -37 degrees but ice crystals meant no wind. Knut was warm in his fur clothes but the females shivered in woollens. Fortunately, the bear hides Smith had provided came in handy and Knut bundled them up. Marj came running outside in only a shawl, with a footwarmer containing a hot brick from the stove, "This will help!" she said and ran back in.

"Thank you!" Lasse called.

"What do you say if we put new winter duds top of the list for all of you on our next trip to Prince Albert?" Knut ventured and they nodded.

At the homestead, by the time he lit the wood stove and the room heated, Lasse's stew warmed nicely on the stove top. She'd also brought fresh buns and with Knut's home-churned butter and cheese, it was a feast. The February days were getting longer but still, lanterns were lit before supper.

"When can we go get Lady and the animals?" Lovisa asked.

"Tomorrow," Knut promised.

"Halvor's a good man, eh?" Mikaila observed and Knut nodded. "He and Greta are the perfect match."

For the Swedish females, having too long hungered for a home, Knut imagined their first night in the country was memorable.

When the girls said, "Good night," and made their way to bed, they were surely enchanted by the sloped roof and wood aroma. Once the candles were out, they would snuggle under their feather tick, listening to the night sounds. The sparkling moon and star-studded sky would shine in amid howling coyotes in the distance.

It wasn't long before Knut heard them whisper, "I forgot how quiet it gets in the country."

"I love this already," but he could hear the underlying mischief in the younger one's voice.

In the master bedroom beside the crackling fire and with coal-oil lanterns extinguished, Knut and Lasse lay in each other's arms. Once again, their fervency ignited and this time with stardust in their eyes, he took the lead. It was fast becoming the second most memorable night of his life.

They slept hard but instinct had him up to rekindle the stove's flame before the last ember died. Tomorrow he would get a load of coal to help make the fire burn longer. After another sweet round of lovemaking that morning, he added more kindling, while she filled the metal dishpan with snow to melt on the stove.

At the appropriate moment, he called to the girls, "It's daylight in the swamp! Time to get up!"

Come May 1904, the up-and-coming community met at a ratepayers' meeting to discuss the condition of the streets, surface drainage, and sidewalks. Total homestead entries were already 88 with 18 applications for patent, 65 cancellations, and 23 abandonments. Businesses agreed to close in the evenings all except mail nights of Wednesdays and Saturdays. Fines of $25.00 were levied for failure to close and the spoils divided amongst the various church congregations. The rail line was expected in August and building the train station was underway. Other buildings left to construct were a public school, three churches, an 80,000-bushel elevator, and a flour and grist mill to produce 100 barrels a day.

The days turned to weeks and Knut and Lasse's promised honeymoon to Iowa came at the end of August once the Canadian Northern Railway established its line. Thinking ahead, he hired a threshing crew to take off his crop.

"My darling," Knut said. "No longer do we have to go slogging across overland trails. This time, we can take the train the entire way."

The four new Canadians were ready to luxuriate in a Pullman sleeper car and to proudly display their Canadian citizenship should it be called for, but that was not a border requirement just yet.

18

Swamp Fever

Melfort and Iowa—*June 1904–May 1917*

It was August 1904 and the constant train vibrations weren't the best for Knut's pregnant wife, Lasse but they had already waited six months to honeymoon. Departing by the Canadian Northern rail line from Melfort, much had changed since his maiden trip in 1902. The first community west now had the name, 'Beatty', in honour of Melfort's first white settler. Like Melfort, the Carrot River Settlement had moved closer to the tracks and renamed itself Kinistino. Besides that, now the South Saskatchewan River was spanned by a new train bridge at Fenton.

At Prince Albert, the Canadian Northern met the Canadian Pacific, bound for the United States border, via Regina, retracing Knut's first steps. Another Mennonite community, Warman, had sprung up, 15 miles north of Saskatoon when a rail line came through from Humboldt. Despite the advancements, the passage gave Knut's household a chance to get to know one another. The novelty of train rides had dimmed, so they focused on cards, tic-tac-toe, and hangman. For Lasse Mikaila, and Lovisa, the sleeping car was luxurious compared to their gruelling memories of sleeping on the seats from Halifax.

Upon reaching the US/Canadian border, they took the Soo Line into North Dakota, then across Minnesota. On the fourth day, they reached Mason City, Iowa, and Knut's brothers. Eli and Jens waited. The farming brothers had travelled across country by horse and covered wagon from Winnebago County. The affectionate reunion had bear hugs all around making the girls giggle. Two days of bumpy travel and one of camping overnight took them the 35 miles back to Knut's childhood home.

His parents, Astrid and Nils, sister, Marion, and half-brother, Wil, waited, plus a whole slew of friends and relations. The welcome was overwhelming and Knut had to tear himself free to make introductions.

Astrid gushed, "You're all so lovely! And with a baby on the way! My heart overflows!"

Nils brewed coffee, "The best in the world," according to Knut.

"Astrid's been baking for weeks!" Nils teased and indeed, the windowsills were lined with pies.

The family congregated, spellbound to hear of Knut's new life in Canada. First came his long walk, the history, and his first encounters with the Indians. Then came Lasse and her girls' fascinating voyage across the ocean, crossing Canada by train, Winnipeg, and the covered wagon leg of the journey.

With whetted appetite, Nils said, "What we wouldn't give to visit you!"

Astrid smiled, "With the train, maybe, one day we can."

Once the crowd dwindled, the family strolled around the farmyard.

"Not much has changed," Knut said, "I'm tickled to see Cisco has a partner," noting a second majestic Clydesdale, this one a female.

At chore time, Knut and the girls pitched in without missing a beat. Astrid and Lasse prepared roast turkey with all the trimmings, with rhubarb pie, and thick cream.

During supper, Marion praised her brother, "Knut, you make us proud! You left home a bachelor and returned a family man!"

At that, Knut put his arm around Lasse and pulled her closer. When Lasse offered to cook supper the next night, Astrid exclaimed, "It's always better if someone else cooks it! I will take the girls on a tour of the orchard."

Upon their return, Astrid confided to her new daughter-in-law, "The girls are so down to earth and we had a good heart-to-heart about the birds and the bees!"

"My stars!" Lasse a little taken aback, patted her hair down, not knowing what else to say.

Come bedtime, she told Knut, "Your mother said the girls are excited for the new baby but a little confused about how that happened."

He laughed, "She would have no compunction to broach that subject! Remember the girls' questioning looks to see Lady and a stray mutt stuck together back home?"

"At least now, they know it isn't the stork!"

One evening on the porch, Knut told Nils about the part he played in getting the Blacks and Swallows incarcerated. Getting another perspective felt good.

Nils's face clouded, "Uffdah! Locked up sounds like the best place for them. Do you suppose they'll be changed men when they get out?"

"I doubt it," Knut stood up and walked to the railing.

"Knut, you're no match for scum of the earth. Watch your back and keep your gun and family close."

"Fighting isn't the answer but protecting my family is."

After two weeks, it was home time and the goodbyes were painful.

Astrid produced a gift, "Unwrap it," she said.

There was his finished portrait taken at the photographer's so long ago. "Thank you!" he said with deep sincerity.

"You're so handsome!" Lasse gushed, "we'll get it framed and hang it in our front room!"

"I kept a copy for us," Astrid said.

Knut bought eight horses from a neighbour to ship home. While Lasse and the girls rode up front in the passenger car, he stayed in the box car to tend the animals. The sweltering July heat was fit for neither man nor beast and drenched in sweat, he sat in the fragrant hay, swatting insects, and hoping for a breeze. The horses instinctively bunched together, switching their tails and shaking their manes, to ward off the horseflies and mosquitoes.

The trip was long but by Regina, a couple of sorrels refused to eat and Knut blamed the heat. Hours later, one had yellowing eye whites and indeed, its lower half seemed extra hot and swollen. Upon closer inspection, other bays did too, and his heart sank. At Saskatoon, when mouths and nostrils swelled and reddened, he knew it was bad.

At Prince Albert, the Canadian Northern authorities allowed the sick horses to switch onto their train. Indeed, to Knut's horror, in the new box car, two horses progressed to lying recumbent and then died. Others seemed to improve for a time but two others laid down and died too. In the end, in a matter of hours and right before his eyes, every one of the eight horses perished, including the black, and the chestnut. Knut was beside himself.

At the next stop, Kinistino, he hailed the porter to notify every rail person with authority about the catastrophe. The verdict was, "You will consult a veterinarian in Melfort for disposal of the bodies and we will send a telegram ahead of your arrival."

"While we seal the freight car, you can clean up in the station's washroom before entering the passenger car," the conductor said.

Upon returning to Lasse, Knut hung his head, distraught, "Every last one of them died."

Sick at heart, Lasse shook her head.

"Those poor creatures!" Lovisa cried.

"There was nothing I could do," Knut lamented. Still feeling dirty, and wondering if he was infectious, he seated himself in a corner, as far away from anyone as possible.

At Melfort, it was time to face the music. The first to arrive on scene was the livery man veterinarian and the medical doctor who did vet work too. His office was above the flour and feed store, one street over. The two donned masks, rubber gloves, and rubber aprons while the train workers opened the sliding box car door. The fetid odour was already starting and swarms of insects met them as they scrutinised the corpses.

"Looks like swamp fever," the vet pronounced as the door was reclosed.

"Definitely," the doctor concurred.

"It's an infectious virus and spreads by blood-sucking insects like horseflies and mosquitoes," they told Knut.

The apprehensive mayor stood at a safe distance, in front of a frightened and growing crowd. Some covered their noses and mouths with hands and hankies.

"The horses were likely already infected when you bought them," the vet said, "the incubation period is from weeks to months."

"They would have had no symptoms, so whoever sold them to you had no idea," the doctor reassured.

"The danger is the high risk of spread," the livery man warned. "The carcasses have to be disposed of immediately, not left to rot or even burned but buried."

The mayor put out his hands in a stop gesture, "The nuisance ground is no option. The disease apparently only very occasionally spreads to humans, is that correct doctor?"

The doctor nodded. Knut felt feverish, and the next he heard was the doctor ordering, "Young man, I need to see you in my office now. We'll let the others load the bodies."

After examination, Knut was given a laxative and directed to the outhouse. Next it was a cup of purgative tea, a purgative, and a bucket to catch his upchucking. After the nasty cleaning out, came a course of intravenous fluid, and a dose of mercury salicylate from a small blue bottle.

The doctor said, "It's a poison for possible bacteria, fungus, or yeast and is to be taken sparingly. Tonight, at bedtime, you can take laudanum. The tincture of opium will help you sleep. Tomorrow, this tonic should help get your appetite back."

"He's infectious, Lasse," the doctor warned, "so if any of you get signs of fever, swelling or jaundice, I want you to contact me immediately."

Knut knew Lasse wouldn't want to risk taking anything when pregnant, and for now, she wanted to go straight home. Regardless, Knut insisted they see the burial through to completion. As a testament to the community, and risking their own exposure, neighbours Jake, Jock, Sean, and Ivar stepped up. The livery man/vet orchestrated transferring the eight animals, at least 1,000 pounds each, using a horse powered jammer. It took over four hours, and once loaded, the wagons made a gruesome processional travelling north out of town. Finished his medical treatment, and not feeling the greatest, Knut and family trailed behind.

"What a spectacle!" Mikaila knit her brows.

At the northern reaches of the farm, and by the light of the moon, with spades and shovels, the men put in a gargantuan effort, hand digging a trench deep enough to bury the remains. Knut helped for a time but feeling worse, laid down on the ground. Lasse mopped his sweaty brow with her handkerchief.

As they finished and turned to leave, Jake and the others came over, "Here, let us help you into the wagon. That was an incredible blow my friend. Make sure you recover soon!"

That night, as Knut lay bundled and shivering on a cot by the stove, he knew Lasse wanted to take him into her arms but deliberately kept away.

She whispered, "It was a sad end to a wonderful trip but at least you got to see your family." He prayed no one else would fall ill.

Fortunately, his case was mild and gradually, he began to feel better. By a stroke of luck, none of the females showed any symptoms whatsoever. Once he felt better, Halvor visited and Knut said, "I don't need those extra horses until sawmill season, so maybe we can take a trip to Alberta for mustangs before I leave for the bush?"

Halvor was interested. "Apparently, mustangs are what people have had to resort to with all the swamp fever."

On a happier note, Lady had visibly gained weight during their absence. When the dog started to fret and couldn't get comfortable, Lovisa said, "She's not acting like herself!"

"She's in labour," Lasse said, and the girls were over the moon.

"We watched the whole birthing process," Mikaila gushed to Greta afterwards, "and we got to meet four healthy puppies!" From Knut and Lasse's perspective, there was no timelier lesson.

That fall, amid chewed shoes and piddles, the household worked around the loveable pups to make the rustic home more baby friendly. The girls made flannelette receiving blankets and diapers, while their mother knitted a christening shawl, and Knut built a wooden cradle. It seemed the whole family was nesting.

Six weeks later, Lasse said, "The puppies are adorable, but they're getting into everything. It's time to find them new homes."

The girls got busy and after a time, Mikaila reported, "We used word of mouth and posters to find places for all but our little Finn."

Lovisa added, "We can't bear to part with him!"

Two days before Thanksgiving, Lasse went into labour herself. Lovisa rode horseback to fetch Greta but the baby boy, Peter, arrived on October 8, 1904, at the hands of Knut and Mikaila. Lasse was now the veteran of four births.

Afterwards, Knut talked a mile a minute, "Things went too far too fast for Greta to help. All I did was catch him, let Mikaila dry him off, then cut and tie the cord."

"Sounds easy, doesn't it?" Lasse laughed, having talked the shaking Knut through it all.

When Dr. Sawyer arrived, he pronounced mother and baby fit as fiddles.

"I wrote in my notes, the patients did fine but the new father could have used some sedation!" Laughter lessened the family's mesmerisation with the physician's black skin close up.

Besides the swamp fever episode, Knut and the doctor had much to talk about. Knut's addition interested the doctor and he said, "Call me Sam. Let's compare notes because I'm going to build a drugstore!"

It didn't take long for the household to discover farming and baby commitments never ended. By daybreak, someone lit the fire ahead of the day's events. By dark, the couple fell into bed, satisfied beyond belief. Knut loved the warmth of his newborn son snuggled against his chest and if the baby stirred overnight, his foot hit the floor first to let Lasse sleep. Knut thought of his mother and sister worrying about his love life years before. In his eyes, he couldn't have found a more perfect woman.

In addition to farming, with any Prince Albert trips, Knut did the promised freighting. Early on, the family came along for their promised furs amongst other treasures. At the Saskatchewan River, before the Fenton train bridge, crossings were by ferry or swimming but in winter it was crossing on the ice.

With plans to build his family a new house, Knut gathered and hauled home several coveted items like a front door with bevelled glass window and ornate kitchen windows with colourful, stained-glass tops. Lasse was thrilled, since they both envisioned the sunlight streaming through the kitchen windows all morning and the front room and entry hall all afternoon.

In bed one night, as they lay talking, Lasse said how pleased she was that Mikaila and Lovisa were so contented with their new life and stepfather.

She stroked his face, "They see what I see, a truthful and strong Nordic man with piercing blue eyes. They look up to you and trust you, because they were too young to remember much about their own father. I think they feel as secure now as they did during the days of their grandparents helping raise them."

He rolled over to look at her and to play with her auburn hair. Her words soothed him. Unfortunately, he heard what she wasn't saying. When, at times, he staggered through the door, drunk as the lord, she forgave him. He wished, but would never say, that like his father and grandfather before him, he hadn't been cursed with the affliction. He hoped his other actions spoke louder than words. Lasse was his queen and the girls, his princesses. He wasn't proud of his drinking and one was never enough anymore.

When baby Peter was baptized, he was a handsome specimen in his beautiful long white christening gown and matching shawl but wailed when the pastor wetted his forehead. All anyone could do was smile. Afterwards,

Knut and Halvor left for a fruitful train trip to the Alberta foothills of the Rocky Mountains. Eight strong and healthy mustangs survived the trip home and went on to live long lives.

That first winter with a baby, Knut insisted, "Lasse, for safety's sake, while I'm away at the sawmill, I want you and the family to move into the village for the winter. The weather is too unforgiving to leave you alone out here."

She hemmed and hawed.

"You can stay at the rooming house and there's a lady to babysit Peter if you want to work. When school closes for the season, the girls can do house cleaning or help you at the hotel. I already spoke to Harry. He's all for it."

Although Lasse felt guilty leaving Greta and Halvor with little Lizzie and no close neighbours, she agreed. Halvor had his hands full with his and Knut's livestock and the Scandinavians knew how unpredictable Mother Nature could be. When Halvor's widowed mother, Helga, moved in, everyone felt relieved. Further, with the high infant mortality rate, Knut and the doctor were on the same page about having the family closer to medical care and the new drugstore.

"If someone needs surgery," the doctor said, "I can operate on the kitchen table at the livery stable and there's a room upstairs for patients to recover. It's better medical service than ever seen here before."

While Knut was away that winter, Lasse did work some at the hotel. After that, to Harry's dismay, she hardly had time. Come spring, it was seeding, when the weather improved, Saturday was a day to prepare for Sunday guests. Folks made special trips to the farm for meals and to take a stroll in the fresh air. Harry and Ida were prime examples.

Although Mikaila and Lovisa were finished school, it wasn't like they had nothing to do out on the farm. The family's lives were happy but full of work. Everything started from scratch from gathering the eggs, to milking, separating the cream from the milk, churning, butchering, and preserving. After a while, Knut built an icebox and the tin-lined wooden unit was a Godsend. It held a large block of ice with a drip pan beneath that got emptied daily.

Sometimes on Sunday, Knut would say, "Let's go for a drive after church and do some visiting," and they would all pile into the buggy.

By Monday, the food coffers needed replenishing. Since every day meant three meals, dishes, and housework, Lasse and Knut appreciated Mikaila and

Lovisa's help. They weren't stingy with praise because much of Lasse's time was filled with nursing the baby and keeping his cradle close.

Tuesdays were wash days. In winter, Lovisa couldn't stop giggling when the frozen stiff underwear and long johns came in from the clothesline.

"See how they stand up by themselves? Here's with the trap door open, and here's with it closed!"

Mikaila added an apron and they both roared.

Knut and Lasse got a kick out of their mischief, "Where is my underwear now?" he asked in spring, once home.

"Being ironed!"

In winter, there were woollens and felts laid out all over the house taking forever to dry, but Lasse rationalised, "It's good for the humidity!"

Wednesday meant ironing, and patching. For the sake of the sad irons, the rocking hot wood stove over-heated the house and everyone sweat buckets. The girls loved to iron but hot pads were needed for the red-hot handles. To them, the tiny iron used for dress frills was like a toy. Thursdays and Fridays were easier, meant for handiwork or letter writing, often continuing at bedtime by candlelight or lantern. Getting baby Peter down to sleep sometimes took hard rocking, and they took turns. Knut had made everyone homemade cross-country skis and that was entertaining but also important in an emergency.

Besides the children's, Lasse and Knut's birthdays fell one day apart on 29 and 30 August. There was always cake and a small gift for the birthday girl or boy.

When Knut was away, he waited anxiously for his loved ones' letters. Out at the sawmill, he would walk two miles into Crooked River twice a week for supplies and to check for mail. He was seldom disappointed. Similarly, his camp mates waited too. Families looked forward to their return mail, so on Sundays, the men often took the time to write home. Being responsible for long faces at home from loved ones leaving the post office empty-handed, wouldn't do.

Knut knew Sweden would always be home for Lasse despite baby antics and Canadian visitors who occupied her time. Cherished letters came from Bjorn and Ava back in Sweden about their two baby boys and that Lasse's father in-law was ailing. Knut knew she wanted to rush over with homemade soup but that was not to be. Confusing as it was, while a new mother, she was also a grandmother to babies she'd never met. Instead of her, it was her own parents filling the role, and that he knew, saddened her.

19

Black Garb

When McLaren and Tessa worshipped for the first time as guests of Emma and Clarice's Holiness Movement congregation, Tessa whispered, "Do you realise we've been Anglican over 50 years!"

Emma and Jock hosted the church service in their home, living the gospel wholeheartedly. On the row of chairs beside the seniors sat Sean, David, Clarice, Philip, four-year-old Birdie and one-year-old Chickadee.

"The theme for today is love and harmony!" The reverend started.

That morning, 30 August 1904, surrounded by born-again Christians, Tessa not only looked forward to the chance to get closer to God but to make her daughters happy.

After the service, the elderly couple and family shook the reverend's hand. "Thank ye fer a most inspirin' sermon!"

"You're welcome! We're happy to have you on this ecumenical day," the leader smiled.

Tessa said, "Emma married into the Holiness Movement church back east and Clarice followed in her sister's footsteps."

The guests mingled and several elders stepped up to welcome them. If Tessa had any misgivings about evangelicals, she laid them to rest that day.

At home, she admitted to McLaren, "Doesnae matter which church, they're all filled with the Holy Spirit."

"A'm glad we went. An occasional visit doesnae hurt."

"Me too but we'll stay Anglican."

Emma and Clarice dropped by wondering, "What did ye think? Isn't the gift of unworldliness somethin' desirable?"

"Ye know we've never been worldly in our entire lives!" Tessa smiled.

"By removin' sin and worldliness, God frees believers from evil thoughts and tempers. His gospel is a second blessin' that transforms sinners into saints."

Sean, sat across the kitchen table, "By sin, you mean drinkin', gamblin', and dancin'?"

"Right."

"Is courtin' women allowed?" he joked somewhat taken aback.

Emma laughed, "Go forth and multiply, me squeaky little brother!"

"Can a ask ye a question?" Sean continued, "why do the women wear black dresses and bonnets?"

"To show an inner holiness and to mark their lives lived separate from worldliness."

Clarice added, "We are deliberately sober and avoid fashion, falseness, and wealth."

Sean and David went outside and Sean said, "A'm stayin' Anglican."

"Me too."

When they returned, Emma teased, "We dinnae judge any other's beliefs. In all faces we see the face of Christ, even yers!"

The boys didn't want to comment on the stark contrast the families displayed when out and about together. Emma, Clarice and families wore black. Tessa and Martha, Anglicans and Presbyterians, chose any colour of the rainbow.

"It's like two sides of the same coin, only different," David said.

Come spring 1905, Sean took out a homestead on the southeast quarter of the same section as McLaren and Philip. All summer his buildings, including a blacksmith shop, came together. One day, friend and neighbour, Knut, rode up with dull ploughshares.

To sharpen, Sean heated them one by one in the coal forge. "Once heated," he said. "Pound each to a thin edge. When they're just the right colour, dip them into water fer the perfect hardness."

"Thank you, Squeaky." Knut tipped his hat. "Don't know what I'd do without you. Say, when are you going to find yourself a woman?" That made Sean blush since he was almost thirty.

The Scottish families were leaders in both church and community and the men attended a meeting of the ratepayers to address village and district concerns.

Jake made a motion that carried, "We've a road grader now, so why not use it, instead of fightin' ruts?"

Talk was to establish a judicial district, and a report came of the theft of money and liquor from Humboldt House. Then, the volunteer fire chief introduced a new firefighting apparatus.

"Basically, it's a big tank of water on wheels with a long hose," he said.

"Ingenious!" Sean was impressed, "a far cry from barrels and buckets!"

"The community is advancing by leaps and bounds. The Carrot River Valley Flour Mill produced its first sack of flour and presented it to Mrs. Reginald Beatty."

Friday, 1 September 1905, Tessa and McLaren headed to town to celebrate Alberta and Saskatchewan becoming provinces and joining confederation. The seniors stopped at Jake and Martha's and found their new barn almost finished. The first barn and a cow were destroyed by a flash prairie fire in April.

Four grandchildren, Toot—10, Fleck—8, Dot—6, and Blue—5, ran up to the wagon for hugs and kisses.

Dot climbed up the side and breathed, "Granny! We're coming too!"

"Be careful ye don't get dirty," Jake admonished, since Blue already had grass stains on his trousers.

Martha and their three smallest emerged from the house all dressed up. After more hugs and kisses, and Jake brushing Blue's pants off, he said, "How was yer church visit to Emma's?"

"Lovely!" Tessa said, "ye have to respect their strict lifestyle."

"Yes," Jake said, "but me family will remain Presbyterian."

Martha nodded, "Jake hopes to join the Masons once there's a chapter close by."

"Now with Saskatchewan getting a Grand Lodge, Melfort can form a charter."

"The ancient brotherhood has a good reputation," McLaren approved.

Jake laughed, "A rancher rode horseback 60 miles to the Qu'Appelle Lodge to receive his papers, then turned around and went home that night."

McLaren echoed. "Livin' 10 miles out, and bein' this old and decrepit, 'tis the dark and cold nights a can't stand."

Toot piped up, "Yer only 64, Grandda!"

They laughed and Jake continued. "If 'tis good enough fer Thomas Edison and the North-West Mounted Police, 'tis good enough fer me. Ye all know I've attended Kinistino Lodge No. 16 in Prince Albert once or twice."

The families went by wagon to Melfort, where 'new province' celebrations happened up and down the streets. Streamers of small Union Jacks decorated the businesses who offered free balloons and noise makers.

"This reminds me of last summer's celebrations for the railroad!" Tessa said.

Across the street, The Hotel's competition hotel had their front veranda used as a podium on the corner of Saskatchewan Avenue and Main Street.

A dignitary in attendance was Territorial Premier Haultain, who gave a speech. "We suggested Alberta and Saskatchewan merge and be called *Buffalo.* Doesn't that have a nice ring to it? However, Prime Minister Laurier deemed the 550,000 square miles was too unwieldy."

People didn't quite know what to think but McLaren winked at Tessa, "The west can't have too much power."

After the speeches came a parade with marching band, costumed riders on show horses, and floats. Foot races and softball followed. Families spread out blankets with picnic lunches, and quenched their thirst with lemonade from apple crate stands. A box social got underway with single ladies having their lunches auctioned off to bachelors.

Sean and David were both front and centre. Sean won a girl named Edith's lunch and David won Sally's. On purpose, they ate within sight but out of earshot of their ever-watchful families.

Tessa remarked on the way home, "The day was certainly a hit and everyone's goin' home tired and happy!"

With summer, the Stoney Creek country school year began and would end with the Christmas concert. Families waited while their children, decked out in Christmas attire, assembled behind the stage's curtain with their teacher. Whether playing Mary, an angel or a tree, all roles were important. The audience joined the carolling and the production ended with a candlelight vigil of *Silent Night.*

A clatter at the door heralded a rotund Santa Claus, wearing a red and white suit with black belt and boots. With a big brown sack slung over his shoulder, his belly jiggled when he laughed, "Ho, Ho, Ho! Merry Christmas!"

The jolly old elf thrilled the children by giving each a Christmas stocking filled with a Japanese orange in the toe, peanuts in the shell, and hard candies.

Little nieces and nephews asked Uncle David, "Where's Uncle Sean?"

"I think he had chores to do."

"Aw! That's not fair!"

By 1906, five more babies had graced the Scottish households since the family's arrival in Melfort. Cream Puff and Kitten for Emma and Jock, Chickadee for Clarice and Philip, and Geordie and Sis for Jake and Martha. With no crop failures, the families' coffers increased and Martha and Emma were ecstatic when their husbands built them large two-storey homes. Officially, it was to make room for boisterous households.

Not surprisingly, certain items had to be shipped from the east. One of those was Jake and Martha's upright pump organ. It was a new and ornate *Karn* made of dark hardwood, with intricate carvings and a bevelled mirror. Inscriptions on the front in perfect gold calligraphy said '*Woodstock, Ontario*' and '*London, England*'. Martha played by ear and decided to tutor any child who might want to learn. Dot was first.

The local flour mill was open a year but was already receiving orders from Liverpool and Glasgow for a carload each of its '*Tiger Lily*' brand flour.

Jock and Emma's eighth and last child, Buddy, was born in 1907 while Jo came along as Jake and Martha's eighth. The local midwife attended both deliveries. The Holiness Movement church got their first bishop that year, and the village of Melfort was designated a town of 500. All were reasons to rejoice with no crop failures and money in the bank.

After the box social, Sean grew sweet on Edith, who came from a neighbouring farm. He encouraged Tessa to get a hired girl and of course, Edith was chosen.

David teased, "Squeaky, ye were sunk from the get-go. She played a little hard-to-get and had ye eatin' out of her hand."

"Ye mean stealin' me heart," Sean corrected. "Edith is lovely, with that dark, curly hair. Don't ye think she has a captivatin' smile?"

"She is pretty."

"Well, I fergive ye fer not bein' quite as smitten as me!"

Tessa noticed that every chance Sean had to help Edith or to get her to spend time with him, he did. In 1909, Sean was 33 years old and it was time. Edith was 10 years younger and a Scandinavian but the two wed at a small

Lutheran ceremony followed by an intimate family supper. She moved in and he was the happiest man alive.

"Now with Edith around, his bachelor house won't seem near so desolate," his mother, Tessa thought.

It was the same year the town of Melfort decided to look into the idea of a telephone system and the doctor provided space for the switchboard. People all around town were either on the fence, praising it or wondering why it was needed.

"Anybody who's had a medical emergency knows why," Jake said. "Pickin' up a phone fer an emergency shaves off precious time!"

By 1911, Jake and Martha's ninth and tenth babies had arrived, Lady Bug and Butter Cup.

"Butter Cup was slated for birth in Prince Albert at the new Holy Family Hospital with the nuns," Martha said. "because the doctor said, 'the Lady Minto is giving me migraines because its new matron is allowin' patients to smoke indoors!'"

Jake filled in the rest. "We planned for P.A., but the bairn had a mind of her own. Thankfully, the Lady Minto served its purpose, even with the smoking. Butter Cup's real name is Tessie."

"We now have seven built-in babysitters, from Toot at 16 to Sis, who's six. They take great care of the three youngest, Jo Jo, who's four, Lady Bug, who's two, and now Butter Cup."

Three months later, Sean's Edith, delivered a healthy baby girl, also at the Lady Minto. Apparently, the sky hadn't fallen in from the indoor smoking. Sean, the new father, strutted like a peacock and got emotional when McLaren suggested they nickname her Penny. Eight months later, Lulu came along as Clarice and Philip's third. To brother Birdie, now 12, and sister Chickadee, nine, Lulu was a gift just for them.

Unfortunately, Sean and Edith were sent a heavy blow when little one-year-old Penny was seized by a high fever and cough, from which she did not recover.

"'Tis shocking fer the young couple, especially Sean, given at 16 he fought fer his own life from diphtheria," Tessa was candid.

Sometime later, Sean, still in a funk, confided, "'Tis hard not to fall into a dark place. A've already had too much of death and dyin'."

All his family could do was support him, listen, and hug him hard. They of all people, knew the feeling of the hard reality.

Families had tractors with steel wheels by this time, and the young adults like 17-year-old Tadpole was proud to drive his father, Jock's, cross-mounted Case. The new tractor made work outside much easier. That year, lives of people in town improved with sewer and water lines and electricity installed. Still, most rural folks lived the way they always had.

Reading the newspaper, the family was appalled. On 30 June 1912, right at supper time, Regina had a cyclone around Victoria Park. Houses and churches were demolished but worse was 28 people killed. The act of God was a stark reminder it could happen anywhere.

By 1914, McLaren and Tessa became empty nesters when David, at 30, tied the knot. He had watched Sean and Edith's love blossom while stricken in love himself since the box social. Sally was an attractive 18-year-old local girl still living at home. They wed at a lowkey ceremony just as World War I unfolded. With McLaren's help, they too set up a homestead north of Thaxted on a northeast quarter.

To everyone's chagrin, Jake and Martha's second eldest son, Edward, or Fleck as they called him, turned 18 and enlisted in the army to fight World War I. All were worried sick but none more than his grandfather, McLaren.

"Please dinnae go," the senior begged, "yer needed here to help with the farm and ye can get an exemption!"

It seemed Fleck was not expecting push back, so rationalised, "Someone has to stand up to the enemy, and that's guys like me."

After their grandson left, Tessa said, "The young man cuts a fine figure in a uniform, ye have to give him that!"

"He's an easy-going sort, who, up to now, hasn't taken stupid chances but he's in no way equipped to go to war," McLaren griped.

"Somebody has to. He has a dry wit and doesnae let much bother him. He thinks bold action is needed to stop that overseas tyrant. We should be glad there's fellows like him willin' to go."

"A suppose so," said McLaren falling into a chair and wiping tears from his eyes. "If somethin' happens to him, I dinnae know what a'll do."

Learning their boy was being shipped to the front, however, pushed Fleck's family to another level of dread where bracing themselves for the other shoe to drop became the norm. With only an occasional letter to go on, the family's life became a roller coaster of fear and uncertainty.

20
Nickel Nose

Melfort *1905–1917*

By fall of 1905, Knut fulfilled the homestead requirements and applied for a patent with Halvor vouching. Months later, after the inspection, Letters Patent were granted and Knut proudly acquired the adjacent 80 acres for $3.00 an acre. The very next year, Peter was almost two and walking and talking, when his new baby sister, Bonnie arrived on Saturday, 23 June 1906. Afterwards, having done the delivery, the gregarious doctor sipped a cup of coffee at the kitchen table. He wanted to monitor the mother's heavy flow for a time.

Knut commented on the hair-raising job the doctor had of making house calls.

"I take anything from dogsleds to railway jiggers to get there," he laughed, "only to find sometimes, the patient is a colicky horse or a cow with milk fever!"

Changing the subject, the physician continued, "You might not know but I'm originally from Ontario and my ancestors were involved in the Underground Railroad."

"Really! I remember tales of that back in Iowa!" Knut exclaimed.

Lasse held her newborn, and both daughters kept tabs on little Peter but they all looked confused.

The doctor explained, "It wasn't a railroad per se but a network of people and safe houses working undercover to get slaves to freedom. They used railroad terms to hide their true actions. Freedom came at the Canadian border."

Knut said, "Right! Slaves were cargo and headed to a safe house run by a station master. The ticket agents made travel arrangements and stockholders gave donations."

"Exactly! A rail line was a freedom route with the destination of Heaven or the Promised Land. Runaways were hidden, rested, fed, and given a change of clothing and money."

"Fascinating!"

Knut continued, "My family swore those old yarns, intertwined with my uncle's experiences from the Civil War, were the gospel truth. Who knows? Even if they never held a shred of truth, they were entertaining!"

Smiling broadly with his sparkling white teeth and flashing eyes, the doctor put his coat and fedora back on, "Duty calls, I must be on my way."

That same year, Lasse and Greta heard that reforms made certification compulsory for ship's cooks. At Greta's next visit, she said, "Without Otto, the ship's crew would be much worse off, don't you think?"

"Yes, and he came with no fancy certificates."

For Lasse, with two babies in diapers, the laundry took on a life of its own. In addition, the Sunday guest meals waned, but neighbours still came and went. Jake and Martha for instance, stopped to pick up a load of lumber from Knut.

Martha was pregnant again, but excited, "The Lady Minto Hospital is in the works named after the Governor General's wife!"

"Wonderful!"

"The door-to-door canvas raised $1,200! And the Victorian Order of Nurses donated $1,000! They're planning 14 beds, two nurses, a servant, and an orderly."

"Amazing!" Lasse replied boiling the kettle.

"There's to be a nurse's training program to go along with it!"

Jake and Knut moved to the front room, and Jake said, "Are you and Lasse going to the 'sand and gravel bee' and supper to build the hospital's basement floor?"

"Probably."

"There's a lot of talk about forming a grain growers association and a co-op elevator to stop the private monopoly."

"Well, the dockage fees are outrageous and maybe we'll see better prices."

When Knut left for the bush, the winter of 1906–07, Lasse wouldn't budge off the farm. It was a winter of blizzards and deep snow, and Knut worried himself sick. He needn't have because with the stockpile of firewood he'd poured his heart and soul into, and Lasse's cache of preserves, it kept them snug. Greta and Helga visited one beautiful day in April to do fancy work and by this time, Knut was back home.

"The heavy snowfall sure took a toll on animals wintering out," Helga said. Lasse loved how the senior taught them her intricate embroidery and crochet stitches.

"Did you know they found cattle trapped and dangling from tree branches this spring?"

"What?"

"Because of the height of the snow drifts," Greta explained.

"That's awful! I wonder how often that happened?"

"Hard to say. On the brighter side, did you hear the Lady Minto has its grand opening on May 15?"

"Yes! All the businesses are closing at three o'clock!"

It seemed most years before or after Knut went to the bush, Lasse found herself pregnant and for the third time, the joy of adding to their family was upon them. Her pregnancies brought an inner glow and renewed vigour she didn't often experience otherwise.

In 1907, the year the hospital opened, Dr. Sawyer took a sabbatical leave for more education in Scotland. Although the community was disappointed, they understood. Lasse was almost a week overdue and Knut dragged his feet about going bush ward. First, he wasn't comfortable without the doctor around. Second, having five winters under their belts, the sawmill crew were quite capable of running the show for a while.

On 7 December 1907, during an awful blizzard, a chubby, red-headed baby boy, they named Paul, made his debut. Lasse, and baby were expertly tended by her family and Knut decided to put off his bush trip until after Christmas. The shiny new hospital would have to see them another time.

By April 1908, a creamery opened in town. Lasse who had always sold chickens, eggs, and cream to The Hotel, now had a second stream of revenue. By this time, Dr. Sawyer was back in town with an enviable and vast assortment of tinctures, liniments and powders. At the same time, he was becoming a political force to reckon with, serving on town council. Simultaneously, a Saskatoon car dealership got cars on the road in the province. In June, news came that the City of Medicine Hat steam wheeler crashed into the Victoria Bridge in Saskatoon and sank. No one was killed but at the same time, a herd of cattle on the bridge stampeded.

A few Saskatchewan communities had phone service but none in the province's northern half. The doctor proposed a town phone system to council in 1909 and offered his drugstore for the switchboard space. Concurrently, road gangs started to build roads and farmers rejoiced at a new variety of wheat called Marquis that matured up to 10 days earlier than Red Fife.

Knut and Lasse's fourth and final baby came on 10 April 1910. She was a red-headed girl, but quieter than the rest and named Gladys. The couple was well satisfied that Knut had been home for each child's birth.

"We had to miss church that Sunday," Knut said. "The girls and I did the delivery but the doctor came racing out afterwards in his little red Rio car."

Peter and Bonnie both started school at Mount Forest country school in 1910. Bonnie was a little too young but well past ready. For Knut and Lasse, watching their youngsters grow up happened in the blink of an eye. Going to school was a big step and changed the dynamics of the household. The children moved from toddlerhood to school-age, guided by their parents plus Mikaila, and Lovisa. One of the family's greatest pleasures was listening to the little ones' prayers at bedtime.

At first, Lasse spoke mostly Swedish, and even though Knut, the girls, and the Eaton's catalogue helped, it was when the children went to school that her English really improved. She had a natural ability with numbers and passed it along to her offspring.

Off the record, at the end of February 1911, Harry and Ida confided their decision to sell The Hotel to a gentleman from Iowa.

Lasse said, "I'm in shock, but happy for you. It's comforting to hear you're staying on to help the new owner establish himself."

By 1912, underground sewer lines were dug in Melfort and come 1913, the railway boom ended. The cities of Regina, Moose Jaw, and Saskatoon had electric street cars and Saskatoon's had wood warming stoves in theirs. Then, with the outbreak of the First World War in August 1914, job markets erupted, this time to include women. Besides farming, freighting, and running a sawmill, Knut was asked to be a cattle buyer for the army. In the meantime, the family was in line for a big shock because Mikaila and Lovisa wanted to leave home and join the war effort. Lasse knew the dreaded day was inevitable.

When Knut gave his wife a questioning look, she explained, "Well, they're well past legal age and can take the train to Winnipeg to work as clericals. I guess it's time they spread their wings."

Lasse seemed more comfortable with the decision than Knut.

"At least, they aren't going to the front," he said, "and it's not like they've never travelled."

"Plus, Kirsten is in Winnipeg, so they can call on her, if need be," Lasse said planning to write Kirsten that night. "They're staying with Ebba and Isak."

Knut knew of the dangers awaiting them, including men, but kept quiet. He couldn't help but worry because he knew Lasse worried too, even though she tried to hide it. "The other four are going to be lost without their big sisters," he said.

Lasse rationalised, "The girls will be making real money for the first time in their lives, and it'll be fine."

"Of course, you know they'll work for poor wages and try to function in a man's world?"

She gave him a wry look, "If they don't get out into the world and meet some young men, they'll wind up old maids, it's time! The little ones are helpful and not that much work anymore."

She was stubborn and Knut gave in, "I can't believe the girls are in their mid-20s and the younger ones are already between four and 10!"

After celebrating Lasse and Knut's birthdays the days before, on Monday morning, 31 August 1914, the family took the grown-up Mikaila and Lovisa to the train station for a painful farewell. Tears marked the end of a way of life but the girls were so eager, no one could stay sad. The family made their way home and tried not to mope. Come afternoon, screeching came from outside and eight-year-old Bonnie came charging in.

"Mother!" she screamed, "the horse kicked Paul in the face!"

Knut and Lasse raced outside to the sound of his pitiful wails. Sure enough, poor Paul's nose was a horrible mess, sitting sideways on his face, swelling, turning purple, and bleeding profusely. They made haste for the new hospital with Peter and Lasse holding towels and ice on Paul's face and Knut driving the team like the wind.

Peter, Bonnie, and Gladys were stopped at the hospital's entryway because no children were allowed to visit.

"What's that smell?" Bonnie asked wrinkling her nose as the children took seats in the vestibule.

A nice, young nurse hurrying past, said, "It's ether."

When Knut laid Paul onto the stretcher, the matron removed the bloody padding. His black and blue eyes had swollen shut and his mangled nose was unrecognisable. Knut tenderly cradled his seven-year-old with one arm while Lasse stroked the boy's red hair.

The nurse asked the patient, "Do you know your name?"

Paul took a long time to answer but said, "It's Paul."

Then she asked, "What year is it?"

When he didn't answer, Dr. Sawyer walked in and said, "OK, that's enough."

After a full examination, he spoke, "It's critical that Paul has immediate surgery. I suspect he has a hairline skull fracture and it's amazing he's still conscious!"

Even though the family sat on tenterhooks awaiting the outcome, Paul did well. They feared a serious head injury but weeks after, even though he still had raccoon-eyes, the little boy was fine. His biggest challenge was learning how to breathe differently but he could still do math in his head like a whiz.

When it came time for discharge, the doctor said, "A hospital bed is far too restrictive for a young boy yearning for fresh air. He can go home to gradually regain his strength and be surrounded by family."

From that day forward, making the best of a bad situation, Knut and Lasse often told Paul how proud they were to have a rich son with a nickel nose. It made him stick out his chest with pride and feel like he was one of a kind. Indeed, the surgeon had replaced the mangled nasal structure with nickel. Although extremely unnerving, the situation had somehow taken everyone's minds off the older girls' departure.

To the community's utter despair, however, their revered doctor passed away the very next year, in March 1915. At the young age of 45, he was unable to recover from a bout of appendicitis. Running a close second on the bad-luck scale, come July 1st, the distant thrumming of prohibition closed in, as Saskatchewan legislators 'banned the bar'.

Lasse received a letter from the girls and realised they had teamed up with Kirsten. Their words, *"She took us to a suffragette meeting,"* rang loud and clear. All Lasse could think of was the radical British women's movement that had smashed windows and wrought havoc in Britain.

Harry told Knut and Lasse, "The pubs may be closed with prohibition but Casey, the new owner, is turning ours into a billiard hall and soft drink store. He has no intention of going out of business."

Before long, a 1916 referendum confirmed the prohibition decision, and it became law. From kitchen tables to board rooms, finger pointing at overindulgences peaked. Accordingly, who could argue that liquor wouldn't hinder a soldier's fighting ability? Shaming wasn't saved for a select few, it was widespread and Knut, himself, really felt it.

At home, he rationalised other uses for liquor. "What about the need to escape life on occasion or sedating our shell-shocked soldiers?"

"As long as they know when to quit." Lasse wrangled. "Alcohol and war don't jive. Not all drunks are happy-go-lucky, like you, too many are downright mean."

"But can't we ever control our own destinies?" Knut asked, chippy at the way the country was run, "does the government have to manage everything?"

They both knew, since the dawn of time, alcohol went in one end and out the other. Officially, those in charge paired patriotic duty with prohibition, "if the Allies were ever to win the war."

Martha came for coffee and told Lasse the latest gossip, "Apparently, Saskatoon's Temperance Colony has been bone-dry since the 1880s and they won't even allow liquor outlets there."

Lasse said, "Knut says men in the pool hall are saying that, 'certain other areas of the city aren't quite so dry because Mounties tend to ignore drinking and houses of ill repute'."

"The general store's owner says, 'A Saskatoon brewery got fined for selling beer as liquid bread'. Now they're restricted to selling two percent alcohol."

Martha went on, "And bootlegging has soared."

Lasse confided, "Melfort can't be much different."

Knut and Lasse visited the hotel.

"The alcohol industry keeps on," Harry said, "the doctors prescribe it, the druggists dispense it, and the clergy fills the chalice for sacraments."

Casey, the new owner said, "I guess between Regina and Saskatoon, doctors are writing over 200 prescriptions a day for the stuff!"

Ida, mentioned to Lasse, "As you can imagine, the hotel supply has dwindled, gone out in favour of people in real need."

Out at Halvor's farm, he and Knut commiserated on the subject as they walked to the barn.

"Cripes!" Halvor said, "you don't have to be a bootlegger to have a still in this part of the world. We've got no shortage of booze-making supplies, grain and berries."

"And everything's still legal to buy, like hops and malt syrup," Knut added.

"Any crock or copper kitchen cooker is suspect," Halvor said with no small amount of disgust, "prohibition has turned common folks into criminals!"

"Even the Mounties shake their heads. I was at the police station one day when Len admitted the loopholes are leading to more corruption than less and those who spout it aren't abstaining themselves!"

Both Len and his partner had been promoted to corporals when a staff sergeant and two more constables had joined their ranks.

Corporal West said, "'Racketeers and moonshiners are smuggling booze across the border wholesale, partly because the US has stricter laws.' At that, he pulled out a newspaper article. It was a cartoon sketch of the border. Canada was leaking alcohol while the poor US below was frantically mopping up the mess."

"Oh, sure!" was all Knut could say.

World War I army enlistments caused the North-West Mounted Police numbers to dwindle. Given national security and alcohol breaches, by 1917, a provincial board of liquor commissioners formed its own prohibition police force.

At the height of all this turmoil, back on the farm, Knut, and Lasse's four children were growing up. The children made their way on foot or by horseback to country school, five miles away. Aside from their schoolwork, household, and barnyard chores, one of their favourite past-times was gopher hunting. They could have cared less about prohibition.

"How many'd ya get?" the boys compared notes.

Since every spring the rodents did extensive crop damage, it was all out war but the teeming rodents were winning. Wheat was produced en masse for the real war but gophers ruined millions of dollars' worth. In fact, human effort hardly dented their numbers. As a result, the government issued free gopher poison and paid a bounty per gopher tail.

"Three cents each can sure add up in a piggy bank," Gladys showed hers half full.

Knut cautioned, "I've put out more strychnine disguised in oats but make sure none of the animals get into it. We've all seen the effects on the gophers, rigid and laying in a 'sawhorse' position. It's never a pretty sight."

"Rats too," Peter said, "laying around the pig house and chicken coop."

"The worst is the wild barn cats," Paul added.

"Yes, they show up from God knows where. Let's check the barnyard," Knut motioned, and sure enough, there was evidence.

"Let's burn the dead ones," Knut said, "we don't want the other animals eating them or they'll be poisoned too."

It was a horrific job to cremate the collateral damage, but the shovels came out and a bon fire was built.

"Every time Mother steps out the door, we see her take the .22 and ping off so many gophers," the boys boasted, smiling at their role model. Knut laughed at his gun toting wife.

On 1 May 1917, *Gopher Day* was proclaimed, and teachers dismissed children early across the province to wage battle. Peter got a .22 rifle when he turned 12, but Paul, at 10, carried a bb gun to try to stun or wing them.

Paul would forever bare the scar of a hole through his hand from accidentally shooting himself with Peter's .22 the year before. When it happened, he was all by himself under a tree in the pasture. He screamed and cried but wasn't supposed to be touching the gun in the first place. He wrapped his hankie tight around his hand to stop the bleeding and found another rag. He figured deep trouble awaited him.

When his mother saw, she exclaimed, "What on earth happened?"

Paul ventured, "Um, my jackknife slipped when I was whittling."

"You better let me have a look," she said, but he made a beeline for the barn and wouldn't let her near it.

"He's worn it wrapped like that all day," Knut said. "The thing has to sting bad."

"Maybe he'll let you look at it," Lasse suggested.

For some reason, Paul did finally allow his father to unbandage it. There was a perfectly round bullet hole gone in through the palm and out through the back of his hand, swollen and turning an angry red. Knut never said a word but soaked it in warm, salty water, then doused it with iodine. The kid already had enough grief with his nose.

"Thank God it wasn't more serious," Knut shuddered to think how it might have gone, "but it was a close call, so tomorrow, they all get a gun lesson."

It occurred to Knut that Peter and Bonnie were more alike, dark, tall, lanky, dry witted, and appreciative of a good laugh. Paul and Gladys were shorter, red-headed, and freckled. Whereas Paul was ready to make others laugh, Gladys was quiet and reserved. The brothers affectionately called each other 'Boos' to rhyme with caboose, which no one understood except them.

When *Gopher Day* came, Bonnie and Gladys worked as a team. Gladys, being smaller, was to flush the gophers' entry hole with a bucket of water while Bonnie waited at the rear exit with a box. The gophers in their underground tunnels would see the water rushing towards them and dash for the back door, but there would be Bonnie. Every time the bigger girl pounced; she made a harrumphing noise that put Gladys into hysterics. When it was over, the children came away with dozens of gophers, and sore sides from laughing. The legendary *Gopher Day* was an enormous success but the coveted *Gopher Shield* went to a school in southern Saskatchewan somewhere between Quinton and Raymore.

21

Obstruction on the Tracks

Melfort and Crooked River—*March 1916–November 1917*

With World War I in its infancy, people at home were just getting their feet wet hearing that Germany had invaded Luxembourg and Belgium. That stairstep to hell, however, was crowded by another exploit entering the world stage. All eyes were on *The Endurance*, captained by the daring Sir Ernest Shackleton, that had taken an expedition to Antarctica, on 8 August 1914. Tragically, five months later, the ship, trapped in pack ice, was ultimately crushed, and sank into the Weddell Sea. Over the next 497 days, with nowhere else to go, Shackleton and his crew were forced to navigate treacherous ice floes. During that time, the world was horrified when a German submarine sank a passenger liner *The Lusitania* during its crossing from New York to Liverpool.

Forthwith, on 21 February 1916, Germany stormed Verdun, France and the battle waged right alongside Saskatchewan taking a monumental first step towards validating women.

Newscasters reported, "The enfranchisement of women, or technically the right to vote, occurred in Saskatchewan on 14 March 1916. The domino effect followed Manitoba's decision in January, and Alberta's in February."

"That would be thanks to the suffrage work of women on the prairies," Lasse said with pride.

Even better news came that spring when the ice melted. Shackleton had launched lifeboats and almost a week later reached the mountainous Elephant Island. It was 15 April and the men recognised the elephant seals with their large elephant-like noses. On 20 May Shackleton and five crew made it to a whaling station, and all the world held their breath over the fate of the others. After four tries, a Chilean steam tug successfully rescued them. It was Knut's birthday, 30 August 1916, and they celebrated Shackleton's harrowing victory after his 24 month and 22-day endeavour.

People worldwide coasted on the joyous momentum but when a provincial election was called for 26 June 1917, women were ecstatic. At roughly the same time as Allied American combat troops arrived in France, the women of Saskatchewan shed their chains of legal invisibility and showed up at the polls in droves. They beamed, even those with family fighting abroad, who otherwise carried the weight of the world on their shoulders. In the afternoon, Lasse lined up at Melfort's polling station behind Greta, Martha, Tessa, and so many others. Like them, she grappled with a confusing mix of wartime emotions from disgust and disbelief to fear and determination.

After voting, the women emerged from the town hall and joined their families waiting in the street. Peter—12, Bonnie—11, and Paul—9 had all crowded in to watch and afterwards, took off to spend their dimes. In the meantime, six-year-old Gladys held her father's hand and went to the post office. Lasse headed for the public restrooms where there was a large room for rural mothers to put their babies down for a nap. They were all to meet half an hour later at the livery stable.

On the wagon ride home, Knut tapped the reins and explained, "Good thing it wasn't a federal election. With the different time zones, the cross-country count doesn't get tallied for hours and by the time we get the news, the election is over."

"Good thing Saskatchewan is all one time zone," Peter said. "But it still takes time for so many ridings."

"For a 12-year-old, you're a smart cookie," Knut said proudly, "the counts trickle in by mail, telegraph, and from those with phones."

Indeed, weeks later, it was confirmed. The provincial Liberals had maintained their strong hold.

Getting into bed, Lasse shared, "There's still a long row to hoe for women but Canada is ahead of the game. Indians didn't get the vote here, and in Sweden, women and even certain men can't vote at all."

"Change is slow for certain things but not for others, like amalgamating the railroads," Knut said, reaching for her under the covers.

In effect, come May, Canada chose to amalgamate the Canadian Northern, Intercolonial, Grand Trunk, and Grand Trunk Pacific into one company called the Canadian National Railway. The Canadian Pacific maintained its status quo.

"Seems bold but maybe the nation will see some savings."

Come July 1917, bad news splashed the front pages of the newspaper.

"A British offensive is floundering in their attempt to drive the Germans from the Passchendaele Ridge in Belgium and channel ports at Ypres."

Knut had brought in a pail of water, then an armload of kindling. "They tried to destroy German U-boat bases on the coast and the continual rain and shellfire on the ridge stalled everything."

Lasse looked up from mixing dough, and asked, "How do soldiers erase those graphic images?"

Knut sighed, "I doubt they can." He came up behind her and traced the outline of her body with his hands, then hugged her soundly. She rested her head on his shoulder.

The anxiety wasn't over because following her 46th birthday, August 29, and to dampen his 42nd year spirits, news exploded. "After Prime Minister Borden saw the carnage abroad for himself, he has determined the Canadian volunteering system which has almost dried up, will never produce enough soldiers to win the war. Stronger measures are needed. As a result, conscription legislation is being implemented through the Canadian Military Service Act until the end of World War I."

Knut groaned loudly. Lasse knew he lived a heightened sense of awareness for those young volunteers already serving and now for those who had no choice. Her eyes glittered as she rubbed his back, knowing his feelings on the subject and his sense of déjà vu. He had deliberately side-stepped the same threat a dozen years before in Iowa. Now, in the blink of an eye, it was a foregone conclusion. So far, he was exempt as a family man and wheat producer but scores of others weren't. All single men, bachelors or widowers between 18 and 41, unless exempted had to sign up. If the fight dragged on, what of Peter and Paul? Still, the prime minister's question of, 'if nothing is done, how will the country face the spent and depleted troops on their return home?' rang a bell.

After Thanksgiving, on 26 October 1917, the news revealed, "The Canadian Corps of 100,000 troops are on their way to Passchendaele with orders to deliver victory."

Lasse watched Knut's face drop.

He pleaded, "God knows we have to stand up to aggression or risk the world's freedom. And surely, 100,000 soldiers is enough to win the battle but dear God, is sacrificing our young men and women the only answer?"

"That's the million-dollar question. How does the world deal with rogue bullies? Who can even understand it?" his wife asked.

"Leaping into war is never the answer!" Knut fumed, "there has to be a better way! Civilians suffer through no fault of their own. Why not target the mastermind himself?"

Lasse changed the conversation's direction, "You know, British, Australian, and New Zealand troops have already tried and failed to capture that ridge so maybe the Canadians can do it."

He sighed, "Evil cannot be allowed to overcome but when does the killing stop? What about falling back on peace and forgiveness? Didn't Jesus say, 'Blessed are the peacemakers'?"

He was right, and without solutions, it was a heavy cross to bear. There was no lulling Knut into a false sense of security. Further, being right all the time was a beast for anyone.

"Maybe one day, sick and twisted leaders and their factions will be targeted, instead of dragging in civilians," she said, "there has to be a way for mankind to save the innocent from those blinded by power and revenge!"

When Knut left for the bush, his hugs were harder and longer. Saying his goodbyes, he murmured to all the family crowded around, "Until we meet again, Godspeed my loves."

As Lasse knew, by the week after Halloween 1917, it was Knut's 15th year wintering in the Saskatchewan bush. With his time in the US logging industry, his experience added up to a good quarter century. Perhaps he could retire in the next decade or so. His usual sawmill crew were standing by and ready. They would prepare ice roads and set up camp. All day, he would be busy assessing timber rights. The afternoon of 6 November, he would walk into Crooked River to pick up supplies and mail and then return to the camp on his usual route along the tracks but it was snowing.

Back at the homestead the next morning, the sun hinted at breaking the horizon when Lasse sluggishly awoke to banging on the front door. Startled, she grabbed a dressing gown to cover herself. There stood a party of her husband's crew with not a dry eye among them. They hung their heads, fiddled with their caps, and shifted from foot to foot.

"Can we speak to you alone?" Olaf motioned her outside. All four children were crowding around wondering what was going on.

She shooed them upstairs to bed, "Go back to sleep and don't worry." She knew it was useless because they were curious and wide awake now. No one could miss the alarm in the air so she knew they would stay hidden on the stairs waiting. It was Keith who broke the news.

"We are so sorry, Lasse. There's awful news. I'm afraid to say but Knut has died. He was run over by a train outside Crooked River."

When the words sank in, Lasse buckled. Numb, her senses deserted her so she didn't feel the morning chill through her night clothes. Cradling herself, she felt her heart thump hard, then she swooned.

A hysterical voice in her head screamed, "How could this happen twice?" But it had, and she felt herself flying apart. With no way out and no detours around such horrific news, an incredible exhaustion dragged her straight down to the floor.

The men rushed to her, imparting their own strength in turns. They held her limp body to them, speaking soothingly, rubbing her back and arms. Alf got a wet cloth for her forehead. Keith found a glass of water. Gradually their strength became hers and eventually, she calmed enough to think. By this time, they carried her back into the front room and laid her on the couch.

Sickened, she blubbered, "Tell me exactly what happened," knowing the children were within earshot.

Before answering, Percy turned to the stairs and brought the children into the room.

The men put their arms around the youngsters, then Keith began. "Somehow, yesterday there was an accident on the train tracks at Crooked River." He paused, making full eye contact, "I'm sorry to say but your father was in an accident and he has passed away."

The children got red in the face and unsure what to do, started crying, unable to take it all in.

Keith went on, "A mixed Canadian Northern freight train had travelled from Prince Albert. At Crooked River, the train men jumped down to start unloading and it wasn't until then that they realised what happened. People said afterwards, the engineer vowed he wasn't aware he had hit anything."

Each man with their arms around a child or Lasse, hugged them a little bit tighter. The children sat stunned, struggling to understand, and looking to their mother for support.

Olaf took over, "The discovery had people walking down the track, trying to figure out what happened and where. It wasn't far from the sawmill, and runners were sent to ask us to help. We raced over and still couldn't believe it was him!"

"By late last night, the official pronouncement was made."

Lasse cried, "He was only 42 years old! Only in Canada 15 short years and married to me for 13!"

For Lasse, it began to sink in that at midnight, Keith, Percy, Alf, and Einar, led by Olaf, had left camp, and rode hard the 45 miles to her farm. They had not slept.

"How could this happen?" she pleaded. "Did he fall? Did his foot get caught? He has four young children for God's sake!"

Nobody said it, but the men and Lasse, wondered what kind of shape he was in when he left the store in order to be run over.

She would normally hesitate in front of the kids but not this time. "Was he drunk? Did he stagger onto or pass out on the tracks?" She looked directly at the crew, "I don't understand!"

"Nobody was there to see."

She stamped her foot, "Somebody knows something."

"For him to pass out doesn't fit." Alf spoke up. "I, for one have never seen him pass out."

"Maybe he was reading one of our letters," little Gladys sniffed, whimpering that it might be her fault.

Keith swung her up in his arms and reassured her, "No sweetie, trains are loud and he would have heard it and moved out of the way."

"And he's crossed those tracks umpteen times and knows the area like the back of his hand," a very grown-up Peter spoke for the first time.

Olaf didn't have to say it because they all knew, "The guy gets comical, repeats himself, and sings but doesn't pass out. That's what he does. That's him." The green chain man was aware that they would have to refer to their friend in the past tense from now on.

"Were the police called?" Lasse asked.

"All we know is the doctor from Tisdale led a coroner's jury."

"They've already ruled it an accident and that's what's going in the newspapers." Olaf sighed. "We didn't want to leave before we knew."

As they spoke, Lasse got up and paced. Her thoughts churned. "How can lightning strike twice? After Bjorn's death a quarter of a century earlier, how could Knut possibly be cut down by the same iron beast?"

She swore and wanted to heave something across the room. The children crowded close and it made her stop pacing for a moment.

She thought, "The children's only frame of reference to understand death is dead animals, and she could see the wheels turning in their heads. Their young eyes were sad and their faces glistened with tears." She decided they felt devastating grief like anyone else and felt their youthful arms encircle her, but her mind raced.

"Where is the payroll money?" her eyes widened, remembering to ask, "were you paid?"

"Payday isn't until this Saturday but the money's gone. No chance you, have it?" Keith asked tripping over his own tongue.

"No. Knut always managed that. He took in cash from board sales, then paid you on Saturdays."

"That's true." Percy said. "He paid us without fail. Once every two weeks."

Lasse pushed to the back of her mind the reports of the raucous Saturday nights after payday. Over the years, Knut had told her stories that would curl anyone's hair.

Keith, backed by the crew, said, "Right after the tragedy, we searched the camp high and low. There was no money. It wasn't like he ever left it laying around but we all knew where he kept it. If it wasn't there, he had to have it on him. All these 15 years and nobody ever touched a cent they didn't have coming."

The looks on the men's faces showed they were counting on the missing money for this Saturday's payday. Questions swirled in her mind. "Did he leave a will somewhere? Could she get access to his business account soon enough to pay the crew? She'd have to hire a lawyer."

"Please get Halvor," she breathed remembering their best friends and closest neighbours, "he needs to know."

Percy took off, hell bent. At the mournful home, the minutes ticked by and people paced or stood and looked out frosted windows, in shock, feeling the paralysis of grief. Halvor burst through the door with Greta and Lizzie not far behind. The elderly Helga brought up the rear. Greta's tears were non-stop, and she, Lizzie, now 14, and Helga, didn't have enough arms to cradle the devastated family. They tried, however, moving from one to the other, then Helga set about making coffee and breakfast.

"There has to be foul play," Halvor spoke aloud for the first time since making his way to Lasse.

The crew members shot him a knowing glance then nodded in agreement. It was an eerie feeling.

"None of us accepts the accident theory," Keith said, speaking on behalf of the others. "I can't shake the feeling that a crime was committed."

Halvor ventured, "My brain and gut say the only ones with anything against Knut are the Blacks and Swallows but nobody's heard of them for ages."

Lasse agreed. "They're the ones with an axe to grind but would they go so far as to murder him?"

"Thieves don't always draw the line at murder. As long as they get what they want, that's all they care," Halvor said. "Payback. Those criminals were locked up for a long time. Nobody knows for sure but they were set for release in 1910. I haven't heard of their return but I've been worrying for the last few years about them coming back."

Lasse was relieved it was out in the open. The house fell into a hush with the group mulling over the situation.

"Even if the coroner and his jury knew there was money involved, without proof, it may not have affected their decision. How do they say it's murder when there's nothing left to investigate?" Greta asked.

"Yet, foul play is rolling around in all our minds and we are suspicious as hell of who we think did it," Halvor summed it up.

Without making a fuss, Helga and Greta poured coffee and motioned for anyone who wanted scrambled eggs and toast to come and dish up a plate. The log house Knut had built was getting crowded with not enough room at the table. Most people ate standing up or holding a plate on their laps. Nobody felt like eating but the food and coffee smelled good. All the visitors thanked the women for their efforts.

After breakfast, a uniformed member of the police knocked on the door and the crew didn't want to leave before they heard what the Mountie had to say. He introduced himself as Corporal Len Grieves and said he had received a telegram about the accident.

He extended his condolences. "I couldn't believe it was Knut. He was a true pioneer in this district and a friend."

He turned to the others, "Normally for an accident, we don't get involved but since it's Knut, I couldn't stay away. If it was a criminal offence, we'd hop on the next train. Plus, the train company has its own police but again, for an accident without evidence to the contrary," he hesitated a moment.

"May I ask questions while I have you all here?"

"It's the perfect time being all of us crew just came from the scene," Olaf said.

"Did any one of you see anybody or anything unusual? Were there tracks or markings that didn't fit? Like horse or human?"

One by one, they all shook their heads.

Keith spoke, "First off, it was snowing. By the time we got there, all the curious onlookers had pretty well trampled the area. People were frantic to figure out who it was."

"We disagree with the accident verdict and think there's foul play," Keith went into detail about the missing payroll and suspicions about the Blacks and Swallows. The others agreed and the cop seemed open to what they had to say.

"If only someone had witnessed anything for us to prove it!" he was almost pleading.

Nobody did.

"I plan to travel to the site and walk around it myself."

"We're almost certain Knut had the payroll on him, but aside from none of us getting paid, we can't prove it was stolen," Einar said.

"And he always paid us on time," Alf sided in.

"I'll play the devil's advocate," the Mountie posited, "he could have blown it on God knows what."

"It doesn't make sense," Keith said, "why, after 15 years, would he suddenly blow it? He's paid us like clockwork all this time. I expect we may never know the answer."

The corporal nodded, "Never say never but that's about it. The accident ruling means he wasn't killed first and dumped there."

"I have one other burning question, but don't wish to offend," the Mountie paused. "Is there any chance he could have ended his own life?"

At first, disgust seized the room, then anger but he was ready for it. In his experience, those closest struggled hardest.

"Of course not!" Lasse almost shouted and the others sided in with her. Now she was riled.

"You understand that when a man makes that decision, he acts quickly? Was there nothing bothering him?" Len asked again.

"The war and conscription but everybody's bothered by that," Lasse said.

"I know it's hard to come to terms with."

Len replied, "I know those types of small-minded men, out for revenge. I promise to pay the brothers a visit." At least he was sympathetic and before leaving, once again extended his sympathies.

After the Mountie left, Halvor took the floor, "Not meaning to sound defeatist, but…" he looked at Lasse. "We know you could try to fight this but the simple fact is you have nothing to go on. Also, being a woman, you might have the vote, but you know women are still non-persons in the eyes of the law."

By this time, more crew members arrived, Sully, the cook, and Ed one of the teamsters.

"You could have a long road ahead of you," Einar added.

"Thank the Lord I have all of you to stand with me being a Swedish woman who speaks broken English," and she started to cry again.

When settled, she spoke quietly, "Nobody is saying it, but we all know that Swedish immigrants in Canada might not be considered as dangerous as Ukrainians or Germans in the middle of this war but we get our fair share of being looked at sideways. We're in the throes of prohibition and a War Measures Act. Knut's drinking was illegal too."

With gentleness, Halvor pointed out, "He wasn't alone. Remember, we have no proof of either foul play or alcohol."

Lasse pleaded again, "His payroll is missing and those brothers spent time in prison in part because of him."

"And me," Halvor chimed in.

That night, after everyone left, Lasse sat on their bed and opened a small bag of Knut's belongings carried home by Einar. She touched the bundle of letters he'd saved and knew he treasured every word.

"Did his pocket watch disintegrate along with him?" she wondered and searched the dresser in high hopes. But no, all she found were his cuff links and underwear. She pulled the clothing to her and tried to breathe in his fragrance. In the bag were extra clothes, socks, underwear, his shaving kit, and a pocketknife he should have had on him. From their closet, she pulled out shirts and other clothes that became wet from the tears streaming down her face.

"How soon will we forget what he looked like?" she cried already knowing the feeling but this time gazing at his handsome portrait on the wall.

The hours lengthened and her mind reeled in between people pouring in to bring food and well wishes. Still the funeral arrangements loomed and she was overcome with a profound sense of loneliness. She would forever remember the day she and her saddened children made their way to the funeral home.

"No child should ever have to do that," she thought but instead reassured, "we must always think of your father with happiness and love because that's what he would want."

She rued, "Why do two sets of my offspring have to carry such a burden? How can I not feel disillusioned?"

For a second time in her life, she fought to withstand shouldering her children's shock and that of the entire community. Most neighbours read the newspaper and accepted it as a tragic accident. The knowledgeable few who thought otherwise stayed silent. The children were coached to keep quiet but the unfairness of losing their father had them crying into their pillows most nights.

The funeral notice invited guests to attend his service on Sunday, 11 November 1917. The horse-drawn hearse left the farm at 12:00 noon and painstakingly, the cortege travelled the seven miles north to their beloved Carrot River Valley Lutheran church near Fairy Glen. Neighbours and friends of every stripe attended, bearing heavy hearts and condolences. It was all Lasse could do to make it through.

During the sermon, the minister spoke of how Knut had arisen from humble beginnings to build his entire life. The cleric beseeched the mourners with pleading eyes and open arms to imagine Knut's soul ascending to and embracing God in Heaven. The wooden casket, carried by six pallbearers, led the recessional for the committal to take place mere steps outside the church doors. When Knut was lowered into the ground, there was no turning back.

At the lunch in the church basement afterwards, the clergyman gathered the family together.

"Knut was a good man," he implored. "He will forever find peace in God's presence and you can visit his grave here, anytime."

The family's first choice was to bury him under a big old tree at home, yet the churchyard was sacred and the law. The problem was the churchyard was too far away and it made their loss all the more permanent. Lasse wanted her family to be able to walk outside and talk to him on a whim but it wasn't meant to be. She and the children nodded, thankful for the quaint church and the thoughtful countryside folks who prepared the lunch.

Initially, Halvor and Greta sent telegrams to Iowa, Winnipeg, and Sweden. It was a hard time around the world, closing in on the end of World War I, and Knut's stepdaughters couldn't get home in time. They arrived after the Armistice in November of 2018, to cradle the family in their arms. Travelling during war was highly discouraged so although heartbroken, everyone stayed put, including his family in Iowa.

As time wore on, the cruel truth was hard to escape, especially when Lasse badgered Greta into sharing what she knew.

Greta started off, remembering back to the day they found out. "When the news registered on Halvor, he screamed 'No'! like a wounded animal."

"It was like he, himself, was hit by the train. He dropped his axe and swayed, ashen and heart sick. Shaking his head, he wept unashamedly, repeating, 'My friend, my friend'."

"When he and Percy made their way back to your house, the truth came out."

"Percy dreaded reliving the memory, 'The train men were met with a grisly sight', and he could hardly speak the words. 'I'm sorry to say but bits of human remains and clothing were stuck to the cars. Evidence was strewn for half a mile west of the hamlet. In the end, Knut could only be identified through process of elimination.' And all Halvor could do was moan."

Greta cradled Lasse as they cried and imagined the horrific scene.

Every fibre in Lasse's being told her that what happened was wrong. However, to fight the honourable coroner jury's verdict without evidence or witnesses might end in back lash. Canadian immigrants were being thrown into prison camps and she didn't feel safe to risk everything. Yet, the wrath of the brothers hung over her like a dark cloud and the four roamed free.

The vision of how she imagined it happening was burned into her mind although she couldn't speak the words. They had followed him, waiting, and watching for the timing to be exactly right. How clever and diabolical to sit concealed in the heavy brush, hoping he was under the influence. The thought of them meeting him, clubbing him to death, stealing his payroll, and dumping his body on the train tracks wracked her with sobs. The train would come along soon enough, the engineer would see the obstruction but wouldn't be able to do a thing to stop it. It was cruel but genius.

By the time the mixed train approached Crooked River, it would have already travelled the lengthy distance from Prince Albert, on its way to Hudson Bay. The rate of speed would be slow with stops at every little port of call. She was angry yet felt sorry for the engineer who might have fought sleep and boredom, hypnotised by tracks and forest. So to receive his personal hand-written apology that included $200, out of the blue, added another layer of complexity.

"Please accept my deepest condolences on the loss of your husband and your children's father. I beg and plead for your forgiveness for the tragic events that unfolded on that fateful day. These funds are a small token but please know they are sent with the utmost sincerity."

Knut's children already knew to fear the marauding ex-convicts. Lasse watched them as amazingly, in a show of courage, the half pints went straight for their weapons, a .22 calibre rifle, a bb gun, a baseball bat, and a sling shot. For days, she saw them come and go, knowing they waited patiently, acting as lookouts concealing themselves in trees at the tops of hills or crouched in the culvert or under the old wooden bridge up the road. Watching for the shadowy criminals, they lay under the attic windows or flattened themselves onto hay bales in the loft. Even the cobwebs under the veranda didn't deter them, lying in wait, stretched underneath for hours.

She wanted to say not to worry, that the men were long gone, but wasn't sure herself. In their young minds, she knew they feared but expected the villains to show. Their hearts ached and burned with a blind rage, wanting revenge for their father's death. The same could be said of her. Furthermore, she didn't have the energy to stop them. She was preoccupied, so they took turns standing guard and doing the chores. All of them hoped every day that the police would ride up with new evidence but that was not to be.

The day of the funeral, Harry from the hotel made a key observation, "I saw those hoodlums boarding a train the day Knut died but never twigged. When I found out, you better believe I stormed over to the police station. The Mountie had already tried to pay them a visit but they were long gone."

"So, there's proof they were back in town. At least for a while," Lasse said, "we can bet the thugs have long vanished."

Ten days after Knut's death, the casualty report returned from the Battle of Ypres. "On November 6, 1917, our Canadian boys have captured the Passchendaele Ridge. With heavy hearts, the massive price paid has met the predicted 16,000, killed and injured."

After that, Lasse spoke to the children at the supper table, "You know how your father felt about war and now we find out the soldiers won the battle on the very day he died. A great win, but I'm thankful he didn't have to hear how the dire losses predicted came true."

Lasse decided Knut would have wondered if the fallen soldiers had a chance to fight or if they were sitting ducks but she kept quiet.

Days later, the newspapers reported, "With conscription the haggling point, December's federal election is the most bitter in Canadian history. At the same time, the Wartime Elections Act, is steadily moving women's rights forward. Soldier's wives, mothers, and sisters, along with female military personnel and nurses will now be allowed to vote. Recent immigrants from enemy countries, are denied unless they have family in the military." In the end, the Borden's Conservative/Unionists beat out Laurier's Liberals.

Once again, Lasse pulled the children to her, this time while outside doing the morning chores. "The hard truth is, your father's death will always be significant to us but do you see how it gets lost alongside the roar of World War I losses? A whole world is in mourning and threatening to lose its morale." The children looked sad and knew their mother held the wisdom of her years.

Bonnie wondered aloud as 11-year-olds sometimes do, "A Norwegian immigrant farmer, run over by a train out in the bush, with no other proof, is simply a tragic accident?"

"That's about it," resignation was solidly entrenched in her mother's voice. "Still, we can't think our loss is any worse than the neighbours whose sons were killed or injured in battle. Your father was no war hero but we can't let the whole world forget he ever lived either!"

It was then that Smith rode up. Speaking of injustice, Lasse had almost forgotten that Indian women were excluded from getting the vote. Hell, their men couldn't vote either but were expected to go to war.

Smith seemed attuned to the mood and said, "We believe those who grieve deeply are standing on the threshold of the spirit world. That makes your prayers holy and strong. With loss, you let go of the past and stop grasping at the future, opening yourselves up to all good things to come."

His words comforted, and Paul spoke. "If we put up a nice headstone at his grave, then he won't be forgotten and we can let go of the past a little." Lasse couldn't help but love that 10-year-old boy.

Knut would be proud of the headstone they chose to mark his life. On the positive side, Knut's grandparents and relatives in Heaven, would be waiting and spared the horror of living through his death. Finally, Knut would never have to witness the prime minister going back on his word to overturn the farm sons' exemption five months after it was put into place. Forevermore, the saying, "What's new on the Western Front," would take on new meaning.

22

The Big House

What would become of them? With the loss of Knut, a bereft Lasse promised her devastated children, "We've reached our quota, so nothing else can happen to this family." She knew it was a white lie but what else could she say?

In the meantime, the search was on to find Knut's will. The day after the funeral, Peter, Paul, Bonnie and Gladys turned the place upside down. Eventually, the boys found it tucked neatly in a corner drawer of his shop.

"Actually," 13-year-old Peter said, handing it to his mother. "It's a message scratched onto the side of a brown paper bag. Looks like he wrote it first with a carpenter's pencil, then went over it with fountain pen."

"The message is dated February 4, 1904, the day we were married," she was astounded, "and he signed it!"

She read aloud, "When I die, all my earthly possessions go to my wife, Lasse, as executor of my estate." At that, she burst into tears, trying not to drip onto the precious paper. The children hugged her and patted her back.

In the lawyer's office, the short, bespectacled man, Mr. William Conway, declared, "Understandably, Knut wanted to protect you, writing out his wishes on your wedding day."

Surrounded by musting dog-eared books, and piles of folders, the learned man rose to the occasion to navigate the estate legalities and sort through Knut's finances.

"But is it even legal written on a paper bag?" Lasse entreated.

"A hand-written, holograph will is definitely legal."

"I expect he had no intention of dying so young, or he'd have done up a more official one." Lasse mused in her best English.

The lawyer replied, "Doesn't matter, pretty or not, this one works and no witness was required."

The main question was their future, that of the farm, and the sawmill. Halvor, and Greta stood by for support as she coaxed herself through the murky depths of life, a second time.

At one point, she confessed to Greta, "I don't know if I'm strong enough to go through it again. The difference is, last time, my parents and in-laws were there to hold my hand."

"You're stronger than you think."

After Greta held her and let her cry, Lasse mustered her resolve, "Mr. Conway is pushing through the red tape. The farm we will keep and the title goes into my name. A logger nearby has offered to buy the sawmill, and I can't refuse. The crew is helping transition it and now I can square away the debts."

The sawmill was the least of her worries. Keeping the farm afloat was no easy task. With Mikaila and Lovisa gone, the work fell squarely on her own shoulders. With little choice, she pulled all the children from school to help. Gladys at seven couldn't risk travelling alone the five miles to school. A Scandinavian bachelor, Old John, lived across the field in a weathered two-storey. He would help for a couple of dollars and a swig of homebrew.

To make up for missing school, Lasse refused to let the cobwebs mount in her children's brains. The teacher shared the needed books and over time, Lasse taught them everything she could about the three R's. Amid reading, memorisation of historical events, handwriting practice, and numbers drills she gave hints about Sweden, "Remember Hedvig, it's a queen, a church, and speaks of where we're from."

Her own abilities with numbers passed along, especially to Paul who naturally found himself at the centre of the grain planning.

Ciphering in his head, he said, "For 50 acres of wheat, running at 40 bushels to the acre, if we can sell it for $2.08 a bushel, it gives us over $4,000."

She checked his calculations on paper, "You're right! That money will go a long way."

He continued, "Twenty-five acres of oats at 80 bushels an acre paying 69¢ a bushel plus 25 acres of barley at 60 bushels an acre and 96¢ a bushel, together is nearly another $3,000."

Every bit helped because realistically, they no longer had Knut's extra income from the sawmill, freighting, or cattle buying for the army. She continued selling produce, eggs, cream and butter to the creamery and The Hotel.

Further, Lasse was aware that her children were doing well with languages. She and Knut had found it comical that their children's native tongue was unquestionably a three-way cross between English, Swedish, and Norwegian. When the world declared war, however, things changed and it wasn't quite as funny.

"For official purposes," she coached, "your nationality is Norwegian and the languages you speak are English and Norwegian."

That was acceptable because it was common for children to assume their father's heritage. In Canada, a country of so many cultures and nationalities, children tended to compare notes on the subject.

"What's your nationality?" they would ask, even though they were all Canadians, their parents must have come from somewhere else. That's how Canada worked.

In fact, Lasse and Knut's children naturally grew up speaking other languages like Danish. That meant they could communicate with elderly neighbours who had not transitioned well to English. Einar's mother was a prime example. Still, based on wartime tensions, in Lasse's mind, it was important for them to identify as Norwegians like their father.

"The Scandinavian neighbours and friends will be the only ones to know the difference, and they will understand."

As Lasse told William Conroy, "Since Knut's death, neighbours and friends treat my family with kid gloves. They encourage us without pity, so we don't lose hope."

"It's a supportive community!"

"Believe me, it's kept me sane!"

"It could be worse. Some women turn to alcohol, become unfit mothers and have their children taken away. Some are committed to asylums," he tried to lighten the moment, "but so are some men!"

Olaf, and others of Knut's crew, who lived locally, were encouraging. They intermittently reminded her, "Knut's wishes can't be forgotten with the lumber he hauled home for the new house."

"It hangs over my head every day," she sighed.

Einar made broad hints like, "It's a shame to see the wood just lying there."

Indeed, through her grief, winter rolled into spring with summer hot on its heels. Out the window sat the pile of perfectly cut dimensional lumber with quack grass and dandelions peeking up around it. The sight was depressing, and she knew the wood would eventually warp. The guilt was killing her. Fortunately, Olaf and Einar had helped the children cover it with tarps in November. But time to use it was growing urgent.

In the meantime, the family took on spring seeding but watching the youngsters made her eyes sting with tears. With the warmer weather came biting insects and dressing in long sleeves and pants, even if it was hot. Further, she worried the children might strain their growing hearts and immature muscles with such heavy farm work.

Peter, wise beyond his years, reassured, "Don't worry, we'll build a smudge, and covering up means not getting stung."

After seeding, one sunny morning, Lasse sat looking out the window and couldn't believe that one solitary wild orange tiger lily had blossomed beside the lumber. Overcome with emotion, she had no choice but to take it as a sign. She'd been lying to herself. She wasn't helpless, she was strong and could do this thing. After bacon and eggs, she went on gut instinct alone.

"I've watched all of us move around like we died right along with your father and today that ends. His dream for a new house cannot die with him."

She had their full attention. "We are going to build the new house ourselves, come hell or high water!"

The children cheered. Finally, she had turned a corner.

"We will all help," exclaimed little Gladys, suddenly happy to pull away from the depressive state no child should ever enter.

This turn of events was exactly what everyone needed. The children echoed Lasse's words, "We'll call it 'the Big House' and it'll follow Swedish lines."

Knut and Lasse's blueprints from long ago showed a spacious two-storey with front veranda and tall windows for sun and fresh air. On the ground floor were the kitchen and dining area, a walk-in pantry, front room, and bedroom. The second floor had a hallway, three bedrooms with walk-in, slanted ceiling closets.

The middle of June 1918, the excavation began. Lasse, the self-appointed contractor, was green as grass about building. She stepped out the measurements to break ground and despite the Spanish Flu, volunteers showed up to help, including members of Knut's old crew.

Keith said, "Knut mentioned your knowledge of building could fill a thimble so we thought you might appreciate our help, and we're gambling the fresh air will keep us ahead of the flu."

Lasse was overjoyed and watched with fascination, their clearing of shrubs and debris to make the land level for drainage. A couple large boulders were pried free and manhandled down the hill, into the ditch out front. With the input of Wilfred, a handyman carpenter, who whistled almost non-stop, the foundation of concrete footings was set to carry the structure's weight. There was no basement, only a small dug-out cellar beneath the pantry.

Greta, pregnant after a decade's dry spell and Lasse, winked at each other, "Remember the whistling curse from the old cattle ship?" Greta asked.

"But now we're on dry land in more ways than one."

"You mean bone-dry," Greta said tongue-in-cheek, "with prohibition and the War Measures Act."

As the dog days of summer wore on, the builders had to substitute perfectly good building days to farm and prepare for winter. Halvor apologised, "Sorry but we have to get caught up with our own gardens and crops but we'll be back."

When berries ripened, it was time to restock cellars. On a berry picking trip to the Pines, along the trail to Fort á la Corne, Lasse's family met the Smiths, who shared a hind quarter of their jumper. It was the choicest part of the animal and Lasse felt honoured, humbly offering a crocheted throw in return.

People speculated about when the war would end and prayed desperately for soldiers to return home, alive. Persistently, the servicemen and women trickled home over the summer months but were thought to unknowingly carry the Spanish Flu because it took off like wildfire. House-building became a hit and miss endeavour and the initial flourish slowed. As the temperature grew chillier and fall was upon them, other days were taken up butchering chickens, pigs, and beef. Icehouses were full which was crucial.

At harvest time, like other farmers, Lasse hired a local threshing crew to take off her crop and was amazed to see so many of Knut's crew doubling as threshers. Indeed, there was Danny, the trim saw man, Percy, the top-loader, and Bill and Ed, the teamsters. Again, her house-building took a beating when volunteers couldn't be in two places at once.

With the house-building ceased for the time being, Lasse cooked hearty meals for the harvest crew twice a day with snacks for coffee breaks. The children pitched in shelling peas, husking corn, and peeling potatoes. They pulled the meals together and hauled water to wash the piles of dishes. Any one of the three eldest could hitch up the wagon and along with their mother, lug food to the field. Serving it hot took real talent but the men's camaraderie was the real reward, even if they had to stay a safe distance apart and wear a mask when they weren't eating.

Lasse heard the crew boss warn, "At suppertime, thanks to the flu, we'll be sitting outside in the farmyard instead of inside the house. Remember! Hats off and hands washed."

Plates were piled high, and gallons of hot coffee, and tea flowed. Once sated, smoking, chewing snoose, telling stories, and teasing followed. "We can't dilly dally because staying ahead of the weather is more of an art than a science."

At the same time, word came of experimental flu vaccines being tried in the United States. It was said they were used on soldiers in army camps and on health staff volunteers. People hoped and prayed the experiment worked.

Despite rain and cold delays, by the end of October 1918, harvest was over, and Lasse's house-building remained stalled. Unexpectedly, Wilfred took ill and scared everyone when he almost died. Fortunately, he rallied to lay low for a steady but lengthy recovery. When one cog went missing, Lasse tried to cover but as usual, she had a full plate herself, and limited skill for house-building.

The Armistice on 11 November 1918, ended the Great War as a ceasefire and not as a surrender between the Allies and Germany. Although the war killed thousands of soldiers, the deadly flu also did a number on Saskatchewan people of all ages and genders. On the same day, it was the first anniversary of Knut's funeral.

Lasse received a letter from Lovisa and Mikaila,

Dear family,

We miss you all dearly! Veterans are returning to no jobs, resenting women like us and immigrants who filled their positions in their absence. There is discrimination towards ethnic groups on the losing side and those of us who walk the fine line in-between, Swedes. We've evaded the issues by keeping our heads down and not making waves. Neither of us has had the flu. We miss you and hope all is well. Love Mikaila and Lovisa

In the meantime, Wilfred's wife, Mary, said to Lasse, "I think if Wilfred had a little medicinal hooch, it would help."

Lasse spoke to Harry, "The Hotel's supply has bottomed out but I know that even a few swallows can make a difference."

Ida piped in, "You no longer need a prescription for alcohol for medicinal purposes, you know? That need is now classed as an 'emergency epidemic measure'. Casey is putting in a big order."

"I'm insulted that hotels and liquor vendors are still on the hot seat, accused of trying to bribe the Liberals to dilute the law further!" Harry declared.

"Good grief!" Lasse exclaimed.

In the end, Wilfred's wife went to the pharmacy and got the scarce alcohol. In truth, Wilfred gained great relief from the brandy, at least to his constitution.

The talk was that Canadian immigrants, like Ukrainians and Germans, even if they were friends and neighbours, were targeted at home as enemy aliens. Melfort people heard how two dozen prisoner of war camps had sprung up across Canada. Even after the Armistice, by the end of February 1919, an internment camp was hastily built at Eaton's railway siding in Saskatchewan. Sixty-five, mostly Ukrainians were transferred there in rapid succession from camps in British Columbia and Alberta.

Privately, people like Lasse, Halvor, and Greta whispered among themselves. "I thought the war was over. How can they be prisoners of war in their own country? They got rounded up and thrown in jail even though they're every bit as hardworking as the rest of us! Are other nationalities getting looked at sideways too?"

Halvor added, "If that's not enough, the prisoners are contending with the Spanish Flu, plus, the aftereffects of a train wreck getting to Saskatchewan."

One night, at Lasse's farm, Lady's pup, Finn, now 13 years old, barked frantically. Lasse thought it was the coyotes again. Out her rustic window, she froze to see a shadowy figure pass the barn in the moonlight. The girls slept but luckily, her 15-and 12-year-old sons had her back.

The man who revealed himself was Ivar, her neighbour from Gronlid, and she called, "Ivar! come inside!"

"Thank you, thank you!" he cried.

"I am so sorry for what's happened to you!" she said, draping his shivering body with warm quilts. She knew he'd been imprisoned. "You're freezing! Come and sit by the fire. What is happening?"

"Knut vas my old friend, so I came here but I don't vant to cause trouble," he apologised. "Yesterday, at the Eaton camp, ve refused to vork anymore and valked avay. The var is over and hanging on is demoralising ewen for the guards. They're as anxious to get home as us. That's vhere I'm going, home to the farm at Gronlid."

At Lasse's surprised look, he promised, "I vill leave wery soon, I just needed a rest and some varmth."

She said, "Ivar, you have my absolute trust and backing. You've worked as hard as any other homesteader and I know you're a rock solid Canadian."

He hung his head and she saw his cheeks were wet with tears.

"Here, please have some hot coffee, and a bite to eat," and the exhausted man gratefully ate and drank. She knew full well that helping him was putting her own family at risk, but Peter and Paul were already saddling and bridling a horse for him.

"Do you dare sleep for an hour?" she asked.

"No. They'll be hot on my trail and I must see my family before I'm deported."

He put on the heavy winter garb Knut hadn't worn in two years and tucked a bag of food under his arm. He turned as he left and said, "It's likely the last time I'll get to see my family. I vill never forget your kindness!"

She reached out her arm and handed him Knut's rifle and a box of shells.

As she and the boys watched him ride into the night, tears welled, "There for the grace of God go I," she cried.

Lasse knew that for Ivar, the reuniting with his wife and family would be bittersweet. Sadly, he knew his discovery was imminent, but was happy for the precious moments.

The newspaper reported, "The Eaton camp prisoners weren't free for long but arrested and moved to a camp in Amherst, Nova Scotia. The Saskatchewan camp lasted only 24 days." Lasse remembered they had passed Amherst, near the Bay of Fundy, on their journey into Canada.

"Ivar can thank God his farm wasn't confiscated or his wife and children imprisoned." Lasse knew he would be grateful that as his accomplice, she wasn't drawn into the fray.

When seeding ended that spring, Lasse and family had put the Ivar situation behind them. By July of 2019, the Big House's structure was framed and tied with anchor bolts to the foundation.

"People are still fighting off, dying or recovering from the flu," Lasse, Halvor and Greta commiserated when they watched Wilfred return to his duties. The man was a shell of his former self.

"He was lucky to survive."

"All of a sudden, we're making headway again," Lasse ventured. "Wilfred says everything gets sheathed with wood next."

Inevitably, each person took on the project with purpose. The vigorous help of the crew, neighbours, and friends produced a symphony of pounding nails, ringing saws, snippets of song, and whistling. It amazed her when friends from town, like Harry and Ida, the two Mounties, the Johnson's, or Marj showed up to help. They came for the house and to do farm work but in general, they loved the fresh air of the countryside.

"With chimney fires a threat," she said, "Knut and I always slept near the wood stove. You know what it's like to wake in the winter to the sounds of silence. No wood popping or crackling means time to act," she laughed, "especially if you've run out of coal. This house, the one Knut will never live in, has my bedroom off the front room. I'll have the kitchen stove and then in the front room, a pot belly stove, for a nice, toasty house."

With the walls up and the roof on, the glass windows were hoisted into place. Lasse rejoiced, "My beloved stained-glass kitchen window and bevelled glass front door! Knut carted those treasures clear across country and I will remember him every single day because of it." Missing him and her older girls was never so pronounced as at that moment when she wished they could be by her side sharing her joy.

"Lath and plaster ceilings help prevent the spread of fire," Alf, the planer, had stepped up when Wilfred stepped back. Alf directed, "Nail narrow strips of wood across the wall studs and ceiling joists and then coat them in plaster. To shape rounded walls, like in the bedroom closets, it's tricky, but can be done. And lime adds to the soundproofing. Can we get any?"

"Our Scottish neighbours have a lime kiln!" Lassie smiled replying matter-of-factly.

The intensive work began but Alf got a kick out of the kids and Lasse appreciated it, "Plaster's fun," he said. "They pretend they're ghosts under all that white powdery dust. Then, until we use the chicken wire, they fashion weird creatures from it."

"Comment sa va? Je suis bien!" she heard the children repeating as he taught them a little French. Gladys exclaimed, "It means How are you? I am fine!'"

With no mechanicals to install, the building schedule steadily improved. Knut had hauled huge loads of wood shavings and sawdust home. Used for insulation, it was stuffed and crammed everywhere, above the rafters in the attic, under the floor joists held up with planks and plywood and poured down inside the two by four studded walls.

"We'll form a human chain handing over buckets of shavings. The children can help." Wilfred was back in the driver's seat. "Everyone knows the shavings will settle, but that shouldn't be for a long time."

Once the lath and plaster dried, the amateur painters lay protective sheets all over the plywood floors and gave the inside walls two coats of white paint. Here they had an assortment of helpers.

"Be careful not to do too much reaching," Lasse warned the pregnant Greta. "You don't want to get that baby's cord wrapped around its neck!"

"That's an old wives tale!" Greta scoffed.

"For the woodworking," Lasse said, "Ted, a finishing carpenter, is here to lead the charge."

Rudimentary stairs were in place but Ted got right to the finishing and before they knew it, he was calling, "Come see!"

"I'm done the stairwell," he pointed, "and think it's what you wanted. It has a nice, rounded handrail and balustrade so nobody falls over the edge. At the bottom are two stair steps leading to a small landing. Then you make a clean half-turn up a run of eight stairs to the top landing. There's a window to the world on the outside wall to enjoy the view as you catch your breath. Directly across from the window are two more steps up to the entry of the second-floor hallway."

When Lasse took a look, she said, "Thank you! It's perfect. The spindles and decorative caps for the posts really set it off."

After the staircase, Ted wasn't finished by any means and the children took every opportunity to slide down the new banister. He constructed the wide wood trim around doors and windows, the crown mouldings, and baseboards, plus, he built shelves in the pantry, kitchen, and closets. Here both Wilfred and

Alf gave him a hand. The baseboards would be attached at the end of everything.

Once they finished, Lasse took on the staining. Doors, window casings, trim, and stairs all required a consistent dark stain and rub.

She said, "Ted will install the tongue and groove wood floors. It's an arduous task."

Ted explained, "The floor has to be smooth and even, so all the pine boards must be shaved and sanded to an exact thickness to avoid breakage. The laying of the floor is tedious so I'll be happy to have helpers."

Then Lasse said, "When it's finished, I will tackle the finishes myself to make the rubbed stain uniform."

Others offered but she declined, "It's important to have one consistent person or we'll end up with a mess. It means I'll be working on my hands and knees," and she groaned.

When finished, every bone and muscle in Lasse's body hurt. Still, she felt proud because the result was well worth the effort.

"Somebody suggested green battleship linoleum for the kitchen floor, but it would be a shame to cover this beautiful wood," she said.

"We can use our braided rugs since that's been the family's pastime most of our lives," Mikaila said.

"Every rag we can spare goes into a thick and colourful rug," Lovisa added.

"One day, I plan to save up enough money to order thick dazzling Persian rugs," Lasse joked. "But not today."

Meanwhile, the volunteers working outside brought the exterior to life. There was no shortage of ladders and scaffolding so more than one level of platforming was wrapped around the outside of the house.

Bonnie said, "Anyone scared of heights doesn't have to feel like they're walking on a tight rope without a net."

Lasse had suggestions to order the most modern asphalt shingles from Sears, Roebuck, and Co. That type were layers of felt saturated with coal tar and waterproofed with sand or crushed shells, then cut into strips.

When she spoke to her woodworkers, she said, "You know, I've always loved the look of wood shingles," and they agreed.

In the end, she ordered them from Ontario. When it came time, it took the group the best part of three days to get the roof and the veranda finished. She was right, the wooden shingles looked spectacular.

With sure-footed scaffolds, the siding went fast. As soon as one side of the building was complete, the painters moved in. Coming behind, the laypersons sloshed on a coat of mellow yellow and trimmed the edges with a rich chestnut brown.

The front veranda was designed for shade and to block out the rain with a roof covering and open sides, all supported by ornate posts. After placing the final brush strokes, the team stood back and admired their work. Something about it filled them with pride, maybe because they sensed Knut was watching and happy.

By December, disappointing word came out of the US that the over 39,000 vaccine doses used in November against the Spanish Flu were ineffective. The family barely gave it a second thought because on a sunny day that month, they finally moved into their new home, despite the freezing cold. At the same time, about a half mile away, Greta gave birth to a healthy baby boy they named Little Knut. The midwife attended and all was well.

The flu waned by April and Lasse threw her own housewarming party as a thank you to all her helpers. The pandemic was officially over, and her small feast, music, and dancing was much appreciated. The Big House with open doors would be another community backdrop for social gatherings.

"Pioneer families love nothing better than to socialise," Paul decided and that was good because he did too.

Throughout the years, sometimes Lasse felt the house was a hollow victory without Knut, but with the children, good friends, and neighbours, she couldn't say she was ever lonely. Over time, she resumed hosting meals for visitors but never as grandly as when Knut was alive. She taught the children to step dance, but it wasn't long before they taught her to do the Charleston.

Tuesday, 15 June 1920, a shocking telegram arrived,

Congratulations are in order. Double wedding ceremony by Justice of the Peace today. Wish us well!

Love, Mikaila and Wayne and Lovisa and John.

Flabbergasted but happy for both, Lasse sent a congratulatory telegram in return. What a far cry from Little Bjorn's grand wedding back in Sweden a decade and a half earlier.

At the grocery store, she heard talk that her old friend, Ivar was deported back to Ukraine from the Nova Scotia prison camp. The grocery store clerk shook his head.

A busty lady in the line-up declared, "Such a tragic turn of events. Our elected officials, just coming through a war, don't know who to trust." Those listening hung their heads.

Halvor and Greta's second son was born in November of 1920 and they named him Ole. Despite everyone's joy at the healthy little boy, other disturbing telegrams came. That decade, one by one, both Lasse's parents and in-laws passed away in Sweden. The men first, then a year later, her mother-in-law, followed by her mother. It seemed all Lasse could do was grieve.

In early 1922, Lasse started to feel awful and lose weight. She was always running to the outhouse and had to get up frequently during the night. Her skin dried out and her hair turned brittle. Something was wrong so she visited the doctor and got diagnosed with diabetes. Thankfully, he was able to prescribe insulin injections thanks to Banting and Best, researchers in Toronto.

Over that decade too, farmers went bankrupt but Lasse was determined not to become one of them. All were frustrated with grain sales. With high freight and dockage fees, farmers banded together and by 1924, sold their wheat through a wheat pool. At harvest time, the pool gave farmers advances on their wheat with the balance paid when the grain sold.

A news report on 16 July 1924, said, "Prohibition has ended but is being replaced by government-owned liquor stores. The ban on alcohol had lasted nearly 10 years and thousands of stills and equipment were confiscated over the past four years."

"It attests to the hardiness of the population!" Lasse snickered.

In 1925, Peter, Lasse's eldest son, turned 21, "I've fallen in love with thoroughbreds and horse racing," he said.

Even though a race might be broadcast on the new provincial radio station, he preferred to have his own horse in the race or attend in person.

Lasse received another telegram on Friday, 17 July 1925.

Dear Mother,

Wish us well! John and I are moving to the Yukon and opening a hotel and restaurant in Whitehorse. Love Lovisa and John.

In the meantime, the family heard a radio report, "Another referendum says the bars have reopened under strict rules. There is no standing, no music, no food, and no women as customers or workers."

Strangely, bootlegging in Saskatchewan proceeded to increase by over 100 per cent the first year after prohibition was lifted. The black market had honed itself to a razor-sharp edge. By 1928, Paul too came of age and loved the bar as a new place to socialise. It wouldn't be until 1935 that women's beer parlours opened separately from men's with no sale of food or other drinks allowed.

23

Farming over a Mickey out Back

Melfort—*1914–1922*

At the back of Martha's mind was always prayers, "God, please keep our son, Fleck, safe, and bring him home alive."

The Scottish woman read the first words of his letter from the war's front line, *"If a eat one more wiener, a'll be barking like a dog."*

The family had learned a good day might consist of ground turnip bread and pea soup with lumpy horsemeat. Wieners weren't likely even available. The bad days could be no food at all or a hard biscuit ground under a shoe and boiled in a sandbag. For that, she worried herself sick.

Fleck wisecracked, *"The last relaxing campfire a had was in the Boer War,"* which Martha knew was total folly because he was no more than a bairn at the time.

It wasn't until after the fact but eventually, the family learned the hard truth. In the Battle of Ypres, their boy was pinned in a foot of water surrounded by the aroma of dead bodies. He refused to succumb to the misery and instead, shared fellow soldier, Del's story, a Dené from Northern Saskatchewan.

Lady Bug, always talking a mile a minute, took it upon herself to grab the letter from Sis's hand to read it aloud and the fight was on.

Dear Family,

According to Del, Inuit elders vow the Northern Lights are departed souls playing soccer and running across the spirit world's ice fields. Their crackling and gyrating, drums up spirit voices yearning to speak with you. Uttering the slightest noise could end badly. Even a tiny whistle, the hint of a tune, or a hum. A say goodbye with spine-tingling chills. Please know that a miss you all!

Love, Fleck.

As far as Martha was concerned, Dot, Aggie, Sis, and Butter Cup were not nearly as naughty as their sister, Lady Bug, nor as outspoken. Lady Bug was a prankster and had her heart set on being a cowgirl and marrying a cowboy.

New Year's day 1918, a haggard Fleck walked through Jake and Martha's door and all five sisters squealed with delight, draping their arms around him, almost knocking him over. His brothers Toot, Blue, Geordie, and Jo Jo, hung back, patiently awaiting their turn. His parents rejoiced yet fought back tears as they all swayed and sang *Auld Lang Syne*. Their boy had been to hell and back but was lucky compared to some.

Martha told Grandma Tessa, "In real life, 'twas the enemy beasts atop the ridge who beckoned him and his comrades. He only alluded to the Northern Lights fer our sakes."

"And fer his own peace of mind," Jake added. "Our Allied boys dinnae take the bait and were some of the few to make it home."

Fleck said with tears in his eyes, "Edgar from Scotland, Del, and me, all made it out together. We were deathly afraid but 'twas knowin' ye all waited fer us, our faith, and pure luck that saw us walkin' out of the Battle of Passchendaele."

Jake winced, "How ironic. Fleck, ye've just come of age yet ye've already lived a lifetime!"

Fleck asked, "Is Grandda McLaren any better after his paralytic stroke last spring?"

Tessa said, "Aunt Clarice is spelling me off with him tonight. Sadly, he's not much better but he patiently awaits yer return."

Fleck couldn't get there fast enough. When he sheepishly entered McLaren's room, the old man threw open his arms.

"We missed ye somethin' awful, me boy!"

Fleck dropped to his knees beside the bed and begged for forgiveness, "Ye were so right Grandda! A should have never gone but we had to do somethin'. Can ye ever fergive me?"

The answer was a foregone conclusion and made the two cry and hold each other tight. They sat together and visited until McLaren closed his eyes, needing to sleep. Fleck and Tessa left the old man in Clarice's capable hands and returned to Jake and Martha's for the festivities.

She asked, "Did ye see his face light up when he saw ye! The invalid's grey, broken body transformed into a healthy, beamin' force of nature."

"Yes, a saw and 'twas breathtakin'." Fleck smiled with tears in his eyes as she hugged him again.

At Jake's home, Tessa tried to brighten the mood, "Thank ye everyone fer takin' turns to help with Grandda."

"We try our best to help move his limbs every day, but he's weak and stiff and the contractures are winnin'. Working around his stiffened joints and keepin' his pain down isnae easy."

In February 1918, then, McLaren was 77 years old. Having lived a full life and seeing his grandson return from war, the pioneering patriarch quietly went to the great beyond. His final breath was quiet and dignified compared to the grating death rattle that had flooded the room for so many hours earlier. The awed family witnessed sunbeam rays shine through the window collecting over his body. His tightly closed eyelids suddenly sprang open and a new light reflected the transfer of his soul to a better place.

Tessa cried, "We're witnessin' the glory of God!"

The well-respected pioneer's funeral was well attended in the Anglican church. The six grandsons who came on the wagon train, all cousins or brothers, functioned as pall bearers and ranged from 17 to 22 years. It was a sad day. Tears flowed because no one dreamt of losing their patriarch so soon. The females filled their handkerchiefs with tears. For Tessa, she imagined his tender reunion with the ones who went before, their three dearly departed daughters and granddaughter.

Jake and Martha learned much later from Chief Eagle Feather, that far away in his camp, when word reached them of McLaren's death, a ceremonial fire was lit. The fire was tended and prayers said until it went out three days later. At that point, the people were satisfied his spirit was released from the earth and had ascended to the Creator. Upon hearing the news, Tessa was amazed and thankful.

Proof that life in the world was precarious was evidenced when, with no notice, a deadly virus appeared that same month. It wasn't choosy and would kill both vulnerable and healthy individuals alike. Canadians joined a world thrust into hand-to-hand combat against a deadly scourge called the Spanish Flu.

After McLaren's passing, Martha and Jake visited Tessa. She showed them some of the items she had added to her girls' special memory box, now to include McLaren.

"I know he's with the girls," Tessa said. "In the box was a lock of his hair, his Bible, and his pocket watch."

"Mother, ye seem filled with the Holy Spirit yerself!" Jake commented.

"A'm bent on helpin' others affected by the pandemic, so a bake loaves of bread fer anyone who needs them, especially bachelors."

"But yer turnin' out a hundred-pound sack of flour at a time!" Jake cautioned, "dinnae hurt yerself!"

"And sewin' masks at record rates," Martha laughed, pointing to the piles sitting on her foot treadle sewing machine. "Ye've turned into a force to be reckoned with!"

"Well, a need to do somethin' with me time!"

"Who better than you to understand the ravages of an epidemic?"

"People have to stay home and isolate!"

Jake said, "Are yer pick-ups and deliveries workin' out?"

"Oh yes, a'm so grateful. A use the clothesline to reel the items back and forth then the grandchildren take turns deliverin' them fer me."

For the better part of two years then, Tessa and her extended family, lived separate existences. Martha worried about her mother-in-law and made sure someone from the family made regular stops. They spoke to her from a distance without hugs or touching, but it was better than making her sick and leaving her alone.

In the middle of the Spanish Flu, and 1919, the grandchildren wedding saga began with Jock and Emma's family first. Three marriages were sanctified between mid-November and mid-December, the perfect time between harvest and spring seeding. Bud, Peanut, and Tadpole found partners within the community but with the virus in mind, the wedding events were drastically scaled down. Normally, small ceremonies would have had larger suppers with all the community invited, however this was no longer an option. It was disappointing but workable. Each new couple, however, took the time after the ceremony to drive past their grandmother's home to wave to her and receive her good wishes.

The grandchildren thanked Tessa profusely for their gifts as did Emma.

"They love the homemade quilts ye stitched into the wee hours of the mornin' but what a strain fer yer back and eyes!"

"'Twas well worth it but yes, me vision is getting worse. I suppose it's cataracts." She knew her wire framed glasses made her look more grandmotherly than ever.

By 1920, with no warning, the Spanish Flu mysteriously disappeared as insidiously as it had arrived and the roaring 20s was born. Three more grandchildren married, all belonging to Jake and Martha. Toot, Dot, and Fleck. For Toot, who married his first cousin Chickadee, it created quite a stir.

Over a cup of tea, Grandma Tessa shuddered to daughter, Emma, "We should've seen it comin' when even at eight years old, he took such a likin' to the little girl."

"A guess, she always was his sidekick."

Consanguineous marriage left some of the family wringing their hands fearful the offspring might be adversely affected.

After great thought, it was level-headed Tessa who intervened, "God knows, the couple will have a heavy cross to bear with the practice bein' banned in parts of the world. In me day, tryin' to block them proved futile because they dug in their heels. Not to mention, fer the rest of their lives, they'll be thrown together at family functions."

"What will be, will be," Toot's father, Jake took his sister Clarice aside.

She whispered, "We won't allow it to affect the good relationship we've always had, will we?"

He shook his head.

The headstrong first cousin newlyweds, swore to change the world, and rationalised, "If 'tis good enough fer royalty, 'tis good enough fer us."

Tessa thought but did not say, "If ye study history, ye know that line of thinkin' dinnae always work out fer the best."

Was it a hard lesson the family had learned too late? Playing almost exclusively with cousins all their lives, what did they expect? All they could do now was to be there to support the couple and to pick up the pieces if need be.

With community gatherings back on, Lasse and children were invited to the weddings. The community loved to dance and children learned at home as was the custom. Lasse's sons, Peter and Paul were 16 and 13 respectively by 1920 and had already interacted with neighbouring Stoney Creek children all their lives. A healthy camaraderie existed during school and community events.

By the time the weddings came around, Tessa observed that Peter and Paul were noticeably good dancers similar to Jake and Martha's two girls, Sis (Miriam) and Butter Cup (Tessie). Peter didn't say much, but anyone could see he had eyes for Sis and, the feeling was mutual.

Sis mooned to her sisters, "A think, 'tis his dark skin and high cheek bones."

What Martha noticed and told her mother-in-law, Tessa, was, "Peter's unassumin' and innocent sidlin' to ask Sis to dance seems to have the girl quite spellbound. A cannae help but chuckle watchin' her follow his lead." Tessa knew the girl was as headstrong as they came.

On the dance floor, the young adults were incredibly light on their feet. To the changing rhythms, they floated, in a magical Peter Pan-like, unison. Lasse decided Peter would always take the lead but had found himself an angel to be bossed by.

Sisters, Emma and Clarice, and their religious counterparts attended the dances, dressed in black, but sat along the sidelines. They enjoyed the fellowship yet stayed true to their beliefs.

Tessa understood that their brothers, on the other hand, were no teetotallers but could take a drink without making it a habit. Jake, Sean, and David avoided gambling outright but enjoyed the odd game of bingo or poker. Their mother noticed over time that they also enjoyed the excitement of chuckwagons and thoroughbred racing, as did she.

Jake and Martha were straightforward about teaching old-time dancing to their children. Tessa and McLaren had taught all their own children but now Tessa was getting too crippled. Butter Cup played the pump organ by ear, and at home, the family took turns dancing around the parlour and kitchen. As a result, Jake's children were comfortable on the dance floor whereas his sisters', Emma and Clarice's children, by rights, should not have been. Sometimes however, out of sight of their parents, the first cousins all danced. Tadpole and Birdie were good sports and as much as they tried, they had two left feet. Unbeknownst to the parents, behind closed doors then, Bunny, Peanut, Bud, Boo, Chickadee, and Lulu learned to waltz, polka, fox trot, and two-step, right alongside their cousins. Anybody could do the butterfly or bunny hop which took stamina but not much talent.

At the latest wedding dance, which was Fleck's, breathless from dancing themselves, the heavier-set mothers, Lasse, and Martha, sat down daintily beside each other on the plank benches skirting the perimeter of the schoolhouse. Tessa sat close enough to be in on their conversation. Thankful for the walls to rest their backs against, the women mopped their brows with crisply starched, lacy handkerchiefs. Both were in the throes of menopause and Tessa knew the hot flashes were no fun.

During the intermission, the schoolhouse floor stopped bouncing. It was a short opportunity to speak normally, before shouting again over the bright fiddle melody, the lofty accordion, and the pounding piano keys. Downstairs, the tables were laden with potluck items for a midnight lunch and the aroma wafted upstairs.

At the break, the men made a beeline for the back door and Martha observed what everyone else suspected, "They'll be farming over a mickey out back."

"You can be sure," Lasse responded and they all laughed.

"A'm well past tryin' to figure out a prohibition law that forces people to resort to such measures. Fer half a dozen years now, with bars closed and liquor outlawed, this is life."

Both Tessa and Martha had seen an almost imperceptible flinch in Lasse and knew that Knut's death was still a sore spot for her. Having spoken to their widowed friend repeatedly, they knew she was a good sport with an even better sense of humour.

Lasse revealed, "In Sweden, they voted against prohibition. Their bars are on the Gothenburg system and even women can go in."

Martha gave her a questioning look. "Really? Well women could keep the men in check rather than waiting outside in the street with the children!"

"Exactly!" Lasse exclaimed, "there, they feed the drinkers, offer games or cinema, and have 'spiritless Sundays'. I think they're addressing loneliness."

"That must make a difference," Tessa said, "but if both parents go in, who looks after the children?"

"Like anywhere, there are grandparents or older siblings perhaps? The newer pubs have balconies for orchestras, or double as tearooms or post offices," Lasse smiled. She used to enjoy her work at The Hotel but as a single parent farmer, everyone knew she couldn't manage both worlds.

Martha and Tessa listened to their friend, marvelling at the forward thinking and common sense of the Swedes.

Martha offered, "A wish these types of changes would trickle over to Canada because although prohibition seemed innocent at the start, the crime is worse with it than without."

"What do ye hear from Mikaila and Lovisa?" Tessa asked.

"They are sophisticated young flappers now. Both married by Justices of the Peace!"

"Congratulations!"

Then Martha asked, "What do ye think about what's blossomin' between Peter and Sis?"

"They make a handsome couple. I am not even embarrassed by my yearning for grandchildren!" Lasse admitted.

"And in me case, great grandchildren!" Tessa added.

Martha spoke of the younger couple. "Paul and Butter Cup are still a bit young and at the experimental stage but 'tis not hard to see the spark. He's all she talks about. How he's so comical and keeps her laughin'. We've heard her say she adores that he can stop a crowd with his step dancin' and jiggin' and works up a tremendous sweat fer his audience. Bein' the youngest of 10, she's a bit of a rebel and if she can get away with somethin' without her older sisters findin' out, then great. Her brothers spoil her to bits and are so much more fergivin'."

Lasse told the story from her perspective, "Paul smokes and Butter Cup wanted to try but soon choked and sputtered. He offered a pinch of snoose and one try had her spitting it out and never looking back. He likes booze, but she said, 'like her dad, she can take it or leave it'."

"That's probably good."

"Eventually, Paul got her to try some of our family's delicacies, Blue Cheese, Limburger Cheese, Kippers, Pickled herring, and Lutefisk. They made her gag so; she drew the line there. I never laughed so hard in my whole life."

Martha and Tessa chuckled, "Actually, she told us the same thing! But notice she keeps goin' back fer more."

"Yes, they have a huge crush on each other, and it isn't goin' away."

The two mothers and grandmother were in their glory.

When the music resumed, a few of the Holiness Movement children, including Tadpole and Bunny hid in the back room behind the stage. They let their cousins and school chums lead them in the latest dances, away from the prying eyes of their parents. Tadpole and Birdie, of course, struggled, and as usual were the brunt of their cousin's laughter which didn't stop them. Martha, Jake, and Tessa were fully aware but never let on.

Jake admitted later that night, "The men outside were commiserating about alcohol production fer the war effort, rather than fer consumption. I know 'tis needed for disinfecting wounds and gun shell powder, but did ye know they use it fer synthetic rubber and plastic, and aircraft de-icin' fluid?"

"Amazin'!"

He went on, "One man wondered why they dinnae at least let us use beer with its low liquor content to help us come alive after work."

Martha just shook her head.

At Aggie's wedding in 1922, the community supper at the school was barely underway when, in the middle of everything, a man ran into the school yelling, "Fire! Fire!"

Everyone rushed outside to see smoke and flames coming from Jock and Emma's house across the field. Those who could, raced to the scene with Jake in the lead. For some crazy reason, he burst into the burning house, taking the stairs three at a time to empty dresser drawers out the window! He got off with the tongue-lashing of his life.

Much later, when emotions and ashes cooled, Jock and Emma ordered a large wooden house from a home builder's association in British Columbia. They used B.C. fir to trim all the doors, windows, baseboards, and for clever room picture rails, and plate racks. Along with the new house, they built a windmill for power with a generator connected to batteries in thick glass containers in the basement. The windmill powered grain grinding, pumping water, and cutting wood.

At the same time, Jake had promised Martha a new house for almost two decades and with the recent fire, they chose red brick to be shipped from the east. Although the two houses were finished differently, adornments ranged from plaster walls, insulated with horsehair and wood shavings, to large verandas. Hoosier cabinets, iceboxes, fancy parlours, and a full third floor attic with upper balcony gave grandchildren room to play. The narrow stairwell to the attic was long and without handrails. Windows on the main floors were unusually large to aid with failing eyesight. Jake and Martha's had hardwood floors and trim, chandeliers, glass pantry doors, and a dumb waiter. Their rich, chestnut brown leather furniture, the grandchildren disliked because it was too cold.

24

Bzzz—I Hear a WASP

Melfort—*1921–1929*

Jake pondered how intolerance happened so insidiously to Canadians. He remembered 1921 when the American Ku Klux Klan spilt over into Vancouver and Montreal. By 1922, they were blamed for sending threatening letters to a Winnipeg French Catholic college, followed by a mysterious fire there, claiming 10 lives. Despite the violence, in a hauntingly familiar trend, the next year, Mackenzie King of the federal Liberals, barred Chinese immigrants from entering Canada. For Jake and his Scottish family north of Melfort, the events weren't impressive but seemed remote compared to the bigger fish they had to fry.

To everyone's dismay, in September 1922, Jock and Emma's grown daughter, Peanut, died unexpectedly. The young mother's swollen tonsils and eventual suffocation caused flashbacks to three decades earlier in Muskoka. The doctor said it was quinsy. After the funeral, held at her parents' home, heart-wrenchingly, Peanut's husband, Les, set about raising their two tiny boys by himself, one aged three months and one, three years. Touchingly, Fleck, the cousin she'd grown up with, laid a pressed lilac bloom alongside her, in her casket.

Two years later, just as the countryside's darkness lifted from having the 10-year prohibition law repealed, the family was caught off guard again. "The Klan has solidified itself in Canada after an agreement signed in Toronto by two Americans and a Canadian."

Wrangling the kitchen dumb waiter up to its full length from the basement, Jake and Martha had stopped to pay attention to the staticky radio, "At a rally in London, Ontario, the Canadian KKK vows it is not lawless or violent and will work to change laws that it does not support."

Finished loading, they sent the lift back to the basement and Martha said, "Sounds innocent enough but why do I have a bad feeling?"

"If they live up to their word, it's one thing but are they trustworthy?"

June 1926 was a difficult month. On the 10th, newscasters maintained, "A dynamite explosion at a Roman Catholic Church in Barrie, Ontario has politicians and religious leaders calling out the violence."

Jake felt suspicious but was it proven beyond a doubt that the Klan was responsible? If they were, the country was treading a dangerous path.

Two weeks later, on June 23, Jake lost sight of the KKK's antics when the family became preoccupied with his brother-in-law, Jock's death, from a stomach ailment.

Stunned and in disbelief, Jake said to Martha, "We've known him ferever and poor Emma never had a chance to finish grievin' Peanut's death and now it's her husband!"

The devastated Emma, with help from her children, held Jock's funeral from their farm home. The day was blistering hot, and the guests, seated on the lawn had removed their hats out of respect. Before launching into prayer, the minister wisely suggested, "Please, put your hats back on for fear of sunstroke."

When the service was almost over, a young man from town galloped up on horseback. "I beg your forgiveness for this interruption," he said, "but I have a dire message."

He handed a note to Jake who read it silently and breathed, "Oh, God no!" then read aloud, *"Grave news. Clarice's goitre surgery here in Winnipeg had complications, and she has passed away. Your devastated brother-in-law, Philip."*

The staggering news cut through the crowd like a knife but it obviously hit Emma especially hard, having now lost both husband and sister. All she could do was hang her head, seeming unable to speak, nor raise a hand or eyebrow.

Tessa cried out for her youngest daughter, and David rushed to steady her. Bitterly, the assembled mourners gasped and sobbed. The gnashing of teeth was widespread, but none more than Clarice and Philip's children. Two still lived at home, Birdie, who was unmarried at 26, and Lulu at 14. Chickadee was 23 and married to Toot. They had two small children and she was pregnant with a third.

Jake watched Martha take charge. She found Sean and convinced him his services were desperately needed. Once Jock's funeral ended, Sean's youthful strength and resolve allowed him to depart for Winnipeg by train, to help Philip escort Clarice's remains home.

After Clarice's incredibly sad funeral, Jake walked across the field to find Emma sitting alone in her hauntingly empty farmyard. Despite the windmill sails quivering in the breeze, she sat on the front porch, beseeching God, "Why have ye fersaken us?"

The rustling leaves caused Jake to imagine the whispers of half a dozen loving spirits surrounding her and he hoped somehow, Emma sensed their presence too.

He said, "Are your children inside?"

She nodded.

"Don't lose faith," he soothed, "between God and the family, we will help ye." He was speaking of her four young adults still living at home, Boo, Cream Puff, Kitten, and Buddy.

"Yer children especially have yer best interests at heart. For that matter, all your brood does but remember, they need ye too. Tadpole with his three children, Bud with his two, and especially Bunny, being a soldier's widow now with five of her own."

Emma nodded and wiped away tears with her apron.

He went on, "Lulu has a soft spot for Peanut's two little boys and after Clarice's funeral, Les thanked Philip for letting the girl spend time with his little ones. She is a Godsend!"

Emma sniffed and seemed to appreciate his words. Something worked because eventually, she discarded her foetal position, and lent a hand to the many places it was needed.

Meanwhile, that summer, Jake awoke in the early hours to smoke coming from his mother, Tessa's farm. He was to learn that her old dog had barked furiously, awakening her to the sight of flames engulfing McLaren's blacksmith shop. Fortunately, it was a building they had deliberately set apart from the others.

When Jake rode up, Philip, Sean, and David were already there, and Tessa said, "It burned to the rafters and just when the bright red timbers collapsed, the boys arrived. We are dumbfounded and when daylight broke, 'twas still too hot to go near."

Philip's tone grew ominous. "'Twasnae hard to see the hoof marks borderin' the site. Looks like somebody torched it."

Sean and David gave grim nods of agreement.

Tessa, shook like a leaf, and croaked, "We need to talk to the police."

They went inside to wash off the soot and David, the youngest, gulped his coffee and rode out.

Corporal Grieves, gracious as always, dutifully took Tessa's statement after poking around the ashes.

He concluded, "The horses were shod. Other break-ins are surfacing, so we have to get to the bottom of it."

Jake, for one, couldn't help but think of the shenanigans from a decade earlier but looking from the burnt rubble to Tessa, he saw fear dancing behind her eyes.

She hid it well but ventured, "A dinnae know what will go up next, the house or the barn," her fear was justifiable.

After the Mountie left, the sons worried amongst themselves, "Fer sure, tin siding willnae save her."

Later that day, over tea, Emma blurted, "Mother, would ye come and live with us? We would love to have ye!"

Tessa seemed surprised, and grappled for the right response, "Oh, a couldnae impose."

"Ye wouldnae be any trouble. A could use yer company and yer help! Both Boo and Cream Puff are to be married next year."

"But to leave this place and all its memories! Ye know how a love bein' in me own home with everythin' familiar." Her voice dropped at the end and there was a long silence. They knew she was grasping at straws.

"Let me think about it," she said. "A guess a'm gettin' a little feebler all the time and livin' alone out here isnae gettin' any easier."

It was McLaren she missed most because to her, he was everywhere. Jake had heard her say she longed for one more sound of his hammering anvil.

"A would feel a lot happier if ye and Emma were lookin' out fer each other," Jake said. "Either that or move in with Martha and me but we've still got six at home, Emma's only got four and only for a short time."

Tessa had no worries as far as crops and farmyard went, with the family taking great care of her. Jake could tell she was feeling her years, with hearing and eyesight failing and finding the stairs difficult but she never complained.

In reality, at 72, she seemed plagued by loneliness and who knew when vandals would strike again?

Eventually, the old woman relented, and clutching her special memory box, moved to Emma's. Slowly, the mother and daughter healed as best they could. In the meantime, Toot and Chickadee moved into the tin-sided house so the old farmyard wouldn't fall into wrack and ruin. Sean's family on the opposite quarter, by this time, had three pre-teen boys and a little girl. Philip and Les seemed more than relieved for all the help.

Jake was thunderstruck that while they grieved, so much had changed, "How on Earth did Saskatchewan folks come to embrace the KKK?"

Then he marvelled at the simple facts. To close the unforgettable year of 1926, two Ku Klux Klan recruiters from Indiana, boldly crossed the border to Moose Jaw to band together the KKK of Kanada, hoping to loom large.

"'Tis like knifing open a wound only for it to scab over a festering sore," Jake said.

He remembered the afternoon in the café when he and Martha overheard the first-hand shaming and manipulation.

A stranger argued, "They say without 100 percent Canadianism, the prairies are the weakest point in the country. How dare we lose the meagre foothold our brave sons fought and died for in the trenches!"

Jake spoke quietly to his wife, "He has audacity, I'll give him that!"

Astonishingly, people nodded, accepting his ideas.

Indeed, over the next days, the radio announcers said, "The $13.00 Klan memberships are flying out the door to eligible WASPs, white gentiles, Anglo-Saxon, and Protestants."

Were the soldiers turning over in their graves? Had the mere mention of betraying patriotism done the trick?

The staticky radio squealed and the announcer claimed, "The Klan's initial rally in Moose Jaw saw 7,000 attending."

Over the airwaves came, "We are a pro-Protestant, white-man's organisation with our first allegiance to Canada and the Union Jack. This is a Christian organisation only, others cannot join. The slogan is 'One nation, one flag, one language, one school'."

And time after time, unrelentingly, they proved their point. The radio announcer said. "Thousands of supporters rallied as the robed and hooded Ku

Klux Klan burned large wooden crosses to the ground. The spectacular blazes were seen for miles."

"Anyone would be intimidated by such a dramatic show!" Jake exclaimed to Martha.

"Or enjoying it!"

Further reports came, "KKK chapters have sprung up across the province. Memberships exceed 25,000 province-wide, with sympathetic, non-members, incalculable."

A grain marketing quota was on, and at the elevator, Jake unloaded his second wagonful of wheat. He mopped his brow, waiting for the agent to cut him a cheque. Another farmer, behind him at the weigh scales got the permission wave and moved his rig inside to release the load of grain into the grated pit.

Inside the office, Alex, the agent, wrote a cheque and tore it off for Jake, then shook his hand. The agent wrote everything in a book, always carrying a pen behind his ear.

The farmer unloading his grain wore green work clothes with suspenders and when finished, entered the office, "Good day!" he laughed, "I'm here to tell you, if you see hoods and robes with a maple leaf on, that's the Canadian Invisible Empire Knights of the Klan."

"How'd you find that out?" Alex asked, writing another cheque but was ignored. Another farmer was lined up on the scale and before he got an answer, added, "Apparently they order the outfits through the catalogue, even women, have joined."

Once Alex did his duty to weigh, measure, and record the next wagonload, the driver moved into the elevator once the first wagon departed. When he wedged the back chute of his wagon open, and grain spilt out, Alex held out a metal can, to catch a sample.

Over the din, Alex yelled, "Gossip has it that the postmaster threatened to fire any employee who divulges names of parcel recipients."

The producer in green, although finished, still hung around, "But you know how fast gossip travels." He snapped one wayward suspender and said loudly, "Under those get-ups, no one can tell a granny from a psychopath. They say they go around on horseback spreading a secret codeword."

"I heard its 'Mac'," the farmer unloading yelled. "Supposed to mean, the plot to 'Make America Catholic', but not much of a secret if we all know."

The man in green said, "The KKK vows to clean up Moose Jaw's riff raff but flourishes there itself."

Jake wanted to say, "It's easy to blame Moose Jaw." Instead, he kept quiet, already intrigued by where this was heading.

"They're blaming Quebec," the man unloading said, "speaking French, having nuns teach it, and crucifixes hanging on public-school walls."

Jake decided Montcalm and Wolfe might roll over in their graves and dared to say, "Didn't confederation spell out French and English livin' side by side? Me parents got married in that era."

The fellow in green said, "Maybe but it's just another piece of paper."

"It's the law," Jake said.

"What about bringing in so many immigrants?" it was the man unloading.

"Right! Well, you have to admit, there is a ring of truth to what they say," the gent in green agreed, "and, what about the income tax that should have ended with World War I?"

"Everyone should question how their tax dollars are spent!" the man in grey said.

"Aren't we all immigrants in this country?" Jake questioned, "it's their lying about being non-violent that gets me."

Even Tessa, at 75, hearing about the conversation, said, "They've hit on some raw nerves."

"It isn't just the idea of straining our school budgets with more separate schools but troubling rumours about poor treatment at the existing ones!"

At the supper table, Martha pointed out, "Remember, at one time we were countin' on the nuns fer the survival of Butter Cup and me?"

Jake nodded and sighed. He sorely missed Jock and McLaren's voices of reason.

Mr. and Mrs. Brown stopped at Jake's one day for a load of hay. At the end of the gate, they met Chief Eagle Feather and his family on their way out.

At their questioning looks, Jake said, "The chief is from the Chagoness reserve. He guided our wagon train and I met him again when we bought lumber at the sawmill for our first house. He always brings us somethin' but it's hard fer him to leave the reserve."

Mr. Brown replied, "Apparently the Indian Agents strictly dole out passes like for selling produce or hunting."

"A dinnae know the rules but we have no quarrel with them," Jake said and motioned with his arm, "Please, come in fer tea before we load yer hay."

"Without bison to hunt, and living on reserves, starvation set in," Mrs. Brown spoke matter-of-factly as she sipped her tea. "Aren't the schools for the children's own good? At least they're getting educated and fed."

"Bein' separated from their families can't be good," Martha replied and the room fell silent.

"They're good neighbours who've helped us, so it doesnae feel right," Jake ventured. "If 'twasnae for them, our whole family might still be wanderin' around lost or stuck in a slough."

"And they have no qualms about fightin' prairie fires!" Martha smiled.

Jake added, "Or going to war. A boy from a northern reserve fought alongside our son."

At that, Jake and Mr. Brown drained their teacups and went outside to load the hay.

Grabbing a pitchfork, Jake said, "Educating their children is one thing but thinking they can take the Indian out of them is pie in the sky."

The man agreed. "Hmm. On another subject, does allowing record numbers of new immigrants into the country make sense?"

Jake silently wondered if Mr. Brown owned a Klan membership. "Couldn't we use more taxpayers? If they're well educated and skilled, this country needs them. Look at the pitiful number of doctors we have, fer instance."

"I suppose so, but I still think the country is going to hell in a hand basket."

Jake sighed. He had no intention of getting into it.

In 1928, hackles rose after a Roman Catholic church was burned at LeBret, and an attempt was made to burn the Regina legislature. Co-operative minded rural folk began to want a divorce from the KKK.

If that betrayal wasn't enough, more news came, "One of the two KKK organisers disappeared with all $100,000 of the membership money. He was intercepted and hauled back to Saskatchewan for trial but released because collecting money was part of the organisation's mandate. At this point, Saskatchewan ties are severed with the American arm but a new locally run Klan has emerged. It vows it is against violence and is merely trying to 'keep Canada British'."

Silent echoes of "bullshit!" were heard throughout the land.

Jake and Martha visited Philip, "The Klan's following has wavered and they were mistaken about homesteaders being easy to rook for long."

"Any God-fearing person doesn't condone violence and that's the way it is." Philip was weary of it all. "A southern farmer, another one joinin' out of curiosity, said, 'the Klan was here to make a fast buck'."

"Maybe so."

Jake said, "A think to most people, burnin' crosses is nothin' short of bullyin' and blasphemy."

"Fer the Klan to pay prostitutes to dress up as nuns was disgraceful!" Martha could hardly speak the words.

"Plus, no one scores points by donnin' hoods and crashin' a church service. That disrespect has no place here. In this country, we have to work together, just to survive."

After the fact, everywhere Jake and Martha went, people talked about the KKK but mostly on the down low. When the two entered the shoe store, Sammy, a Jew, was measuring a lady's foot.

She wore a lovely red hat and Sammy had brought out a pair of pumps from the back. Slipping one on for size, she started, "Once the Klan did their damage, they slithered home."

Another lady, in a fur-collared olive-green wrap wanted oxfords. Turning around and seeing friends, she said, "They had the nerve to call Canada the dumping ground of the world because of our immigration policy!"

Jake figured Sammy looked uncomfortable being outnumbered by WASPs.

The one with the red hat answered, looking directly at Jake and Martha, defending herself in front of Sammy, "They made people believe foreigners were taking over. Yet, they twisted the truth. Its infuriating how they inflated statistics!"

Jake tipped his hat at Sammy as he and Martha headed out the door to the public rest rooms. "We're only looking and you're busy,"

"Is there no place to get away from this subject?" Jake asked his wife.

In the rest room, Martha said later, an old woman rocked away in a wicker rocker and said, 'The Klan were clever, listenin' to people's complaints'.

A younger woman took a chair and let her toddler run free in the big room. She sighed, "There already were questions about Catholics, Jews, Negros, and the French before the Klan ever arrived. But preservin' Britishness by blamin' everythin' from gamblin' to prostitution on them, wasn't fair or right!"

The elderly lady shook her head and finished with, 'Even Indians moving to town were blamed'.

The battle of attitudes and labels, however, became all-consuming and inhuman. Unfortunately, out of the mouths of babes the negatives snowballed. Insidiously, school children either brought the derogatory terms from home or adopted them from others. Unquestioned worldwide, the practice of hateful rhetoric and nicknames stuck and at its all-time high, it became quite acceptable to use ethnic slurs against for instance, Krauts, Bohunks, Japs, Chinks, and dirty Indians.

Sadly, in January 1929, the old pioneer, Tessa, passed away at Emma's home. Tragically, siblings Jake, Emma, Sean, and David were now officially orphaned even if they were all grown up. Their mother was 78 years old and this time, the family, although bereft, was better able to cope. The matriarch and role model from a past era would be sorely missed but at long last, she and McLaren were together. Her special memory box secured a permanent place of importance in Emma's home and now they added mementoes of the matriarch.

"'Tis soothin' to know the good company she'll keep in Heaven," Jake reassured Emma.

"Yes, even if she never lived to see a pension," Emma replied.

"Even though she was technically eligible fer the last couple of years."

"In a way, 'tis a blessing because she would have had to pass the ludicrous means test to prove she hadnae earned more than a dollar a day in the past year."

At the 6 June 1929, election, the Conservatives swept to power for the first time in years. The new Liberal opposition accused the Conservatives of being a front for the Klan. The Conservatives utterly rejected the accusations not wanting to associate with a group that spewed hatred.

Meanwhile, Klan memberships dramatically dropped, hand-in-hand with a plummeting economy as the world entered a depression. Jake wondered if some wished they had saved their $13.00 for a piece of pie and a cup of coffee with a friendly neighbour.

25

A Festering Sore

Melfort—*1927–1929*

Times were good in 1927. The world was changing, and Lasse, at 56, wore pants instead of the long skirts she'd worn all her life. She hadn't cut her hair for decades and her lengthy, fully greyed hair was parted in the middle. Sometimes she wore a crown braid or twisted it into a sassy milkmaid braid, further back on her head.

Trading seed for purchases was common and that's how the family became the proud owners of a new-to-them, shiny, black, Model T Ford. The four-door coupe had a canvas roof and running boards. She got a driver's licence with no test and proceeded to jerkily drive it home, screeching the tires, grinding the gears, careening around corners and almost missing one. Her sons were hysterical with laughter, one in the passenger seat and one in the rear. At home, Halvor snapped a photo of them standing in front of their prized possession. When the film was developed, Lasse was pleased to see the picture included an old wagon's hitch in the corner, a sign of the changing times.

The day they brought the car home, Saskatchewan was the third most populous province and electricity was being dangled like a carrot under their noses. It was a decade after Knut's death, and as far as Lasse was concerned, electricity was a nice dream but like other farmers, she either didn't or couldn't opt in.

"Of course, I want to lighten our workloads but without a gas or wind turbine or living close enough to tap into the municipal supply, who can afford it? Better yet, who isn't afraid of it?" she defended.

So, the town had electricity and that led to a strange phenomenon.

"Come nightfall, there's two worlds. The countryside, that's black like the inside of a cow, and the town, that's lit up like a Christmas tree."

That didn't stop farmers from socialising the way they always had. "Coal-oil lanterns do the trick," she said.

With new inventions and the catalogue, Lasse warned, "Times may be good, but we have to be careful with our money. The truck and tractor made a big difference outside, but inside, nothing's really changed."

Bonnie, 21 and Gladys, 17 knew exactly what their mother meant.

Bonnie shared "There's talk of indoor water systems. Oh, not to have to pail water!"

"Oh yes but loads of money, I suppose," Gladys countered.

"It would be magnificent, but the farm has to come first," Lasse sighed.

Furthermore, Lasse was comfortable the way she was. Part of that was how she was raised in the old country. She'd realised long ago that for her, Sweden would remain frozen in time. Keeping their birthplace alive wasn't hard for the older girls but more legend for Knut's children, all born Canadian.

She rued, "By the next generation, the knowledge we hold of Sweden could be all but forgotten."

More worrisome was that it became obvious to her that a smattering of her neighbours had probably purchased Klan memberships. There was no way of knowing for sure. As an immigrant herself, she felt a sick sense of betrayal, knowing everybody from curiosity seekers to hate mongers could jump on the bandwagon, buying into the propaganda.

This particular afternoon, she put the finishing touches on a batch of cookies when a knock came on the front door. Most entered through the back, so it seemed odd. She was happy to see her old friend, the Mountie, Len, standing outside on the familiar veranda he helped build. The Big House was nearly a decade old and she hadn't seen him for ages. Him arriving out of the blue had her concerned.

After an awkward moment, he asked politely, "May I come in?"

She nodded and held the door open but her heart pounded. It was obvious he grappled with something.

"Please sit down," she motioned and caught her breath. "How about coffee and a cookie?" The thought of stomaching bad news had her guard up.

After pouring his coffee, he took a bite off the macaroon and began, "I've known you for a long time, Lasse," he paused, "and I'm crossing a fine line here but you need to know."

Slowly, he described his experience. Lasse learned that at the latest Klan rally, in this, his final year of police service, Len happened to be part of the patrol. He was haunted by something oddly familiar about one group of the robed and hooded figures.

"One limped and another had a purplish-scarred hand, then, it hit me. There's no doubt, the Blacks and Swallows are back." At this, he took another sip of the aroma-filled brew.

Her cup sat untouched and he watched the colour drain from her face.

"A decade ago, even if they hadn't skipped town, we had nothing to hold them on," he said.

She felt like someone punched her in the gut and her face showed it.

Still, she measured her words. "Thank you. My children and I have spent our lives trying to forget those men. For years, we have endured fear and loathing, always watching for signs of their return."

Len nodded, seeming to know only too well. Lasse realised one of the drawbacks of his job was seeing lives shattered and derailed from crime.

"And now that they're all grown up, these men decide to return?" she spat sarcastically.

"Arrogantly so but maybe sloppily too," he supposed.

He shouldn't have said it but did, "If they thought they got away with murder, then one day, they might slip up."

For Lasse, this was surprising because no official had ever uttered the word murder. She felt grateful hearing his words but wrung her hands, uneasy to open old wounds. Conflicted, she felt fear bubbling inside. In essence, Len had admitted he thought they were guilty too, and it was like removing a weight. Now she had a dilemma. Should she share the knowledge with her grown children or not?

After the Mountie left, scared of her children's reactions, she paced the floor, talking to herself, "There isn't much any of us can do about it anyhow, and those men are dangerous."

In the end, she decided, "They need to know."

Indeed, when the four grown children heard, Peter and Paul stomped and fumed, then got very quiet. When the two 20-somethings became even more closed mouthed, Lasse figured something was up. Still, she made no effort to stand in their way and almost hated herself for it. It wasn't until sometime later, well after the fact, that they spilt the beans.

Peter started, "Watching over our shoulders and turning the other cheek had gone on long enough! You know that, Mother."

She nodded.

"So, we commandeered Halvor and Smith to start digging around. We know violence is never the answer, but how about teaching a lesson?"

Paul continued, "First, Smith and Swift Arrow tracked the brothers' whereabouts. As usual, they were hiding in plain sight, squatting in an old hunting shack beside the river, way off, near Fort à la Corne. The evening in question, the place sat empty, so the girls moved in first, to drip syrup onto the beds, and scrape bird droppings into the sugar bowl."

"Oh, my word!" Lasse exclaimed.

Looking directly at Bonnie and Gladys, she shook her head, "You girls were there too?"

They nodded without a hint of guilt.

Peter said, "If that wasn't enough, Halvor helped us go inside and set coil-spring muskrat and weasel traps where the brothers might step. No permanent damage intended, just a good snap of pain to give us the upper hand. Since it got dark, we had the element of surprise, and hoped our crazy plan might work."

"We hid in the underbrush and waited," Paul built the moment. "The birds had stopped squawking to herald our presence, when the brothers rode up. We watched and held our breath. The first two, the self-important ones, Jeb Black and Gib Swallow jumped down, and strode into the shack first. Then came snapping traps, squealing pain, and roaring curses!"

Bonnie snickered, "I'm sorry, but we had a hard time keeping a straight face!" she looked at Gladys.

"Owen Swallow and Amos Black, not smart enough to hang back, tore in after them, only to add their yowling to the din."

"It was perfect!" Gladys announced glibly.

Peter took over, "The door was flung wide open so wearing our flour-sack head covers, we brought a barrel of tar and bags of feathers up close. We felt no shame to rise up and blitz the four of them, which we did!"

"No words were spoken but we struck while the iron was hot." Paul breathed. "They fought, shrieked, and cursed but it was over in minutes and they weren't in any position to carry out their threats."

"You almost had to feel sorry for them," Paul said, reaching into his pocket and pulling out his father's pocket watch, "until I saw this dangling from Jeb's hand. If that's not proof of their guilt, I don't know what is."

As Paul handed the watch to Lasse, Peter denounced, "With only lukewarm tar, I didn't feel sorry for them, they didn't even get burned, only sticky. Still, seeing Father's watch, they deserved it!"

Lasse's face clouded, showing total shock. "Oh, my stars! We knew they were guilty all along! Still, I can't believe you did that!" she started.

Her children's faces dropped, not really expecting a tongue-lashing.

But she surprised them, "No wonder you didn't feel bad. Those men finally suffered some consequences," she was not going to admonish her children because she felt no remorse either.

"Now," she went on, "even if they're never formally prosecuted, they get to go on living even if your father can't. I feel vindicated and all I can say is thank you. If you're hit first, you hit back. A single pocket watch can't prove anything so case closed, let's never breathe a word of it again."

In fact, not another word was spoken on the subject outside the household. If the Mountie had any suspicions, he didn't let on. From their perspective, the Blacks and Swallows disappeared again and for Lasse's family, they hoped it was forever.

People were preoccupied with the Klan and days later, Lasse heard innuendo that certain residents felt sheepish about being duped. 'The Organisation', its preferred title, eventually disappeared from sight too, the four dastardly brothers with it. Unfortunately, like the microbes of the Spanish Flu, the Klan sentiment was never truly gone, persisting wherever a host could be found.

By 1928, the Royal Canadian Mounted Police replaced the liquor commissioner's police force and Paul, at 21 came of legal age. He spent time carpentering, ciphering, or reading history and hid his alcohol to not disappoint his mother. Peter, on the other hand, would rather raise, race, and show thoroughbreds than anything.

After the fact, they found out Bonnie and John had gone off to a Justice of the Peace. It was a sign of the times, but Lasse felt gypped because Bonnie was her third daughter to do so. Given the late harvest, a small supper was held at the bride's home. It was a humble gathering but appreciated.

The next year, Lasse wrote a letter to Bjorn, Ava, and boys.

Over at Halvor's one day, Lasse and Greta raised their smiling faces skyward having received the best news anyone got in a long time.

"For the first time ever, women are recognised as persons!" Greta clapped.

Echoing her sentiments was Helga, "The walls of Jericho are coming down!"

The radio newscaster said, "Today, October 18, 1929, women can run for the senate thanks to the Famous Five from Alberta, including Nellie McClung. They campaigned the Supreme Court and their 'Persons Case' overturned Section 24 of the British North America Act to recognise women as persons under the law."

"This is only the first step. Now there's hope for women to change the status quo and become professionals," young Lizzie quipped.

"The sky's the limit. But even property ownership and birth control would help." Gladys raised her eyebrows.

"Don't expect the road to be smooth. Expect opposition!" wise, old Helga spoke, "can I top up your tea?"

Lasse answered, "You're right," and held out her teacup.

"On the other hand, imagine working at a profession and getting paid in line with what men get!" Greta proposed.

"And not being forced to have a man sign a loan for you," Lasse interjected, "unless of course, you're a widow."

Halvor had come in from checking his livestock and after they told him the news, he said, "It could be lifechanging. Somebody in Kirsten's situation, trying to get away from an abusive husband now isn't forced to live a life of poverty. She could make it on her own, at least hypothetically."

Greta agreed. "Imagine that. Not destined for a life of housework!"

"Well, working out of the home is one thing but men can't have babies. Someone still has to address that tiny detail," Halvor threw in. "Maybe they'll figure out a way to hatch them under a light!"

Everyone laughed at his jesting.

"Whatever happens, it won't be overnight. Everything starts off small and takes time to grow," Lasse said.

"Well, the seeds are sown. Let's hope this giant gain doesn't get twisted beyond all recognition." Halvor had an inkling of how society worked.

"Faith, the size of a mustard seed, can move mountains," Helga spoke, "overcoming fear and doubt goes a long way to breaking through a brick wall!"

"Exactly!" Lasse loved the woman's wisdom.

Black Tuesday, 29 October 1929, caused financial disaster with banks collapsing and people panicking. The stock market crash ended the roaring twenties and sent the global economy spiralling into the Great Depression. Lasse watched in horror as everything lost value. People resorted to returning their cars or like Lasse, converted them into Bennett Buggies; the horse-drawn autos without gasoline.

When it hardly rained, and the crops suffered, grasshoppers moved in, and Gladys, the youngest at 19, wondered, "What can we do to make ends meet?"

Greta stopped by and joked, "We've always traded hand-me-downs and the flour bags these days are stylish, stamped with floral designs!"

"Real trend setters!" Gladys laughed. Lasse knew she was embarrassed to have to resort to such a thing but grateful just the same.

Greta and Halvor's daughter Lizzie, was already 22 and two other sons had been added to the mix. Little Knut was 11, and Ole, the afterthought, was 10.

Around town, poverty reigned. No one could miss those who wore tire strips strapped to their feet, tied on with binder twine for rubber boots. Others used cardboard for shoe soles. Lasse's and Greta's youngsters refused to stoop to those levels and kept traplines going, chopped wood for sale, cleaned neighbourhood houses, and shone shoes for every penny they could get. The families had milk cows and shipped cream, plus sold eggs year-round, plus had all their own meat and vegetables. It truly saved them.

December 1929, Peter married Jake and Martha's daughter Sis (Miriam). The inter-marrying of Norwegian and Scottish families sent a message at the demise of the Ku Klux Klan that the younger generation refused to be subverted by racism or hatred. They were fully supported by their families and community.

Lasse sat down one evening and wrote a letter home to Sweden,

My dear family,

Peter and Miriam's wedding the first week of December was lovely. Peter looks the happiest ever. The ceremony was in the Presbyterian Church with supper at Stoney Creek School. Our two families pooled resources and I baked a wedding cake. Even though people are hard up, their generosity was amazing and appreciated. The Conservatives are in power and we've had the worst drought, grasshoppers, and lowest wheat prices ever. Don't worry, here in the north, we're better off than in the desert-like south. Grain growers got paid $1.00 a bushel up front this year, but the international price fell to 50¢, so it will take the Pool elevator 20 years to pay off the debt. In the meantime, grain is being smuggled to the states for better money. I miss you dearly!

Love, Mother.

26

Combining Families and the Circle of Life

Melfort—*1930–1958*

By summer 1930, despite the Great Depression, the provincial Conservatives took control of the province's natural resources, something the Liberals had never done. Winter's early arrival had crops snowed in. When finally, the threshers could go, Lasse, Gladys, and Paul spent the morning wading through snowdrifts to shake snow off the sheaves. They tried to shoo their mother back into the house but she refused.

"I'm only 59!" she argued.

From a distance, Paul saw Smith set his brake and jump off to help after gliding across the snow towards them on a dogsled. The dogs yelped for a time, then settled in to await their master. When the work was done and after tea and biscuits, Paul showed off his six tobacco tins full of gopher tails ready to turn in for the bounty. Not only that but he had a multitude of stretched weasels, rabbits, and other small animals to cash in for their fur.

"Come spring, crows' feet and eggs are worth money too, to save the crops," Paul said.

The talk turned to the land and the government controlling the natural resources.

"My people shake our heads at how the government thinks they can own Mother Earth."

Lasse agreed, because it was the truth.

Before Smith left, he helped Paul put a jumper's hind quarter inside the icehouse. Then the family waited for the threshers.

Paul was 23 and said, "When the depression lifts, let's look into buying one of those new self-propelled combines."

Lasse laughed, "You're funny!"

292

"Well, how about a pull-type?"

"In the meantime, see what I got?" he produced a ticket stub for the Irish Sweepstakes. "If we won, we'd be set!"

"Aren't those illegal and aren't we in a depression?" Gladys gave him a funny look.

"It's the chance of a lifetime, even so!" Paul was bewitched, "it's for charity and if you win, it's $140,000. If you don't buy one, you have zero chance."

"The question is, will the ticket ever hit the drum in Dublin?" his mother scoffed. "Don't you think the seller could pocket your money or sell you a counterfeit ticket?"

"I'm not the only one buying them!" he defended.

He saw her forced to admit, "I guess $2.50 is a paltry sum if you win but don't forget, you could get pinched by the authorities in the meantime!"

Of course, the threshers came and went and Paul didn't win the sweepstakes. He had to shovel grain in the bin and the barley bothered his eyes. All summer, he hauled lumber home from his Fort à la Corne sawmill to build a bungalow for him and Butter Cup, or Tessie, as he called her. It would stand several hundred yards west of the Big House.

Paul felt his mother wasn't the kind to interfere in their marriage. Between the two of them, they would make sure Tessie wasn't lonely, being separated from her big family.

He reassured his fiancé, "We'll have the garden, then two rows of poplars and lilac hedges between us. Our one-story building will be easier to heat, to change storm windows, and to dung out eaves-troughs than the Big House."

"I like the idea of the cistern under the house, the hand pump in the kitchen, and a rain barrel," Tessie exclaimed. "Our little house will be cosier than what I was raised in and certainly with fewer children!"

Paul knew she loved her siblings and wondered about contending with nine of them her entire life.

"Can we have half that many? Paul asked and idled closer to sneak a smooch."

"We can start with one!" She'd made up her mind on that front long ago because by the time she was 11, her oldest siblings had already married and left home. As the youngest, she spent her teenaged years living alongside half of them. Paul's family was similar with two older sisters left home long ago.

He wasn't joking about the bungalow being warmer. The Big House's wood shavings had settled to the bottom long ago. Used to sacrificing, Lasse never grumbled because keeping her wood/coal stove stoked was part of life.

"The gustin' north winds off the Arctic, must blow right through her place," Tessie said. "No wonder she sleeps on the main floor!"

Paul's mind was a flurry of planning and he barely heard her.

"We'll need a space fer the pump organ Mother and Dad promised me," Tessie reminded. "Dot doesnae have room and she and I are the only ones who play."

"The organ's too tall for the east wall's piano window, so it has to sit against the south wall."

"It's nae supposed to go against an outside wall!"

"Sorry, but it can't be helped!"

After a moment's thought, he said, "What about me building you a set of cupboards for our kitchen?"

"If ye make them wall-to-wall," she beamed.

Tessie respected his abilities and how he had sacrificed his own education to save the family's farm upon his father's death. Amongst other things, she was attracted to his humour, talents with numbers, and carpentry skills. They weren't just going to be spouses they were best friends.

In the meantime, Lasse received a letter from Kirsten in Winnipeg.

Hello Lasse,

It's been forever since we talked and aren't the Dirty Thirties just that? Even if your crops are better than in the south, you can't win with bottomed out grain prices. I'm scratching out a living doing gardening, baking, and mending. It's better than living with that brute, alone on his farm. I heard Saskatoon women had a sit-in strike at city council looking for aid. How ridiculous that men can get it but not women! I hope all is well with you and look forward to hearing from you soon! Love Kirsten.

Paul read his mother's return letter.

Dear Kirsten,

Peter and Miriam celebrated their second anniversary and live on a farm a mile south of us. Bonnie and John live halfway between the two farms and are expecting their second baby but their first little girl is already a treat. Greta and I are sending a box of clothing and dry goods for you to use or share. We live day by day too and are thankful for intact soil, not blown away like in the south. With all the farm bankruptcies, I had a stranger show up touting a new scheme. He said, "To prevent the banks seizing land, they're proposing the government assumes title so the farmer can lease the land back." I politely said, "No thanks!" Then talked to my neighbours who wonder if it isn't communism dressed up in sheep's clothing. Farmers are against it and I, for one, want no part. I love getting your letters. Write back!

Love Lasse.

PS Men are too proud to take handouts and some ride the rails, looking for work. Every so often one shows up here, looking for a good meal.

On Halloween, 1932, Paul and his lovely Tessie left the farm in the Model T and horror of horrors, stayed away overnight. Paul saw that Lasse and Gladys tried to appear surprised when they returned.

His red face clashed with his red hair but he proudly announced, "Congratulations are in order! You can now call us Mr. and Mrs!"

Elated, they all hugged, never admitting that eloping was getting old, even if easier. He and Tessie had stopped at Jake and Martha's on the way by to share the good news and get Tessie's things.

Her father, Jake, sighed, "You have no idea what a relief it is to have our tenth and last child married off!"

Martha only smiled through her tears.

Back at their new home, Paul could finally do what both he and Tessie had waited for. He carried his new bride across the threshold and they were never happier.

A week later, Tessie's parents hosted a small reception and Paul heard Martha tell Lasse, "We're thrilled to have two of our daughters married to two of your sons."

"Two sisters marrying two brothers! How unique! We're happy too. It's been coming for a long time. Growing up four miles apart, something was bound to come of it."

Sadly, in 1932, Peter and Sis's first baby son was a stillbirth and they buried him under a tree, along a fence line north of the house. 1933 was the lowest point of the depression, but Paul and Tessie had their first baby girl in

July and named her Marion. Peter and Sis weren't far behind in October with a baby girl, Bernice. Bonnie and John had produced a third child, Dale, in addition to their little Hattie, and Clarence. The cousins became lifelong friends and Paul knew Lassie was in her glory.

By early 1936, Lasse read to Paul and Tessie, what she wrote to Bjorn and Ava. Paul could see that it was hard for his mother to face but his legendary half-brother, whom he'd never met, seldom wrote anymore.

Dear Bjorn, Ava, and boys,

Aside from the depression, things are going well. Your half-siblings, my older three, are married and living close by. In March of last year, Gladys married a strapping young man named Charles. He's the adopted son of Scottish farmers west of here. The two farm across the road from his parents and close to the Mount Forest school. I am now an empty-nester and getting used to it but Paul and Tessie live in the same yard and that helps. By June 1935, we've seen men riding the rails for the second time. They left B.C. relief camps in droves bound for Ottawa to demand work. You know at one time, gangs of men worked building railroads, bridges, and roads but not now. By July, one of their meetings in Regina turned violent. Believe it or not, the federal Liberals won a majority in October again! I miss you all but am losing hope we'll see each other again in this world. Love Mother.

June of 1936, Tessie's uncle David and his wife, Sally, moved to a warmer climate on doctor's orders for Sally. David sold the farm and he, Sally, and six kids moved to Chilliwack, British Columbia, the warmest city in Canada. At 52, David temporarily delivered milk door-to-door. His leaving was a blow to the family, especially to Sean.

The afternoon of July 25, Paul was working in his shop and heard a loud crash. He wasn't in time to see his mother, Lasse, fall backwards down the back steps of the Big House. With hammer still gripped, he sprinted, unaware of the mallet sliding through his fingers.

"Mother!" he screamed, dropping to his knees alongside her sprawled body. Shaking her was of no use; she was gone, and he knew it. She had breathed her last breath.

"Tessie!" he screamed. "Please come!" he sobbed and his wife came running from the garden, two little girls trailing behind. The scene was grim. Lasse was an awful shade of purplish grey and laying stone still.

Paul couldn't think straight but was aware that his wife feared dead bodies. Nor could she have ever seen him look so stricken. Still, she took charge and after covering his mother with a sheet, their shock settled somewhat.

Neither knew what to do except sit quietly beside her unmoving body. Finally, Tessie said, "You have to go find help." Shakily, he started for the barn to saddle up, no point in wasting time hooking up the Bennet Buggy. He could imagine Tessie speaking soothingly to little Marion and Alice. "At 65, Grandma has grown tired and gone to Heaven."

His mother's words echoed in his ears, "If I ever give in, I'm done for," and it seemed true. As his horse galloped away, he couldn't erase the sight of her lifeless corpse, covered with a sheet, and his wife and sweet little girls sitting with her. All they could see was her feet sticking out covered with her new, Queen Quality Lace-Up shoes she was so proud of.

Racing south, up and down the hilly road and over the creek, he felt sick and heartbroken, and could scarcely think. "Get Peter, Bonnie, and the undertaker," he told himself.

The closest sibling was Bonnie but no one was home. He tried to remember his mother's face and felt panicked until she flooded back, then thought, "You and I haven't been apart more than a night or two my whole life. I wonder what I'll do without you?"

He found his brother, Peter, and broke the news. Peter groaned, then stayed silent but tears coursed down his cheeks. All he said was, "She never got back to see her beloved Bjorn or Sweden," he turned to Sis, "you need to go and help Tessie."

At the undertaker's, the mortician was gone on another call. A little boy, whose leg was hurt in a log rolling accident died from gangrene. Peter and Paul felt dreadful but could do nothing but wait respectfully, all the while dying inside for themselves and the little boy's family.

It seemed an eternity when they finally returned to the farm. In the dark of night, Tessie and Sis, who had rushed over, still sat outside, guarding their mother-in-law's body. Three little girls, Marion, Alice, and Bernice were sound asleep on their laps. A gun was propped against the house and they had built a bonfire. A dimming lantern flickered, causing shadows to dance across both women's faces.

The two brothers assisted the undertaker to gently load their beloved mother into the back of the coach. Watching the transport vehicle drive off, Paul and Peter hung their heads and wept all the more. When they got around to asking about the gun and the fire, Tessie explained how she was worried about skunks or raccoons.

When the family went to the funeral home, Paul admitted, "For me, making arrangements stirs up memories of our father's death 19 years ago."

"This time, we're all grown up and should cope better but no one's ever ready to say goodbye to their mother." Peter choked out the words.

"No one's ready to become an orphan overnight either," Gladys and Bonnie wiped their eyes.

"Remember, she's finally found peace," the undertaker consoled as he he'd done a hundred times before.

When asked to bring clothing for the deceased, it was the sisters-in-law, helping Lasse's daughters. to choose her wedding dress.

A prayer service at the funeral home's chapel, the night before the funeral, wasn't private but meant for family and close friends. All of Knut and Lasse's children attended, including Mikaila, and her daughter, Helen, from Winnipeg. Lovisa came from Whitehorse.

In her open coffin, Paul believed his mother looked angelic with her silver hair offset by a pale seafoam dress and adorned with crystal rhinestones, Knut's wedding gift.

After prayers and lunch, the mourners sat in the pews with the casket open at the front of the chapel, reminiscing and storytelling. They sensed her spirit's need to be part of this intimate tribute and Paul truly believed it was. Paul remembered Knut's stories of Smith telling about the wakes his people held and it seemed similar. Before the coffin was closed, Bonnie asked that her mother be covered with her favourite woollen throw.

Lasse's funeral was a large gathering at the Carrot River Valley Lutheran church where she was buried beside Knut. Friends poured into the quaint country church and listened to the pastor pray and speak of her incredible life. Greta and Kirsten's eulogy caused tears of sorrow amid precious laughter about their old friend. The pastor invited others to celebrate her life by coming forward to speak of their memories of her. Harry and Ida were first with hotel and house-building stories, followed by the Mountie Len, who spoke of her determination, then Halvor and Greta about her strength and valued friendship. Even Smith and members of Knut's sawmill crew, attended, plus those who had helped build the house, threshers, restaurant patrons, storekeepers, and on and on. Her doctor and lawyer had predeceased her.

When it was over and the family went back to the farm, they couldn't help but pay tribute to their forlorn-looking Big House. "It's filled with her belongings, but looks so lonely and silent now," Peter said sadly.

"For a house usually filled with sunlight, there's not even a shimmer," Paul added remembering his life there with fondness. "Like it's grieving the loss of its owner." Inside was a different story, Paul felt her spirit everywhere and hoped his siblings did too.

By December 1936, Tessie's Uncle David wrote home from Chilliwack, and anyone stopping by Jake and Martha's could read his letter.

Dear family,

Chilliwack, compared to Melfort is balmy fer December. With the warm, humid weather, we already see an improvement in Sally. The new electric street railways out of Vancouver are a sight! I start a farm job tomorrow. Being a milkman is a noble profession, but I do have farming in my blood. We miss you all!

Love; David, Sally, and family.

On the Scottish side of the family, two years later in 1938, Tessie's Aunt Emma, died.

Tessie explained, "I'm sorry to say she died in Bunny's vehicle while being rushed to the hospital."

Tessie, Paul, Peter, and Sis paid their last respects despite a raging blizzard. It seemed the entire community had done their best to turn out to the Salvation Army Barracks for her funeral.

The minister's tribute was, "Emma, a good Christian woman of sterling character, has gone to the great beyond. She was a good neighbour, always ready to assist in times of trouble. Having endeared herself to all, her family and community will sadly miss her."

When Emma died, Tessa's special memory box was given a new home, placed in a prominent place in Tessie's parents', Jake and Martha's parlour.

With all the deaths, the number of memorial items were almost outgrowing the box.

Shortly afterwards, alarmingly, they noticed Jake, walking to the barn with his hands clasped behind his back. On the way home, Paul told Tessie, "I hate to say this but your father says he's losing the feeling in both arms."

Indeed, Tessie's father, Jake, had no control over the condition which soon became obvious. He finally admitted, "Me arms are useless and just hang at me sides anymore."

The former going concern, had his hips stiffen and it was like rigor mortis was taking over his body while he was still alive. Suddenly, he could no longer do anything and he complained of a roaring in his ears. Rocked to the core, the entire family prayed for resolution. The affliction spread to his legs and no one was ready for the day he collapsed.

Later, Martha told her children, "Thankfully, Toot was here helping and he and I struggled to put your father to bed."

"A think he's paralysed," Toot claimed with dread.

The grown children living close by offered to help, but Martha sighed, already tired, "Ye can spell me off sittin' with him while a sleep. He's extremely proud, if not a little pig-headed," she said, "he willnae let anyone do his personal care, except me. A can't possibly do everythin' so a've asked Toot and Chickadee and their four children, to move in to help with the farm."

Tessie was one of the siblings who took turns sitting with her father, and she often took her three children with her. Besides the two girls, they now had a two-year old son, named Richard.

She told Paul, "The girls were fascinated watchin' Grandma give Grandda a dill pickle to suck, to help with his dry mouth!"

Shortly after, Martha was beside herself when she told the others, "Now he has no facial expression or voice. He only moves his eyes. A told him to blink once fer yes or twice fer no."

Jake blinked his answers while the doctor examined him and pronounced, "It's creeping paralysis, and I'm sorry but there's no cure." At that, Jake squeezed his eyes shut as tightly as he could and a tear splashed down, into his ear. Martha clasped his hands in hers, trying to impart strength.

27

The Link

Scotland to Halifax, Nova Scotia—*August-October 1939*

On Sunday, 27 August 1939, the world heard, "Poland has ordered a partial mobilisation against Hitler's troops."

War seemed inevitable and a Scottish man, James, leaned against a ship's guard rail, ready to depart Liverpool. Born in 1900, his age went with the years and it wasn't simply the war making him leave Scotland.

His mother had said, "Ye tried but 'tis not yer fault yer the second son with few prospects in this bleak job market."

"Clerkin' was worse than readin' an intensely borin' book," James said.

No one mentioned the dismal failure of his bar exam. Too late, he and his classmates discovered that polo and the classics didn't prepare you for a profession.

"Entering the clergy is out of the question, even though a do love God."

His mother agreed. "And thank God purchasin' a military commission went by the wayside," she said, "after Edgar's trials and tribulations, your father would never have considered it."

James's 46-year-old brother, a veteran of World War I, usually clammed up about the war, except to James. More than once, Edgar's Gaelic brogue rang out over a slamming cane. "For yer own good, never sign up!"

Edgar's painful recollections were of the trenches and bombed-out wastelands but he was preaching to the choir.

"A wouldnae hurt a fly and they'd have to drag me kickin' and screamin'," James said, "if a could be classed a conscientious objector, a would!"

"When the archduke and his wife were assassinated on June 28," Edgar went on. "Bizarrely, people seemed to think the soldiers were going on an excursion to Paris or something! They were not!"

But James's military call came mid-July, and he hauled himself in for screening.

Afterwards, kicking his shoes off at the door, he said, "Thank God fer poor colour vision! A can't tell red from green, so a'm barred from service. Plus, a cannae stand the sight of blood so bein' a medic is out."

Edgar sighed with relief, "Imagine some recruits memorisin' the colour chart bein' so desperate to get into the service! Brother, ye have literally dodged a bullet!"

Their father warned, "We should have known when Chamberlain allowed Hitler to annex Czechoslovakia a year ago. The Munich Agreement was the start of a slippery slope."

Suspicions ran amok and Edgar predicted, "Anybody with half a brain could tell somethin' was afoot. Hitler's spent the last six years rearmin', ever since he became Chancellor in 1933."

"And outright defied the Treaty of Versailles to reduce arms from 1919!" their father sounded frustrated.

In that moment, amid squawking seabirds back on the ship, the memory of James's father gave him a sinking feeling and he capped those thoughts for the time being.

It wasn't just individuals with suspicions, Poland certainly knew and were on the alert as newspapers reported, "Three Polish destroyers have left Poland bound for the United Kingdom to avoid capture in a potential German invasion."

Things were heating up.

Despite the Great Depression, going abroad could whisk James away from the rumblings of a dreaded war. He would put his best foot forward and emigrate to the colonies to live in fresh air and wide-open spaces. If all he had to offer was good breeding, well, that was something.

James overheard his father, "He's no drinker, fortunately, one drink is his limit."

"And what an adventure!" his mother responded, "the Canadian West has such romance with the fur trade and Indian maidens. Maybe it will mend James's tattered love life," she wrung her hands.

His friends said, "Yer caramel eyes bewitched that married woman."

"Whose husband is in utter denial, a might add," added another.

James finally admitted, "The affair is over. She's a pyromaniac! The elderly lady whose house she burned is left wearin' gloves to protect her severely burned hands."

"Her ridiculous spouse thinks someone's out to get her. Denial and cover-up doesnae help."

The local shrews and gossips euphorically spread the rumour of James's affair as part of a rigid old-world society. They churned out victims, exposed secrets, and dumped scoundrels on their heads. Their tongue-wagging was only interrupted long enough to acknowledge *Kristallnacht*, the Night of Broken Glass on November 10, 1938. Windows of shops owned by Jews were smashed throughout Germany, the annexed Austria, and Sudetenland in Czechoslovakia. Almost a hundred Jews were killed and thirty thousand forced into concentration camps.

Not just Poland, hackles rose throughout the world.

Faced with leaving home forever, James wondered, "Will me mired life here pale compared to where a'm headed?"

"Yer sure ye dinnae want to take a passenger ship?" his mother asked, "we could easily afford the $30 ticket direct from Scotland."

"A chose a cattle ship departin' Liverpool because the adventure will keep me occupied."

His mother went on, "The only thing ye know about workin' with livestock is from the grapevine or a book, right? Apparently, workin' cowboys in Calgary have told Scottish lads to obtain a cowboy kit."

"'Tis woolly chaps, spurs, and a wide-brimmed Stetson," James wasn't the only one talking to friends of friends. "Sounds far-fetched to me but do ye suppose that applies to cattle punchers on a ship?"

Edgar got the joke. He'd gotten his wife to round up a set of work clothes, boots, and suspenders for his brother.

On the ship, James's thoughts were of yesterday, when the train from Scotland took him to Liverpool. In the English city, he'd made his way to a lodging house owned by one of the steamship lines. Apparently, the accommodations were much improved from years gone by. Dirt and over-crowding did tend to ruin things.

They awaited the ship but paperwork, a medical, and vaccinations took priority. In between times, he sat beside others on wooden benches. Hearing his Scottish brogue, one man with a distinctly British accent, told him about

Liverpool's port. "Did you know most of the port's stone was granite brought in from Scotland in the early 1800s?"

A scuffle erupted, just as James replied, "No, a dinnae,"

Out of the blue, a young ruffian nipped another lodger's bag. The middle-aged male victim roared and a security guard gave chase. Minutes later, the guard returned, out of breath, with the bag under his arm.

"The culprit dropped it two alleys away."

The angry victim cursed, until a Cockney cleaning woman scolded him for his own gullibility, "Don't yer lump of lead head know the confidence tricksters run Helter-skelter? The Penny-come-quick are as old as the earth?"

When news came that the ship had arrived, James was finished screening and hailed a cab bound for the harbour.

The Brit taxi driver helped with his luggage then asked, "Have you ever seen the Port of Liverpool?"

Not waiting for an answer, the cabbie rattled off his spiel. "It's a 24 hour a day, enclosed, seven-and-a-half-mile dock system running from Brunswick Dock in Liverpool to Seaforth Dock, in Seaforth. It's the most advanced port system in the world. At the same time, it's isolated from the high tides."

Pulling into the harbour, James sickened at the sight of the large monstrosity of a ship with peeling paint he was supposed to board. After dragging his luggage including trunk, barrel of china and linens, satchel of clothing, and violin across the planks, Captain Galen greeted him. The captain was German and spoke through an interpreting member of the crew.

"We should reach Halifax roughly the middle of October," the captain said. "I won't make any promises but about six weeks, dependent on weather, mechanical problems, other ships in distress, and the unpredictability of the cattle themselves. The men will show you around."

As they set sail, looking back towards the shoreline, James watched people waving and getting smaller in the distance. A split second of panic made him feel like bolting. This was a German ship and the captain was German! Hanging on, he realised that was ridiculous. A lump welled in his throat at the thought of his dear mother. Would he ever see her again? He might as well be going to the dark side of the moon.

Trying to pick himself up, he looked forward to shedding the old ways of lords, ladies, and strict protocols. Canadians were a new breed. They were said to have mostly started out poor so had few expectations to elbow their way through society and James looked forward to a more even playing field. Unless someone was a no-good-lazy wastrel, poverty was no disgrace in Canada.

He thought, "A may be many things, but lazy is not one of them. With the allowance from me family, perhaps a can find work and stay afloat."

His father had assured the family when they first talked of his leaving, "James is not truly a remittance man. Those days ended after the First World War. Surely a remittance lifestyle willnae be tolerated durin' a depression with the economy and empires crumblin'."

James wondered, "Who knows whether Canadians will even accept the shirt-tail relative of a remittance man?"

After the sailing got underway, an older Norwegian cattle-puncher named Carl, who had interpreted for the captain, looked James over and motioned for him to follow.

Carl said, "I've learned other languages over the years but might not always get it right. We left from Hamburg and with stops, it's a tramp's ocean route. As a stockman, you'll feed and care for the steers. Your berth is down below."

In the bowels of the ship, the smell was foul. The area was hot, noisy, and he had to duck. He expected the cattle wouldn't be the only ones thrilled with the fresh air when they hit shore. Being the typical gentleman, he'd brought a formidable amount of luggage. The biggest was a brown steamer trunk that had heavy brass locks and corners. In it were rackets, a small easel, and silverware. His fine bone china and linens were in a barrel. With no room, all he could do was jam the barrel, trunk, a satchel of clothing, and encased violin into a corner.

Carl simply rolled his eyes and smirked at James's arsenal, knowing full well the belongings would be soaked before long. When he and Carl headed towards the cattle pens for introductions, James was struck at how elderly the crew was.

A lanky Swede named Hans took over the orientation on how to keep the steers alive. The most important check was the gates or animals might leap overboard thinking they could swim ashore. The kitchen's livestock was a milk cow and calf, chickens, geese, pigs, sheep, and goats. James understood it was simple, honest work, where he would get his hands dirty.

The week before, on August 23, the Germans signed a non-aggression pact with Russia. If anyone could keep the Germans in line, it might be Stalin but why was he befriending Hitler? As a result, James's' confidence began to plummet.

Working with cattle was exhilarating, and every day, the workers had several hours to themselves. Card playing was a favourite pastime but toasting with watered-down rum in a beer mug was not. Fine if he drank. Both alcohol and water were rationed, and fresh water being scarce, for him, hydrating with spirits was difficult.

His thirst worsened with supper from big hunks of lumpy bread and salt junk they said was beef called 'old horse'. Chewing the portion doled out, James thought longingly of the tin of sweets his mother had tucked into his belongings. If only he could get to it, but unpacking would mean upsetting everything and not worth the effort.

Hans said, "The laws are changed about schooling for cooks but we hung onto Otto, who was grandfathered in."

Shortly after eating Hans said, "I'd advise you to drag a hay bale up into the fresh air to sleep. Lay your jacket underneath you."

James said, "Let's hope the creepy crawlers keep to themselves."

Hans laughed, "If you get over-hungry and stand in the galley, Otto might share the occasional handout." It worked when he was tossed a couple crusts of bread.

That evening when it was time to sleep, James couldn't. He never undressed, so got up and climbed the companionway to the deck. There, he found an opening to lean over the rail between a coil of rope and a lifeboat. The water roared past the hull below like a hot knife slicing through butter. He wondered how fast eighteen knots was supposed to look. After a while, dizziness forced him to sit and he allowed his thoughts to drift. His eyes welled at the thought of his father. The dear man had up and died two weeks before James had set sail.

The doctor said, "Massive heart attack," but the family witnessed it disguised as a stomach ailment with nightly indigestion and heartburn. At the thought, James's own nausea worsened until he was forced to lean over the rail and lose his entire supper. Lumps, and all, slid down the side of the rusty vessel.

Wiping his mouth, and feeling a little better, he turned away to lean back against the rail. His brother, Edgar, was the heir, and although James might have been jealous, he was happy for him. If not for Edgar and his mother, James might have lost his nerve.

With the weight of the world on his shoulders, he felt sleepy so turned to go back. A hen ran across his path and he thought of the bread crusts stashed in his pocket. Sprinkling crumbs at the front of her cage, she returned to her nest without squawking. The air was fresh, and the wispy clouded moon sent slivers of light. No one else seemed awake in the world. Settled against the hay, it was quiet, and he fell into a deep slumber.

He heard the laughter of two little girls playing with rag dolls. They wore ribbons in their long dark auburn hair, white dresses, and polished shoes. Their mother appeared, and he was astounded by her beauty and the love she radiated towards them. She too wore a white dress and her long auburn hair, looked freshly brushed. It was carefully pulled to one side and fell in front of her shoulder. She spoke softly with a distinct Nordic accent, then sat down beside them as they played. When she turned to face him, he could see tears rolling down her cheeks.

At dawn, he awoke to livestock and the crew coming to life. Strangely satisfied, the would-be cattleman shook off the remnants of the dream and looked forward to crossing the English Channel.

When he casually mentioned the dream to Hans and Carl, they got a funny look, "We knew a woman once almost like you describe," then went on about their business.

Hans said, "We'll round the tip of southern Great Britain and leave from the port of Plymouth, a city in Devon. It will take time to cross over to Cherbourg Harbour in Normandy, northwestern France. This is the second largest artificial harbour in the world and is infamous as the port where the *Titanic* made its final stop."

For James, the day was a mix of hard work, interspersed with card playing, and kibitzing. His co-workers relished the ship's biscuits and rum but not him, especially since the biscuit was unleavened bread and nothing but flour and water. So far, the diet was left wanting with too many hard peas and too little fruit. Thankfully, there was fresh milk and eggs from the cook's animals and it seemed the man did his best. The stop in France caused no issues.

James tried hard to fit in and to keep to himself, unaware that he could become a source of entertainment to the others. He didn't see himself as a snob but had been schooled since birth to believe he was superior.

That night, finally out of the channel and adrift on the ocean, he was back on his bale. Every bone in his body hurt and with the weather changed, it felt like his temples were squeezed in a vice grip. James prayed for protection from a storm and eventually dozed. The wind smelled of rain and crossed his face like the softness of a woman's breath.

He drifted deeper and heard a voice whispering:

"Jimmy, where are you?" He could see the woman, wandering along the deck and trailed by her little girls. This time they were dressed for a trip, with coats and hats. Again, she called, "Jimmy, answer me." How did she know his name? In the throes of sleep, he tried to speak but the words wouldn't form.

All his struggling to answer her only woke him up. Then he tossed and turned, fully disturbed by the images. Strangely, he was growing fond of this woman. Morning came much too fast. A threatening storm had veered away and taken the rain with it. His prayers were answered.

"I saw the dream woman again," James said.

"I think you're haunted or obsessed," was all Carl would say.

But Friday, 1 September 1939, brought terrible news. The radio reported, "Germany's air force, the *Luftwaffe,* ground troops, and tanks, the *Heer*, have invaded Poland. World War II has begun."

At that point, it was hard to find someone on board who didn't feel incredibly vulnerable, even the captain and other Germans.

Within days, more word came, "The United Kingdom and France have declared war on Germany and are mobilising."

That relieved the ship's occupants somewhat. Unfortunately, disappointing news came on Sunday from President Roosevelt. "The United States will officially stay out of the conflict."

James lost count of the days after that because like others, he was in and out of seasickness with rough waters. There were women and children on board, often working to pay their fares with mothers clucking over their children.

One little girl with long blonde hair, maybe five, made her way down to the cattle stalls and asked him, "Can I help?"

She was little enough to put her hand beside his and help carry the pails too. "My name is Sadie, what's yours?" Sadie was lovely and sweet and they became instant friends. Her mother would shoo her away often but still he felt protective over the little girl.

On Sunday, September 17, they were a goodly way across the ocean when more shocking news came. The newscaster was grave, "A German submarine *U-29*, has torpedoed the Royal Navy aircraft carrier *HMS Courageous* off the coast of Ireland. The British warship carried 48 aircraft and is the first of the war to be sunk. The carrier had turned into the wind to launch her aircraft, putting her directly in the submarine's path."

All ears were tuned in, waiting for more information as the report continued, "The ship capsized and sank in 20 minutes. It was a depressing blow since the *Courageous* had just left the port at Plymouth and was on an anti-submarine patrol off the coast of Ireland. *U-29* had stalked her for hours."

People felt physical pain knowing their ship had been in the vicinity only days earlier. It was more than frightening.

"Of the 1,259 crew, 518 were lost, including the captain. Those who escaped were picked up by a Dutch ocean liner. Two escorting destroyers hunted the rogue submarine for hours without luck."

The crew in the galley exchanged sober looks. Everyone wanted to worry aloud but no one dared. Magnifying problems could foster panic in close quarters and was never a good idea. The idea of the submarine lurking in the ocean's depths, was terrifying.

"Surely, the Germans won't harm a ship from their own country!" was their only recourse.

James kept busy. He found a rope to recoil, checked the pen gates, and tightened a hinge. Then, he counted the steers, anything to keep his mind occupied. Indeed, the sensitive children vibrated with the taste and feel of fear in the air. At the next meal, Sadie, for one, was teary and cried when faced with salty meat again. At least, the food distracted them all from the bigger issue.

James went to bat for the little girl, "Otto! Cannae, we switch it up fer oatmeal with milk from the cow fer these bairns?"

The old cook met the challenge and afterwards said, "I'm happy they lapped it up and forgot about things. No child should have to worry about the threat of torpedoes. I was saving a pudding of flour, suet, and currents but tonight everyone needs a distraction. It's Lasse's recipe, a woman I once knew."

The ocean-goers ate their troubles away and awoke to a howling wind. White caps and choppy water propelled the ship forward at a surprising hilt.

James's first thoughts were, "Let's hope our luck holds out."

James wasn't the only one thinking of the *Titanic,* particularly with the *HMS Courageous* laying at the bottom of the ocean.

"They were only 400 miles south of Newfoundland and 20 miles away from the *California,* an ocean liner with its radio operator off duty," Carl said. "Their distress signal went unheard."

Hans went on, "And about an hour and 20 minutes after going down, 700 were rescued from lifeboats by a Cunard liner, the *Carpathia.*"

James could fill in the rest, "They dinnae have enough lifeboats or any practice usin' them. Since 1913, lifeboat drills and round-the-clock radio watches are mandatory."

"Yes, and an International Ice Patrol monitors for icebergs in the North Atlantic shipping lanes ever since."

Regardless, James was happy when the wind died down. As the days continued, they encountered other small squalls from time to time. One day, the crew was heartened to see an albatross flying around the ship. To them, it meant good luck because the bird supposedly carried the soul of a mariner trying to help them.

On Thursday, 28 September 1939, across the air waves came, "Warsaw, Poland has surrendered after valiantly fighting back with snipers and taking German soldiers prisoner. Germany and the Soviet Union, however, took control and the *Wehrmacht* troops went on full parade to flaunt their victory."

Watching the men set out bird snacks and fussing over the albatross, James had time to remember Edgar's story and what he had tried to shield James from regarding war.

"The trenches were hell, and that's the kindest thing a have to say," Edgar coughed, painting a grisly scene.

"It rained non-stop, so we could barely see and were freezin' cold with numb fingers. Soldiers lay shot and dyin' all around us or drowned in shell holes." The veteran gasped for air. "If not that, the trench fever, trench foot, or gangrene would set in."

James shook his head at the macabre aspect of World War I.

"A'm not lookin' fer sympathy, a just want ye to understand," Edgar pleaded.

"A do," James assured.

"The snipers were relentless, and the fire and smoke devastatin' but nothin' compared to the constant roar of artillery that drove men crazy." He filled his lungs to get the rest out. Still, his eyes glazed over.

"All against the backdrop of scurryin' rats capitalisin' on the rottin' corpses."

He was silent for a moment. "That's somethin' I cannae bear to think about. A pair of rats reproduces about 1,000 a year."

Edgar stopped short of telling James how it affected his marriage but James already knew. Edgar's wife had spilt the beans.

"Rats and people dyin' were what his nightmares were made of," she said. "He couldnae sleep with me because between gaspin' fer air, the night terrors, and his flailin' limbs, he was either hittin' or kickin'. Fer me own safety, a had to sleep apart from him. One time, a awoke to him sittin' bolt upright, shakin' me by the shoulders. He was sobbin' violently, yet sound asleep."

Edgar went on, "The capstone, of course, was madness. Men either committed suicide or simply gave up."

Edgar was at the Battle of Ypres alongside the Canadians when the Germans launched their first attack of poison gas. "With no protection, all our side could do was urinate into our hankies and clamp them over our mouths and noses."

"Oh, no!"

"They thought they had us, but we kept fightin'. To everyone's surprise, the enemy suddenly retreated and vanished back into their rat-infested holes."

"Like me, many veterans came home with gas lung or shell shock," Edgar's voice trailed off and James was fully aware he wasn't expecting to live a long life. In fact, he was in the end stages of lung damage, miraculously surviving this long.

28

Old Jimmy—The Remittance Man

Atlantic Ocean to Melfort—*28 September 1939–1992*

After the capture of Poland, for two weeks between 28 September and 15 October 1939, the cattle ship's occupants were over it and yearned for Canadian shores. Hearing how Germany and Russia divided the spoils of Poland between themselves didn't help their sketchy Thanksgiving meal.

When the ship finally docked at Pier 21, Halifax, squawking sea gulls heralded their arrival. Immeasurable relief flooded James, who gingerly stepped down the gangplank ready to embrace the land of the free. Like others, he would endure the rigorous immigrant screening, then catch the soonest Canadian National Railway train west.

Canada had officially declared war a month earlier, and there was evidence of military personnel everywhere. Emotions ran high, blending fear with pride for people in uniform. With mixed emotions, James kept a low profile.

During the customs experience to gain Landed Immigrant status, the room buzzed with patriotism, most having a brick wall attitude towards the aggressors. James's heart-ached for the fresh-faced volunteers arriving on troop trains. Was there no other way?

He thought of Edgar's words, "The brave but naive souls will see the world but somewhere between honour and horror, they'll meet mankind's darkest side. They'll run blindly into hellfire, learnin' to kill or be killed, and perform acts of sheer barbarism they never dreamt possible."

With military personnel everywhere, James bought a sleeper car train ticket for Winnipeg. After freshening up and boarding, he was struck by a distinct sense of déjà vu.

His seat was beside a Calgary family, and the husband said, "Senseless, bloody war but both the Calgary Highlanders and the Saskatoon Light Infantry were mobilised after Poland was invaded."

His wife said, "And don't you know, the boys see serving their country as the thing to do. A convoy of our troop ships with protective craft escorts is sailing to England soon."

Her husband was sceptical, "They'll have to do some fancy foot work to avoid the German U-boats," and everyone agreed it would be dangerous.

Along the route, James had tried to read a book but found the sights far too distracting. Aside from the military troop trains, he'd enjoyed seeing the beauty of each province, and was in awe of the sprawling countryside with so much open space. A little time spent recuperating in Winnipeg couldn't hurt before the final leg of his journey to Saskatoon. It was a full week before the train arrived there on Sunday, 22 October 1939.

In the central part of the city, the Victorian splendour and gleaming marble of the Fort Garry Hotel on Broadway called to him. Between dips in the pool and time in the restaurant, he took in the sights. Portage Avenue thrived and the city itself was like a hornet's nest, bustling to keep up with a world at war. Crowded armouries spilt over into other buildings and the place crawled with flight crews on their way west for training. On the streets, James met everything from pilots to gunners, who were joining the ranks of all the flight training schools across the country. Shopkeepers scurried to anticipate the needs of the bustling population and it seemed like the Great Depression was lifting.

By Halloween, James left the Manitoba city, jostling in the same spaces as military travellers, and arrived in Saskatoon the night of November 1st. After a good stretch, he sent a telegram home to Scotland with news of his safe arrival. From the station on 1st Avenue, he could see the Bessborough Hotel and could have walked the few blocks east down 21st Street.

The four-block cab ride was ridiculously short and the cabbie laughed when James said, "Luggin' a steamer trunk and barrel is nought an easy feat."

Once checked into the impressive riverbank hotel, he bought a postcard featuring pictures of the hotel itself. The one-cent stamp filled him with pride seeing Britain's two young princesses, Elizabeth, and Margaret Rose.

At breakfast the next morning, a slightly older gentleman folded his newspaper, stood up, and offered his hand in acquaintance. Cecil was a large barrel-chested Scandinavian dressed in a suit and puffing on a fat Havana cigar.

"Do you think there's any truth to Hitler denying he has designs on Rumania?"

James laughed, "A wouldnae believe a word!"

"Me neither. What do you think of the Bez? Seven years ago, it was built to look like a Bavarian castle but the depression left it unopened until 1935."

"'Tis stunnin'!"

Cecil used his trouser cuffs to flick his cigar ashes, then drained his coffee cup.

"I'm off to Western Lighting for a vacuum cleaner," he chuckled, "then, it's Sterling Shoes to buy Aladdin Hosiery for my mother."

"Nylons?" James asked, winking.

Cecil laughed.

That afternoon, mulling over where to put down roots, James took a stroll downtown. A small crowd gathered outside a coiffure salon window where the sign said 'croquingnole marcel waves'. Seeing their uniformed admirers, the women inside smiled coyly and continued their activity.

James moved on. With no intention of buying, he walked to Boyd Bros and looked over the new Chevrolets and Oldsmobiles. He bought a driver's licence with no test for 25¢ and took the Olds for a test drive past the university, hospital, and swimming pool. Suitably impressed and back on foot, his last stop was the Picardy Candy Shop to buy a box of chocolates.

Back at the hotel, eating a steak supper, he skimmed the newspaper. It was no surprise that Hitler gloried in his defeat of Poland. "Is Lithuania next?" the writer asked.

Another story queried, "Is Russia's friendship with Germany cooling?" They could only hope.

Friday, 3 November, James and Cecil took a walk around the hotel after breakfast. It was slower going and on 24th street near City Hall was the HMCS Unicorn Naval Reserve building.

Cecil explained, "They recruit and train for land, sea, and air."

James remembered Edgar's eagerness to sign up.

"On the one hand, a feel great respect fer those willin' to fight but on the other, all a can see is the image of me brother," James admitted.

"Is he a Great War veteran?"

"Yes, and scarred for life."

Cecil shook his head, and they eyed the recruitment centre's boat shed. Suddenly, with the river so close, the training became far too real.

James sighed, "Like lambs to slaughter."

"Some will fall, no doubt."

The two men sat on a park bench at the City Hall square, and Cecil said, "I brought my mother to the city in June to see King George VI and Queen Elizabeth. We only caught a glimpse as they whizzed by but at least we saw them. By their last stop, at Melville, they said the crowd was bigger than either Regina or Saskatoon's population!"

James thought, "A saw them at Balmoral two years ago."

That evening, feeling restless, the Scotsman thought of taking a dip in the salt-water pool but instead, opted to explore more of the hotel. The Adam Ballroom was empty, except for a man in the shadows who tipped his fedora and said hello. James nodded in return, then strolled across to the dimly lit Terrace Lounge and stepped out onto the balcony. The air was fresh and cool and, in the twilight, a beaver slapped its tail in the rushing river below, while a flock of geese honked overhead.

Back inside, James wandered past the Salon Batoche and other meeting rooms before retracing his steps and climbing the stairs to the third floor. Here was a small, tired looking woman, obviously having a bad day because she didn't make eye contact. Ascending the spiral staircase to the top made him gasp. The tenth floor had high slanted ceilings and stark white walls. Being the city's tallest building, a small garret-type window on the front wall gave a spectacular view of the city. For a time, he watched mesmerised, as ribbons of green and yellow light shimmered across the night sky. Since it was nearing bedtime, regrettably, he tore himself away.

The enormous, winding, staircase was much more fun to go down. Ahead of him, he heard the laughter of children sliding down the banister and expected to gain on them upon rounding every bend but never did. He wondered why they weren't tucked into bed for the night.

Saturday, November 4th, at breakfast, Cecil said, "I know you're pondering where you might land next. I'm leaving for the little one-horse town of Guernsey this morning for a late Thanksgiving dinner with my mother.

Would you care to join us? You could sink your teeth into some home cooking and take in a beautiful countryside!"

James didn't hesitate, "Thank ye, a would be honoured! What are ye drivin'?"

"A 1937 Buick that I bought at the General Motors plant in Regina."

James needed no further coaxing. Upon settling his hotel bill, he found the opulent facility charged $3.00 a night and 25¢ per meal.

Cecil was a good driver but with pluming cigar smoke, James rolled down his window a crack. The vehicle tore down the rough road with a rag stuffed in a golf-ball size hole in the windshield. While marvelling at the countryside, James recounted his hotel explorations from the night before.

Cecil snorted, "You do know the Bez is haunted, don't you?"

"Really?"

Cecil's version of the children on the stairs, the haggard lady on the third floor, and the man with the fedora in the Adam Ballroom caused a bell to go off in James's head.

"A think a may have inadvertently made their acquaintance!" he sputtered, "maybe 'twas best a was totally oblivious!"

"More than you bargained for, eh?" Cecil laughed and coughed, almost choking.

Eventually, James changed the subject. "Is Guernsey named after the island in the English Channel?"

"Yes. Like many other Canadian places, named after the old country."

Upon arrival in the village, they headed directly for Cecil's mother's home.

"She'll be cooking up a storm and loves to feed people so you know you're welcome."

"Thanks for inviting me!"

Rosemary, in her 60s, was outfitted in a house dress and apron and the smell of roast turkey wafted out the door. She shook James's hand then embraced her son and squealed with delight over the vacuum cleaner and hosiery.

Cecil carved the turkey, browned to perfection with meat falling off the bone. When they sat down to eat, James's mouth watered. Heaped high in her expensive china bowls was a delectable spread with an assortment of colours, textures, and aromas from mashed potatoes and gravy to ambrosia salad, and cranberry sauce.

Rosemary patted down her wavy hair before Cecil said grace. James was already in seventh heaven when she topped off the main course with pumpkin and apple pies, smothered in freshly whipped cream.

"A cannae believe what a've been missin'," James praised. "This meal was extraordinary! Thank ye fer includin' me!"

They sat at the dining table talking for a while and inevitably the talk turned to James's trip and the outbreak of war.

James said, "We had anxious moments at sea when war was announced! Then, right behind us was a submarine sinking a British aircraft carrier."

"Oh dear! How I despise war!" Rosemary spat. "I can't believe the world is forced into it again!"

"Me too," James admitted. "Bein' a pacifist, a'm lookin' to find a place where I willnae be run out on a rail."

After a moment, Rosemary said, "Melfort has Scandinavians farmers who are on the same page as us. I have an old friend living there."

James felt hopeful.

Cecil offered, "We could drive you! Mother, would you like to go for a Sunday drive tomorrow to take him to Melfort?"

It appeared one thing she loved was driving in the car because she jumped at the chance.

Before going to bed, Cecil pulled out a pipe and a pouch of tobacco. "My father used to smoke this before he passed. I'm more of a cigar man. If you want, they're yours."

"Well, thank ye! A love the pungent smell but never smoked one."

Although James coughed and sputtered at first, he found the pipe soothing. Edgar couldn't ever tolerate such a thing.

The trip north took place Sunday morning, 5 November and one of the biggest joys was listening to the radio. The car had a built-in Motorola with push buttons and pre-set stations. James wanted to take them to a restaurant but they wouldn't hear of it. Rosemary had already packed turkey sandwiches for lunch. They included him like part of the family because for them, the trip itself was a joy and helping others was in their nature.

When they dropped him off, on their way to see Rosemary's friend at the grocery store, James handed her the box of chocolates he had saved for just such an occasion. In return, Rosemary gave him a tin of rolled and buttered lefse, sprinkled with brown sugar and cinnamon. He thanked them, hoping one day to meet again.

At first, he wandered around, making inquiries at multiple places about opportunities for work but after a time, rested on a bench across the street from the big stone post office. The plaque said it was built in 1912 and it crowded the full street corner of Main and McLeod.

A middle-aged local farmer in coveralls and straw hat came along and introduced himself as Paul. They got to talking about nothing much and as usual the talk turned to the war.

"I don't like it one bit," Paul said and James was quick to agree.

James ventured, "Ye wouldnae know of any work opportunities around here, would ye?"

Paul hesitated at first, "Well, perhaps. First, tell me about yourself."

After James told his story, including working with cattle, Paul invited, "I'm looking for a farm hand if you're interested."

James replied, "Yes, I am."

"Room and board is included."

The deal was struck and Paul helped James load his belongings into Old Bessie, the Chevy car, and they drove off. James was thrilled by the countryside and when they got to the farmyard, Paul explained, "My mother's Big House has sat empty for three years since she passed. She and my father were the original homesteaders."

After introductions to Paul's wife, Tessie, and the children, Paul showed James the ropes. The chores meant feeding, watering, and dunging out pens and stalls. Paul had an assortment of livestock and the friendly dog was a black and white border collie they called Brewster.

Meals were at the kitchen table in the family's bungalow and after supper, James walked across the yard, 'home' to the Big House. He sat on the veranda, trying his new pipe and watching the sunset. It was a great finish to his first day. The family taking an evening stroll, couldn't stay away, and wandered over to sit with him.

"The nights are cooling off," Paul said, "one of these days we're in for snow, can't you smell it in the air?"

"A'm looking forward to it!" James said loving snow, "please, wait here a minute."

He returned with Rosemary's tin box and the lefse treats were a hit.

After saying good night, and all alone, he felt contented laying in the dark listening to the hoot owls. The background chorus of frogs, crickets, and howling coyotes gusted in with the fresh air from the bedroom window. The only ominous reminder that the world was at war was the occasional flight school planes flying overhead. You could hear them but not see them. Apparently, pilots in training were practicing their night flying with no lights. Snuggling under his warm quilt he thanked his lucky stars for Canada.

After a sound sleep, he awoke remembering a dream and was mystified about the reappearance of the auburn-haired woman and her two daughters.

James wrote a letter home to his family.

My dear family,

I have arrived and found employment on a farm north of Melfort, Saskatchewan helping do chores. I stay in the Big House, an empty two-story in their yard. Paul, the owner, is Scandinavian and his wife, Tessie is Scottish. Sunrises and sunsets are staggering from my wicker rocker on the front veranda where I smoke my pipe. Now don't be upset because the pipe was a gift from the Guernsey fellow who drove me to Melfort. The Big House is rustic with a five-gallon drum heater for wood and coal but the place is only 20 years old. It remains glorious with hardwoods, stained-glass windows, and a bevelled glass front door. I take meals from Tessie's kitchen. Last night's was fried chicken with rhubarb and strawberry pie, scrumptious! The two enchanting little girls, Marion and Alice are six and four, with a one-year-old brother, Richard. Tessie has her hands full, so I play a role in entertaining the little ones and vice versa. Paul says snow is on the way! I miss you all.
Love James.

By 1940, distrust of Hitler was palpable with nearly all of Western Europe under Nazi control. The Fascist leader, Benito Mussolini envious of Hitler and seeking glory, joined the Axis powers on 10 June 1940. Between the Fall of France and the impending Battle of Britain that summer, a sensational evacuation of Allied troops from Dunkirk had Brits regaling in the streets. It was then that Winston Churchill, prime minister of Britain in his first month of office, gave the people a morale boost, still warning that danger was not over.

His unforgettable words were, "We shall fight on beaches, landing grounds, in fields and streets, and on the hills. We shall never surrender."

The three-month fight over British skies kept the Luftwaffe at bay and despite the bombings, King George VI gained respect for remaining at Buckingham Palace even when it was bombed repeatedly. Still, the cost was thousands of Allies and Germans who lost their lives.

Once again, Churchill, in appreciation for the Royal Air Force and Allied air crew, famously went on record, to say, "Never in the field of human conflict was so much owed by so many to so few."

Still, the danger mounted when in September 1940, partly based on tensions with Great Britain and the United States, Japan signed a Tripartite Pact to join Germany and Italy, the Axis powers.

Shortly after, James received a telegram:

"Your family's estate was bombed. They are presently unaccounted for."

A devastated James unable to sleep or breathe, paced and wrung his hands agonising over their fate. It was only days later, however, that relief came.

"Your mother, brother, and family are safe." And James finally exhaled. Ultimately, the battle moved over the skies of Germany and Hitler called off the attack.

While war raged overseas, life at the farm ticked on. The children loved storytelling after meals, especially their favourite about Nessie, the Loch Ness monster. Paul was building the children a flat-bottomed boat for spring to cross the flooded creek to get to school. Otherwise, they had to stay over with Uncle Peter and Auntie Sis for days on end. James helped, and the children started calling him, 'Old Jimmy'.

Occasionally, Old Jimmy took the train into Saskatoon and sometimes brought home gifts for the children, like big, woollen scarves in winter. He didn't tell anyone but he'd met a nice lady, Phyllis, in Saskatoon, a shoe saleslady. The relationship was complicated, however, by her jealous ex-husband.

"A know he's volatile," James said to her, "but maybe if ye married me, he'd settle down." She shook her head, always worried the brute would do something rash. When James begged, she still refused. Over time, he came to accept her decision.

At the farm, Paul told Old Jimmy the stories of Knut's death and the suspected brothers. James heard about Lasse, her first husband's train trestle accident, and her coming from Sweden on a cattle ship. He wondered if the presence he felt in the house was her.

No neighbour seemed to take offence to him living in their community but consistently referred to him as a remittance man. He decided, it probably had more to do with his Scottish brogue, than his stance against war, or that for a time, he received money from his family across the ocean. With their bombed-out estate, however, the money couldn't continue. For him, to be lumped in with the real remittance men who built Cannington Manor in the Athabasca District in 1882 gave him a touch of pride.

Sitting at the breakfast table on a regular Wednesday, 13 August 1940, a flustered Scottish cousin, Ronnie, knocked at Tessie and Paul's door.

"Come in, come in," urged Tessie. "What's wrong?"

He said, "It's yer mother!"

He sat and wrung his hands, "A'm sorry but Martha has laid down on the bed beside yer bedridden father, Jake, and died."

Tessie swayed and Paul went to her.

"The heavy load of caregivin' must've been too much fer her." The 29-year-old, Tessie, crumbled into Paul's arms and Old Jimmy gathered the children around him.

Ronnie, whose mother was Grandma Tessa's sister, came out west to help with the first harvest in 1902, and never went back, sick of stones too. To get the news to Tessie, he was the only one in the immediate vicinity with a car.

When she, Paul, and the children rode back with him, Old Jimmy went along. The doctor pronounced, "I'm sorry, but Martha died of aortic stenosis, a bad heart valve."

Martha's funeral service was from the Presbyterian Church with interment at the Mount Pleasant Cemetery. Chaos ensued surrounding paralysed Jake's ongoing care, but the family stepped up. Jake, of course, only able to move his eyeballs and relegated to bed, missed his wife's funeral. Old Jimmy stayed with him so the family could attend the service. He would do it for Tessie, and he would do it for Paul, who still stung from the loss of his own mother.

Tessie took her turn caring for and doing Jake's laundry. One winter's morning, she sent a box of freshly laundered clothes to school with Marion and

Alice in the caboose for Uncle Toot to retrieve. As usual, the little girls picked up several cousins along the way.

By late afternoon, it was threatening darkness, and there was no sign of the children or caboose, The parents worried, so Paul and Old Jimmy struck out on homemade cross-country skis to search. Coming up the last hill, was eight-year-old Marion, driving the team with only a caboose floor, no walls or roof. Alice clung to her sister for dear life.

Upon reaching her father, Marion cried, "The caboose burned down! We looked out the school window and saw it on fire! A neighbour man came and put it out."

"And Grandda's clothes are all burnt up!" Alice sniffled.

The little girls had dawdled all the way home, thinking they were in trouble.

"It's okay," Paul reassured. "We thank God you're not hurt. I can build another caboose and Granddad has other clothes."

The men figured one of the little cousins had accidentally hooked the box of clothes while exiting the caboose, knocking it onto the red-hot coal stove. The clothes would have smouldered a while, then kindled into a glorious blaze.

Eventually, Tessie's sister, 38-year-old Aggie, living near Lenvale, took in her infirm father. Jake's care was heavy but her husband and the other family members helped.

In the meantime, by 1941, Bonnie's husband, John found work in the British Columbia forests and they moved to the coast. All the family were sorry to see them go but John was an entrepreneur and an inventor. Soon, he made a name for himself in the B.C. logging industry, inventing a portable sawmill.

The attack on Pearl Harbour by the Japanese happened Sunday morning, 7 December 1941. The first news reports never made it to the airwaves until after 2:30 p.m., a half hour after Paul's 34th birthday celebration began and the partygoers gathered around the radio. With over 4,000 Americans killed or wounded, it was no surprise to hear the United States had joined the Allied war effort. Now, the Pacific War and World War II merged and a couple of days later, Germany declared war on the United States.

On 4 June 1942, came the Battle of Midway, a small island in the Pacific Ocean halfway between Japan and the United States. Americans secretly cracked the Japanese code and caused Japan to suffer heavy losses. It was a major turning point of the war.

At the same time, Old Jimmy received word that his brother, Edgar had passed away. Knowing it was coming wasn't the same as when it actually happened, and Old Jimmy cried his eyes out. The children stayed close, surprisingly understanding of their old friend's sadness. They drew him pictures, fashioned him bracelets, and wrote stories to brighten his spirit.

"Thank you," he said, "in time, I'll feel better."

The country rationed sugar: one cup per adult per week but no one complained because it meant more for the soldiers. They could also get two dozen tea bags. The women shared recipes for tomato soup cake, Kraft™ macaroni and cheese, and lime Jello™ filled with olives, sweet pickles, and celery.

Another turning point was the Battle of Stalingrad on 7 July 1942, when Old Jimmy had returned from a weekend in Saskatoon. On the same day, Marion, turned nine. Alice would be seven in August, and their brother, Richard was four. Marion got a new bicycle and the other two didn't, so feeling sorry for them, Old Jimmy shared his red liquorice sticks. The household learned, after the fact, that the battle that day on Russian soil was the most catastrophic of the war but one from which the German army would never recover.

Old Jimmy's daughter, Lily, was born August 1942 and she became the light of his life. It was the same day, August 19, when Canadians led a catastrophic amphibious attack at Dieppe, France. With delays and other errors, the Allies, mostly Canadians, lost the cover of darkness and met with severe losses. Old Jimmy thanked God every day for his life in Canada and his loved ones, Lily and Phyllis.

When school started that fall, there were bumper crops and Marion and Alice rode her new bicycle to school. For three miles there and back, Marion pedalled for all she was worth and Alice rode on the handlebars. It was hard going for Marion but worse for Alice's rearend. Still, for the few warm months, life felt free.

During the war years, Canadians supplied over half of Britain's wheat and flour, bacon, cheese, eggs, and evaporated milk. Old Jimmy saw that Paul's children never knew poverty having their own garden, meat, and dairy, nothing like food shortages around the world.

Further, the community looked forward to Saturday nights and the family included Old Jimmy, if he was home. In the summer, they loaded up for town in their grey Chevy, Old Bessie. For winter, they rode in a caboose on sleighs pulled by horses. The adults shopped and visited while the children played and ran around the lit streets. The high point for Marion and Bernice was pooling their money to share a waffle at the greasy spoon.

The Second World War years moved forward, and the fighting overseas killed bodies, spirits, and minds. The plethora of deaths forced Old Jimmy to face a moral dilemma every day. Did pacifism have a place in the face of extreme evil and in a just war? There were pros and cons.

His thoughts were interrupted when Paul's visitor arrived. It was a friend from town who brought a message. Paul looked shocked but read:

Dear family,

I am heartbroken to tell you that my fourteen-year-old daughter, Helen, has drowned in Lake Winnipeg when there swimming with friends.

Love, Mikaila

Paul was speechless. His poor dear sister! All he could do was send a return message of condolence.

"Tragic news of the loss of your darling daughter, please accept our deepest condolences!"

He had only met Helen once, at his own mother's funeral. Mikaila would be devastated and might never recover.

A convoy of 130 ships filled with Canadian soldiers left Halifax for England on 1 July 1943. It was a proud but sickening moment for Canadians.

By November, Sean was struck a blow, when Edith, his wife, died at 57 from a stroke. He loved his children and grandchildren but it wasn't the same without her. After three decades of marriage, he sorely missed her.

That year, Italy was in chaos, their king had resigned, and Mussolini was on the run. On D-Day, 6 June 1944, the Allies dropped British and American paratroopers onto the German-controlled beaches of Normandy, France, intending to liberate Western Europe. The Germans put up a massive fight and the Allies' losses were extensive but they hung on. In the end, for the first time in the war, the German soldiers retreated rousting them from France and the Netherlands. There was light at the end of the tunnel.

That summer, Paul hired neighbouring members of the James Smith Indian Reserve to build a pole fence around his pig barn.

Old Jimmy wrote home.

My dear mother,

How are you? I am taken up with my new love, Lily, your granddaughter, and her mother, Phyllis who live in Saskatoon. I see them as often as possible but it's complicated by her ex-husband. Paul's friend, Smith, an old-timer from the Indian reserve, has sent his son and family to assist with a building project. They set up tipis across the road and entertain us by the hour watching their activities. When the women bake Bannock, they share it as a treat. Paul pays the workers on Friday nights, and they leave and return about Tuesday. I miss you every day. Love James (incidentally, they call me Old Jimmy!)

During World War II, seven years after losing Martha, on 7 September 1944, Jake was on death's door. By the next afternoon, he took his last breath. Now officially orphaned, pregnant Tessie and her siblings were heartbroken but felt for him, it was a blessing.

The minister commended, "Jake was a true pioneer, serving a quarter century as trustee and president of the country school board. He raised a large family and made their home a welcome gathering place for community activities."

Four decades after the wagon trek and homesteading, he was laid to rest beside his wife. Finally, they would see their loved ones on the other side. The family's special memory box was added to but replaced by a bigger mahogany box and Tessie took it to her home for safekeeping. Toot and Chickadee inherited Jake and Martha's home and quarter.

Hitler ordered his last great offensive at the Battle of the Bulge on 16 December 1944. The snow was deep on the French soil, heading towards Germany. Despite the inexperienced Allied troops, they stubbornly refused to surrender. The fight waged for weeks until amazingly the Germans retreated.

On Christmas eve, Tessie and Paul's fourth child, a baby daughter, named Sharon, was born at the Melfort hospital. It was three months since Jake's death, and mother and baby came through with flying colours.

During their 10-day hospital stay, Paul, back at home, brought out the photo albums. One picture was of Paul's mother, Lasse, with Paul and Peter, standing in front of their new 1920s Model T. Old Jimmy could have sworn the grey-haired, heavier-set woman was the lady with the auburn hair from his dreams. Paul told of his father, Knut's journey to Saskatchewan and Tessie's grandmother, Tessa, facing a diphtheria epidemic. Something felt familiar to Old Jimmy, and he scratched his head.

When Tessie and the new baby came home, the remittance man went along to town and bought the family a wooden mantel clock. They proudly displayed it atop the china cabinet, and he taught the children how to wind it.

The winter of 1944–1945, the Allies pushed into Germany only to discover mass graves and other horrors beyond belief. Half dead, skeleton-like prisoners of war were liberated at multiple concentration camps. Names like Auschwitz and Birkenau became synonymous with gas chambers and mass murder. Over time, the Allies pieced together the nightmarish events. Tragically, unimaginable estimates came in as 6,000,000 Jews exterminated. The world was never so mortified.

January 1945, the final year of World War II, closer to home, news came of a murder and the death of Tessie's nephew, Garth. He was her sister, Dot's youngest son, and was a lead telegrapher in the navy. Garishly he was discovered floating face down in the New York Harbour. Aghast with blood curdling suspicions; enemy Axis spies were all anyone could talk about. Suddenly, the war had entered their own back yard.

Paul, Tessie, and Sean travelled the 60 miles to attend the Nipawin funeral. They went to Dot's home first to console her and her eldest son, Earl, also a seaman, who got bereavement leave from the navy.

Supporting the family at the church, the mourners stood together in the pew, and Paul seethed with disgust, "Spies, treachery, and saboteurs!"

"That is exactly what the Allies fight against," Sean agreed.

The casket was closed but inside it, Garth was outfitted in his best dress uniform. At the service, led by the Canadian Legion and Auxiliary, his mother was presented with a folded Union Jack flag. Afterwards, she sobbed out the words, "My baby was only 23! I am honoured that the pallbearers were his comrades, all navy seamen outfitted in their best service dress uniforms."

As the crowd delivered their condolences, Earl remained stoic with a faraway look in his eyes. The mourners heard over and over, "Garth was a hero who deserved the highest tribute."

The sting of Garth's loss was lessened for some, when on 30 January 1945, over 500 Allied prisoners of war were rescued from a Japanese POW camp at Cabanatuan, in the Philippines. During a nighttime raid, United States Army Rangers, Alamo Scouts, and Filipino guerrillas did the heroic liberating but not without their own losses.

Come 28 April 1945, the Italian dictator, Mussolini, disguised as a German soldier, was shot and killed while crossing to Innsbruck, Austria in a truck convoy. He was recognised and he and his mistress were hung head downward by their captors. Italy celebrated his death and returned their country to democracy.

8 May 1945, was declared VE Day (Victory in Europe) when the Germans surrendered, and Nazi leaders signed the surrender documents. People around the world rejoiced.

On 6 and 9 August 1945, however, the world stood by horrified, when, in retaliation for Pearl Harbour and ongoing Japanese concerns, the United States dropped two atomic bombs on Japan. One over the city of Hiroshima, and the other over Nagasaki. Defeated Emperor Hirohito made the announcement of Japan's formal surrender over Japanese radio, and days later, on Sunday, 2 September 1945, the war ended. Almost every country in the world was affected and all expected the process of rebuilding to take decades.

The summer of 1945, after years away, Lovisa, from the Yukon, surprised them all with a visit to Paul and Tessie's farm, and Mikaila joined them from Winnipeg. Paul, Peter, and Gladys whom the women had helped raise, were thrilled. Bonnie, firmly entrenched in British Columbia, couldn't be there. Well-to-do Lovisa enthralled Old Jimmy, being such a vibrant woman and the owner of a hotel and restaurant. After commiserating about days gone by in the Gold Rush, and the end of the war, Old Jimmy told them snippets about his life story and about his odd dream connections. To his dismay, Lovisa howled with laughter.

He answered, "Whatever it was, there's really no one left to ask, is there?"

Mikaila, however, didn't scoff, "I believe that creatures who dream enter the dream plane through the sleep portal. It's the place where mortals meet souls. I attend séances myself to connect with Helen," she said matter-of-factly. Helen was her deceased daughter!

Paul was flabbergasted, and thinking his half-sister was slightly touched, changed the subject. He told them about Bonnie's experience as a widow now, still living at the coast.

"One of the notorious brothers paid her a visit and she shook like a leaf the whole time. Bonnie was convinced Gib Swallow would kill her, but the man appeared to have found a conscience."

The sisters only stayed one more day, then returned home. After that, the Melfort pioneers took another hard hit when David, in British Columbia, and Philip at 98 years, both died in 1949.

"Clarice needn't have worried 50 years earlier that her suitor was 23 years older because he outlived her by exactly 23 years," Tessie said.

A big change came in 1949 when Saskatchewan Power inaugurated the Rural Electrification Program. Power poles and power lines were strung alongside roads, and yard lights shone in farmyards with the flick of a switch. Suddenly, rural Saskatchewan was no longer dark with houses and barns lit up and new appliances easing every aspect of their lives.

Come the 1950s the children had grown and were being married. In 1950, Marion met a strapping young man from Ethelton, a community to the southeast. As it turned out, he was the son of Troy, who her grandmother had met on her covered wagon trip through the Greenbush forest in 1903. Marion gave birth to her first son.

The next year, Uncle Toot, dropped dead from a heart attack at the age of 56. Chickadee, plunged into uncertainty, felt unable to manage the farm and family, and frantically cast around for a solution. It came in the form of a housekeeping job serving two bachelors in another community. The drawback was she couldn't take her two little boys, the youngest of her six children. Needing the money and unsure what to do, she contacted the St. Patrick's Catholic Orphanage in Prince Albert. It became the home of her two boys, six and eight years old. The facility was newly opened and sadly torn, she left them in the care of the Sisters of Charity of the Immaculate Conception.

Four years earlier in January 1947, the original orphanage holding 122 children was levelled by fire in the wee hours of the morning. It was 45 degrees below zero and six young girls and one Sister perished. A second Sister was seriously injured when she slipped from the icy ledge of an upper story window.

The two little Protestant boys, thrust into the foreign world of a Catholic facility, learned to survive without benefit of their parents. Chickadee visited when she could and did her best to work hard and pay for their boarding fees. Children were there for good reason and sometimes it was whole families of up to 14 siblings if their mothers or fathers had died.

In the meantime, on 6 February 1952, King George VI passed away and a whole new chapter opened for Canada. His daughter, Queen Elizabeth II, began her reign over the Commonwealth at the tender age of 25.

For the next generation, in most households, a new fridge was followed by an electric stove, a clothes dryer, and finally a television. Like the others, Sean's family were early to get power and machinery and he lived until July 1958. His Lutheran funeral service was well attended as the last living child of the original wagon trekking pioneers, McLaren and Tessa.

Paul and Tessie's children were producing grandchildren by July 1961, Marion had three and Alice two. Peter and Sis's daughter Bernice also had two. Old Jimmy, whose birthday went with the years was only 61. At one point, he grew terribly ill and Paul took him to the hospital where he lingered for a time, then passed away. He had left a hand-written will and in it he bequeathed everything he owned to Phyllis and Lily, except his fiddle that went to Tessie.

He left a letter explaining his investigations over the years during his travels back and forth to Saskatoon. Killing time waiting to see the loves of his life, he had spent time digging for information.

My dear family,

Thank you for all the kindness you showed me all these years. I wanted to leave you knowing the truth about the Blacks and Swallows. The three men gained Jeb's approval by doing his dirty work. Jeb, the puppet master, is serving a life sentence in the Prince Albert Penitentiary. Amos and Owen are locked up in psychiatric wards in North Battleford and Weyburn, as dangers to themselves and others. Gib is relegated to an abandoned cemetery with a rotted wooden marker. Wild grass grows high, and headstones are desecrated by vandals. Gib developed a conscience in the end and drove himself to dangle from a rope. I was told Amos and Owen have repented their sins.
Best regards,
Your friend, Old Jimmy, the remittance man.

For over four decades, the family believed the scoundrel brothers had gotten away with murdering Knut. Although the Blacks and Swallows were never legally held responsible, they did suffer consequences. Perhaps Knut's children could finally stop looking over their shoulders.

In 1971, Tessie had proudly reported, "My two nephews raised in the orphanage are now grown men. Today, one is an RCMP officer in the Northwest Territories and the other is a firefighter in Ontario. On March 10, she passed away while visiting her youngest daughter in Yorkton. By 1992, Paul followed from a stroke, living in a nursing home."

Epilogue

Saskatoon—*May 2021*

On a busy Saturday in May 2021, as restrictions eased from the COVID-19 pandemic, Grandma had her youngest grandson at her house after a game of flag football. For lunch, the seven-year-old was downing an entire can of Alphaghettis™, one of his all-time favourites. He was telling her stories and suddenly remembered the one about the great grandmother who was married more than once.

The little boy tried to remember, "I think she had one husband who died when he fell off a bridge, but another one died too?" His grandma smiled and pulled up a picture on her iPhone.

"Do you know what this is?" she asked.

"Oh yes, that's a train trestle bridge and we see one every time we go to the lake."

Grandma explained, "My great-grandma's first husband in Sweden was the conductor who died on a train that went into a river when the trestle broke, Then her second husband, your great, great, great grandfather died when he was run over by a train at Crooked River."

The little boy nodded because once again, he recognised the stories he had heard since he was little. He raced downstairs, sat on the organ stool and began to pump the pedals. The ancient *Karn* bellowed up and he began to tap out a tune to *'Three Blind Mice'*. Built new in 1906, the organ made of dark hardwood, with intricate carvings included a bevelled mirror. Gold inscriptions on the front said *'Woodstock, Ontario'* and *'London, England'*. Grandma looked at the framed photo of her great grandfather and glanced at the three paintings she had completed of the train track area at Crooked River where he lost his life.

The grandma said, "I want you to remember that our family has a special memory box, an old Bible, and a beautiful gold pocket watch to look at some day when we have time."

Those original souls from over one hundred years ago left an impression on their part of the world and would not be forgotten five generations later. Their countless offspring thrive producing a multitude of professionals living around the globe.

The End

Bibliography

Abandoned Rail Lines in Saskatchewan. Sask Trails. http://sasktrails.ca/wpontent/uploads/2015/11/Abandoned-Rail-Lines-Sask.pdf accessed February 5, 2020.

Abbra, Charlie. (September 8, 1955). *A Pioneer Talks About the Old Log Drive.* The Western Producer: http://saskhistoryonline.ca/islandora/object/PrairieRiver%3A31877

Acosta, Anna M. MD, Moro, Pedro L. MD, MPH, Hariri, Susan, PhD, & Tiwari, Tejpratap S.P. MD (December 2020). *Epidemiology and Prevention of Vaccine-Preventable Diseases. Diphtheria.* Centers for Disease Control and Prevention. www.cdc.gov accessed February 10, 2021.

Adamson, Julie (2012). *How did Saskatchewan Pioneers Homestead?* Saskatchewan Gen Web. www.aumkleem.wordpress.com accessed May 16, 2022.

Admin (October 29, 2018). *How quickly can rats multiply in your facility?* Rentokil. www.rentokil.com

Amery, Fiona (September 16, 2021). *Do the northern lights make sounds that you can hear?* The Conversation. www.theconversation.com accessed November 10, 2021.

Anderson, Nancy Marguerite. (January 11, 2014). *The Smell of Furs.* https://nancymargueriteanderson.com accessed April 17, 2022.

Andreola, Karen. (1997). *The Atmosphere of Home.* Homeschool World. www.home-school.com accessed January 28, 2022.

A project of the Saskatoon German Days committee. *Egg money: a tribute to Saskatchewan Pioneer women.* Regina: DriverWorks Ink.

Armstrong, Jerrold. (1980). *Kinistino The Story of a Parkland Community in Central Saskatchewan in Two Parts: Book 1. Melfort*: Phillips Publishers.

Assistant Secretary for Environment, Safety & Health. (May 1993). *EH-93-4 The Fire Below: Spontaneous Combustion in Coal. Environment, Safety & Health Bulletin.* U.S. Department of Energy, Washington, D.C.

Author Unknown. *11 creatures from Scandinavian folklore you should know.* Scandification. www.scandification.com accessed October 10, 2021.

Author Unknown. (November 3, 2014). *19th Century Lumberjacks Were Kinda Crazy.* All About Canadian History. www.cdnhistorybits.wordpress.com accessed March 17, 2022.

Author Unknown. *20 Prayers for Healing That'll Bring Peace and Strength in Hard Times.* www.womansday.com accessed March 7, 2021.

Author Unknown. *1900 Horse-Powered Farm.* Living History Farms. www.lhf.org accessed January 16, 2022.

Author Unknown. *1920s Coats, Furs, Jackets and Capes History.* Vintage Dancer. www.vintagedancer.com accessed November 22, 2021.

Author Unknown. *1930 – 1939 – Wish You Were Here: Saskatchewan Postcard Collection.* http://digital.scaa.sk.ca accessed April 3, 2022.

Author Unknown. *Abandoned rail lines in Saskatchewan.* http://sasktrails.ca accessed January 20, 2022

Author Unknown. *About Roleau.* Town of Roleau. www.townofroleau.com accessed April 24, 2022.

Author Unknown. *A journey through time on the way to Hamburg's first subway line.* The history of Hochbahn. www.hochbahn.de accessed March 9, 2022.

Author Unknown. *Alberta and Saskatchewan join Confederation.* Office of the Commissioner of Official Languages. www.clo-ocol.gc.ca accessed January 30, 2022.

Author Unknown. *Almighty Voice Jailhouse.* Canada's Historic Places. www.historicplaces.ca accessed February 22, 2022.

Author Unknown. (October 22, 2018). *An 1867 Dance.* Blog. Royal Scottish Country Dance Society. https://www.rscds.org accessed September 26, 2022.

Author Unknown. *Atlantic Ocean.* https://www.britannica.com accessed December 6, 2021.

Author Unknown. *Bessborough.* Heritage Saskatchewan. https://heritagesask.ca accessed April 3, 2022

Author Unknown. *Best 10 Trails and Hikes in Duck Lake | AllTrails.* https://www.alltrails.com accessed July 29, 2022.

Author Unknown. *Birdlore: Albatross: The Lucky Charm?* World Bird Sanctuary. http://world-bird-sanctuary.blogspot.com accessed September 26, 2021.

An Engineer's Aspect Blog. *Birs Bridge Collapse. The Moenchenstein Railroad Bridge Collapse – June 14, 1891 – An Engineer's Aspect* blog www.anengineersaspect.blogspot.com
accessed December 23, 2019.

Author Unknown. (May 29, 2014). *Bone Dry Saskatchewan (Throwback Thursday).* Law Society of Saskatchewan. Toronto World. July 1, 1915. www.lawsociety.sk.ca accessed February 1, 2022.

Author Unknown. *Role in World War II of Benito Mussolini.* Britannica. https://www.britannica.com accessed December 8, 2023.

Author Unknown. *Building A Society. Saskatchewan. A Pictorial History.* www.jkcc.com accessed April 6, 2022.

Author Unknown. *Canada's Premier Dog Sled Race.* Canadian Challenge. www.canadianchallenge.com accessed February 24, 2022.

Author Unknown. *Canada Time Zones.* Time Temperature. https://www.timetemperature.com accessed September 9, 2022.

Author Unknown. (June 16, 2019). *Cattle Die as Maysora Docks in Israel.* The Maritime Executive. https://maritime-executive.com accessed September 11, 2022.

Author Unknown. *Cherbourg.* www.en.normandie-tourisme.fr accessed August 24, 2021.

Author Unknown. *Clapton.* Lenvale & Clapton School District. Melfort & District Museum. https://www.facebook.com accessed October 9, 2023.

Author Unknown. *CN Police Service.* www.cn.ca accessed August 6, 2021.

Author Unknown. *Confederation 1867*. (September 14, 2018). The Canadian Encyclopedia. https://www.thecanadianencyclopedia.ca accessed September 26, 2022.

Author Unknown. *Covered Bridges: A Part of New Brunswick's Heritage*. Gouvernement Nouveau-Brunswick. New Brunswick Provincial Archives. https://archives.gnb.ca accessed September 24, 2023.

Author Unknown. (April 20, 2022). *Crop sharing or cash rate land rental agreements – which is right for your operation?* FCC Knowledge. www.fcc-fac.ca accessed June 1, 2022.

Author Unknown. *Did you know we had to ration food during the war?* www.cbc.ca accessed April 4, 2022.

Author Unknown. *The Dieppe Raid 19 August 1942*. Government of Canada. https://www.veterans.gc.ca accessed December 7, 2023.

Author Unknown. *The Different Types of Liquor – A Bartender's Guide*. Crafty Bartending. www.craftybartending.com accessed June 29, 2022.

Author Unknown. *Diphtheria*. Mayo Clinic. www.mayoclinic.org accessed February 29, 2020.

Author Unknown. *The Dreamscape – Plane of Dreams: r/Dn Behind the Screen*. https://www.reddit.com accessed October 18, 2022.

Author Unknown. *Early 20th Century Loggers*. Heritage Newfoundland & Labrador. www.heritage.nf.ca accessed March 16, 2022.

Author Unknown. *Elephant Island: Five Facts You Need to Know*. Expeditions. https://global.hurtigruten.com accessed October 14, 2022.

Author Unknown. *Elephant Island*. Earth Observatory. https://earthobservatory.nasa.gov accessed October 14, 2022.

Author Unknown. *Equine Infectious Anemia (Swamp Fever)*. Saskatchewan Horse Federation. www.saskhorse.ca accessed February 21, 2022.

Author Unknown. *Exploring Horse Colors: A Guide to Equine Color & Patterns*. Horse Racing Sense. https://horseracingsense.com accessed August 27, 2023.

Author Unknown. *Forensics. A partial print of the history of forensic science*. Archives Hub. www.archiveshub.jisc.ac.uk accessed March 11, 2022.

Author Unknown. *Fort à la Corne National Historic Site of Canada.* www.pc.gc.ca accessed March 12, 2022.

Author Unknown. *Freight Swings.* The Encyclopedia of Saskatchewan. www.esask.uregina.ca accessed February 25, 2022.

Author Unknown. (June 21, 2014). *Gabriel's Crossing – in Saskatchewan Historical Markers – Waymarking.* https://www.waymarking.com accessed July 29, 2022.

Author Unknown. *George VI (r.1936-1952) – The Royal Family.* https:///www.royal.uk accessed September 23, 2022.
Author Unknown. *Town of Hague.* www.townofhague.com accessed February 23, 2022.

Author Unknown. *Historical Trails. Trail Basics – Supplies. Trail Center Mercantile Store.* National Oregon/California Trail Center. www.oregontrailcenter.org accessed October 27, 2021.

Author Unknown. *History of Amsterdam.* Things To Do In Amsterdam. www.thingstodoinamsterdam.com accessed October 6, 2022.

Author Unknown. *History of Asphalt Shingles.* Canadian Asphalt Shingle Manufacturers' Association. www.casma.ca accessed January 13, 2022.

Author Unknown. *History. Town of Osler.* www.townofosler.com accessed February 23, 2022.

Author Unknown. *History of Saskatchewan and The Old Northwest. Fraternal Societies in Saskatchewan.* Electric Canadian. www.electriccanadian.com accessed January 29, 2022.

Author Unknown. *History of Warman.* City of Warman. https://www.warman.ca accessed September 30, 2023.

Author Unknown. *History of the Women's Rights Movement.* National Women's History Alliance. www.nationalwomenshistoryalliance.org accessed February 5, 2022.

Author Unknown. *HMS Courageous.* www.en.m.wikipedia.org accessed August 24, 2021.

Author Unknown. *Homesteading: Dreams and Realities.* US History II (OS Collection). www.courses.lumenlearning.com accessed November 10, 2021.

Author Unknown. *Influenza (Flu). 1918 Pandemic.* Centers for Disease Control and Prevention. www.cdc.gov accessed December 13, 2021.

Author Unknown. *Kristallnacht.* Holocaust Encyclopedia. www.encyclopedia.ushmm.org accessed August 24, 2021.

Author Unknown. *Lath and plaster.* Wikipedia. www.en.m.wikipedia.org accessed September 15, 2021.

Author Unknown. *Leptospirosis.* Britannica. https://www.britannica.ca accessed January 3, 2024.

Author Unknown. *Their Majesties on Holiday 1937.* www.britishpathe.com accessed April 3, 2022.

Author Unknown. *Manure.* East Multnomah Soil & Water Conservation District. www.emswcd.org accessed November 5, 2021.

Author Unknown. *Medical Conditions That Can Keep You from Joining the Military.* www.military.com accessed August 24, 2021.

Author Unknown. *Medicine.* Melfort & District Museum. https://www.melfortmuseum.org accessed November 8, 2021

Author Unknown. *Medicine – Dr. Shadd.* Western Development Museum. https://wdm.ca accessed January 12, 2024

Author Unknown. *Melfort.* The Encyclopedia of Saskatchewan. www.esask.uregina.ca accessed March 20, 2022.

Author Unknown. *Montmagny (Town and Country).* The Quebec History Encyclopedia. http://www.faculty.marianopolis.edu accessed September 8, 2022.

Author Unknown. *Moving to Sweden? Then these 20 pointers will come in handy.* www.sweden.se accessed December 6, 2021.

Author Unknown. *Never in the field of human conflict was so much owed by so many to so few.* UK Parliament. https://www.parliament.uk accessed December 8, 2023.

Author Unknown. *Objects | Edwardian shoes. Women shoes. Vintage shoes –* Pinterest. https://www.pinterest.com accessed November 21, 2021.

Author Unknown. (June 13, 2021). *Old Scottish Sayings, Scottish Words and Slang Your Granny May Have Used.* www.scotlandwelcomesyou.com accessed July 29, 2021.

Author Unknown. (December 13, 2006). *The Origins of Some Scandinavian Finger and Toe Naming Rhymes.* Mama Lisa's Blog. www.mamalisa.com accessed September 19, 2021

Author Unknown. *The Philippine-American War, 1899-1902.* Office of the Historian. www.history.state.gov accessed May 31, 2022.

Author Unknown. *Plymouth.* www.visitbritain.com accessed August 24, 2021.

Author Unknown. *Port of Liverpool.* Wikipedia. www.en.m.wikipedia.org accessed April 2, 2022.

Author Unknown. *Production.* Stats Canada. www.www66.statcan.gc.ca accessed November 11, 2021.

Author Unknown. *Protective clothing. Clothing can offer protection from biting insects.* www.who.int accessed August 7, 2021.

Author Unknown. *Québec.* Peter auf Tour. Travelling the USA and Canada. https://www.peter-auf-tour.de accessed September 8, 2022.

Author Unknown. *Raid at Cabanatuan.* Wikipedia. https://en.m.wikipedia.org accessed January 12, 2024.

Author Unknown. *The rise of the Axis and the breakdown of relations with the U.S.* Brittanica. https://www.britannica.com accessed December 8, 2023.

Author Unknown. *Saskatchewan Rail Network.* Minister of Highways & Infrastructure. Saskatchewan rail map. www.ontheworldmap.com accessed January 20, 2022.

Author Unknown. (March 7, 2008). *Saskatchewan Road and Railway Bridges to 1950.* www.pubsaskdev.blob.core.windows.net accessed February 22, 2022.

Author Unknown. (1894). *The Settler's Guide or The Homesteader's Handy Helper.* Montreal: William Foster Brown & Co, Publishers. https://electriccanadian.com accessed February 28, 2021.

Author Unknown. *Stars and Stripes: The American Soldiers' Newspaper of World War I, 1918 – 19. Timeline (1914-1921). A World at War.* Library of Congress. https://www.loc.gov accessed November 16, 2023.

Author Unknown. *Stockholm to Hamburg by train.* Railcc. www.rail.cc accessed March 9, 2022.

Author Unknown. *St. Patrick's Catholic Orphanage. 1903-1973: Prince Albert, Saskatchewan.* University of Calgary. https://digitalcollections.ucalgary.ca accessed October 16, 2022.

Author Unknown. *Sweden. Daily life and social customs.* Britannica. www.britannica.com accessed September 19, 2021.

Author Unknown. (2016). *Swedish Cottage Style.* Nice Space. www.nicespace.me accessed February 8, 2022.

Author Unknown. *Swedish Krona.* Oanda. https://www1.oanda.com accessed October 10, 2021.

Author Unknown. *Telecommunication.* Encyclopedia of Saskatchewan. University of Regina. https://esaskuregina.ca accessed September 21, 2021.

Author Unknown. *Tikinagan – Moss Bags.* The Arrow Newsletter. Manitoba First Nations Education Resource Centre Inc. www.mfnerc.org accessed January 6, 2022.

Author Unknown. *Time Zones in Sweden.* Time and Date. https://www.timeanddate.com accessed October 12, 2022.
Author Unknown. *Train Schedule Halifax – Montreal.* Via Rail Canada. www.viarail.ca accessed May 4, 2022.

Author Unknown. *Transport in Saskatchewan.* Saskapedia. https://saskapedia.com accessed October 10, 2023.

Author Unknown. *Travelling in a Covered Wagon. (Prairie Schooner, Conestoga Wagon).* www.saskschoolsinfo.com accessed October 27, 2021.

Author Unknown. (August 24, 2019). *Transport in Saskatchewan.* www.saskapedia.com accessed February 22, 2022.

Author Unknown. *Treaty 6.* Indigenous Saskatchewan Encyclopedia. www.teaching.usask.ca accessed February 22, 2022.

Author Unknown. (December 31, 1914). *Troops Shoot Duck Hunters. Canadian Soldiers Enforce New Regulations With Fatal Effect Near Buffalo, N.Y.* The Chilliwack Progress. www.newspapers.com accessed January 27, 2022

Author Unknown. *Uniforms and equipment. North-West Mounted Police uniform.* Canada. Royal Canadian Mounted Police. www.rcmp-grc.gc.ca accessed March 7, 2022.

Author Unknown. *Victorian Christmas: In the Classroom and the Home.* Diefenbaker Canada Centre. www.diefenbaker.usask.ca accessed February 18, 2022

Author Unknown. *War of 1812 Overview.* USS Constitution Museum. https://ussconstituionmuseum.org accessed December 10, 2023.

Author Unknown. *Western Canada's largest railway bridges.* Forth Junction Project. www.forthjunction.ca accessed February 21, 2022.

Author Unknown. *Politics – Dr. Shadd.* Western Development Museum. https://wdm.ca
Accessed November 18, 2023.

Author Unknown. *Witness the beginning of World War I with the assassination of Archduke Franz Ferdinand on June 28, 1914.* Britannica. https://www.britannica.com accessed August 21, 2022.

Author Unknown. *Women's 1920s Shoe Styles and History.* Vintage Dancer. www.vintagedancer.com accessed November 11, 2021.

Author Unknown. (December 6, 2017). *Women's Shoes: 1929 versus 1936.* Witness2fashion. www.witness2fashion.wordpress.com accessed February 6, 2022.

Author Unknown. *World War II. Sept 1, 1939 – Sept 2, 1945.*

Author Unknown. *The World Wars. To get a drink you have to sell!* http://villedemtl.ca accessed November 10, 2021.

Baerwaldt, Margaret. (March 4, 2015). *Tisdale.* The Canadian Encyclopedia. www.thecanadianencyclopedia.ca accessed December 10, 2021.

Baird, Craig (2020). *The KKK Thrives in Saskatchewan.* Canadian History Ehx www.canadaehx.com accessed June 4, 2021.

Bates, Christina. *"Beauty Unadorned": Dressing Children in Late Nineteenth-Century Ontario.* https://journals.lib.unb.ca accessed April 15, 2022.

Beal, Bob, MacLeod, Rod, Foot, Richard & Yarhi, Eli (July 8, 2021). *North-West Resistance.* The Canadian Encyclopedia. https://www.thecanadianencyclopedia.ca accessed September 2, 2023.

Birbeck, Andrew & Hastings, Karen (January 13, 2021). *11 Top-Rated Day Trips from Stockholm.* www.planetware.com accessed December 6, 2021.

Bishop, Mary F. (May 5, 2021. *History of Birth Control in Canada.* The Canadian Encyclopedia. www.thecanadianencyclopedia.ca accessed May 9, 2022.

Blainey, Geoffrey (1966). *The Tyranny of Distance: How Distance Shaped Australia's History.* Macmillan Publishers

Bonney, Margaret Atherton. (November 1980). *Days of the Sawmills.* The Goldfinch 2 (2) 2-4.

Border Entries – Library and Archives Canada. *Border Entries Before 1908.* www.bac-lac-gc.ca accessed January 26, 2021.

Brach, Tara. *In the Lakota/Sioux tradition.* Earthmonk. www.facebook.com accessed October 17, 2022

Bridges, Alicia (May 19, 2018). *The same but radically different: Newly revealed footage shows 1930s Saskatoon in full colour.* www.cbc.ca accessed April 21, 2021.

Brien, Natassja. (November 7, 2018). *First Scandinavian Mission Church – The Heart of Winnipeg's Scandinavian Community.* http://heritagewinnipeg.blogspot.com accessed March 13, 2021.

The British Library. *Sailors' Language – Lobscouse and Dandy-Funk p.xii.* www.vll-minos.bl.uk accessed February 15, 2021.

Brydon, Mrs. Charles. *Pioneers Battle Fire.* Canadian Bush Plane Heritage Centre. www.bushplane.com accessed March 10, 2021.

Busby, D. I. in discussion with the author. June 8, 2021.

Butts, Edward (February 6, 2006). *Almighty Voice.* www.thecanadianencyclopedia.ca accessed February 17, 2020.

Canada History Project. *World War I: Women Get the Vote 1916 – 1919.* www.canadahistoryproject.ca accessed April 10, 2021.

Canadian History Museum. *Our First Old Age Pension 1915-1927.* www.historymuseum.ca accessed March 22, 2021.

Carlson, Teresa (curator). *Sisters United: Women's Suffrage in Saskatchewan. (1876-1985).* Diefenbaker Canada Centre. https://www.diefenbaker.usask.ca accessed November 18, 2023.

Carryer, Simon. *Sea Transport in the 1930's.* www.pelgranepress.com accessed January 13, 2020.

Carson, D.M. & Ricketts, S.W. *Equine Infectious Anemia (EIA).* VCA Animal Hospitals. www.vcahospitals.com accessed February 20, 2022.

C. Cecil Lingard. (April 1, 1938). *Pioneer Statesman.* Macleans. www.archive.maclean.ca accessed April 6, 2022.

Centre for Disease Control. *Diphtheria Symptoms.* www.cdc.gov accessed March 7, 2020.

Chakrabortty, Aditya (Thursday, March 17, 2022). *Western values. They enthroned the monster who is shelling Ukrainians today.* The Guardian. www.theguardian.com accessed March 17, 2022.

Chief Buffalo Child Long Lance. (February 1, 1929). *The Last Stand of Almighty Voice.* Maclean's. www.archive.macleans.ca accessed February 23, 2022.

City of Melfort. *History of Melfort.* www.melfort.ca accessed March 10, 2021.

City of Regina. *Regina History & Facts.* www.regina.ca accessed February 8, 2021.

City of Saskatoon. *History.* www.saskatoon.ca accessed June 28, 2021.

Collins, Robert (1980). *Butter Down the well. Reflections of a Canadian Childhood.* Vancouver: Greystone Books. A Division of Douglas & McIntyre Ltd.

Coluccy, John M. Ph.D., & Hendricks, Kassondra. *Understanding Waterfowl: Flocking Together.* Ducks Unlimited. www.ducks.org accessed July 6, 2021.

Committee of The Kinistino and District Historical Organization (1980). *Kinistino The Story of a Parkland Community in Central Saskatchewan in Two Parts: Book 2.* Melfort: Phillips Publishers.

Community Stories. Canadian Military Heritage, Saskatoon, Saskatchewan. *Saskatoon and the Second World War Experience. Saskatoon Military Effort from 1939 to 1945.* www.communitystories.ca accessed April 21, 2021.

Confederation Debates (1865-1949). *House of Commons, 18 April 1902, Canadian Confederation with Alberta and Saskatchewan.* www.hcmc.uvic.ca accessed March 10, 2021.

Conners, Terry. Department of Forestry. University of Kentucky. *How to be Successful with your Small Hardwood Sawmill.* www.esf.edu accessed March 22, 2022.

The Cotton Ball Conspiracy. (1993). *Regina: from Pile o' Bones to provincial capital.* www.wordpress.com accessed February 8, 2021.

Craddock, Derek. (Feb 1, 2022). *Remembering the tragic St. Patrick's Orphanage fire, 75 years later.* PA Now. https://panow.com accessed October 16, 2022.

Crooked River History Committee. (1990). *Forest & Mills to Farming Skills. Crooked River – Peesane & Districts.* Altona, Manitoba: Friesen Printers.

Cunningham, Maria. (October, 2023). *There's a Cure for That: Historic Medicines and Cure-alls in America.* Oregon Health & Science University. https://www.ohsu.edu accessed January 3, 2023.

Deibert, Dave. (October 17, 2018). *Raise a glass or roll a joint: A look back on prohibition in Saskatchewan.* Saskatoon Star Phoenix. www.thestarphoenix.com accessed September 19, 2021.

DeMain, Bill. (January 3, 2012). *When the Car Radio Was Introduced, People Freaked Out.* Mental Floss. www.mentalfloss.com accessed April 12, 2022.

Dempsey, Hugh A. & Filice, Michelle (May 28, 2019). *Pitikwahanapiwiyin (Poundmaker).* www.thecanadianencyclopedia.ca accessed February 8, 2021.

Development of the Saskatchewan Milling Industry. *Illustrated Inventory of Flour and Grist Mills in Saskatchewan.* www.mhs.mb.ca accessed February 23, 2022.

Dobrowski, C. (contributor) (1982). Hudson Bay & District Cultural Society. *Valley Echoes 1900-1980. Life Along the Red Deer River Basin, Saskatchewan.* Inter Collegiate Press.

Donovan, Blair. (October 2, 2020). *23 Something Old, New, Borrowed, and Blue Ideas for Your Wedding.* Brides. www.brides.com accessed July 29, 2021.

Dyck, Bruce. (July 28, 2005). *Dirty Thirties: fact and myth.* The Western Producer. www.producer.com accessed September 20, 2021.

Eagle, Jean Scott (October 1973). *Our Coming West. Section D. The Trek.* Moulton, Sandra (July 1995). *1842-1995 Ashdown & Scott 1841-1995.* Prince Albert: Gateway Printers.

Editor. (February 3, 2014). *Dining Out At The Dawn Of The 1900s.* KDLG. https://www.kdlg.org accessed September 24, 2021.

Editors. *Great Depression History.* History. www.history.com accessed April 4, 2022.

Editors. (March 3, 2020). *Treaty of Versailles.* History. www.history.com accessed January 4, 2022.

The Editors of Encyclopaedia Britannica. (September 22, 2006). *Holiness Movement.* www.britannica.com accessed April 16, 2021.

The Editors of Encyclopaedia Britannica. *Ostend Belgium.* www.britannica.com accessed February 16, 2021.

The Editors of Encyclopaedia Britannica. *Wagon Train. North American History.* Britannica. www.britannica.com accessed November 3, 2021.

Ehman, Amy Jo (2017). *Saskatoon. A History in Words and Pictures.* Lunenburg, Nova Scotia: MacIntyre Purcell Publishing

El Fakhry Tuttle, Myrna (August 30, 2019). *Why is Canada a Bilingual Country?* Law Now. www.lawnow.org accessed July 2, 2021.

The Encyclopedia of Saskatchewan. *Eaton Internment Camp.* www.esask.uregina.ca accessed March 12, 2021.

The Encyclopedia of Saskatchewan. *Kinistino.* www.esask.uregina.ca accessed March 23, 2021.

English to Scots Gaelic. Google Translate. www.translate.google.ca accessed August 3, 2021.

English to Swedish. Google Translate. www.translate.google.ca accessed August 4, 2021.

Enss, Chris. *Getting Personal On The Frontier: Mail-Order Brides.* www.historynet.com accessed March 23, 2021.

Ethics Guide. *Pacifism.* www.bbc.co.uk accessed April 21, 2021.

Excerpts from the Original Electronic Text at the web site of the Eris Project, Virginia Tech. *Winston Churchill Speech before Commons (June 4, 1940).* Hanover College History Department. https://history.hanover.edu accessed December 7, 2023.

Fairfield, James and The Mother Earth News Editors. *Running a Small-Scale Sawmill Business.* Mother Earth News. www.motherearthnews.com accessed March 16, 2022.

Family Tree for Ole Christian Gunderson. www.myheritage.com accessed December 31, 2019.

Federal Reserve Bulletin. (October 1924). *Farm Prices of Grains.* Fraser – St. Louis Fed. https://fraser.stlouisfed.org accessed November 11, 2021

Ferencz, Ben. *The Greatest Trial the World has ever Seen.* Tedx Talks. www.youtube.ca accessed February 5, 2022.

Ferencz, Ben. (November 19, 2020). *The Last Living Nuremberg Prosecutor: Ben Ferencz 75 years Later.* www.youtube.ca accessed February 5, 2022.

Ferland, Lisa. *Life in the 1800s, I mean, in a Swedish stuga.* Knocked Up Abroad. www.knockedupabroad.com accessed February 8, 2022

Fictum, David (January 24, 2016). *Salt Pork, Ship's Biscuits, and Burgoo: Sea Provisions For*
Common Sailors and Pirates. https://www.csphistorical.com accessed January 13, 2020.

Flynn, Connie. (2018). *The History of Ceiling Fan.* Modern Fan Outlet. www.modernfanoutlet.com accessed October 23, 2021.

Fokker, Anthony. *500 Years of Dutch Design.* www.kingdombythesea.nl accessed February 16, 2021.

Forsyth, Garry (2018). *The story of the charismatic pioneer, Dr. A.S. Shadd, who was a driving force in the early development of Melfort.* www.melfortmuseum.org accessed March 27, 2021.

Fox, P. (February 2020) in discussion with the author.

Frana, Philip L. (1995). *Smallpox: Local Epidemics and the Iowa State Board of Health, 1880-1900.* The Annals of Iowa 54, 87-118.

Fraser, Carol (February 24, 2006). *Matthiasville Cemetery Draper Township, Muskoka District, Ontario.* Interment. Cemetery Records Online. www.interment.net accessed August 4, 2021.

Freed, Mrs. Robert James. *A True Story of Pioneer Life.* Moulton, Sandra (July 1995). *1842-1995 Ashdown & Scott 1841-1995.* Prince Albert: Gateway Printers.

Friesen, Gerald (1987). *The Canadian Prairies A History.* Buffalo: University of Toronto Press.

Gagnon, Erica. *Settling the West: Immigration to the Prairies from 1867 to 1914.* Canadian Museum of Immigration at Pier 21. www.pier21.ca/research/immigration-history/settling-the-west-immigration-to-the-prairies-from-1867-to-1914 accessed May 21, 2021.

Galbraith, H. in discussion with the author on June 24, 2021.

Gaudry, Adam (September 9, 2019). *Gabriel Dumont.* The Canadian Encyclopedia. www.thecanadianencyclopedia.ca accessed June 17, 2021.

Gibeault, Stephanie. (October 22, 2019). *Why Does My Dog Herd My Kids?* American Kennel Club. www.akc.org accessed November 3, 2021.

Gilmore, James. *The St. Lawrence River Canals Vessel – Maritime History of the Great Lakes.* http://www.maritimehistoryofthegreatlakes.ca accessed September 8, 2022.

Gjenvick. *Transatlantic Ships &Voyages. Crossing the Atlantic Like a Seasoned Ocean Voyager.* www.gjenvick.com accessed December 23, 2019.

Gjenvick Archives. (Est. 2000). *Wedding Fashions, Weddings & Anniversaries. Wedding Dresses and Gowns 1880s-1930s.* www.ggjenvick.com accessed February 11, 2021.

Google Translate. *English to Norwegian and English to Swedish.* www.translate.google.ca accessed July 21, 2021.

Google Translate. *English to Scots Gaelic.* www.translate.google.ca accessed August 2, 2021.

Grotsky, H., (2019) in conversation with the author.

Gunderson, David (2009). *Ancestors of Ole Christian Gunderson.* Genealogical Research.

Gunderson, David (2009). *Descendants of Ole Olsen Putten Tokerud.* Genealogical Research.

Gundersen, Mathew Paul (July 13, 2020). *Norwegian Phrases: Common Sayings in Norway.* Life in Norway. www.lifeinorway.net accessed August 1, 2021.

Hallowell, Gerald (November 13, 2020). *Prohibition in Canada.* The Canadian Encyclopedia.www.thecanadianencyclopedia.ca accessed March 18, 2021.

Halton, Clay. (August 27, 2023). *What is Black Tuesday? Definition, History, and Impact.* Investopedia. https://www.investopedia.com accessed December 6, 2023.

Harris, Mary (Mar 15, 2017). *Remember This? The Ku Klux Klan would forever regret their expansion into the Town of Barrie.* www.barrietoday.com accessed June 6, 2021.

Harvey, Steve. *Scandinavian People Traits: Your Guide to Scandinavian Features.* www.scandification.com accessed March 16, 2021.

Harbour's Review. *Oostende Port.* www.harboursreview.com accessed February 16, 2021.

Harris, Karen. *8 Things You Didn't Know About Real-Life Covered Wagons.* History Daily. www.historydaily.org accessed October 26, 2021.

Harvey, Steve. *Scandinavian People Traits: Your Guide to Scandinavian Features.* www.scandification.com accessed March 16, 2021.

Helstrom, Cheri. (2015). *Forever Changed.* DriverWorks Ink: Regina.

Henry, Natasha, L. (January 31, 2020). *Underground Railroad.* The Canadian Encyclopedia. www.thecanadianencyclopedia.ca accessed September 23, 2021

History of Bridges. *Bridge Failures – Most Famous Bridge Disasters.* www.historyofbridges.com accessed December 23, 2019.

History. *This Day in History. 1912 April 15. Titanic Sinks.* https://www.history.com accessed January 14, 2020.

Hobbs, R. Gerald, Hobbs, Helen (December 16, 2013). *Holiness Churches.* The Canadian Encyclopedia. www.thecanadianencyclopedia.ca accessed April 16, 2021.

Hopper, Tristin. (August 28, 2018). *Here is what Sir John A. Macdonald did to Indigenous people.* National Post. https://www.nationalpost.com accessed September 1, 2023.

Howard, Joseph (1952). *Strange Empire Louis Riel and the Métis People.* Toronto: James Lewis & Samuel.

Hucl, Pierre The Encyclopedia of Saskatchewan. *Wheat.* www.esask.uregina.ca accessed March 19, 2021.

Huddle Staff. (October 28, 2016). *New Brunswick's 7 Most Haunted Places.* Huddle Today. https://huddle.today accessed September 24, 2023.

Indigenous Corporate Training Inc. Blog. (June 23, 2015). *Indian Act and the Pass System.* www.ictinc.ca accessed June 7, 2021.

Iowa Official Registrar. (1902). *Iowa Legislature.* www.legis.iowa.gov accessed January 14, 2020.

Iowa State University. *Department of Military Science Subject Files, RS/13/16/1.* Special Collections Department, Iowa State University Library accessed January 14, 2020.

Jacot de Boinod, Adam. (June 9, 2014). *The ultimate guide to Cockney rhyming slang.* The Guardian. https://www.theguardian.com accessed December 8, 2023.

Jarvis, Dale (July 27, 2019). *Whistling at the Northern Lights.* www.thetelegram.com accessed April 18, 2021.

Johanson, Mollie (July 12, 2020). *What is Crewel Embroidery?* The Spruce Crafts. www.thesprucecrafts.com accessed April 25, 2021.

Karras, A.L. (1975). *Face the North wind.* Don Mills: Burns & MacEachern Limited.

Kaur, Japneet. *6 Haunted Places in Montreal That Will Scare You To Death With Their Spookiness.* Haunted Montreal. Travel Triangle. https://hauntedmontreal.com accessed September 24, 2023.

Kennedy, Rita. Travel Tips. *Landmarks in Le Havre, France.* www.traveltips.usatoday.com accessed February 16, 2021.

Kent, J. (1985) in discussion with the author.

Khan, Safdar, A. (November 2013). *Overview of Strychnine Poisoning.* Merck Manual. Veterinary Manual. www.merckvetmanual.com accessed September 25, 2021.

Klein, Candice (June 3, 2020). *Temperance colony or sex trade boom town? Saskatoon's little-known history.* www.cbc.ca accessed March 16, 2021.

Knafla, Louis A. *Law and Justice.* Encyclopedia of Saskatchewan. www.esask.uregina.ca accessed March 11, 2022.

Ladd, Marsha. (January 11, 2014). *Historical Treasure: Mrs. Potts' sad iron.* Tribune-Star. www.tribstar.com accessed September 21, 2021.

Lambert, Cindy (March 10, 2020). *Prohibition Stills and Mash.* Wine History Project of San Luis Obispo County. www.winehistoryproject.org accessed March 4, 2021.

Latimer, Kendall (August 18, 2017). CBC News. *KKK history challenges idea Sask. Always welcomed newcomers: expert.* www.cbc.ca accessed April 4, 2021.

La Trier, Wilfrid (February 25, 1903). S.E. Dawson, Printer. Full Text of *"Report of the North-West Mounted Police, 1902".* www.archive.org accessed February 22, 2020.

Lawlor, Alexa (May 26, 2018). *Memorial garden to offer education on Eaton Internment Camp.* Saskatoon Star Phoenix. www.thestarphoenix.com accessed April 10, 2021.

Legaspi, Rexy. (February 11, 2021). *What Comes Next? What to Expect When You're Building a Home from the Ground Up.* The Plan Collection. www.theplancollection.com accessed September 15, 2021.

Legion Saskatchewan Command. *Military Service Recognition Book.* www.sasklegion.ca accessed February 24, 2020.

Leith, Annabelle (July 9, 2018). *Foraging in Sweden's forests: what to look out for and when to pick them.* www.news@thelocal.se accessed February 12, 2020.

Lundh, C. (2003). *Swedish Marriages. Customs, Legislation and Demography in the Eighteenth and Nineteenth Centuries.* (Lund Papers in Economic History; No. 88). Department of Economic History, Lund University. www.lucris.lub.lu.se accessed February 9, 2022.

MacDonald, Norbert. (Spring, 1973). *A Critical Growth Cycle for Vancouver, 1900-1914.* BC Studies, (17). www.ojs.library.ubc.ca accessed January 27, 2022.

MacDonald, Ron (May 8, 1965). *Klan Gained Hold in Saskatchewan.* Saskatchewan News Index. Winnipeg Free Press. https://library.usask.ca accessed April 19, 2021.

Maenpaa, Sari (April 2001). *From Pea Soup to Hors d'oeuvres: The Status of the Cook on British Merchant Ships.* The Northern Mariner, pp. 39-55. www.cnrs-scrn.org accessed January 16, 2020.

Margis, Matthew (2016). *America's Progressive Army: How the National Guard Grew out of Progressive Era Reforms.* Graduate Theses and Dissertations, 15764. https://lib.dr.iastate.edu/etd/ accessed January 14, 2021.

Maritime History Archive. *Cowboys of the Sea: Cattlemen aboard Merchant Vessels.* www.mun.ca accessed January 15, 2020.

Marsh, James H. (September 11, 2013). *Montcalm, Wolfe and the memory of the Battle of the Plains of Abraham.* The Canadian Encyclopedia. www.thecanadianencyclopedia.ca accessed July 2, 2021.

Marsh, James H. (July 9, 2021). *Railway History in Canada.* The Canadian Encyclopedia. www.thecanadianencyclopedia.ca accessed December 9, 2021.

Marsh, James H. (January 7, 2022). *St. Lawrence River.* The Canadian Encyclopedia. https://www.britannica.com accessed September 8, 2022.

Maryland Fire and Rescue Institute. (June 9, 2010). Drill of the Month. *Ventilation/Firehouse*. www.firehouse.com accessed March 14, 2021.

McCartney, Duane. (July 8, 2021). *Prairies' first Black doctor left lasting legacy.* The Western Producer. https://www.producer.com accessed November 18, 2023.

Melfort Board of Trade (July 1952). *Melfort…The Heart of the Carrot River Valley*. www.peel.library.ualberta.ca accessed March 10, 2021.

The Melfort Journal. (July 9, 1980, July 9, 2003). *1904, 1905, 1906.* Accessed at the Melfort Museum, Melfort, Saskatchewan September 14, 2022.

Mellows, Phil (October 21, 2017). *Nationalize the Pubs.* Jacobin. www.jacobinmag.com accessed April 17, 2021.

Merriam-Webster. *Cowcatcher/Definition of Cowcatcher by Merriam-Webster.* https://www.merriam-webster.com accessed April 5, 2021.

Meyer, Roy W. (Spring 1968). *The Canadian Sioux. Refugees from Minnesota.* Minnesota Historical Society. www.mnhs.org/mnhistory accessed February 1, 2021.

Mindling, Charles Thurman (Spring 1949). *The Grand Army of the Republic in Iowa Society and Politics.* University of Iowa's Institutional Repository. Iowa Research Online. www.ir.uiowa.edu accessed January 14, 2021.

Mistatim & District History Book Committee. (1983). *From Forest to Field 1903-1983. Mistatim and Districts.* Humboldt, Saskatchewan: Humboldt Publishing Limited

The Mob Museum. *Bootleggers and Bathtub Gin – Prohibition: An Interactive History.* https://www.prohibition.themobmuseum.org accessed March 4, 2021.

Moulton, Sandra (July 1995). *1842–1995 Ashdown & Scott 1841-1995.* Prince Albert: Gateway Printers

Moulton, S., (September 15, 2022) in conversation with the author.

Moulton, Sandra (February 2002). *Stoney Creek School and District.* Melfort Journal.

Moyles, Trina. (May 20, 2021). *From the fire tower: a lookout's view of Alberta wilderness.* CBC Radio. www.cbc.ca accessed January 6, 2021.

Mukhtar, Saqib. *Routine and Emergency Burial of Animal Carcasses.* Texas A&M Agrilife Extension. www.agrilifeextension.tamu.edu accessed February 20, 2022.

Murnan, Tom. *Dinner in the Diner During the Golden Age of Rail Travel.* The International Wine & Food Society. Americas. Omaha and Council Bluffs Branches. www.iwfs.org accessed April 22, 2022.

National Museums Liverpool. Maritime Archives & Library. *Information Sheet 13. Emigration to USA and Canada.* https://www.liverpoolmuseums.org accessed January 13, 2020.

Nielsen, David. (November 11, 2019). *World War II Facts, Turning Points, Battles, and More.* www.familysearch.org accessed April 4, 2022.

Oakhill Homestead. *How to Keep Livestock Water From Freezing.* www.oakhillhomestead.com accessed March 31, 2021.

Oberholtzer, Cath. *A Womb with a View: Cree Moss Bags and Cradleboards.* www.ojs.library.carleton.ca accessed December 10, 2021.

Oberholtzer, Cath. *A Womb with a View: Cree Moss Bags and Cradleboards. The Tic-A-Nogan.* www.ojs.library.carleton.ca accessed April 7. 2022.

Owen, Wendy. (Autumn, 1989). *Manitoba History: The Cost of Farm-Making in Early Manitoba: The Strategy of Almon James Cotton as a Case Study.* Manitoba Historical Society. www.mhs.mb.ca accessed June 16, 2022.

Oyeniran, Channon. (February 19, 2019). *Sleeping Car Porters in Canada.* The Canadian Encyclopedia. www.thecanadianencyclopedia.ca accessed March 8, 2022.

Pannekoek, Frits & Filice, Michelle. (September 13, 2016). *Mistahimaskwa (Big Bear).* www.thecanadianencyclopedia.ca accessed February 8, 2021.

Parks Canada News Release. (November 12, 2021). Toronto Canada. *Government of Canada commemorates the discovery of insulin on 100th anniversary of this life-saving medical breakthrough.* https://www.canada.ca accessed January 6, 2024.

Pitsula, James M. (September 21, 2020). *Canadian viewers of HBO's 'Watchmen' should know the KKK helped bring down a provincial government in 1929.* www.theconversation.com accessed April 18, 2021.

Plante, Trevor, K. (Summer 2000). *Researching Service in the U.S. Army During the Philippine Insurrection.* Vo. 32. No. 2/Genealogy Notes; National Archives. www.archives.gov accessed January 15, 2021.

Prairie Berries. *History of Saskatoon Berries.* www.prairieberries.com accessed March 19, 2021.

Provincial Archives of Saskatchewan. *The Spanish Flu in Saskatchewan – Saskatchewan's First Female MLA.* www.saskarchives.com accessed April 10, 2021.

Public Health Division. Ministry of Health & Long-Term Care. *Diphtheria Guide for Health*

Care Professionals – Ontario.ca. www.health.gov.on.ca accessed February 29, 2020.

Queen, G., Captain, U.S. Navy (1999). *Navy Military Funerals.* Navy Band. https://www.navyband.navy.mil accessed December 9, 2023.

Quinlan, Alexander, Mann, N.E & Heard, Stawell. *Cookery for Seamen.* University of Chicago Press.

Ramsey, Doug & Everitt, John Cater (October 2007). *Manitoba History: Called to the Bar: An Historical Geography of Beverage rooms in Brandon, 1881-1966.* Manitoba Historical Society. www.mhs.mb.ca accessed April 11, 2021.

Robinson, B. in conversation with the author March 11, 2022.

Rogers, Randal & Ramsay, Christine (2014). *Overlooking Saskatchewan Minding the Gap.* Regina: University of Regina Press.

Rollings-Magnusson, Sandra (2018). *The Homesteaders.* Regina: University of Regina Press

Ronca, Debra. *Why were women on ships considered bad luck?* HowStuffWorks. www.people.howstuffworks.com accessed July 5, 2021.

Room, Robin. (2001). *Sweden in an international perspective: alcohol policy and drinking habits.* Centre for Social Research on Alcohol and Drugs, Stockholm University. www.robinroom.net accessed February 8, 2022.

Rose, Michael. *The Ship to Nowhere.* Montreal. www.archives.macleans.ca accessed January 13, 2020.

Roy, R.H., Foot, Richard. (October 22, 2020). *Canada and the Battle of Passchendaele.* www.thecanadianencyclopedia.ca accessed May 10, 2022.

Rubenstein, Daniel, I. *Bothersome Flies: How Free-Ranging Horses Reduce Harm While Maintaining Nutrition.* Frontiers. https://www.frontiersin.org accessed August 27, 2023.

Ruddy, Jon (April 1, 1967). *The Sweeps.* MacLean's. www.archive.macleans.ca accessed April 26, 2021.

Ruta McGhan, Patricia J. *Pink Lady's Slipper (Cypripedium acaule Ait.)* U.S. Forest Service. https://www.fs.fed.us accessed April 16, 2022.

Ryan, Timothy (July 1955). *Voices of the Past -The History of Melfort and District.* Melfort and District Golden Jubilee Committee

Saskatchewan Archival Information Network. *Prince Albert.* www.sain.scaa.sk.ca accessed February 22, 2020.

Saskatchewan Archives. *Homesteading.* www.saskarchives.com accessed February 8, 2021.

Saskatchewan Archives. *Homesteading. Land Records. Provincial Archives of Saskatchewan.* www.saskarchives.com accessed February 28, 2021.

Saskatchewan Archives. *Saskatchewan.* www.saskarchives.com accessed February 28, 2021.

Saskatoon Star Phoenix Archives. (October 29, 1918). *Relief for the "Flu".* www.thestarphoenix.com accessed April 18, 2021.

Schwinghamer, Steven and Raska, Jan (2020). *Pier 21: A History.* Ottawa: Canadian Museum of History, Canadian Museum of Immigration, University of Ottawa Press.

SeaRates By DP World. (August 2005). *SeaRates.* www.searates.com accessed February 15, 2021.

Shire, Timothy W. (November 29, 2007). *Pioneer Inland Terminal. The New Murphy's Siding.*
http://www.ftlcomm.com/ensign/homeTowns/crooked/murphys/pioneer/pioneer.html accessed February 5, 2020.

Shotwell, James T. *Alternatives for War.* Foreign Affairs. www.foreignaffairs.com accessed January 9, 2022.

Siggins, Maggie (1991). *Revenge of the Land A Century of Greed, Tragedy, and Murder on a Saskatchewan Farm.* Toronto: McLelland & Stewart Inc. Simpkin, John (September 1997). First World War. *Trench Food.* Spartacus Educational. www.spartacus-educational.com accessed April 18, 2021.

Simpson, Harley. (July 2, 2017). *12 Reasons You Should Visit Manitoba.* Culture Trip. www.theculturetrip.com accessed May 13, 2022.

Simpson, Michael John & Filice, Michelle (March 31, 2016). *History of Powwows.* The Canadian Encyclopedia. www.thecanadianencyclopedia.ca accessed January 20, 2022.

Smith, Denis (March 13, 2020). *War Measures Act.* The Canadian Encyclopedia. www.thecanadianencyclopedia.ca accessed November 10, 2021.

Smith, Peter B. (2009). *Prairie Murders. Mysteries, Crimes and Scandals.* Toronto: Heritage House Publishing Company Ltd.

Sperando, Andy. (May 1, 2006). *The people who work on trains.* Trains. www.trains.com accessed March 8, 2022.

Staresinic-Deane, Diana (2012). *Lessons from a Kansas graveyard: What a 1903 outbreak of Diphtheria can teach us today.* www.wordpress.com accessed February 29, 2020.

State Historical Society of Iowa – Iowa Pathways. www.iowapbs.org accessed February 16, 2020.

State of Minnesota. Department of Administration State Archaeologist. *Burial Grounds.* www.mn.gov accessed February 9, 2021.

Status of Women Canada. *100th Anniversary of Women's First Right to Vote in Canada.* www.cfc-swc.gc.ca accessed April 10, 2021.

Stillwell, Ted W. Portraits of the Past. (February 11, 2014). *Pioneer leader to caravan: 'Wagons ho!'* Leavenworth Times. www.leavenworthtimes.com accessed October 26, 2021.

Stonechild, Blair. *Indigenous Peoples of Saskatchewan.* Indigenous Saskatchewan Encyclopedia. www.teaching.usask.ca accessed February 6, 2021, and July 27, 2022.

Sturrock, Dudley (May 15, 1932). *Wanted on Voyage.* www.archives.macleans.ca accessed January 13, 2020.

Stuska, Sue. *Equine Health. Introducing a New Horse to the Herd.* Eclectic Horseman. www.eclectic-horseman.com accessed April 13, 2022.

Sutherland, Tricia & Waiser, Bill (November 19, 2019). *Opinion: The case for the exoneration of Chief One Arrow.* www.thestarphoenix.com accessed February 8, 2021.

Sutton, Philip (June 30, 2011). *Maury and the Menu: A Brief History of the Cunard Steamship Company.* https://www.nypl.org/blog accessed January 13, 2020.

Sylvestre, Jason & Demmans, Carson (2015). *Strange Saskatchewan.* Lunenburg, Nova Scotia: MacIntyre Purcell Publishing Inc.

Tate, Bro. M.W. *Historical Sketch of Freemasonry in Saskatchewan.* Freemasonry in Saskatchewan. https://skirret.com accessed April 16, 2021.

Tattrie, Jon. (January 22, 2015). *Alberta and Confederation.* The Canadian Encyclopedia. www.thecanadianencyclopedia.ca accessed January 30, 2022.

Tattrie, Jon. (February 3, 2015). *Saskatchewan and Confederation.* The Canadian Encyclopedia. www.thecanadianencyclopedia.ca accessed January 30, 2022.

Taylor, Alan. (June 19, 2011). *World War II: Before the War.* The Atlantic. www.theatlantic.com accessed August 23, 2021.

Taylor, Alan. (June 26, 2011). *World War II: The Invasion of Poland and the Winter War.* The Atlantic. www.theatlantic.com accessed August 23, 2021.

T. Buddy, (August 8, 2020). *Moonshine Can Still Cause Health Problems.* Verywellmind. www.verywellmind.com accessed October 23, 2021.

Terras, Astrid. *Muskoka History: A brief review by Astrid Terras.* www.freepages.rootsweb.com accessed June 19, 2021.
Thatch Creek Historical Society. (1980). *Tales and Trails of Thatch Creek. 1905-1980.* Regina: W.A. Print Works Ltd.

Thomas, Sue (April 3, 2019). *How 2 women scientists helped by Grand Rapids, created whooping cough vaccine.* www.mlive.com accessed March 7, 2021.

Town of Neepawa. Neepawa: Land of Plenty. *History & Heritage.* www.neepawa.ca accessed June 12, 2021.

Train Geek. *CN Tisdale Subdivision.* https://www.traingeek.ca/wp/trains/class-1-railways/cn-in-saskatchewan/tisdale/ accessed February 5, 2020.

Train Schedules. www.rome2rio.com accessed January 28, 2020.

Triebe, Madelaine. (December 18, 2016). *The 17 funniest expressions in Swedish (and how to use them).* Matador Network. www.matadornetwork.com accessed August 4, 2021.

Trimble, Marshall. (March 23, 2017). *Did Old West Trains Have Bathrooms?* Truewest. https://truewestmagazine.com accessed April 16, 2022.

University of Alberta Library. *Prince Albert.* http://peel.library.ualberta.ca/bibliography/3474/reader.html#0 accessed February 21, 2020.

University of Toronto Library. *Canada Sessional Papers Maps (1901-1925).* www.maps.library.utoronto.ca accessed February 27, 2020.

Vaccines and Immunization: Epidemics, Prevention and Canadian Innovation. Diphtheria. www.museumofhealthcare.ca accessed March 7, 2021.

Veterans Affairs Canada. (April 20, 2017). *Canada Remembers Women on the Home Front.* www.veterans.gc.ca accessed March 17, 2021.

The Volunteers. (1831-1902). *Demystifying the Citizen Soldier.* www.jstor.org accessed January 15, 2021.

Waiser, Bill. (January 30, 2018). *History Matters: 1939 royal tour turned Melville into Saskatchewan's largest city for a day."* Saskatoon Star Phoenix. www.thestarphoenix.com accessed April 11, 2022.

Waiser, Bill (2018). *History Matters. Stories from Saskatchewan.* Stories originally published from the Saskatoon Star Phoenix.

Walker, Lt. Col. Drayton E. *A Resume of the Story of 1st Battalion, the Saskatoon Light Infantry (MG) Canadian Army Overseas. During the War.* www.saskatoonlightinfantry.org accessed April 21, 2021.

War Museum. *Canada and the First World War. History. Conscription, 1917.* www.warmuseum.ca accessed April 10, 2021.

War Museum. *Canada and the First World War. History. Farming and Food.* www.warmuseum.ca accessed March 22, 2021.

War Museum. *Canada and the First world War. Passchendaele.* www.warmuseum.ca accessed March 20, 2021.

Wascana Park. *Wascana: Interpretive Panels: Pile of Bones Creek.* www.doftw.com accessed June 18, 2021.

Waymarking. *Birs Bridge Collapse 1891 – Munchenstein, Bl, Switzerland Railway Disaster Sites onWaymarking.com* www.waymarking.com accessed December 23, 2019.

Weeks, Linton (June 11, 2015). *Dirty Dancing in the Early 1900s.* NPR History Dept. www.npr.org accessed April 16, 2021.

Wells, Paul (Jan 11, 2019). *Canada's angry, divisive politics are as old as Canada itself.* www.macleans.ca accessed June 6, 2021.

Western Development Museum. *A Brief History of Agriculture in Saskatchewan.* www.wdm.ca accessed February 2, 2020.

Whelan, Corey. (Aug 25, 2020). *How to Say Grandma and Grandpa in Different Parts of the World.* Reader's Digest. www.rd.com accessed June 13, 2021.

Whitcomb, Dr. Ed. (2005). *A Short History of Saskatchewan.* Ottawa: Dollco Printing.

Widds, Randy William, (1992). *Saskatchewan Bound: Migration to a New Canadian Frontier.* Great Plains Quarterly. 649. https://digitalcommons.unl.edu/greatplainsquarterly/649 accessed January 26, 2021.

Winger, Jill (April 10, 2019). The Prairie Homestead. *How to Whitewash Your Barn and Chicken Coop.* www.theprairiehomestead.com accessed March 9, 2021.

Wikipedia. *August 1939.* www.en.m.wikipedia.org accessed January 4, 2022.

Wikipedia. *Battle of Verdun.* https://en.m.wikipedia.org accessed November 16, 2023.

Wikipedia. *Canadian Confederation.* http://www.en.m.wikipedia.org accessed September 26, 2022.

Wikipedia. *Conductor.* www.Wikipedia.com accessed January 26, 2020.

Wikipedia. *Conductors/Guards in Europe/Switzerland.* www.Wikipedia.com accessed January 26, 2020.

Wikipedia. *District Municipality of Muskoka.* www.en.m.wikipedia.org accessed June 1, 2022.

Wikipedia. *Draft horse.* www.en.m.wikipedia.org accessed January 16, 2022.

Wikipedia. *Holiness movement.* www.en.m.wikipedia.org accessed March 21, 2021.

Wikipedia. *Ku Klux Klan in Canada. Policy and Propaganda.* www.en.m.wikipedia.org accessed June 7, 2021.

Wikipedia. *List of rail accidents (1890-1899).* www.en.m.wikipedia.org accessed December 23, 2019.

Wikipedia. *List of rail accidents (1900-1909).* www.en.m.wikipedia.org accessed July 1, 2021.

Wikipedia. *Outward holiness.* www.en.m.wikipedia.org accessed March 21, 2021.

Wikipedia. *Pullman Company.* www.en.m.wikipedia.org accessed June 27, 2021.

Wikipedia. *Ross rifle.* www.en.m.wikipedia.org accessed March 11, 2022.

Wikipedia. *Royal Canadian Mounted Police.* www.en.m.wikipedia.org accessed July 7, 2021.

Wikipedia. *Saskatchewan Provincial Police.* www.en.mwikipedia.org accessed December 9, 2021.

Wikipedia. *Sawmill.* www.en.m.wikipedia.org accessed March 15, 2022.

Wikipedia. *Stairs.* www.en.m.wikipedia.org accessed September 15, 2021.

Wikipedia. *Swedish emigration to the United States.* www.en.m.wikipedia.org accessed February 8, 2022.

Wikipedia. *Treaty 4*. www.en.m.wikipedia.org accessed February 9, 2021.

Wikipedia. *Treaty 6*. www.en.m.wikipedia.org accessed February 9, 2021.

Wikipedia. *Winnipeg Victorias*. www.en.m.wikipedia.org accessed May 12, 2022.

Wiki Visually. *Mistatim, Saskatchewan*. www.wikivisually.com accessed March 20, 2021.

Williams, Holly (July 3, 2020). *How Britain is facing up to its hidden slavery history*. BBC. www.bbc.com accessed July 8, 2021.

Willmore, Chris (2019). *Reginald Beatty. Stories of Indian Days. O-ge-mas-es. Relates many incidents of early life in the west.* www.onlineacademiccommunity.uvic.ca accessed February 24, 2022.

W. Sarah. (December 18, 2012). *Swedish Common Women's Dress in the mid 1800's* A Most Peculiar Seamstress Blog. www.peculiarseamstress.blog accessed February 7, 2022.

W. Sarah. (January 7, 2013). *Swedish Common Women's Dress in the mid 1800's – Underwear.*
A Most Peculiar Seamstress Blog. www.peculiarseamstress.blog accessed February 7, 2022.

Youngdahl, Karie. (September 26, 2018). *The 1918-19 Spanish Influenza Pandemic and Vaccine Development.* The history of Vaccines. www.historyofvaccines.org accessed January 10, 2022.

Young, Rachelle (April 30, 2020). *Five ways researchers find whales in the open ocean*. Oceana. Protecting the World's Oceans. www.oceana.ca accessed June 13, 2021.

Your Living City. (June 26, 2020). *Swedish Wedding Traditions: Customs and Culture*. Stockholm. www.yourlivingcity.com accessed June 27, 2021.

You Tube. Annette. *20 Norwegian Words for Everyday Life.* www.youtube.com accessed July 7, 2021.

You Tube. *1930s Dublin Ireland, docks, Livestock Export.* www.youtube.com accessed January 13, 2020.

YouTube. MrShoptaw. (September 28, 2015). *Best of the Historic Steam Sawmill.* www.YouTube.ca accessed March 15, 2022.

You Tube. *Covered Wagons of the Oregon Trail.* www.youtube.com accessed October 31, 2021

You Tube. Scotia Droning. (September 24, 2016). *Cruise ships in Halifax Harbour.* www.youtube.ca accessed September 9, 2022.

YouTube. Rappold, Patrick Matthew. (July 18, 2018). *From the Sawyers Perspective Sawing Hardwood Logs.* www.YouTube.ca accessed March 15, 2022.

You Tube. (June 23, 2016). *Fur Trapping – Coil-spring trap sizes explained.* www.youtube.com accessed June 7, 2021.

You Tube. *How Norwegians Speak English. Norwegian Accents and Dialects.* www.youtube.com accessed July 7, 2021.

You Tube. *How Swedish women got the right to vote.* www.youtube.ca accessed December 6, 2021.

You Tube. *How to Identify red pine (Pinus resinosa).* https://m.youtube.com accessed April 16, 2022.

You Tube. *Livestock Transport: Take a ship tour onboard MV Becrux.* www.youtube.com accessed January 13, 2020.

You Tube. *Norwegian American (English Subtitles).* www.youtube.com accessed July 7, 2021.

You Tube. Scott Singer Cruises. (March 18, 2019). *Norwegian Gem Docking At Halifax.* www.youtube.ca accessed September 9, 2022

You Tube. Erin. (July 6, 2021). *Scottish Slang.* www.youtube.ca accessed July 7, 2021.

Yue, Wenhui. (June 2, 2020). *1868.* 1860-1869, *19th century, year overview. Fashion History Timeline.* www.fashionhistory.fitnyc.edu accessed June 1, 2022.

Zak, Luke. (July 10, 2020). A Brief Dive Into the History of Lead Paint. Zotapro. https://zotapro.com accessed September 17, 2022.

Zuehlke, M. (2001). *Scoundrels, Dreamers & Second Sons. British Remittance Men in the Canadian West.* Toronto: Dundurn Press